HEARING

Library of American Fiction
The University of Wisconsin Press Fiction Series

HEARING

by
Jael

Joyce Elbrecht and Lydia Fakundiny

THE UNIVERSITY OF WISCONSIN PRESS
TERRACE BOOKS

The University of Wisconsin Press
1930 Monroe Street
Madison, Wisconsin 53711

www.wisc.edu/wisconsinpress/

3 Henrietta Street
London WC2E 8LU, England

5   4   3   2   1

Printed in the United States of America

Library of Congress Cataloging-in-Publication Data
Elbrecht, Joyce, 1927–
  Hearing by Jael / Joyce Elbrecht and Lydia Fakundiny.
    p. cm.—(Library of American fiction)
  ISBN 0-299-21300-5 (cloth: alk. paper)
1. Dwellings—Remodeling—Fiction. 2. Historic buildings—Fiction. 3. Women historians—Fiction.
4. Voodooism—Fiction. 5. Florida—Fiction. 6. Diaries—Fiction. I. Fakundiny, Lydia, 1941– II.
Title. III. Series.
  PS3555.L24H43 2005
  813'.54—dc22
                                                    2005011641

Terrace Books, a division of the University of Wisconsin Press, takes its name from the Memorial Union
Terrace, located at the University of Wisconsin–Madison. Since its inception in 1907, the Wisconsin
Union has provided a venue for students, faculty, staff, and alumni to debate art, music, politics, and
the issues of the day. It is a place where theater, music, drama, dance, outdoor activities, and major
speakers are made available to the campus and the community. To learn more about the Union, visit
www.union.wisc.edu.

Juba this Juba that
Juba killed a yella cat
Get over double trouble Juba

Juba up Juba down
Juba all around the town
Juba here Juba there
Juba Juba everywhere.

—Early African American "Patting Juba" Song

Contents

Acknowledgments

Joyce Elbrecht and Lydia Fakundiny wish to give their profound thanks to colleagues and friends who read early versions of this novel: Ann Boehm for her characteristic honesty, Stuart Davis for his quick-witted comprehension, Margaret Nash for her sensitivity to form, Nancy Osborn for her understanding of literary reception, Nancy Raine for sounding textual depths with her poet's ear, Anthony Rossi for his empathetic grasp of character, and Sandra Siegel for tenacity and openness in negotiating her scholarly position vis-à-vis our work. And to those readers who responded with gratifying enthusiasm to our final version: Holly Laird, whose critical cast of mind ranges with ease over the compass of literary imagination; Andrea Lunsford, whose attunement to detail prompts an ever closer attention to getting it right; Marj Haydon, whose intelligence inspires that loving focus needed for creative work; and Sheila Moermond of the University of Wisconsin Press, whose discerning judgment of literary quality and professional guidance launched our manuscript on its journey to publication.

HEARING

1

Trail of Seduction

You know I love you, Jael," Sam said, giving me a lift to the airport this morning, "but none of us has much time any more, not a minute to waste, and—nothing to do with us, makes no difference to me personally—I've been thinking you might want to, you know, position yourself better. For the future—purely for your own good, a kind of safety measure."

My flight out of Athena was on the ground. I boarded, Sam's advice fresh in my mind. I value his opinion; he goes back to the mid-eighties when I was teaching full time on the tenure track. Academia didn't agree with me (a colleague once described me as "overly intellectual"), but Sam made the scene more inviting. By his senior year, he'd arranged so many exquisite little private picnics, walks, music sessions, and country excursions for the two of us that the nature of our attraction became pressingly, if not publicly, obvious. What with people on the alert for sexual harassment, we were reasonably discreet. Waiting, that is, until his last class with me was over and I'd rushed to turn in his A (he's smart and ambitious). We had a couple of great years before new projects and interests crowded out our relationship. When good sex has been free of obligation and jealousy (a rarity in my experience), it's easy and natural to keep up a friendship through the years. For Sam, this trip I'm on is unnecessary, if not a bizarre irrelevance, just another distraction from the really important things.

A straight shot from La Guardia to New Orleans and upgraded too. Business class in exchange for my seat on an earlier flight, the kind of trade-off you half resent because you've been more than obliging. Merely a matter of getting what you deserve when not landlocked classwise. I lean back with a mid-morning coffee and consider my route over to Florida's Gulf coast.

The fine specimen next to me in the aisle seat is wearing one of those Italian silk suits women always want. Soft, nubbly. Late forties, the male Caucasian body at its most appealing age to my mind, trim, muscular—could be bi—closed laptop astride his genitals, IBM compatible. In such public settings he commands appreciation, I'll hand him that. Tinkling his drink, jaunty as a baseball pro closing a multi-million-dollar deal, eyes agleam with the sporty bravado they get when it's been patience and distance long enough. What's needed here for a truly cosmopolitan run is a little acknowledgment, and he's strictly not one to brake on turns. Usually they wait for cruising range with seat belts unbuckled. But this airborne community has barely lifted off common ground and it's already time for my travel fortification. I dive into my briefcase and surface with a dozen sheets of the most dense, absolute nonsense computers can generate, every element scaled, cropped, flipped, modified beyond recognition, overprinted, no telltale repetitions:

4

It always works, more or less; I count on meaningless marks. They introduce just the right amount of alien without that fatal exotic-erotic combo. Just enough to put them off. This one crosses soft Italian silk legs, lets his *Journal of Neurosurgery* drop to his laptop and inclines his torso toward me, jaw clasped firmly, head slightly cocked. The usual approach mode of the more aggressive types, what we have here is a slimmed-down Buck Mulligan, muscle-toned by success. Squints sideways, confident of making out something familiar on the page in my hand, some clue to a key.

I adopt the concentration of an overworked writing teacher marking student papers: harried, harassed, hurried, nothing showing to waste time over. As unsuggestive of Titian's woman-flesh, and as unnymphean, as an empty schoolroom. Margins fill up with my minute stabs at random. After years of rehearsal I've got it down pat, face-feel perfected, that look of narrowed intensity stupefying the run of professionals when they shed the wary blandness of their social masks. Even the off chance of access to the code of some multinational's industrial secrets probably wouldn't add enough to *this* bottom line.

He bears down on a face-search and, buddy-boy, I'm no beauty—well, the eyes maybe, large, hooded, some kind of ethnic mix going back too far to call. But the nose, that settles it. A utilitarian beak, evolved to break apart and brush aside mud globules from worms too colorless for human sight. A probe for seas, puffin-like. Still, some of those early Florentine portrait profiles, now they—but my God, the mouth. No lipstick, not even a chapstick slick. In fact, not a soupçon of makeup on a face that could at least have highlighted its theatrical potential. Lacks imagination, commonplace drudge dressed like she's not, traveling on her company's expense account.

He slumps back in his seat and gives me a final up-and-downer. Sure I'm the mouse he sees, too starved to squeak, he runs his eyes over me openly now like an old-time inspector concluding a quality control review. With that dismissive way they have of expelling breath when there's nothing at stake, he completes the valediction by shoving his journal aside and opening his laptop. Back to business, reconnaissance over. It's the early 1990s and he's into future shock.

Back to immediate practicalities for me. Car rental, roadmap. Funny I forgot the one with the route Harding penciled in red—the very route she herself drove, back in 1977. A shrink would accuse me of some kind of resistance to Harding's wheel tracks.

If only I had a touch of that genius exhibited by Luria's mnemonist: not memory's distorted recollections but immediate sensory recall.

The specificity of solid detail. Imagine having push-button access to all that startling, unbelievable array of sights, sounds, smells you call your "past" with no loss of sensation, images and feelings available at will. So what if you have no idea of what's going on or why, who does? Flash up that rocky island-studded coast on the Adriatic, stop off in Dubrovnik twenty years ago, trek again in the Himalayas whenever you please: invisible rampages of energy, unchartered combustions of emotion, mental sallies spilling out every pore, as concretely felt as the silken nubbles beside me. With that kind of access to the past, where's the pressing need for a future? I'd dead-end this writing business like the droppings of an extant species. Leave it off like Rimbaud left off poetry.

But then Rimbaud was a male teenager with good personal reasons for disappearing from the cultural scene, whereas I'm forty-three, female, and unlikely to fare well in exotic trading places. I'd be willing to settle for a lot less like, say, total recall of Harding's map with the red trail of her drive from the New Orleans airport to the north Florida coast, my route immediately laid out before me, as clear as the steward and stewardess squeezing the drink-cart by. Not that I'd understand any more than I do now, but why have to think beyond the normal disability of sensory amnesia to get some place? I mean it's not like I'm looking for transcendent meanings, I'd just like a better mental mode of accommodation for getting around.

Still, my nonsense fort has its consolations and I lapse comfortably enough into the usual semiconscious state. He's booting up. Serious handicap, this having to make do without his desktop online oomph. Reasonably certain I've become the right amount of alien to keep his eyes off me (if not his mind off serendipitous pleasures) I slide my hand into my briefcase and caress the diary. Old leather as soft-skinned as a smooth fat baby. A gift to Frances Boullet from her father on her fifteenth birthday, the year the Civil War began. She wrote most of it, but there are four—no, five— different hands. Maria-Louisa was still writing in it the summer Harding spent down there. I hate to give it up.

Harding thought I should have it. "Intellectual loner, Southerner resettled in the Northeast, mistaken by academia for one of its own," so she once described herself. Elizabeth Harding Dumot, from whom I took my first and last course in "literary theory" in the early '70s. (Discovered I had a talent but small need for it—theory always already soaks my experience and fragments it like rainwash even without the steady pound of an academic deluge.) It was sixteen years ago, in the summer of '77, that she restored the old Boullet House and found the diary there, and still its story has never been told. But how could it be? Don't private stories, insofar as they remain private, vanish without trace? What survives (dead or alive) has only the public existence displayed in fossils of privacy—consider the well-kept cemetery as a classic instance. Time's transformations of privacy, with all their power and horror and beauty, into the public things that make up our world may log their agents but never their dynamic. A great, pure mystery without beginning or end, not subject to investigation.

The restoration itself was a different matter. Of that Harding gave detailed accounts to any who would listen: this-old-house yarns of community corruption, all the mess you have to work your way through when you commit to rehabilitating a historic property—the politics of place and time that trap you in any passionate engagement. Never a word uttered publicly, though, about what was in the diary or how she got hold of it, the private story growing at the fallow core. My mission is to take the diary back. Back to the antebellum home Captain Boullet built for his daughter Frances, the diary-keeper. Back to Tarragona (an earlier Florida settlement, some claim, than St. Augustine). I know my way around the West Coast. Naples, Marco—I've even cruised the Ten Thousand Islands—Fort Myers, Sanibel and Captiva, Sarasota, Tampa, all the way up to Cedar Key. But never beyond, along the northwest arm toward Alabama, where Tarragona is—the Panhandle, where the spent force of hurricanes from the Caribbean twist into tornado funnels that dip down into the Deep South.

This is nothing like returning an animal to the wild, a creature's natural habitat. Restoring a strictly cultural object to its original place, in these times, feels more like one of those familiar pornographic acts necessitated by our participation in global affairs. Like a public show of the diary's body, of its sheer feel and weight when I hold it, of the way it parts, falls open in my palms and nestles there, pulsatile.

A woman like Harding suddenly trekking off in mid-career to parts unknown and buying a run-down old house out of the blue can innocently, even naively, stir up a medley of chance. Uncover relics of privacy like the diary. Harding has a positive genius for such unintentional reactivation of hidden circuits.

After she'd restored and sold the house, she settled back into her teaching, her academic persona. To all appearances nothing had changed, and a good decade passed before I asked the why-question. Never had I *thought* to ask why she got into it in the first place—more the naif then than she, I was too busy during those years processing her story of restoration's perils. Not to mention the politics. But there it was one mellow fall day in the late '80s, idly popping up over coffee in her backyard patio—a miniature version in Athena, New York, of a French Quarter courtyard glimpsed from, say, Dauphine Street.

"Why?" She got that look that's so much hers it's like a DNA print. Her body goes still in mid-movement like someone spotting a familiar form in the distance, and her talk outs slowly, then faster, finding its way by seeming to lose it.

"There's a kind of heightened promiscuity that grips everyday life up here when winter drags on and on." And in response to my lifted eyebrow, "No, no, not casual sex, just cold weather magnifying all the day-to-day brutalities of living, those indiscriminate little unwanted intimacies—at the office, in faculty meetings, the supermarket, the parking lot, you name it—strangers and half-strangers and people you'd think would know better rubbing up against your nerves like rock salt. Morning, noon, and night, walls of black-smudged snow hulking over sidewalks and always more on the way, whiting out the landscape in these scenic Finger Lakes. You suspect the entropic principle has won out and brought the old reliable round of nature to a dead stop. No April—cruel or not—this year, you think, and that sunburst of color on the figured rug by the window as you wake—brilliant yellow, green, flecks of cobalt—must be hallucinated. Sure enough, the colors go slithering back under a blubbery skin of sameness; before you're out of bed, they've retreated with something like an evolutionary gratitude for cellular origins. Oh, my dozen or so seasons up here have brought adjustment, meaning I can snug into our downy gray comforts good as anybody, on the coldest night. But like any normal infant I fret after a spell of ignorant bliss—when younger it might have been 'Light, Color, Action'; by then, at a ripe forty-two, it was the one word 'Light!' Age, you see, merely increases pleasure in the freedom of surface activity, the vivid play of things on the skin."

Maybe—I reached awkwardly for some interiority to her why-answer maybe a touch of anxiety-induced obsessing over the direction her life was taking . . . or not taking? (By that time I was already on the lookout for such vines of doubt in myself; they fasten on you before you know it.) Her flow of words turned me squarely back to her own experience: "No crisis in my life, inner or otherwise, no upsurge of radical alienated consciousness, all of which I suffered to such romantic extremes in adolescence and beyond that the inevitable leavings more than compensated for any repeat performance. No creeping glandular onset of menopausal falling-off or emotional neediness. I wasn't even down in the mouth—just, as I've said, the usual abrasive bondings, paroxysms of space that squeeze the quick of matter like machines graphing body parts."

I can hear Harding's voice, more familiar to me than my own, at almost any time, almost at will: "So call me Hagar, minus angelic visitation and son. It was latish March, droves of students off on so-called spring break—shedding the drab and the cold, all the mundane terrors. The more dramatic variety, Lord knows, none of us is ever for an instant allowed to forget, as if we need prompting to how and where in the world things could be worse, as though we've somehow escaped twentieth-century barbarism if we're not in the very thick of its terror. Didn't we watch Vietnam burn over dinner? And the nightmares of Cambodia, Biafra, Ethiopia, El Salvador—East Timor despite the news blackout, we knew anyway—and Haitians by the boatload, hanging on God knows how. Civil wars and tribal wars and fallout from the old War on Communism, famines and floods, earthquakes, tortures and disappearances, mutilations both newly experimental and traditional, genocide, mass graves and rapes, and refugees. Always the refugees. I can hardly remember who they all were or in what order, but always the women running with their children, eloquently elegant as they drop, a scarf or coat half blown off, old people starving and ignored, bodies hacked and pieces mingled like a multi-national gathering. Smash, beat, bludgeon, cut and gut, bomb and burn without notice, shoot and gas without limit . . . we're not to transmit such knowledge—oh no, not even to speak of it, that's the media's job—we're to shut it in our cellular makeup where the bounds of our safety send out recurrent chemical beeps like an alarm built into a home surveillance system.

"So, what with all that, needless to say, no news cameras showed up in my vicinity when the sun didn't shine at the vernal equinox. Nothing newsworthy about the perennial drip of the commonplace poison, the sting of the daily solution with its bromides—where violence hangs around like a blood relative. Let's just say it was a better quality of the ordinary I was after that spring—color, warmth, ripe fruit lusciously within reach, plump juicy figs in my case; where I come from they're ordinary as an apple up here."

The age-old traffic of trivia, the human ethology of pushing and pulling so constant it's like a part of our natural environment. What Harding wanted was to get away from the names and badges around her. The primitive batter of life institutionalizing itself. Why trek down to Florida out of the blue that March day in 1977 and buy the Boullet House? Yearning for the eternal return of the sensuous engendered desire for a place where life could be practiced like a violin.

The Italian silk suit, laptop in sleep mode, is literally breathing down my neck as if we're in on this together. Does he think we're sharing a hymnal in a church pew? I shut the diary, slip it pointedly back into my briefcase. My animus glances off him like the close call of a slap in the face. Wrong tactic Juba girl, I chide myself, you've cracked the fort. And he barges right in.

"Pardon me," he says slapping himself on the forehead, "I can't believe what I was doing! Me of all people looking over somebody's shoulder at a private document like that, completely forgot where I was for a minute there . . . belonged to your grandmother probably—hmm?"

"Yes." I often lie quite automatically when angry—nothing equals it for throwing people off without them suspecting.

"Oh brother, what can I say? No disrespect intended for sure. When my sister and I were kids, well, we got into my mother's diary. Darned if she didn't catch us on the first page. A woman and her diary—hell to pay if you go between 'em. Definitely not *liber quem omnes legant*—know what I mean?" He slaps his forehead again with his palm. "Just thinking about it gives me the guilts."

I carefully file the nonsense sheets still on my lap in a briefcase pocket.

"Can't *believe* I got caught again. Like putting a time bomb on the seat between us. And me the world's great libertarian, strictly no intervention." More forehead activity and rapping softly: "Bad toy / naughty boy / got no sense / makes Mama tense / big fat baby / crying for maybe / *quid refert mea / paucis horis—*"

"Excuse me," I interrupt, prim as you please, grip my briefcase, and squeeze past him on my way to the toilet. Recalling the zipless, I lock myself in and reflect on my perturbation. The diary is slated to become part of an exhibit and I'm delivering it to the Boullet House for that purpose. So what's this, where do I get off with this sense of ownership? This urge to lay claim to it, protect it and care for it like a personal belonging. A piece of my private, very private property.

And wasn't I pleased, even flattered, when Harding asked me to prepare it for publication? Had a pricey replica made for that purpose, and on my desk at home, at this very moment, lies a laboriously annotated transcript. *They* made the decision and I, it seems, am the primary agent of change in this process of going public with it. I'm their writer, the one supposed to know how to bring out the diary's potential. Stage its opening on the commercial front.

Shred it! I consider ripping up the filmy pages and stuffing them down the toilet, leather binding and all—deal with the replica and the transcript later. The insistent knock of the stewardess aborts this option. We're preparing to land, the light has been flashing for some time.

"Be right out!" I yell and sway back to my seat seconds before we touch ground. Snappy, smooth landing. A few clap: Southerners returning to native soil, the ease of regional accents and bonds, their weather and their way of life. Guess I'll go on with mine too—writing this and that to be taken into the hands of any old body looking for a quick read.

Or will I? I remember what Harding once called her "early prophetic failure." Just married, straight out of college, she'd managed to land a job on the basis of sheer gall, without a scrap of experience, on the *New Orleans Item*. She did okay with Mardi Gras balls and features about touring violinists and ballet troupes, even got praised once for an interview with the famous Southern novelist living across Lake Ponchartrain on the Bogue Falaya River. But sent to the Irish Channel to get a story on the sniper killing of a soldier in South Korea after the war and listening to the mother reminisce tearfully about her son's love of TV—"Billy's dream was to manage a station for our troops over there"—for nearly an hour, Harding quietly slipped away without recording so much as the names of surviving family. Not even enough facts to fake it.

I on the other hand am at my best when doing legwork. I end up with more than I can ever possibly use. Call it genius or drudgery, how I get it doesn't bother me. All part of the project—a matter, as I see it, of entering into life rather than violating it. My confidence in my capacity to surf the flow free of ostensible interference has never been greater. No problem with the writing itself either, I actually look forward to that part. But publication—something about it . . . no, not that either, I've moved past any but ordinary compunctions on that front. It fills pockets with pennies, after all.

The plane has emptied and my seat belt's still buckled. The stewardess is giving me a watchful look. I grab my carry-on and make a long nonstop dash for the lobby where I plunk down to deliberate undisturbed. There's an expectant gaiety in the air. In the Big Easy traces of it flit about even in the international airport. I'm nothing if not responsive and feel more lighthearted already, more my usual self.

I can always abort this mission. It's a free country, right? Or make a detour. Mexico, Costa Rica, the West Indies—Havana by way of Santo Domingo, look it over before Castro's day is done. Or check out Haiti during Aristide's exile. Chile, Argentina, by way of Ecuador and the Galapagos, evolution's tourist haven. No problem. Anything's possible.

Not a trace of Aschenbach's tiger crouched in the gloom as Harding lifted off that March day, not long after Jimmy Carter's inauguration in the bicentennial year. Headed south, no set destination, in the existential vacuum of holiday freedom. Five days' worth including travel time. Didn't stop to call on anybody she'd known in New Orleans during the years of her marriage—handed over a traveler's check and wheeled straight out on to Airline Highway and kept going in her shiny Mercury Cougar smelling like it just rolled off the assembly line. Posh model, if something of a gas guzzler, mid-size bargain at economy rate. Her fleece-lined winter coat chucked carelessly in the back seat—a little fillip of narcissism to initiate her escapade—the barest contact with one of several gadgets, and the window slid down. Warmth laid itself across her shoulders, limbs relaxed. Dispossession had its advantages, but *having* without *possessing* now that was luxury! And ah the extraordinary ease of it all, the usual tedious maneuvers from flight reservations to rental cars arrayed, for once, into a frictionless *fait accompli*. The sure powerful joy of getting what you go for.

Midday traffic was thinning out on Chef Monteur, where the radio promised sunny days through the weekend and old Highway 90 eased her, on strains of Verdi, along the narrow lake-bounded flat of land toward the Mississippi coast—*A quell'amor, quell'amor ch'e palpito* . . . love, love, pulse of the world—this was an all-time favorite and she was singing along gloriously with Victoria de los Angeles . . . *misterioso, misterioso altero, croce delizia, delizia al cor* . . . until the spit and roar of static engulfed them both. But her home state greeted her with a mild radiance, not yet the torpor that takes hold when heat plays paradoxical tricks like an antipsychotic drug.

Down the highway a piece a local station was playing the blues. Harding has musical addictions and here already two of her top hard-core fixes, opera and Delta blues, had come to her unbidden. Half-shuttered Mississippi Gulf coast towns lounged on her landward side, still in their winter vacancy: Waveland, Bay St. Louis, the old beach homes surviving hurricane after hurricane at Pass Christian. Traffic picked up at Gulfport, crowding homeward at Biloxi. And ahead, just off the highway, sleepy old Ocean Springs where Walter Anderson made great art behind the thorns of a Cherokee rose.

And my own trip down here? Will the pragmatic nineties open on to a more realistic take, based on my own experience now? No mere tale told by another. Is mine a play within a play? I switch on my pre-millennial version of Zen: forget your intellectual impasses, let them disappear into the color of things around you. Move on, access another network. As the poet said, I'm no Hamlet nor was meant to be.

Get in your car and make it fun, "car" being a synonym for "escape" here. As a Hungarian émigré of the '56 revolution, there's nothing I appreciate more about the USA than its federation of spaces allowing safe passage for us refugees from one to the other any time, usually by car. You can correlate what's in front of you with what you've been led by somebody else's story to expect. Life is all a matter of story-maps. Isn't that the social dimension we naturally move around in from birth?

So, why not? Why not now experience firsthand, if not Harding's excitement of return from her self-imposed exile, then that of an immigrant moving through the locale of her story? However fast we immigrants catch on to the indigenous role of car and gun in guaranteeing U.S. citizenship, we keep looking for confirmation—keep on trying to correlate what's around us with what we've been led to expect.

Which reminds me, I have neither gun nor car.

Do I have a reservation? No? In that case I would probably do better with one of the smaller agencies, other side of long-term parking. I take his advice—glad I always pack light—and conclude shortly that the entrepreneurial frenzy of the '80s has changed things for good. It's been morning in America too long (for some at least) and make-my-day-kick-ass time's in the driver's seat. Nothing's easy in the post-Reagan-Bush supply-side aftermath. Insisting on the vehicle of my choice—at a discount, yet—as I've been vaguely fantasizing, would betray a Rip Van Winkle mentality: escape must be prescheduled under supply/demand conditions. Failing that, play the game, get in line, take it or leave it. Hang around until "something" comes in.

Said with a no-problem, rest-easy-but-we're-in-a-hurry-here smile: "Hmm . . . *acaso una hora, acaso un día, acaso . . . juntas todos los días.*" His cheerful helplessness ticks me off less than most; I'll try my luck here.

I grab a croissant sandwich, fat city, and take a seat inflexibly molded to the generic human butt. No hassle, life in the territory of plastic means you never have to worry about defacing anything but yourself. I eat too fast for my own good, settling into the big-hurry-no-worry mode.

There's a steady stream of drop-offs and drive-offs. A sense of urgency hums around me as if we're all averting imminent personal defeat by shrewd attunement to what comes in and what goes out. Employees at terminals, phone pinched between shoulder and jaw, thumb through piles of forms, drop asides to one another in various creoles, disappear and reappear through an unmarked red door—all with that half-snappy, half-languorous festival air typical of Caribbean workplaces and with a sweet-faced lack of concern for all clients. Equality: all us chickens here getting a chance to grab a piece of whatever's left. With all the corporate downsizing, seven years is max for a job anyway.

Decidedly not the New Orleans Harding lived in during her married years in the late 1950s and '60s, city of indolent streets where no car ever parked curbside in front of your house unless to visit you or your neighbor. Homeowners uptown were said to forget to lock up after dark. More baby-boomers were expected. Harding, in tune with the times, bore two in the early '60s, both girls.

I stretch my legs and consider following her path to the letter from here on. The word-path of the tale told held in my memory.

Cat-king of the highway, Harding's Cougar pointed its factory-polished nose east on the new Interstate to Alabama, lapping up the level miles across Mobile Bay toward the Florida Panhandle where the hidden lure of sugar-white beaches always to the south tempts the traveler to take any and every exit. Late that afternoon she turned off at Destin, the sea Aegean blue, all but one hotel still shut fast. Pairs of retirees promenading along the open beach front. No cars whizzing by and no motorcycle fume or engine roar shattering the sunset, calm, unspectacular, a light brush over the face of things before the dive down.

She got out and faced the sea to watch the turquoise rim of water billow into the twilight, then, circling back west from Destin, crossed over the slip of sound and down an old beach road where the flat scrub-grown land loped away in grassy dunes to the open Gulf and her day's wandering revealed itself, after all, as the roundabout nearing to a goal. An unpremeditated homing. Without map or effort at recall (or like me, tale told) she'd steered the Cougar through the sea-filled night to the Sands Hotel on Tarragona Beach, body of childhood summers—blue-green glitter through white curtains early in the morning, salt air a flutter of joy; crabs scurrying in the tide's rich fringe and seabirds turning on the wind for slow beneficent hours; ripe Indian peaches coating fingers with a sticky bouquet and the cool cleansing gush of an outside shower; the sting of ice-cold soda pop at the back of the throat, sweet Gulf oysters and shrimp with soda crackers for supper, the nearness of stars nesting in the soft night and, later, their distance, in the roll and drone of the tide from sleep to waking to sleep. Journey's end.

The Cougar's wheels crunched to a stop, the engine stilled like a great cat at rest. Boarded up, balconies perilously sagging, the old Sands had the look of property condemned to the wrecker's ball, or a hurricane to finish it off. Head lights cut, Harding leaned forward momentarily blinded.

Feeling revives, plucks at the heart in backward reaches—something more surfacing in memory by the softer light of moon and stars . . . a weightless anxiety . . . a snowy white gown reddening at the hem. Far enough into middle age not to flirt with fancy on a holiday she took it to be no more than a troubled eidolon, an old dream fragment perhaps, too brief for asking "whose?" or "where?" or "was it I?" before it sank back, tugged under and out into the deep, and the forgotten island summers gathered, crested, and flowed benignly, promisingly, through her.

But Harding, like other Southerners with long memories of delightful low-cost accommodations on the water, is nothing if not a sensible traveler, ever on the lookout for what may come in handy later on. While the cool moonlit vastness of the Gulf was cradling sleepers long ago in their spacious balcony suites on the seaward side, she'd already taken note of the neon flash down the two-lane beach road: "Gulfview Motel. Just one block from the water. Always open. Reasonable rates." Musty clean with hand-me-down Holiday Inn decor. No billowing white organdy curtains or giant humming fans.

The morning after: Sunrise paled the horizon into infinite blue and the Cougar, solitary beast of the chase, already cruising Tarragona Beach from end to end and down the short perpendicular side streets. "The Island," as they used to say—a sparsely developed spit of sand back then, with a highway running down the middle. So called after Tristán de Luna, one of the colonizing Spaniards whose names children memorized in school (textbook illustration: gaunt, bearded, armor-clad conquistadors disembarking from their ships as awed aboriginals congregate nakedly at a distance). More densely settled now but still something of the same feel about the place thirty-five years or so later, the clumps of cottages here and there along the main strip—a little grubby with obsolescence but recognizable—something familiar, too, about the now-defunct gas station, too close to the road, with its single pump locked in rust and Pegasus still flying above it. And the old beach concession, shut down for the winter, and the public pavilion behind it time-covered in graffiti. Lone survivors in crowded commerce with strangers.

At the main intersection Harding turned up the ramp of a new four-lane causeway arched over the placid expanse of DeLuna Bay toward the town opposite, the once scrappy colonial settlement of Tarragona—Spanish, then by turns English, French, and Spanish again, straggling along its lovely deep harbor—offering yet the promise of natural shelter that had drawn four centuries of seekers. Replicating itself by fits and starts during those rapacious centuries, with the unruliness of places always about to boom. Down below to her right, a dwarfed remnant of the old drawbridge buckled in the water amid a forest of warnings. "DANGER! Keep Off!" "No Access." "No Fishing."

From the fine curve of the Bay on the other shore, tongues of green reached lushly inland with hints of rooftops spaced well apart. Bayous— where some of Tarragona's fine old families would surely live, their days stretched out in a wealth of sameness, time slowing to the sensuous dimensions of spacious homes shaded by cypress and oak at the water's edge festive with birds feeding. Bayou Sanchez, Bayou Ribaut, Bayou Caroline— soon their names would roll off her tongue. Not quite at the exit ramp the old bridge alongside and below the causeway resumed its broken way to town amid more danger postings. A few early risers, intent on a little forbidden fishing. (Any mention of the old bridge would later elicit insinuating looks about goings-on out there in the dark.)

And there it was—she'd already come too far!—the very icon of inexhaustible satisfaction itself, high up on its white marquee: a huge coffee cup open at top and bottom, fumes curling aromatically upward and a coffee-brown river sloshing out below, a raft of letters rising and falling, riding the waves like surfers: T-H-E B-O-T-T-O-M-L-E-S-S.

Eagerly, Harding joined the stream of cars converging on the flat-roofed cinder-block building that housed the Bottomless Cup Café.

One long ago summer she'd discovered her power over the icon's existence to be absolute—as long as she didn't get too close—squinting one-eyed at the farther shore from the old drawbridge (the only crossing to town back then), boldly advancing toward the desired shape, index finger at the ready, way past where she was allowed on her own, until the instant she spotted it—now! Faster than a blink, the tip of her finger flew over the open eye. Like a pin-point star in the dome of night she could make the cup—that loomed so huge when you were right up under it— come and go with the flick of a finger.

No amount of explaining by adults (or those aspiring, like her brother, to grown-up attitudes) could dispel the perplexity of the cup's bottomlessness—and turned around, its infinite plenty. Never ran out of coffee, they said with a conspiratorial wink. She'd watch as seconds were poured for customers, and thirds, time after time. Alone in the dark of her bedroom at the old Sands, tide rolling and fan whirring and white curtains billowing, she'd imagine herself bobbing with the letters in a coffee-brown sleep that flowed nowhere. Nowhere, the very test of survival. Nowhere: the measure of Utopia.

"More coffee, ma'am?" Made fresh, and satisfyingly bitter with a last bite of buttered biscuit. There'd been short refills aplenty, more turned down in-between, and still this sweet languor over a cooling cup, tuned to the music of the black-haired waitress's voice directed here, there, among the gregarious hum of the old Bottomless.

Unchanged as far as she could tell, lingering on the memory of that early developmental struggle with the duplicities of metaphor. "Jack be nimble, Jack be quick" was, quite possibly, the only true natural wisdom of childhood: agility is the answer. After such nightly bouts with the unbounded, you simply jumped, undamped and undaunted, into the next mystery.

"We'll be moving this fall! Come see us in the Historic Quarter, only minutes from here," read a notice beside the cash register. Counting out change on a little green mat, while supplying directions to the old Quarter, the waitress gave Harding the flash smile—the one that commits to nothing and asks nothing in return but does both with impersonal friendliness.

"You may be seeing me again for lunch."

"Our dessert special today is walnut cream pie," she said with that softening upturn of a question, dark eyes briefly consulting those of her customer.

"Same recipe as in the old days? I've been gone a long time."

"Should be coming out of the oven right about now." Already a distancing tone concealed with perfect courtesy her shift of attention to the couple next in line.

One tended to forget in the wintry deeps of involvement up North, not the difference the surface makes but the ease of it. The sunny smoothness of the surface.

It's past 3 p.m. and I've drifted off into the spirit of the Crescent City when I'm paged. "Señorita Juba to the counter, *por favor,* Señorita Juba."

Success. The smiling young Latino agent processes my Visa and points to a little two-door Dodge Shadow in the parking lot. Blue, washed, and allegedly serviced. *"Con mil amores,"* he murmurs, dropping keys into my hand.

The one next in line behind me fixes on them like the Wolf on Little Red Ridinghood. I grab the packet containing my rental agreement and a road map and I'm out of there, goodbye airport. On the other side of town I swing off I-10 to Chef Monteur through Gentilly. Outside the city limits on the old highway to Mississippi the beehive of traffic thins until, New Orleans less than a half hour behind me, there's only my Shadow gliding through the stretch of marsh, past roadside camps on their stilts. Coasting to the tempo of an earlier, unhurried environment afloat between Lake Ponchartrain and Lake Borgne. A warmish late spring day, lightly overcast.

I settle down and bask without a thought as to the question of the diary's future, so swept along am I in Harding's tracks over the Pearl River and into the Magnolia State, as announced on a solitary billboard bearing the state flower of Mississippi, which, having given birth to her, decreed her, she feels, a monster of minor parts (in the old sense of both having too many and at least one too few). A state where such freaks might relax and nap unseen—like me, I feel.

Soon other signs—for the Grand Casino, Lady Luck, Treasure Bay, Gold Shore, and Casino Magic looking appropriately Disneyish—come thick and fast but fail to perturb this laid-back charm. At Bay St. Louis new malls line the highway and traffic slows, the Gulf softly nudges the Point like a flattened sky. I'm definitely enjoying a sunny rapport with Harding sixteen years after the fact and ease appreciatively by the old waterfront homes at Pass Christian. It's a different scene from what I'd expected along this coast, a distinct scent of money in the air, beaches sparkling clean as though swept down each morning. Gulfport coming up . . . Biloxi next, home of Jefferson Davis.

Traffic shoots past like a space lift-off and my gas gauge is on empty. The Grand Casino, a block-long monument to kitsch in violet and blue-gray, blue and red, offers uninhibited access—every shade of fun and excitement, come and get it. And there, there ahead, a flock of white ibis, like a fluttering clothesline flung into the sky.

I swing into a Texaco station, edge up to one of its sixteen pumps and insert the 87-octane hose. Across from me a couple of them, handsome, thirty-something and feeling it, top off with super unleaded. A half-full minibus squeezes past with all cheering, throwing out their arms at us, opening their palms in crap-shooting gestures. It's the President Casino's private shuttle bus, free rides for all takers.

The two across from me rumble with volcanic energy. "Hoo-ee," one of them hollers, "I'm gone crack some dice and slice some decks tonight!" "Yea-ho," yells the other, "Bi-luck-si ain't enough luck-si to hold me. I'm gone break some pots."

I realize I'm moving into the development boom of gambling adrenaline from Gulfport to Biloxi and decide to cut over to I-10 again. Where the pace is smoother. Over Mobile Bay, on into Florida's panhandle, on Harding's heels. I even drive the extra leg to the white sands and Aegean blues of Destin and circle back the way she did. The gush of evening rain has tapered off to a drizzle so slight and fine it seems a mere landward exhalation of Gulf water. In time for my arrival on DeLuna Island the cloud cover pulls apart, one or two bright stars pop out.

Harding's childhood haven—the old Sands—was demolished years ago. No surprise. A complex of well-kept time-share villas, each with private pool heated for year-round use, has inherited the name. Not a ghost of the old fishing bridge, though. Safety first.

From the causeway Tarragona is a rag of patchily phosphorescent Gulf weed strung along the deep harbor. Nightlife has either shut down already or requires minimal illumination. At the very last moment, as the causeway ramp slopes into a four-lane commercial strip, I spot the white marquee like a piece of outdoor conceptual art looming ahead on high stilts. No building under it but the same wafting fumes with bottomless cup and muddy river beneath, redesigned as a stand-alone pointer for the Old Tarragona Historic Quarter: T-H-I-S W-A-Y, in the broad shaft of an arrow piercing the coffee waves. I follow the arrow, ignoring drivers rudely cutting past and in front of me left and right. Couch potatoes on the prowl—a little prime-time pizza maybe, tank up for Letterman. Catch Wal-Mart before they close.

But the Bottomless Cup Café, relocated in the Quarter since Harding's time, is dark. I note signs of activity in one or two upscale drinking establishments and down the street there's a nice little iron-balconied terrace restaurant advertising bed and breakfast. Shades of the *Vieux Carré*. In less than an hour I'm dead to the world.

No markers for the old Quarter in the 1940s when Harding was a child—nobody'd have thought of mentioning the town slum.

It was a different story when she arrived there in the late '70s with historic reclamation set off by the Bicentennial in full swing. Packaging of the past for eye-appeal was nowhere more evident than in the welcome center for visitors—high-beamed, hollow-toned, detailed and polished to perfection. Staffed by college students—bright-eyed types politely coached in how to relate to the public and seemingly untouched by protest movements of the previous twenty years—it had been Tarragona's railway station once, though that sunny March morning it resembled none Harding could recall from the age of trains. "Authentic" restoration failing to preserve the objects of memory.

Plenty of free parking, though, and stacks and stacks of last year's Bicentennial Guide for the taking. Foldout map inside, for suggested walks through the Historic Quarter, site of the town's first waterfront settlement—a maze of cottages in a variety of styles, many already restored to a high finish: Diaz House, Renfrew House, Quiroga House, among others, all bearing the family names of their original owners and minutely rendered on the map. Not exactly to scale, explained one of the visitor-friendly welcomers, but like really picturesque, you know.

From the welcome center (YOU ARE HERE: Gateway to four centuries of Old Tarragona), Harding found her way down busy Cadiz Boulevard to Hernando Plaza, shown on her map as a colorful square of walks radiating from a central pavilion, with perfectly miniaturized gas lamps and Charleston benches spaced casually among springy ringlets of shrubbery and ancient live oaks primped with Spanish moss. At its bottom edge, the wrinkle-silvered waters of the Bay, and along the top, across the broad avenue—where she now paused to orient herself—an imposing structure identified as the Hernando Inn, with carriages circling around a graceful fountain at the front entrance. Round about 1838 when, according to the map's legend, Captain Claude Francis Boullet ("patriot and merchant of the city") had the Hernando built in atypical style out of imported Havana brick, the port of Tarragona was on a roll. One of those boom eras that literally altered the landscape.

"Why, yes ma'am, plenty of rooms at the Inn, nice big ones. None of 'em ever been cut up, just like the day they was built." Was she wanting something by the week or the month? The anxious little woman at the reception desk looked worn out beyond her years. (Later, Harding would come to know her as "Miss Annie," general drudge to the neighborhood.)

In Harding's experience, wherever an old part of town is attracting money after decades of neglect ("rehabilitation" was the official lingo in Tarragona circa 1977) you need a good nose for what's rising, what's falling or leveling off, what's so run down it's past rising or running down any further, and what may be one thing looking like another. Cultivate this critical organ of detection and you're likely to catch a pretty reliable whiff of the prospects.

"Not this visit," she answered inhaling deeply, "just looking." If any ghost of former affluence (one of the ladies and gentlemen, say, shown alighting from their carriages on the Bicentennial map) lingered about the Hernando, it wouldn't be apt to hang out in the foyer. Not among those vinyl hulks cluttering the great expanse of Italian marble floor—a lovely celadon and rose domino pattern under half a century of grime. A teenage boy, skinny and slack-jawed, with a lank mop of yellowish hair, gaped down the winding marble staircase like the specter of some young beauty assessing her social purview.

"The boy cain't hep it, ma'am, he don't mean no harm." And then to him, "Stop ya starin', Jimmy Hurd—come on down, lady ain't stayin'."

Outside, local populations of birds and squirrels, stray dogs and cats were congregating by the ruined marble fountain. The same look there of hardened neglect, as if leery of post-Bicentennial display—as though withdrawal were the only available defense against history's upscale triumphalism. Amid law and real estate offices, title companies, architectural firms, and tourist boutiques housed in a sprightly mix of rehabilitated frame cottages around the Plaza—effusively balustraded two-story Victorians alongside more reticent shotguns of the time and, tucked here and there like self-effacing rarities, three or four cottages of the century before, all with their tastefully color-coordinated shingles of occupancy—Captain Boullet's grand old Caribbean hostelry stood glumly aloof. If you can't go with the flow, well then, stand firm on the difference.

The Plaza that morning was all soft Bay breezes and doves' wings brushing the sandy ground under moss-festooned oaks. Composed as a picture. On Harding's map, it sloped down to a stylized mass of wavelets populated by sea monsters among which galleons of old steered their perilous course, homing to port or headed out to DeLuna Island and the open Gulf. Irregular grids of streets spread away from the Plaza's three landward sides: Saragossa, Valencia, Blanca, Arriola, Jerez, Altamira, Villalonga, Aguilar, Cadiz, with St. George, Lavallet, Ribaut, and Caroline adrift among them.

Flotsam of Europe's great powers plying colonialism's hungry seas. How might the winds of reclamation be blowing? It happened, while she was idling over the topography of restoration—mercury hitting seventy and enraptured syllables of *Traviata* singing in her head (*A quell'amor quell'amor ch'e palpito . . .*)—that her hand strayed down the back of the iron bench she was sitting on and encountered a plaque.

Placed by the Tarragona Garden Club in fond memory of
Letitia Hart Cane (d. 1959) beloved wife of Randall Cane, Jr.,
whose pioneering commitment to the rehabilitation of America's
oldest continuous community has been an inspiration to all.
Everywhere in evidence, that brilliant North Florida March day. All down the little crisscrossing streets and lanes—in all the moans and groans of rehabilitation, the cacophonies of ripping, pounding, hauling, scraping, and bedecking that signaled, like the cries of a healthy newborn, a fresh and vigorous community in the making, a more genteel, more harmonious order. Mrs. Randall Cane, Jr., ready to issue forth in taste and decorum, finished down to Athena's shield carried lightly on her left arm.

Harding was avidly taking it all in, yards and walkways spilling over with demolition mess, every turn of the old Quarter's transformation. Taking in, as well, the fact that the entire Historic District seemed to be making itself over as a kind of small-business park. "Does anybody *live* here?" she asked a workman swigging an RC on the porch of a Greek Revival cottage, post–Civil War, that advertised itself as the "future home of Segovia Designs, Ltd."

"Not me," he chuckled, more as an aside to his coworker. He was a family man, new home out past the city limits on the Alabama side. Had to think about what kind of neighborhood the kids would grow up in.

She'd already drawn her own conclusions from the upwardly trending staff at the welcome center, the blank stares all around at her mention of residential areas. One eventually broke ranks—the old Quarter was "really taking off," he said, and (lowering his voice) would have long before now except there was this, like, public housing project close by, a place called Segovia Villas. On the rough side. So she followed her nose: commerce rehabilitating the southern end of the Quarter nearest the waterfront at a hectic pace (the Hernando Inn was the big holdout), residents were bound to follow. Were most likely there already, stashed away on the ground floor of restoration somewhere—studio apartments piggy-backed to boutiques, that kind of thing.

Harding's organ of detection flared as she cut back to the Plaza's trafficky north end, then headed for the "fringes" behind the Hernando, the grid of streets primed to rise next—as a residential neighborhood, if her nose could be relied on, proximity to the housing project notwithstanding. Wasn't there always an enterprising set, blind to class and color given the right opportunities? Ace in her hand: the local community college, due to go four-year any day, within walking distance.

What she noticed first was the quiet. Entering the alley alongside the Hernando she'd stepped through some gap in the rattle of traffic and reclamation into the sheltered domestic space of noon—a sudden sweetness of Carolina jasmine in the air, yellow trumpets of it twining through an espalier of woody wisteria over the soft-colored old brick of a high wall backing a deep double lot. A massive forged iron fence rimmed the grounds of a two-story frame house fronting the next street, Valencia. Large, the white paint flaked off its clapboards almost to the wood, the yard a landfill of cast-off appliances and trash. A pack of mongrel dogs ranged sullenly in the shade of the wall. Space galore, though—plant a terrace there, leave the old fig tree, still bearing, erect an arbor at the back draped with a branch of wisteria from the old wall.

She closed her eyes the better to see it, the garden yielding itself to her with all its power already rooted in her, then followed the fence down the alley and left along Valencia Street to the front. It was shabby, with that muffled look houses get that's like shame in a person, but solid and level on substantial brick piers, pre-Civil War she guessed—tall ceilings if it hadn't been messed with, well-proportioned rooms, ample light, cooled naturally by drafts from the Bay making a breezeway through the central hall. No hint of *art nouveau,* no anticipation of any modern turn. A structure entirely reflecting dependence on its past, built for work and leisure inside that spectacular old Spanish fence. In marked contrast to house and yard the fence—eight feet tall no less—was in well-nigh perfect condition, its iron palings free of rust. As if to declare the true state of things. Proud, seeming not so much to shut out the world as to frame and secure it within.

Beside the locked gate hung a notice colored and lettered like an old pub sign:

Heritage Homes Inc.

FOR SALE

Margaret Avery: 722–2511

She made a note of it, eyeing nearby properties in varying degrees of dilapidation and potential. The rambling old cottage across the street, not as striking but pleasant, showed signs of work about to begin.

Back down the alley again, to size up the jackleg addition at the rear—knock down that eyesore, restore the old gallery with its row of French doors opening out to greenery and shade—then once more to the front, where boughs of a great live oak arched across the yard toward second-story dormers. Head between two iron palings, reading past marks of decay, neglect, abuse, Harding studied the handsome cypress entry, the floor-to-ceiling windows along the veranda. What was such a house for if not to be lived in?

Or—and here was the question at the heart of her vision that brilliant spring morning—what was life for if not to be lived in such a house?

Across a Hepplewhite table from Margaret Avery of Heritage Homes, No. 12 Hernando Avenue, Harding learned that, in the very Quarter where a run-down historic shack could bring upward of fifty thousand, the Boullet House (going back, interestingly enough, to that same Captain Claude Francis Boullet who'd put up the Hernando Inn) on its deep double lot, with its authentic seventeenth-century Catalonian fence and spacious interior might be bought for substantially less. Except for that ugly addition, no one had tampered with the house since it was built about mid-nineteenth century. Exclusive listing: once-in-a-lifetime opportunity. The Committee for the Preservation of Historic Tarragona, a private group of developers, had indicated a willingness (which had, to Harding, an odor of eagerness) to sell cheaply for all cash.

To someone prepared to begin at once—that was the only hitch—a buyer in a position to do a quality restoration, naturally. True, that block of Valencia was still something of a frontier in the Historic Quarter. The Boullet House was the key. Harding took this to mean the Committee had its eye on the whole block and more, but only after someone else made the first move—took the major risk. They were underwriting a pioneer at a bargain-basement price.

"It does need everything in the world done to it, you realize, but the potential—well, you can see for yourself. Now that it's on the market, it won't last long—care for a look inside?"

"Sorry," said Harding, "I'm not seriously interested at this time—what with only a couple of days in town it would have to be today, but really . . ."

"The Wentworths won't mind a bit," Margaret Avery shot back, all poise and business in her sea-green linen suit, already dialing their number.

Late that afternoon Harding walked down to the beach below the derelict old Sands and slipped off her shoes. Already the folly of it was crystal clear. This pull to the Boullet House had all the heft and feel of a compulsion, a paraphilia of sorts. If you know what it's like to be hopelessly infatuated, you'll readily follow her in arriving at an answer. Or perhaps in not arriving at one.

Premise: Compulsions feed on the tension between an uncanny knowledge of their objects and an extraordinary ignorance of them. The excitement thus generated turns first to agitation, then frequently (unfailingly, Harding would have insisted) and rapidly to pain—the foolishness in them reducing one to the very depths of humiliation. Time, will, sheer strength—not to mention money, the savings accumulated since her divorce, the promise of a modestly comfortable future as she moved on through her forties and fifties toward retirement—all at stake. Hers was the worker's risk of sliding into the iron clamps of poverty, oppression, violence, that three-headed monster ever on the prowl for the unattached woman. (No escape for one in three, said the statistics.) Sheer endurance, resignation, hard work—the odds were good these would still suffice to ward off the first two heads. But violence? The pure terrifying craziness of that energy, the denial of refuge, utter lack of mercy, narrowly utilitarian judgments, blind eye for consequences—here, images crystallized in quick succession like a condensation of the whole story: a tri-colored beagle, unremarkable except for the bloody crust of mange over all except its head and running down the legs and feet between swollen toes, abandoned beside the Gulf many summers ago—a cripple returned to the wild—and she, a child on vacation with her family, feeding it, keeping it alive in its hideout on the edge of a salt marsh, understanding so well its cast-off condition and yet concurring finally in her father's assessment, as it stood helpless in front of them, tail tucked and head down, eyes shifting, "Looks like she might have been a good little hunting bitch, no good now, poor thing," before he pulled the trigger and she helped him dig the hole. What held her most in this spontaneous reel of memories was the fact that except for an occasional subdued whine so brief it was no more than a hint of sound, the beagle was mute from the day she found it dumped on the marsh's edge to the moment it died.

Yes, to yield to this absurd desire for a run-down old house would be to court ruin. To risk losing all she was least willing to lose. She could simply leave. Now. Get back in her rented Cougar and drive away forever, go on with life knowing she'd made the prudent choice. She could—but she didn't want to. The love object promised (as always) satisfaction so compelling as to turn any move away from it back into itself (despite her sense, even then, of an ignorance concealed in her infatuation). In adolescence, when she'd accommodated to nearsightedness rather than wear glasses, her normal experience was of a clear and vivid state of things up close rapidly fading out at a distance; so now, she adjusted to not seeing her way through the reach and depths of violence in the offing. You can't die here and now but once, she told herself with a dry acceptance of dire consequences.

On to the sole consideration that gave her pause: her children, Helen and Vanessa, in their teens, soon to be college-bound. To risk her own future was one thing, to gamble away theirs unpardonable. The old Gulf-side hotel sagged toward her down the slope of sand as if offering counsel. Out and back, out and back in perfect concert, flocks of sanderlings chased the tide's foamy fringe teasing her feet with its withdrawals and narrow misses, this undirected sun-warmed energy signifying for her the right distance for playing life out to the end. Only a slight imaginative shift in the delusionary depths and heights of passion opened the vista where responsibility for Helen and Vanessa led down desire's lane. For *their* sake the risk *must* be taken.

Harding watched her shadow leap away into the waves luminous with sunset, shrink and swell, divide and reunite in their undulations. She was putting herself on the line. The alternative? To deny herself. Watergazing, she concluded, may foster gay delusion, but how else is one to get a good look at what goes on out there?

The Bottomless Cup Café has changed hands more than once since relocating to Tarragona's old Quarter, full range of gourmet coffees and teas now, pastry chef (member of Cuban family who owns the downtown bakery) also caters. Not the rich homey fare of Harding's childhood but a culinary displacement she tends to favor as much as I do.

I sit in one of the bay windows and order a local favorite, a guava puff, feeling windblown and tingly and uncharacteristically at peace. Up with the sun, I drove back over to the Island and walked—and walked. All up and down the wildlife refuge covering the eastern end. Looked out to sea a lot with some dim expectation that an inspired resolution of my problem would settle on me before breakfast. Not a whisper. Not a clue about how to go public with the diary as instructed, without letting others get their hands on it. I waited and walked and marveled at the whiteness of the sand under my feet stretching mile after mile—the kind of terrain where answers, as unsummoned as problems, should settle on you not with the strength that moves heaven and earth but with the comforting warmth of the sun.

This Beckettian condition of waiting holds no appeal for me; I'm an investigator at heart, the kind who turns things upside down looking for what's wanted. Upside-downs, quietly fingered, offer untold treasures of fascination. And there's plenty of time yet; the diary and I are not expected till late afternoon. I consider telling them I've lost it or it's been stolen or a maid mistakenly threw it in the trash or neighbors' children destroyed it or dogs maybe . . .

I pay up, resisting the lure of a second guava puff to go. Compliments of the pastry chef bringing out a fragrant fresh tray of them. More stranger-friendly than when Harding was down here restoring the Boullet House, Tarragona has the provincial feel of older American towns doggedly offering themselves to history buffs, sniffing at the scent of their desire, devising a past that satisfies, satisfaction tapped at the source. Such are the skills of manufacturing raw material for the tourism industry.

Back to the trail. My Shadow scoots past police headquarters to the old railway station on Arriola Street where, squeezed in beside a sporty Mercedes parked in the shade, I surreptitiously pop open the trunk. Just checking—diary in briefcase, all safe and sound. No point lugging it around and being tagged as a business type when I can pass for just another tourist. Several are being welcomed inside the center for visitors. They have an international look about them, some arty, well-heeled, receiving directions to a nearby four-star French restaurant. Anticipating the noon repast by several hours.

"Yes," replies the young attendant, a Bicentennial Guide with walking map (like Harding's) is available on request. Five-dollar contribution suggested, special fund for local beautification projects. The Guide has become a collector's item—am I a collector? He has a crisp manner, pleasantly formal in jacket and tie, Southeast Asian if I know my cultural quilt, but with startling blue eyes.

I accept one of the new revised maps, distinctly unpicturesque but free of charge. The phone rings and he answers snappily, "Welcome Center, Will Wentworth speaking."

"I'm wondering," I blurt out when he hangs up, "if by any chance you're related to Jeremy Wentworth who used to live in the Boullet House?" And died there, I don't say. Harding found the body—her entrée to Tarragona that summer she came down to take possession of her impulsively acquired property—downstairs in the back wing, Captain Boullet's old quarters. Propped up in a hospital bed, dead as a doornail and staring wide-eyed across the room at her. Just him and the family garbage, the rest having already moved out. Like a smell so pervasive it becomes the air you breathe, old Wentworth haunted her subliminal life virtually from then on.

"My great-grandfather. Except for my Uncle Billy I'm his only living male descendant," comes the proud reply. "Passed away when I was a toddler. Did you know him?"

To be asked at my age if you knew somebody's great-grandfather has a disquieting effect and I shake my head in forceful denial. "Not personally, but I'm interested in the history around here . . . the old families, like the Wentworths . . . good old English name . . ." I don't mean to be emphasizing that side of things and I'm relieved when he responds with a gracious incline of the head, as if acknowledging his own well-known and accepted place in society. Not hung up on ethnic labels.

I cruise down to the Plaza and pull in by a restored eighteenth-century cottage as nicely proportioned as a Shaker bench. Authentic to the nines. And speak of the devil: the shingle out front reads "Greeley Connor, Architectural Consultant." Pipe-smoking Bostonian, MIT, hailed in Harding's time as Old Tarragona's official expert on all matters historic. Still on top of things after all these years, just as she predicted.

"A pity there's no way to cut corners in this kind of work," he'd offered in response to her tale of squandering more than a week over demolition and building permits at the Office of Planning and Construction downtown—where she was viewed by suitefuls of clerks and assistant supervisors, at several echelons of bureaucracy, as having an attitude.

Only the Supervisor of Municipal Construction had the power to issue a permit for a historic building, they said. And only after the most thorough review of cost estimates—who would do the work and how and on what schedule—and of course only after the Preservation Board approved her architectural plans at its monthly meeting. Not all cities looked after the interests of property owners the way Tarragona did. Greeley could understand her frustration, but you had to allow the process to work. Had she been advised that no permit would be issued to her personally? That was never done. Never. Only licensed contractors got permits, including demolition permits, those above all.

Impossible to countermand the message: don't mess with our historic homes, leave them to the professionals. "Greeley has a contractor's license, didn't I tell you?" was Margaret Avery's contribution to Harding's problem. He was architectural consultant to the Board, moreover, of which she was herself a member. An arrangement could probably be made.

It was. Plans drawn, permit issued, followed by unscheduled five- to ten-minute drop-ins two or three times per week by Greeley Connor, now Harding's consulting contractor, fees unspecified. As unquestioningly confident as though mediocrity were a matter of good genes, he never had to prove a thing. His single-minded dedication to getting it right said it all.

Authenticity, Greeley would intone, is the yardstick of any serious restoration. And of course code compliance. "Without code compliance" (said in the matter-of-fact way of one alluding to a shared existential condition) "you'll never get a certificate of occupancy." A language species Harding instantly recognized after her years in academia, the institutional syntax not to be transgressed even here.

I decide I may as well leave the Shadow parked in front of Greeley's place—it's legal—and amble through the Plaza down to the water's edge. Still there, the bench with the plaque on it dedicated to Mrs. Randall Cane Jr., inspiration to all. Time-mellowed, along with the restored cottages surrounding the Plaza, and not an irreverent scratch or scar on any part of it. Like Harding I nestle in, let the sun do its thing through the frayed ozone layer. My easy-to-read map of Tarragona has a blow-up of the Historic Quarter on the back, informative and to scale. Oh but I miss those galleons—and sea monsters. Like grotesques in the marginalia of illuminated manuscripts they highlight dimensions of meaning that're always there, even when unrepresented.

As though to make up for the lack, public buildings—City Hall, the new Performing Arts Center—flash their locations in stamps of little red brick structures here and there all over the downtown. My eye stops on the Tarragona Public Library, an avenue of investigation opening to me.

On my way there I get sidetracked. Down a short block between the business and the historic districts my Shadow spins around in a U-turn, not so much on impulse as from an involuntary response to a familiar name on one of the office buildings. *The Tarragona Sentinel.* Grown bigger and better (two additional sections since Harding's time, plus entertainment insert on Thursdays). On request, the old issues from late August '77 are obligingly stacked before me by an intern, crisp as the morning they arrived on Harding's front porch her last week in Tarragona—those marathon days of finish-work and the town, fangs bared, claws gory, moving in on the Boullet House, exposing the monstrous configuration of its polity in news clippings she'd hastily crammed into a manila folder. Once back in Athena, she placed them before me like proof sheets of her restoration story, and I studied them with a diligence due the Rosetta Stone. I'm smitten now with a desire to look at them in their original context, to handle the sixteen-year-old pages of newsprint.

The real thing, all here. On top, the electrifying front page of Monday's issue, August 15, 1977: Jake Landry's corpse spiked face-up on that magnificent Catalonian fence circling the Boullet House. He's wrapped in an old KKK robe—family heirloom from Reconstruction days, it comes out later, hand-sewn for one of the two Evans brothers employed in younger days at El Inglés, along with the victim's grandfather, Jacob Landry, who ran the plantation for the Howards, maternal grandparents of Frances Boullet. Name the kinfolk and you place the person. Turning the pages and watching the story unfold in its graphic day-by-day novelty carries for me, as it did for Harding, that strong sense genealogy brings of knowing exactly who people are. Understanding more about what's going on than is told.

There're few in the daily news before me whose kin I don't recall from the diary. The Hurds and the Wentworths, of course. Poor old Doc Shibbles, holed up next door to the Boullet House and always on the watch. Randall Cane of Segovia Crescent, the third of that notable name— unscathed by it all as usual. And the two expecting me at the house later today—Maria-Louisa (the *Sentinel*'s "Creole Woman," known locally as "Miss Mary Louise") and Aimée Hulin (member of Tarragona's social elite and niece of Randall Cane, coming to Maria-Louisa's aid in promotion of Haitian art). One way or another everybody got in on the act—reporters, cops, thrill-seekers, old-timers, various of the gainfully employed and the perennially unemployed—because, one way or another, everybody was already part of it. Greeley Connor, architect, with his Bostonian cachet. Tony Krasner, roofer, who liked being around the glamor of money old or new, while the victim, Jake Landry (as devilishly adept with a pencil and sketchpad as his plantation overseer grandfather), ran the town's drug trade. Confessions made, retracted, remade. Harding, too deep into Tarragona's past for her own good, managing a hairbreadth escape, unconvinced that the Evans men (her father-and-son team of plumbers) were guilty of murder as charged, eyewitness testimony and her own fear of them notwithstanding.

What a lot you have to know to decode the news! Wednesday's centerfold spread on the old Howard Plantation ("Then and Now"—with authentic pre–Civil War sketches amid cutting-edge historical theorizings about their peculiarities) quickly spawned a letter to the editor from one "Jon, Last of the Alligator Indians": to correct an error of fact about his great-grandmother. A lady not so dark if you've read the diary.

I really should be on my way, but sheer nosiness—about whether the plot unraveling before Harding drove out of town left any knot afterwards—gets the better of me. Week after her departure, August 22–29, 1977: none of this have I seen before. Stills of the accused, Tom Evans and son Aubrey, from a national newscast, dignified to the hilt—big on self-vindication. Dribbles of opinion or confabulation disguised as follow-ups. A flood of letters, most in favor of dismissing charges. One writer makes no bones about the general consensus: "Let's face it, Jake Landry getting himself killed sooner or later was not that big of a deal." Late in the week staff writer Roland B. Markit (last-ditch effort to keep the story, by now almost buried, alive) waylays the senior accused's wife in her neighborhood Winn Dixie. Mrs. Evans declines to answer questions but repeats several times, "Tom's just saying what he thinks is best for the family and I'm the one who knows."

That does it. Clearing up the old mystery of who killed Jake Landry that summer of Harding's restoration is not what I'm down here for (and, anyway, I think I have a pretty good idea where her skepticism about the guilt of the Evans men was coming from). I refold August 29 and stack it with the others.

"Got everything you need?" the intern inquires in passing.

Have I? "Guess so," I reply. Naive member of the public never quite sure of what's what with a media spin. We smile understandingly at each other as I make for the exit.

The Historic Quarter is well behind me when I turn into the small parking lot of the Tarragona Public Library, an unremarkable two-story brick building from the 1950s. After 1 p.m.! Not the pedestrian lunch-hour bustle you'd expect downtown. At the convenience store across the street they have all-beef hot dogs sizzling on a spit. I order one with everything on it, shrink away from the coffee dregs on the hot plate and choose an icy coke in an old-style bottle instead; haven't had one of these in years.

From fast food in a sweaty car to the library's central air, set so low I'm shivering. Downstairs it's like summer camp. High school and junior high kids, on special research projects, crowding one another at the rows of terminals with internet access, even the online catalogue stations in full use. Three assistant librarians are serving the needs of youth. I interrupt one to ask where the Frances Boullet collection is located. (Still regretting she'd had no time for the public library that summer, Harding reminded me of it as I was leaving Athena.) Expressionless, he slinks into the cubicle behind the check-out counter to consult the librarian—sixtyish, tortoise shell glasses on a matching chain around her neck.

She sets her glasses in place and peeps around the corner of the partition before coming out, a bit puzzled by my query. "You must mean . . ." She smoothes wisps of gray hair escaping from her bun and steps with Old Southern hospitality from behind the counter. Up the stairs we go to an out-of-the way wing on the second floor. "There, 'Captain Boullet's Library,'" she reads from a brass plaque on a handsome large table inserted lengthwise in a horseshoe of shelves, "nice to see someone take an interest, hardly anybody does anymore. It's an unusual private library, what's left of it, donated to us by Randall Cane III."

"This is not all of the original collection?"

"Less than half, we've sold off the rest over the years in our annual liquidations. With Dr. Cane's consent, of course—mostly the fiction, whole sets of novels and short stories, poetry too, all replaced with modern editions. Readers like their classics better glossed these days, more information about the author and so forth. Is this the material you're interested in?" She points to a printed notice casually propped against tall gray steel bookcases along the wide back of the horseshoe, dated May 11, 1936:

These handsome wooden bookcases, with their rolling staircase,
originally stood along the upstairs north wall of the Claude Francis
Boullet House. A unique collection of books by or about women is
shelved thereon.

"Handsome wooden bookcases?" I ask, looking around.

"Sent to the Boullet House recently, at Dr. Cane's request. The present owners are negotiating to buy back the collection—I thought you might be representing them."

"I'm not . . . looking for anything in particular," I lie, "only curious about what Tarragonans were reading in the early part of the century." She starts to say something but smiles uncertainly—unconvinced, I feel—and slips back downstairs.

I browse through the titles down one side of the table. *History and Theory of Money; Palace of Minos; Modern Treatment of Wounds; His-*

tory as Past Ethics; Some Heretics of Yesterday; Beginnings of Writing; Histoire d'Haiti; Pathos of Distance; Dante and the Early Astronomers; Progress and Poverty; Harmonics; L'empereur Dessalines; A Grammar of the Maninka-Bambara-Dyula Dialects. A History of Architecture on the Comparative Method; Traumatic Injuries of the Brain and its Membranes; Ruines: ou Méditations sur les révolutions des empires; The Axe Laid to the Root . . . many more on the structures of things—the brain, language, the sense organs. The workings of power in configurations from family to nations and corporate bodies. And technology, its expansion of life-possibilities and its cultural narrowing of them. Travel in every nook and cranny of the world, the flora and fauna, the cultures. My kind of books, all shelved alphabetically by author, and largely from the last half of the nineteenth century and early decades of the twentieth—it's like running across an old bookstore where your personal leanings are frozen and re-flected back to you in the life-span of another. A quick spot-check turns up no name plates or other marks of ownership inside.

On a hunch I settle in front of the ersatz steel bookcases at the back, the women's books—a likely repository for guidance as to what I, over and above the passing whims of my own desire, should do with the diary. For what or whom was it destined?

Hmmm . . . Louisa May Alcott's *Work: A Story of Experience;* Djuna Barnes, *The Book of Repulsive Women;* Michael Field, *Long Ago; Secret History; or, The Horrors of St. Domingo* by Mary Hassal; Nella Larsen's *Quicksand* and *Passing;* Gertrude Stein's *Three Lives; Hit* by Mary Walker—Phyllis Wheatley, Sara Winnemucca's *Life among the Piutes,* and, yes, another candidate, Mary Wollstonecraft. I'm spellbound—expecting to find, if not an outright message, then any number of clues as to where and how Frances Boullet might approach my problem. It's *her* problem after all. The personal problem lingering after death, unresolved: disposal of life's leavings.

I remove an armful respectfully from the first shelf and begin my search with Alcott, scanning the pages for telltale marks: checked or underlined passages, marginal comments, an exclamation point maybe, a question, an impetuous "yes" or "no." A scratch, a doodle.

Nothing in any of them, not so much as a dog's ear or an inclination to fall open at some favorite page. And yet all these books look and feel much handled. I push them aside and go through a second pile, then select—the first to hand being an early British translation of Freud's case study of Dora—works considered provocative or controversial in their time, unusual enough to have elicited some response. Great fun, this, randomly pulling out and riffling through Frances Boullet's books, not a few unknown to me. A good hour has elapsed since I gave up any expectation of help from her with the problem of settling my piece of her estate. There's only this, and it can be explained in any number of ways: the determination—evidently a conscious discipline—to leave no trace of herself on what she read.

I stretch and peer at the notice about the "handsome wooden bookcases, with their rolling staircase." The date on it—May 11, 1936—sends me running downstairs and out to the car where I look up Maria-Louisa's diary entry about how she came to be living down the street (still "the fringes," in Harding's time) from the Boullet House:

> MAY 2, 1936. I am today in receipt of the deed to a cottage on the last block of Valencia Street where the rag-tag immigrants live along with assorted poor and colored—this in return for giving up all claim to the property of Frances Florida Boullet, deceased.

Just as I thought, Dr. Cane made his "bequest" to the library only days after this piece of behind-the-scenes horse trading. Did any word of it leak into the public domain, I wonder, and what face was put on it there? Back at the reference desk, I request *Sentinel* microfilm for the month of May 1936.

The afternoon has passed and I'm barely getting started. Observing me with that cautious absorption people feel when dealing with those of unbalanced enthusiasms, the librarian leaves for the day—Maria-Louisa and Aimée will be expecting me within the hour. But here it is, May 5, 1936, among other items of purely local interest on the front page:

Haunted House Passes to Trust

The old home of Captain Claude Francis Boullet at 321 Valencia Street, occupied after his death by his daughter Frances Boullet, has been placed in trust by Randall Cane Jr., Esq. According to his son, Randall Cane III, soon to open Tarragona's first mental hygiene clinic, "It's the only way to ensure preservation of the property's historic value."

Maria-Louisa Bernard, the colored woman living in the house, reported to police that Miss Boullet, nearing ninety, disappeared late last year along with her Haitian companion. A teacher at Segovia Elementary, the woman purports to be Frances Boullet's closest living relative.

"One look at her, and you can tell she ain't a Boullet," opined Mr. Jake Landry, an employee at Cane & Wentworth, through whose offices the Bernard woman has agreed to relinquish occupancy of the house. A document leaving the property to her, supposedly penned by Frances Boullet and witnessed by one

Jonathan Redman Howard, himself deceased since 1923, is believed to be a forgery.

Neighbors report having seen the two old women, one white and one colored, or ghostly beings like them, in and around the house on Valencia Street, long rumored to be haunted. According to Mr. Landry, the Bernard woman has been "using the premises for making and selling hoodoo potions." Mr. Landry has been appointed resident caretaker. The extensive holdings in Captain Boullet's library will be donated to the Tarragona Public Library.

A little more than a week—that's all it took, and nothing about any horse trading. Rid of Maria-Louisa, Randy Cane couldn't get the last traces of Frances Boullet out of the house fast enough. Her books. Presented to the library in her father's name. The definitive cleansing.

Upstairs I run a fingertip over the few remaining titles on the steel shelves. Virginia Woolf, *A Room of One's Own,* Hogarth Press edition. This one I take out and open. From the bottom of the title page the bold black letters of Zula's distinctive hand leap out: "AND O FLORIDA WHAT A ROOM!" A message from Zula—or, as I've just read in the *Sentinel,* Miss Boullet's "Haitian companion."

Hardly to be construed as a voice from the grave directed to me, reality being not merely what you make of it. But putting what you get hold of to your own use, like transplanting flowers from the banks of a creek to pots for patios, changes the particulars of the situation you're in. Zula's words convince me—even if, say what you will, I'm already predisposed to agree: putting the diary back where it came from would, under present conditions, make a public object of it. A display item for museums and sideshows—dignification and degradation in the same gesture.

I've at least got this much straight: the room Frances Florida Boullet made with Zula is not to be disallowed. My mission's not to return the diary to its place in their sanctum but to help them hold their own there.

How, then, to dispose of it?

Back on the track of Harding's tale—still a few minutes left before my rendezvous at the Boullet House—I head for the Hernando. Looks about as down and out as a crack house and the traffic is something else. Kids of all ages and rainbow colors milling around the littered marble fountain, swigging cokes and trading little rap numbers. Adults of both sexes coming and going with proprietary ease, some with babies strapped to their chests.

I edge past them into the foyer. More people, all ages and kinds. People draped over assorted chairs and couches as though waiting for the next bus out, or for a relative or cabbie to pick them up. People tapping impatiently on a reception counter that looks like somebody's cast-off formica island, behind which a youngish-looking, fair-haired man sorts through keys, taking his time. Thrusts them at guests on demand with gleeful satisfaction.

Not so young up close—past thirty now, same skinny slack body, it's got to be Jimmy Hurd. He makes noises in my direction but, lacking Harding's quick grasp of idiolects, I can only stare back open-mouthed. As uncomprehending as he.

"Give the lady her key Jimmy." A little old woman has darted out from behind a warped plywood partition where she was evidently on high alert. "Boy needs your name and number ma'am."

Jimmy's talking a blue streak and gesturing at me. Head flips up and down as if it's been wound up when I say, "I don't have a room here, I'm from out of town."

"We might keep you outta the rain till you get your papers," says the old lady, giving me the once-over. "You got luggage to store?"

I'm having trouble reading the situation and the fact that this is my first time down here seems insufficient reason. What could have brought such an uptick of business to the old Hernando, obviously long over the hill?

"Is there some kind of convention at the Inn?" I ask.

"This ain't a inn going on for over two years now, we're sheltering the homeless on a temporary basis. Families mostly, gov'ment-subsidized. Now the economy's picking up there's a big developer from over at Palm Beach set to buy the place and turn it into condos with a shopping arcade on the ground floor, Mr. Greeley Connor he's in charge of the plans. You a tourist?"

"Kind of, I came to see a place a friend of mine restored. The Boullet House on Valencia Street."

Jimmy gets all fired up, stabs the air back and forth with both hands and shouts, "Awee! Awee!" A word I recognize at last from Harding's stories: his version of her name. After all these years he still remembers, but whatever else he's telling me goes over my head.

"Shush up, boy!" Miss Annie—it can't be anybody but Annie Hurd—raises her voice to a pitch compounded of authority and desperation in equal parts. "He's talking about that secret room they found over there ma'am—guess that's what you come down here for. The opening ain't till tomorrow and they don't want more'n five or six in it at a time, thass what I was told." She eyes me sharply and adds, "It's by invitation only, guess you got one already."

A sandy-haired couple in their late twenties with three kids, squarely on the middle-class rung, pushes forward. Papers in order—the man spreads a sheaf of them on the counter. I nod my thanks to the Hurds engrossed once more in the temporarily homeless.

From the Hernando I turn down the alley as unprepared for the real thing as if I'd never inhabited the Boullet House in the intimate surrogacy of hearing Harding's tale of its restoration. A spirea hedge has taken hold along the ancient iron palings, screening the profusion of growth within. Artful growth, knowingly planted, lovingly nurtured, carefully pruned and weeded to shape desired spaces with the look of the untended and the unintended. The old wisteria still twists along the ten-foot brick wall at the back—under its shade, a picturesque nook yielding an architectural sense of a garden of pleasures enclosing pleasures opening on to more pleasures enclosing still more.

And the house itself, serene with the promise of domestic spaces within—how differently I'd pictured it! Not sinister, exactly, but obscurely and subliminally disturbing somehow—more brooding, more like a toned-down Addams cartoon of a house. My provincialism shocks me; I'm still the Eastern European immigrant taking on her American identity by way of the likes of the *New Yorker.* The normative Northeastern chauvinisms. This is a thoroughly Southern house with a Caribbean flavor, no turrets, no twists and turns, no gingerbread histrionics. No Hawthorne gables either—not even any Southern gothic redolence of horror.

I realize that what I've been inhabiting in my writer's imagination is not the house Harding fell in love with but the nightmare of restoring it. The ordeal it became for her almost from day one, when she opened the door on Jeremy Wentworth's corpse. The brutalizing of herself, the unanticipated physical and mental ravages—she'd taken for granted there would be able workmen to give shape to her vision while she herself would turn a hand to the odd bit of aesthetic tinkering more or less at her pleasure, looking in on them daily if necessary.

On Greeley Connor's advice, Johnson Ware was hired for the demolition. A man of few words who strictly set his own schedule.

"Tomorrow, Mr. Ware?" This was right after getting her hard-won permit. It should have been little more than a week's work for an experienced wrecking crew.

"Could be tomorrow, yes'm."

But it wasn't. And not the day after. No choice but to start on the interior woodwork herself, prying it loose piece by piece, room by room. Caked with decades of paint and dirt, it would need to be sent out for chemical stripping and, later on, remounted, refinished.

About a week of tomorrows passed when who should come moseying in at last but Ware's adolescent crew. Without Ware. Holes were knocked in walls and ceilings all over the downstairs. Lots of holes, all different sizes, wildly at random. Same thing next day. Plaster and lath nipped her legs at every turn, the house a guerilla war zone—not a gutting job but the hit-and-run of resistance.

Several days later, about mid-morning, the green dump truck lumbered into her drive and out climbed Mr. Ware himself, grim and concentrated like an expert about to defuse a landmine. Looped some heavy chains around the tottering brick columns under the add-on at the back of the house and secured the other ends to the rear of his truck, the boys, tense and expectant, lined up alongside. Mopping his forehead, Ware slid into the driver's seat, the engine wheezed and coughed, and the old truck lurched and jerked forward in response to minute hand signals from Mo, the ablest member of the crew. In clouds of dust the jackleg addition came crashing down, dragging a piece of the gallery along with it. Cheers and high fives all around. With chains in tow, the boys scrambled up into the empty bed of the truck already bumping triumphantly out the drive, then down Valencia Street as though late for an urgent appointment.

More days of waiting. Moral: he who controls demolition controls restoration's progress as surely as the Preservation Board or the City Building Department. Somehow the work would have to get done without depending on any of them. Appalled by the madness of what she'd undertaken as one summer's job, anxiety nested in Harding like an environmental threat. Waspish facets of it multiplying and sharpening her infatuated vision with the close-up focus of compound eyes.

Nothing's more tedious than going on and on about how hopelessly in love you are—or were. Harding never talked about it but her whole story reeked of it. How her entanglement with the house pushed her resources—physical, financial, emotional—to and beyond their limits; how it swept her up in the pornographic theater of communal life and laid out her place in Tarragona amid its European leavings of sexual politics, social strata, racial tensions. The postcolonial violence of these our postindustrial times. And she herself collaborating with all the usual—performing love acts on the house, revitalizing its parts member by member, giving herself up to it lavishly, gut for gut, daily shaping and being shaped by it. Living with the ooze and muck of it, putrid and invigorating, transformed and killing, whatever it came to, this spiritual blow job.

So love affairs go, and why not with a house? Doing it with an old wreck. Certain confessions, "I fell in love with this cat," or "this view," or "that book" (the possibilities for love objects are endless) are no mere metaphors for the drama of desire's crimes and betrayals any more than "Jim" or "Ib'n Hassan" or "Jael." Proposition: Objects of passion always mold your desire into the form of the whole world offering immediate access to whatever you want. Open. Enter the apocalyptic abyss.

Fall in, fall out. The house as object of her desire revived slowly by her lovemaking to something suggestive of its original condition. But the more it showed itself for what it was, the more her desire shifted away from it. That old paradox of love's fullness of time playing out: the erotic spell dispelled in yielding to seduction.

But of course—perils of Pauline—she broke loose. Cut the perilous tentacles of meaning. Sold the house meticulously restored inside and out, at no profit, almost exactly fourteen weeks to the day after her arrival. Infatuation over, worked through. Literally, in her case. *Finis.* Packed up her personal belongings, drove back to her daughters (ready for their summer with father to end) and to her teaching job at Athena College (where the question all such institutions spawn would echo up staircases and down hallways in more or less of a welcome: "Have a good summer?" meaning, is that article or book ready for publication yet?) Perhaps her desire shifted away from the house because, as the restoration neared its end, the future called for no fresh love acts to be performed. Merely the routines of maintenance work. The repetitions of everyday tender loving care.

But I think not. I think her desire waned because the irresolvable difference between her and her love object—disguised in premature union—turned out to have little interest for her. Which is another way of saying she'd had her fill of the house early on in the restoration and finished it less out of desire for it than out of a hunger for freedom— I think, too, she moved away from it *because* she'd found satisfaction at the heart of it.

And release from what is too limiting, too private. Release bounds off from satisfaction like a dog from a leash. She saw what we always see when we end an affair: a discrepancy between the love object as it is in the world and as it might be in an ideal universe (one created solely by us true lovers).

But that's finished; no more corrupting tentacles from the old story of ruin and restoration pulling all into complicity with it. After these many years since she bought, restored, sold it and drove away, the house looks as she first envisioned it—gracious, welcoming. A home to be lived in for a lifetime and passed on.

Well-maintained down to the apple-green-tinted white of its clapboard siding, the dull russet trim, the umbered gray of outside shutters. The veranda in deep shade. Light-filled floor-to-ceiling windows, the sparkle of mullioned panes. And the cypress entry with its patina of care, the bronze shiplock. Not a trace of Harding's plight taints her work, everything just as she said. I step back to the curb, look up and down Valencia Street—restored as far as the eye can see in both directions. I seem to be the only living thing in sight at the moment, like an accidental figure in a heritage print.

Behind the Spanish fence the great gnarled oak arches streetward past the tops of the palings and over my head, and gently back to the veranda, laying veils of moss over the shuttered dormer windows. Inside, they're five feet off the floor with recessed seats, deep alcoves you can climb into for reading. Frames for taking in views beyond.

The windows, the diary. They go together like outside and inside. Space and time.

Harding's love affair with the house had reached the locked-in phase that sultry Wednesday in June she found the diary. Couldn't pull out of the deal now—too much sunk into it already—and couldn't really afford the risk to health and well-being of staying on; slave to her project and she knew it, crouched up in those dormer alcoves with the stink and chaos of demolition all around her, working loose casements stuck fast in layers of oil paint, blow by blow with hammer and chisel. No exit from the house of bondage, no way out but through it inch by inch on grimy, bleeding knees. Harding's not footloose like me.

Down in the street they moved across her line of vision like figures passing in and out of a TV monitor. The family from the Hernando—Miss Annie steering her senile mother-in-law along the sidewalk and, trailing after, the hunchbacked Dollman with his basket of little handmade mannequins and his toothless grin, and Jimmy, his adolescent double. Barefoot as usual. Then a couple of Hernando transients or semi-permanents, shuffling around the corner from the alley in a wobbly alcoholic daze. Or, as people said, drugged out of their minds.

Tap-tap and scrape, lead-dust with each breath. The casement opened to sweet Gulf air at last, Doc Shibbles's white scalp gleaming up at her through the screen of oak leaves. This way and that, in sync with the back-and-forth of his garden hose down the sidewalk, the daily pre-sunset lustration kept precisely to his own frontage. Not a foot beyond into hers or his neighbor's on the other side.

On to the next window. Crack and crunch—this one popped open with unexpected ease and swung out, Harding's head close behind. From the sidewalk, eyes turned up at her so searchingly she felt them outlining her own gaze through the spreading twilight. The olive-skinned woman of color wearing a dark green turban, face intelligent with aging beauty, nodded as if satisfied with what she saw, not a greeting but some private confirmation, and walked on. This was Harding's first encounter with Miss Mary Louise.

Two more windows to go. The big front room Harding had thought of as her future library was growing dim and still she hunched to her task with chisel and hammer, monitoring comings-and-goings below. Stephanie Wentworth, flaxen-haired nymphet—blatantly pregnant again —waddling toward town. The Hurds home-bound from the Seven-Eleven, and the busy little man who seemed to turn up everywhere in the old Quarter barging past, cigar at arm's length, as though to avoid dropping ash on his patent leather shoes. A hiatus, and then Mr. Stavros, Sr., recently retired, and his Norwich Terrier, twilight dimming the brisk step of his white linens down the block to where Cadiz Boulevard cut off the restoration area from its shabbier fringes.

The sill at the western end of the room spelled trouble. Mounded with cracked plaster, bare laths on the ceiling above stained and bulging—an old leak. Out in the trunk of her car, she rummaged for the cordless police spotlight picked up at a yard sale back home in Athena and made her way back upstairs without turning it on—more than anyone I've ever known Harding has what seems like the capacity of the blind to move through familiar surroundings in the dark. Standing on the seat of a broken-backed chair pulled out of trash the Wentworths left behind, she shone her light at the casement.

Blistering paint, much of it flaked off. The lever looked ready to turn, easy job. She heaved herself up on the ledge and reached for it— a violent sneeze, eyes tearing and burning, she set down the light and pinched her nose, holding her breath, and strained past heaps of debris toward the window. Couldn't quite make it. Gingerly, she burrowed forward through the moldy plaster one foot at a time. More sneezing and tearing—then a crack like an unsound tree splitting open, and she was falling. Down, down in a rain of rubble.

A split second later she landed hard in darkness.
After the shock of passage: uncontrollable trembling. And disengaging themselves in consciousness one by one—scraped elbows, knees, shins, a dull throb through the left ankle sprained in childhood, blood pulsing in her ears like a storm-driven tide. Nothing broken though, no gashes. No internal stabs of pain.

It was cool, inexplicably cool and fresh. She felt around for something to stand on, pull herself back up through the jaggedly lit opening made by her fall, but touched only rotten planks, damp hunks of plaster. In her jeans pocket was one of the many matchbook remnants she'd plucked from the wrecking crew's careless litter of cigarette butts and candy wrappers. Not a spark on her first try, but the second match hissed and flared—the place was cavernous! Aswarm with innumerable others surging from the darkness on all sides. If—the crazy thought came like renegade neurons firing—if they had something to do with the drug-ring rumored to operate out of the Hernando, she was in for it, no point running. Maybe a deal. Cut a deal with them, offer the house as a front, herself if necessary. Her hand jerked and the flame went out. She took a deep slow breath and held it, listening. Nothing.

Stepping tentatively in what she supposed to be an easterly direction, parallel to the library wall, she struck another match, took several more trembling steps, struck another. No partition in sight. On in the same direction, fighting a sense of something uncannily animating the shadows beyond her little match flame—there, the pale figure of a woman in a crowd of others. Her attention locked on the spectral figure looming as if enthroned above a great oblong chest and, after the match died, on the spot where she'd been.

What saved Harding from panic was fury. Tearing off another match she confronted the commanding presence with its firefly flutter. Dazzling whiteness, but no head, just a hook looped into a strap suspended from a high ceiling beam directly over the chest. A dress on a hanger. And the chest? She pushed and heaved but there was no budging it. The match sputtered and went out and something with the wraithlike touch of a spider's web slid down over her in the dark—the dress, dislodged by her rough experiment with the chest. A long white dress with the weight and texture of raw silk.

Whatever this place, she felt she must be just about in the middle of it, eight yards or so in either direction judging by the length of the library on the other side of the wall; no wider certainly than the window seat she'd crashed through, six feet at most. Overhead, a foot or more and higher at some points, all the way up to the attic floor elsewhere. Arithmetic is a wondrous antidote to seeing ghosts, like bringing a scene into focus by simple lens adjustment. Things had been carried here, a big heavy chest or, more likely, material for making it. In pitch darkness Harding began to feel a Pythagorean calm, certain she was alone even as her sense of a surrounding multitude became ever stronger.

Three matches left. When she'd stepped off fifteen feet past the chest she lit the first and held it out searchingly. There ahead of her, a short flight of stairs against the end wall.

On the bottom step she was in the dark again. Another step, feeling her way with both hands up the wall of the staircase—encountering a metal rod about the length of her forearm, that turned ninety degrees straight down. A low rumble overhead and the distinctive scent of a cedar hatch opening. She bolted up the last few steps and bumped the top of her head, the matchbook dropping from her hand. Two hatches, then, one above the other, opening and closing independently. Back down a step, fingering the wall again and fighting claustrophobia until—flush by the handrail, just where it ought to be—another rod. More rumbling and blackness gave way to the diffuse dark of early evening pouring into the library through the open casement.

Tremulous and energized as though cued to appear on stage, Harding went straight for her spotlight—still poised on the ledge of the ruined window seat at the other end—then back through the open panels and down the stairs with her beam on low, entering the mystery deliberately now, moving unsteadily in a vertigo of wonder aglow with color: green and indigo, scorched ochre, intense yellow, turquoise and cochineal, blood orange beside violet, rich ebony black, sienna and umber, stark white on white, luminous pastels, sky blues and celadons—a festival of color upon color, the spell of it drawing her into the quintessentially sensuous magic of sheer existence flashing its primeval radiance. Plants, animals, reiterated like afterimages, as if answering questions about themselves, mountain masses pulled out like organs from valleys where water circulated in pulses: a river appearing and disappearing. Frogs and salamanders, snakes and bugs pursuing their lively commerce through flowering vines twined over hewn beams and rafters, birds lighting in their smooth-planked recesses. And the trees! A mahogany forest, oak, pine, fustic, rosewood and logwood, satinwood and laurelwood. Coconut, palm, breadnut, avocado, almond, groves of apricot, banana, mango, orange, lemon, grapefruit. To her left, a vista as though through an open window: rows of workers in fields of vegetables and rice along a path to a village crowded with the same dark-skinned people busy at their crafts, none pictured in detail, only in structural essentials—a head, a torso, limbs moving through a plane of whites to take on their existence in color.

Wherever any figure—rock, plant, animal, or human—was fully rendered, it astonished with a solidity revealing no more than the singular ordinariness of whatever is, the unceasing specification of a spirit of motion amassing—here, there, everywhere—a democracy of things affirmed, even guaranteed, by their sheer materiality. Each with a being unshared by any other, yet each somehow the other in all its difference. Anything in this world might at any moment become something else—plants, insects, humans starting to feel like animals, animals like plants—as if what is happening or what a thing becomes were purely a matter of chance in the play of motion, its uniqueness nothing but the moment's residue manifest in the material transformation of this into that. Here: a tall jet-black man in tatters with a goat's hoof around his neck, earless and powerful of body, leaping over a red clay ravine as if air were his natural element. Like a god. Or a demon—like the giant snake, there, wrapping itself around a tree from floor to ceiling, enormous eyes peering down at her from a green human-sized head amid painted joists and planks.

At the four corners of the enclosure sea and sky met—in one, birds circling over a ship, fish swarming its hull, deck spread with food like a lavish table; opposite, a woman emerging from the sea into the light of a strong sun; in the third corner, a streak of lightning reflected eel-like deep in the water; and in the fourth, a rainbow arching over the sea and undulating on its surface—nearby, a smoky anhinga dried its wings on a giant marou tree shading a waterfall. Harding felt herself placed in a world not so much adrift between sky and sea as secured by them at the four corners of its reach, four possible openings. Even the elegant geometry of what appeared to be an air circulation system—designs in black and white radiating from grilles, large and small, along the walls—reinforced her sense of an abstract order. Where was she? What had she fallen into?

Slowly she swept her light over the chest at the center, pausing on its frescoed side panels. Images separated as if framed. A dark, lovely man with a rope around his neck, eyes like raging lights. A trunk stacked with money. Bloody, sinuous hands twirling a small star-shaped object. A tall woman in French Empire fashion, charcoal-skinned, intently studying her reflection in a mirror. A basket of figs with herbs in bloom; a gold-spangled necklace; a sleeping alligator. Two ancient women, one fair and the other brown, face to face, smiling in a curious excess of vitality. A brimming goblet. A riderless white horse staring into the blackest of nights. The images had a surrealist feel but without plumbing psychical depths, no hint of figures floating up from the unconscious—nightmarish not in the dream sense but in the way that events or objects perceived in ordinary waking life can come suddenly clear in startling isolation, suspended like abstractions yet with the hard finality of the indisputably real. At her feet, in a creamy heap, lay the dress, the hanger still hooked to an embroidered cloth slithering lizard-like over one end of the chest. Moved by an instinctive regard for the dead, she smoothed the silk against her own body—a dress made for a smaller woman, its elegance of another time, the high-fitting collar, full sleeves, long narrow cuff—and looped it back in place.

Again she passed her light over the chest's frescoes, their strange beauty wrenched free of narrative meaning. Still. Frozen, while the surrounding space pulsed with a single great impulse to life, motion. A miniature face—one of several in cameo-like relief—leapt into her light, arresting her arm's movement. The Hurd boy? No, not Jimmy's face—this mask projecting its white horror at me, she thought, with the remembered shock of walking in on Jeremy Wentworth, his look of bellowing agony fixed ashenly in death. Yet it wasn't old Wentworth either. Still the conviction lingered that she knew this face, familiar as a distant relative passing in and out of one's home during childhood.

Nearby, three painted wood-pegged drums hung from one of the high rafters. A nudge at the largest and it swayed to and fro in a swirl of déjà vu that rapidly took on the authority of real memory: six or seven years ago, a colleague of hers back from the West Indies—Haiti, was it?—after a semester of field work with students, collections of ritual objects joining ceremonial masks from Dahomey, Andean textiles, and other anthropological booty in his roomy professorial home. The prize, a pair of finely crafted decorated drums—Rada drums, one missing, he'd said—suspended a little to one side of a drafty Victorian entry above a bold-figured Kuba rug of some antiquity. Swaying lightly when the door opened.

Ceremonial drums. Artwork suggesting a cosmology. Rough-hewn rush-bottomed chairs pushed against the walls as though to make a clearing. An immoveable, chest-high oblong box with a jumble of objects on top—pots, bottles, jars; beaded gourds; a painted calabash with small polished stones in it; a basket of tiny iron crosses; sculptures of carved wood, iron; a little hand bell, a conch beside a bamboo flute, notched sticks, sequined flags loosely wound around pieces of cane, a pitcher. She picked up a shell from a basket of them—a delicate pattern painted inside—then another and another until it clicked: they were motifs from *vèvè,* designs for summoning the gods. The *loa.* Some of which, like the coiled form of Damballa in one of the little sculptures, she recalled from her married years in New Orleans where reports and pictures of the *cérémonie* had been as surreptitiously popular as the tabloids.

A *caille-mystères,* then: house of the spirits. She had fallen into a voodoo sanctuary, a place for initiates to bed.

Minutely, she examined a group of clay vessels and wiped each in turn with a handkerchief. No dust. Picked out one or two delicate branchings of coral from an enameled box and let them drop back with a click, tested the weight of a hand-worked iron chain, rattled a gourd, put the minuscule bell to her ear and listened to it tinkle. Sniffed at aromatic liquors in stoppered bottles and at tiny dishes of dried herbs: lavender, basil, angelica, eucalyptus, anise, rosemary, lemon balm, hyssop. Ran her fingers over carved figurines and peered into covered earthen jars containing unidentifiable powders. Stirred the contents at the bottom of an iron pot with a wooden stick.

Bits of fiber, a fancy button, seeds, horny slivers, strands of hair, decomposing snips of plants. The leavings of everyday life made strange.

She was standing before an altar. All those old rumors about the long dead Frances Boullet—*this* was behind them? Sold her white birthright for an African knowledge and put it into practice? No simple harmless recluse but a macabre power—a dangerous one, not to be discussed, and passed over quickly if her name came up. One of those to be avoided, that was the message. And so, it had become clear to Harding, was Frances Boullet's house. Boarded up for a time after her disappearance—dead, it was believed, but no corpse to prove it—then run down by the Wentworths, themselves shunned, until she, an outsider, chanced on it one blue seductive day in March. She fingered the dyed burlap altar cloth and tapped cautiously at the frescoed sides. The impulse came and went to fetch hammer and chisel, break open the ochre-stained masonry seal between base and top, look inside. Gently, she lifted the creamy silk skirt from the end of the altar to let it hang clear.

And there, amid the clutter of ritual objects lay an old leather-bound book on a cloth frayed at the edges to a smooth fringe, overstuffed-looking at the fore-edge, like a favorite volume with too many place markers in it, the odd postcard or wildflower pressed among the pages. On the spine was the numeral "XL" over Frances Boullet's name stamped lengthwise in gold, and, on the face page, this inscription in a clear old-fashioned hand:

My Last Writing, wherein the years from December 24, 1860 to
December 5, 1935 are recollected in decoupage.

A diary. Thick with sheets snipped off an inch from the binding, new sheets of the same size and quality pasted neatly to the stubs—a recycled volume of sorts in a variable longhand, prettily calligraphic in some parts, then breaking away at a slant and growing dense, at moments rapid to the point of illegibility; fluid and plain elsewhere, like the face page. One and the same writer though, if she was any judge. Presumably Frances Boullet.

But no, two other hands had made the final entries—a brief one, a mere few lines in strong brushlike strokes, followed by a new writer wielding a clean broad-nibbed pen. Then a run of blank sheets. Harding turned back to the beginning and smoothed the page as though in anticipation of reading, a gesture so habitual to her in the presence of a book she'd been on the point of forgetting that it was already past ten p.m.—on her feet since sunup, not a bite of food since midday—that she was desperate for sleep. As if intuitively complying with some etiquette of the place, she nestled the diary back on its faded apricot cloth under the doubled-up hem. Nothing casual about the position of the dress.

Another puzzle came clear on the way out: the unexpected head room, a foot or more, under window seats that were at shoulder height in the library. Fingers poked through an iron grille at the bottom of the inside wall told the story: the floor of the library, the whole upstairs in fact, was raised, with a hollow layer between it and the downstairs ceiling. All there from the beginning, then, the sanctuary and its secret, strategically built into the house.

Harding gathered her belongings, double-checked all the downstairs windows and locks, shrinking back from the pungency of cigar smoke around her car even before she noticed the glow and heard his voice.

"Evenin, Miz Dumot, thought you was a burglar." The one Annie Hurd had addressed as "Jake" earlier that evening. Lodger at the Hernando Inn, more or less permanent, said to know everything that went on in the old Quarter. Knew her name, that much was certain, and knew a short cut in the dark through her backyard.

The gate to the Boullet House stands slightly ajar as though someone has just slipped out. What am I doing here? For sure I didn't have to come the roundabout way I did; they have a modern airport in Tarragona. Direct flights to and from LaGuardia daily. It's more than a whim, this following in Harding's footsteps with the idea that I'll get my sense of direction straight, uncover my bearings. Just as you can stop seeing what you live in daily, a tale told by another can become so familiar it sidles off, silent, not so much into unreality as into irrelevance, or the gulf of the commonplace, or the homogenized hum of the universe where it can no longer be entertained, heard again.

I'm after a full restoration of sight and hearing. To use my own eyes again—like there, inside the fence, the mature hydrangea and oleander mingling now with showy bromeliads and dense, shade-loving fern. More than the expressionist startle of details, more than the impressionist continuum of a tale told. More. More than realistic remains, modernist memories and postmodern memorials. Tracking Harding, literally along her infatuated trail to this house, I've only this year passed her age that summer in 1977. Time enough for me to see more clearly where she was then—I'm leery of infection.

On the gate is the little bronze plaque she put up:

321 Valencia Street

Claude Francis Boullet House, 1857

Restored 1977

And below it, a sign for the Haitian Gallery of Vaudun Art. "Open by Appointment and by Chance." I step through, reach back for the pull.

The satisfying heft of the gate closes me in and Harding's walk leads me up the wide, beautiful steps made of the old Spanish bricks she salvaged and laid with her own hands. On the veranda I pause to orient myself. It's working; the house is assuming the tactile clarity of dreams, the ghostly feel of memories undergoing the shock treatment of restored sensation.

And here I am inside, bronze doorknob still in hand, chimes announcing a visitor fading out. No one appears but the sweep of the cypress staircase invites me up its satiny bowed treads. I approach, set one foot down with care as if scaling a rock face, clutching the thought of the diary like a handhold and breathing as though I've entered a rarefied air, the thinness of excitement anticipating the choke of anxiety.

This surge of feeling, this symptom of passion, startles me. Is that what I was driving through last night like the soft patter of rain? And this morning, cooled and sure. It's this passion—of love, is it?—I've come here to underwrite, read out of myself, then get on with my own life. Yet here I am sailing along with a calm buoyed by the feel-good of well-being, the easy crest of a long slow wave rolling into that extraordinary mildness at shoreline. You would think I've come home. To a proper home, I mean, where I'm *at* home, traveling into a solitude peopled by my own busy crowd. An impossible position to be in on the staircase of a house that will never be mine. Proposition: Lovers experience their passion as the wax and wane of impossibility jerked into reality.

At the top I'm as giddy as an understudy making her big entrance, no longer caring whether I've got any reason for being here or not. I'm about to charge into the library, the huge front room with the dormer alcoves, when a casually chic, darkly blond woman about my own age appears in the doorway—all smiles, with a shushing index finger to her lips.

"Come." She ushers me back down. "You're having supper with me, no excuses." At the bottom of the stairs she looks hard at me and says, "So you're the one Harding charged with the diary?"

"More like I took charge, actually, or so it feels. I'm Jael B. Juba. And you're Aimée, right? Are we going out some place?"

"No." She secures the gate by remote and throws the bolt on the handsome shiplock. "I live here now—apartment in the back, including

Captain Boullet's old bedroom. When I divorced James it was the perfect answer."

"And Maria-Louisa?"

"Still in her adorable little shotgun down the street. That whole block's been rehabilitated except for her cottage, which makes it more picturesque than ever. She's eighty-six this month, walks over here every day and does almost as much work in the garden as me. Talk about a green thumb. She wanted to be alone in the sanctuary this last night before the opening."

We enter the room where the Wentworths, in prerestoration days, congregated around their giant TV console—an elegant sitting room now. Harding once said she'd never encountered Aimée Hulin without the shock of experiencing a fatal flaw in that elegance, the lightning streak of vulgarity modifying perception of her like an epiphany: "A class thing, the mark of what Southern aristocrats still consider, but no longer call, 'white trash,' which Aimée definitely is *not*. Marvelous how this vulgar streak, when it appears in the 'good ole families,' as in English royalty, gets mixed in with, if not wholly transformed into, self-aggrandizement. Their way of glamorizing elements of trashy taste, an unconscious aesthetic alignment of the upper and lower classes that manages to work like a put-down of the stodgy middle." This had led me to picture Aimée as a slimmed down version of the media's authentic flower of trashy taste, Roseanne. Short on manners except when stylized on occasion or displayed for personal gain. Gushes of sentiment when least expected but insensitive to all except family and friends, whom she protects (bitch with heart of steel) or destroys as self-interest dictates. The clichés of romance, in other words, played out as comedy of manners.

If Aimée ever flirted, as the young often do, with any such scenario, she certainly has cleaned up her act—with a touch of formality like a line of respect drawn for others.

"Please," she says, handing me a glass of pale sherry, "feel free to explore downstairs all you want. I'll call when ready."

I take my time browsing through the suite of front rooms on either side of the wide hall, each full of Haitian art and artifacts, my mind dancing from one spectacular thing to another, making notes (a whole wall of Lafortune Félix's paintings above a long table of sculptures by Louisane St. Fleurant!) on what calls for closer study another day. Back again in Aimée's sitting room, I see she's left the door open to her bedroom—Captain Boullet's once upon a time—where Harding found old Wentworth's corpse. I enter gingerly. Along the opposite wall French doors open to the back veranda—Aimée's moving among an abundance of plants there, a serving dish in each hand.

I linger in the bedroom. The impression of harmony is so assured and its intimacy so engaging you don't notice at first how varied the decor is. A room where you feel the strangeness of return as if unexpectedly entering your own place forgotten and unvalued for generations, kept and swept by the seasonal broom year after year, forever offering its proprieties of comfort and caress.

In this balm of sensuous satisfaction, individual pieces step forward—decorously, only when invited—and recede with a curtsy to give place to others. The magnificent lacquered bamboo bed opposite the French doors, its gauzy silk canopy reflecting light from two chandeliers like a weave of crystal threads. Next, edging its solid frame toward me by some fraction of an inch, a painted breakfront lodging a laptop with a stack of printouts beside it, and, pushed back a bit, a wrought iron and wire chair contoured to the body, plump with a down cushion flashing a rusty yellow and white geometrized mayfly. Plants in celadon-glazed cylinders shoot thin spears toward the ceiling on each side of the breakfront already inching back into place. And now comes a pair of what I at first take to be Venetian chairs beside a small sycamore table holding a tole lamp, a pile of books, a notepad. Then on a stand at coffee-table height, a papier-mâché tray, its green, yellow, and rust bucolic scene blending with the bloom of orchids in a semi-circular glass planter.

It's the chairs that do it. They don't recede but stand quietly before me unwilling to be dismissed—neither originals nor reproductions but reminiscent of all the eighteenth-century painted Venetians I've ever seen, as if fixing not the idea of them but the range of their possibilities. But then the breakfront suggesting, as it does, definitive embodiments of English painted pieces is not itself, I realize, English. As for the others: the sycamore table, French but not really; the ebonized bench, Chinese with those inverted feet and a fat moiré-covered cushion, but not Chinese really. Not even imitation Chinese, I decide, as it minces back to the foot of the bed. Nor are these furnishings exactly "in the style of" this and that—they so precisely evoke object-experiences from a past not their own that I feel mildly disoriented. Like jet lag in an exotic and absorbing culture.

My dis-ease is palliated by the tray, unmistakably real English chinoiserie, with its delightful rural scene, and the tole lamp just as reassuringly eighteenth-century New England. The multi-leveled glass planter's contemporary for sure, of local craftsmanship most likely. I check out some old ivories ranging from thumbnail size to several inches, both Asian and European, and, under the nest of japanned tables holding them, an intricate nineteenth-century ivory picnic basket. Then a very early Flemish wall tapestry and, beneath it, a striking bronze surrounded by jades and enamels. I'm admiring a Celtic head from a collection of ancient and medieval coins when Aimée beckons me through one of the doors and I follow her out.

Something's off—we're not on the back veranda Harding described but inside a lush garden room with French doors, duplicates of those to the bedroom, opening out over wide brick steps into the garden. Yet this is certainly where the veranda should be.

I make no effort to hide my confusion and Aimée loves it. "My dining space," she sweeps out an arm. "Floored with the very same handmade Spanish bricks Harding used for the front steps. Remember? The ones she left so neatly stacked along the fence on Doc Shibbles's side?"

"I . . . I remember—is he still around?"

"Been dead for years. But Maria Zamora's still over there, inherited the house and, to everybody's amazement, a flush bank account—we all thought he was penniless, never spent a dime—so she right away had the house fixed up and refurbished, no problem with the Board, it's not old enough to be on the historic register. She dresses up fit to kill and breezes through house and grounds over there like Marie Antoinette escaped from the mob. You'll see her at the opening tomorrow, I'm sure."

On the stone table in front of me—a tureen of chilled soup; plates of berries and melon balls, sliced tomatoes, cucumbers, peppers, and other raw vegetable bits; cheeses and barbecued ham; a crispy loaf of bread and a Chilean wine.

"So what do you think of Harding's folly?"

I know she means the house but I'm still hung up on the decor. "This table," I begin, "I can't place it, so polished you forget it's stone . . ."

"Does it remind you of something?" She's in her element, leading me on.

"The sculpted legs—something Mesoamerican about them, but of course it's not . . . doesn't look like anything Mesoamerican I've ever seen. Feels Preclassic though. If the Olmecs had it in their cultural orbit to make a garden table this would be it—unsettling somehow, like some of those gorgeous not-quite-this, not-quite-that *objets* in your bedroom."

"Really? And how does my garden room come off for you?"

Ferns, palms, greenery of every description dotted with white, yellow, and rusty orange blossoms, two natural fiber hammocks strung side by side in a corner, a Persian lusterware cat peeping from yellow blossoms cascaded down a primrose jasmine tree—a room both luxuriant and domesticated. Any number of items from the other Americas give it a Pre-Columbian look, as if they belong here, down to the Toltec stone warrior outside at the garden entrance.

"We-ell," I'm unsure about the effect of what I'm about to say but she's asking for it, "the table—and its setting extended into the garden— reminds me of afternoons in the country. No one particular real afternoon, and it's much more than a reminder, as though what we're sitting in here is the concrete original of every idyllic afternoon in the country minus irritations like heat, humidity, bugs, the reek of livestock, picky aunts, crying babies, sibling rivalries and hurts, legitimations of self, lineage, territory, even provincial proprieties and perspectives. It's the civilized original freed from itself, freed to be the past it never was and the future it never will be."

"I can see why Harding passed the diary on to you."

The furnishings putting me out of joint are mostly of Aimée's design, fabricated under her supervision in a shop at the college by students. Well over a hundred have worked on this table alone in the last five years. They rib her about being a wastrel and a perfectionist, can't understand why each thing should be subjected to the accidents of so many apprentice hands to become just what she wants.

"Rendering the precision of the random, are you?"

"Not a bad way to put it, the kids call it 'chance-crafting.'"

I've hit the right note with Aimée; her smile has a trusting spontaneity in it. What I can't understand is how she got by with such a breach of historical authenticity as closing in an antebellum veranda, and I pose my question directly, the way Harding would.

"How in the world did you pull this off—some powerful new member or influence on the Board? Some postmodern turn forced by the '80s maybe?"

"Getting warm. A few years ago Uncle Randy resigned and was replaced—no, not by me—by Maria-Louisa."

"You're joking! Miss Mary Louise on the Preservation Board? A Caribbean *mambo* of ancient lineage talking blueprints with Greeley Connor?"

"Who's still architectural honcho, by the way—but the garden room went up the year before her appointment, not long after we took the Boullet House off Chris Stavros's hands.

"Let me get this straight. A major alteration violating every commandment in their book was approved by Randall Cane III *and* Greeley Connor, not to mention Margaret Avery and the other dyed-in-the-wool authenticators?"

"Well, yes and no. When I decided to celebrate the end of the Reagan era by divorcing James, I needed a place of my own, and—well, the arrangement with the Stavros law firm, their offices downstairs and our art gallery upstairs, was working out fine, but then Chris's dad died and his daughter graduated from law school about that time—Alex, the younger one, is going the same route—so with all of that, Chris felt called on to follow through. The parental cottage was past due for an authentic facelift anyhow, and with no expenses spared it was just the place for Stavros & Stavros to carry on the family business, younger generation included—as Maria-Louisa and I do here in our gallery, you might say. Couldn't have been more ideal for us. The garden was already established by then, and the back veranda—oh, the veranda was fine, but if I could have only one interior of my own for the rest of my life it would have to be a garden room, without it I'd take to the woods. This was the obvious place for it."

"And the Board," I press her, "how ever did you get by with it? Your garden room—delightful as it is—is about as far from an 'authentic' antebellum veranda as you can get. Who or what could be so mighty as to go against the grain of history?"

"A deep, dark secret in Uncle Randy's life, that's what. As Maria-Louisa says, every man marches to the beat of his own body."

"Is the secret . . . uhm . . . a matter of public knowledge?"

"Probably wouldn't make much difference anymore to anybody but him and, of course, Aunt Sophie—this happened ages ago, back in the twenties—but who's to predict the effects of scandal? No, it's not something to be noised around, not until they're gone anyway. Uncle Randy was always my beau ideal when I was growing up, urbane, strong, fun, but caring about things that matter, nobody could match him and old as I was when I found out, I was shocked. One of those passionate adolescent affairs—he was just fifteen at the time—with Jeremy Wentworth's little sister Annie. Doc Shibbles had an album with a picture of them looking like Romeo and Juliet, Uncle Randy pretty and lithe, Annie lovely and delicate. She got pregnant, of course."

"Not the Miss Annie who runs the Hernando, the one you see there with Jimmy?"

"The very one, incredible as it may seem if you knew my uncle. The Wentworths were definitely on the skids by the time he took up with her even though Jordan was still a partner in Grandfather Cane's firm, nominally anyway; he had a weakness for drink that got passed down to Jeremy— debts too, growing like kudzu month after month and mostly held by the Canes as mortgages on Wentworth property. They could have foreclosed on Jordan ten times over but chose not to, or so I always heard. Who knows what really happened."

"Noblesse oblige?"

"Something like that." Turns out that back in the early part of the century, when Jeremy Wentworth was a boy and Randall Cane III hardly out of diapers, Aimée's grandfather, Randall Cane Jr., drew up a complex trust with himself as trustee—distributions solely at his discretion—and Jordan Wentworth as settlor and beneficiary, along with his issue, of any income above and beyond the debt burden of properties held in trust. Jordan placed everything, all he had left, in this so-called Wentworth Trust and signed it.

I lift an eyebrow but refrain from commenting. After all, this involves Aimée's own family and she seems willing enough to tell more.

"When Jordan Wentworth finally passed away in an alcoholic coma, Jeremy was suddenly yanked off the sidelines and made a junior partner in the law firm—it was 1927 by then and he'd been waiting so long he viewed himself as a victim of neglect and maybe more. Word was they took him in to keep him under control—every now and then somebody in my family would up and say 'the devil himself can't be any meaner'n a drunk Wentworth.' You see, the Canes always believed Wentworth men tend to excess, like a hankering after a time when the gods pull out all stops and no holds barred in their fight for survival—*Götterdämmerung*."

"Sounds like Jeremy was considered something of a business liability."

"That and then some. The Canes always did pride themselves on their sense of honor and they would have wanted to keep him on a short leash—the drinking, for one, but more in case he ever got wind of Uncle Randy's deep dark romantic secret. A story of mutual blackmail—the Canes and the Wentworths."

She stops. We've arrived at the point where further understanding of a situation inevitably calls for something like gossip and, I, primed for this revealing take on Tarragona's eminent and respected Randall Cane III, urge her on.

"Such a long, ugly story . . . maybe after dinner," she adds quickly, seeing my disappointment, "if you're up for it."

It's after ten when I pull on to the causeway that spans Tarragona Bay. I feel compelled by a need to be on the water tonight—the glint of impenetrability already winks on each side of me. Like a vast eye my Shadow floats over.

I check in at the snazzy new high-rise hotel on the far tip of the Island. Top-floor studio overlooking both Gulf and Bay, special promotional midweek rate. On the balcony the salty expanse can be inhaled with that sense of release you get when you return from your inland life to the sea. Maria-Louisa's having her last night in the sanctuary before the opening tomorrow—I'll not deny myself a last night with the diary, in suitable surroundings. It's still mine. Nothing said (nothing explicit anyway) about leaving it there during my long supper with Aimée.

Aimée in her garden room. She stays with me now like a thought-experiment in the appeals and perils of Edenic restoration. My peculiar sensitivity to the bodies of others again—in learning to conceal it as all must (not doing so marks you as mental) I often experience a temporary possession by their bodily spirit. Aimée-pouring-out-coffee, so graciously at home in those spaces where Nature and History meet in converging lies and lines of design.

I reminded her of where she'd left off. "All right, then," she began, "back to 1927, Roaring Twenties, and who do you suppose is working as an errand boy and general factotum for the Cane and Wentworth law firm? Still in his teens then but already had that knack for making himself indispensable."

"Let me guess," I said, "he never did catch on that there can be too much of a good thing and that his insider knowledge could get him shot and dumped over a fence half a century later—how's that?"

"Bull's eye. Jake Landry came out of his momma's womb prepped to rise on the misdeeds of others, and so I guess it was no accident he ended up brokering a marriage between little pregnant Annie Wentworth and one James Stuart Hurd, last of an old and sickly Scottish family going back to the Royal Scots of King George's War. They were dirt-poor and James's mother, who lived with him here in town, was given to understand she might be able to set up her own trust for the benefit of James and his progeny, funded in full—terms unspecified—by the Cane family. So not surprisingly Mrs. Hurd signed right away and, with the promised sheaf of deeds in hand, made the case to her son that they were worth the marriage vow.

"Well, James Stuart Hurd had a bad speech impediment and he may already have been slightly humped even then, but he was no dummy when it came to figuring out that a bunch of papers may not amount to a hill of beans. Or maybe it was his mother having second thoughts. Anyway, they noticed pretty quick that he had no access to the trust's assets or any income from it—my grandfather Randall Jr. retained absolute control as trustee—so they held out for a carrot and Jake Landry obligingly cooked one up: the Hernando Inn. James would take over management of it, and then some. The Hernando was about to be acquired by the Wentworth Trust and could easily be slipped over to the Hurd Trust with nobody the wiser—the day the marriage vows were spoken. That was the deal: all future profits to flow directly to James Stuart Hurd who, along with his mother, the young bride, and the young bride's child, would enjoy lifetime occupancy of Captain Boullet's family quarters on the first floor. For a young man in not so robust health and entirely without other prospects it looked like a windfall.

"Nobody ever consulted Annie, of course, and by the time it got to her the whole marriage package was a done deal. Even at that, she agreed to it only on condition that brother Jeremy would never find out about her affair with young Randy Cane or anything to do with the arrangement. She adored Jeremy and was afraid of him, afraid for herself, I think—in these parts, family dishonor still justified extremes of punishment back then— but even more afraid he might kill Randy, who'd once looked up to Jeremy as a kind of mentor. And she was probably right, everybody always handled Jeremy with kid gloves right up to the end. Uncle Randy used to say nobody should ever give Jeremy cause for what he called "hereditary tendencies," meaning, so we all inferred, a fatal pull to bring the world down to the Wentworth level.

"So the newlyweds moved into the Hernando and started running it— or Annie and Mrs. Hurd did, James never was much more than a janitor. A girl child was born, Katherine Stuart Hurd, named after her grandmother. Eerily pretty, according to Maria-Louisa—I got this entire story from her—lovely in that frail, bloodless-blonde way. He took care of the child from the beginning while the women kept the place going between them and tried to fix it up, but it kept on running down, probably due more to the Depression than to any lack of management skills on their part. Little Kathy failed to thrive, never went to school, and was never seen without James Stuart Hurd even throughout her teens and twenties when old pictures show her looking like a wraith of a child stretched tall. I gather she could talk as normally as anybody but seldom did, and the two of them had less and less to do with anybody else—Maria-Louisa remembers them jabbering to each other with the greatest ease in the cadences of his speech impediment, like a dialect exclusively adapted to them, she says.

"At thirty-four Kathy died giving birth to a little boy—they called him Jimmy. Everybody knew who the father was and he became a pariah overnight. James Stuart Hurd always had been at the edge of respectability and hung on only by virtue of his family name, and after Kathy died he crashed like a dive bomber without a target into the pits of local low life— Florida, I'm here to tell you, is second to none in its representatives of that social echelon. Gradually he turned into one of the local 'characters,' the Dollman so-called, the only name we kids ever knew him by. He always blamed poor Jimmy for Kathy's death and did his best to ignore him.

"Annie cared for the boy like part and parcel of the job she'd taken on with her marriage contract and, to the very end, lived with her lawful husband as if wedded to a split consciousness. The marker she placed over his grave when he finally died disavows him completely.

> The beams of our house are cedar,
> and our rafters of fir.

I have this theory that what Annie was memorializing in this bit from the Song of Songs was a higher mode of marriage, and the 'house' she had in mind, I'd be willing to bet, was a little log cabin over at El Inglés, built by my great-great-great-grandfather on the Howard side when he brought his family down from Virginia. Reminds you of a chapel—it's hard to forget—and I'd swear it was the scene of her love affair with Uncle Randy. Still there, it and the old blacksmith shop, they're the only original buildings left on the plantation and he keeps them in pristine condition, as authentic as the day they were built. It's his way of preserving the memory of that pure youthful passion for Annie, I suspect.

"Not fir, though; the cabin's built of cypress—cedar and cypress—a little poetic license there, maybe, but I can't imagine her having James Stuart Hurd, alias the Dollman, in mind when she put up that gravestone. They do say, though, there was a wisp of something in the frail twist of his body, like the beauty of a mayfly's wings, when he married her, like an ephemeron—until you watched him talk, that is, when his jaw would clamp down and draw that white, white skin into a skull-mask with a vent for muffled sounds coming out between the clack of his teeth. Still, there's the touch of soul on his face when you see it in the sanctuary—that's *his* head on the sarcophagus, twisted around on his neck and looking back at you.

"He gained weight after Kathy died, lost height and got more humped, and was never seen without that basket of homemade dolls. We all knew about the insides of those dolls when I was growing up—the pregnant female ones at the bottom filled with pot and coke, brown for pot, white for coke, and the big-muscled males on top, appropriately loaded down with the hard stuff. I guess you know it eventually came out he was peddling for Jake Landry. That basket drew attention away from his Dorian Grey degeneracy—what's more disarming than a basket slung over somebody's arm, even the poor old Dollman's arm?—but nothing could take away my teenage horror of him. I used to shiver and shy away from passing him in the street, and I knew even then there was some unmentionable thing to do with him and the Wentworths and, somehow, with Frances Boullet, something unspeakably wrong from way back and definitely *not to be associated with us*—the Canes or any of our friends.

"Sounds pathetically hush-hush, I know—like *AIDS* still is in some quarters today—'bad blood,' they used to say, but we're talking now about the '60s, when the whole Quarter, running down for decades, finally went to pot—pun intended—with Jeremy Wentworth in the Boullet House roaring drunk or stoned out of his mind most of the time. We privately dubbed him 'King of the Fallen Court' because he used to hang out in the alley back of the Hernando surrounded by his admirers, all like him blighted offshoots of our best families, or claiming to be. The Hernando became their second home—'the Palace' was what our crowd called it then, with Jake Landry standing guard over everybody and everything, and drink and dope flowing freely all around. The Fallen Court got so out of hand by the early '70s our parents started talking about cleaning up the old Quarter before it was too late, and that's when the Preservation Board, which started out as a ladies' garden club presided over by my grandmother Letitia, was made over into the historic watchdog it is today, with Uncle Randy as chair. People started buying up the old wrecks down here and restoring them for offices and businesses. Everybody who was anybody got in on the act; you'd think they'd been commanded by the gods of civic duty. Even the old winos of the Fallen Court developed a burning interest in the topic of restoration—it was like their pride of distant, very distant, ownership was being reclaimed—and the Dollman's business picked up steam; he was all over the place. I'm sure Harding remembers him well. After her time, poor James Stuart Hurd went steadily down. *Literally,* year by year. You could see him getting closer and closer to the rubble of the gutted houses he rummaged through for bits and pieces to make his dolls, and finally he just doubled over so he couldn't drag his basket around any more. Along about dark the summer before he died in 1989, he'd be scuttling around the grounds of the Hernando on all fours, like something bound to earth. Doc Shibbles came to the funeral and killed himself later that same week. Heroin overdose, same as Jeremy Wentworth.

"To the end, Shibbles maintained there're families in Tarragona that carry 'demon blood' through the male line—the demon was supposedly holed up in the Boullet House and would periodically break loose as long as any of 'em were alive. In his suicide note Shibbles implored Uncle Randy to lead a mass 'self-disposal' of all these doomed men so they could die secure in the knowledge of having destroyed the demon, and just in case there was any doubt about who he had in mind, he left a list of the endangered families: Hurds, Wentworths, Evanses, Simmonses, Canes. Uncle Randy released a statement to the *Sentinel*, I recall, expressing compassion for his old friend and fellow physician whose anguish and misplaced concern for others was brought about, in Uncle Randy's professional opinion, by the delusions of paranoid disorder causing him to take his own life, that kind of thing."

Aimée was only about halfway through her story when she side-tracked to a distressing theme. "But that's enough of the demon," she said, "you've read the diary and know the facts. I've never even laid eyes on it. Of course I've heard what's in it and more, from Maria-Louisa, but that's not like the real thing I'm sure."

She paused and looked directly into my eyes but I was unforthcoming, just gave an of-course nod of agreement and waited.

"Sure you want to hear this entire rambling horror story, uncensored?"

"The more rambling and uncensored the better, I need to catch up—I'm behind times."

"Where was I?"

"The endangered Cane family."

"Oh that—you realize that Uncle Randy doesn't have a superstitious bone in his body, but vibes from Frances Boullet and her house have rankled and festered in him like an ulcer ever since I can remember. I grew up hearing about the family curse going back to my great-grandfather, old Judge Cane—he and his wife Lucy, it was said, suffered more than other victims of the 1918 flu epidemic around here, their fevers lasted so long and ran so high their skin mottled until it dropped right off their bones. And then Grandfather Randall burned to death during a family reunion over at El Inglés—"

Aimée broke off and looked away, but turned resolutely back to me with the reckoning of Randall Cane Jr.'s last hour.

"It happened late one night—he loved to ride over the plantation when the moon was out—he'd picked up a lantern and walked to the old log barn, a small one-story more like a big crib for storage with a threshing floor in the center, no longer used for anything except storing hay, and with bales of it stacked around the sides to the ceiling it must have been like a well-built tinderbox—at the kindling point, the way old wooden buildings get sooner or later down here. It was like a flashover; nobody could get to him even though they could hear him scream. Uncle Randy later identified the charred remains by the gold repairs in Grandfather's teeth. There was an iron bit across his skull with shreds of leather bridle still attached to it, and the story went around he'd snarled himself in the bridle while trying to harness a new stallion, a beautiful but unruly albino, with a reputation for refusing to take the bit. He'd been locked in on the threshing floor of the old barn and must have trampled Grandfather—got away, flat disappeared. This happened in 1950, the year I was born.

"And coincidence, coincidence, the old Shibbles home next door—been there since at least the War of 1812—burned to the ground that very night with Doc Shibbles's mother inside. People claimed that set Doc off on his nutty conspiracy theories, with him swearing the albino was hitched to the live oak in front of the Boullet House that night—he'd seen it clearly, pawing the ground in the light of the fire. And what with him carrying on about the demon on a white horse and Maria Zamora telling anyone who'd listen that the 'old ones' were coming and going every night at the Boullet House—she meant Frances Boullet and Zula, of course—tongues kept wagging all during my childhood. Kids would whisper to each other across their school desks about the old haunted house down in the Quarter, like we had some special reason to worry—all the Canes, me included, but Uncle Randy most of all. A lot of 'em around here honestly believed Frances Boullet had the knowledge of how to come back from the grave, and that Uncle Randy was destined for a death even more gruesome than his daddy and granddaddy.

"They say he used to poke fun at the ghost stories surrounding the Boullet House and dismiss them as 'superstitious malarkey' and 'paranoid fantasies.' But by the time I came along, it seemed Uncle Randy couldn't so much as bring himself to call the house by name—he'd say 'that piece of Old Tarragona Trust property' or 'the sea captain's home,' meaning Captain Boullet of course, and never a peep about Frances and her crowd. Only when it became clear that Harding meant business with her restoration did he utter the name Boullet again, and then only with the adjective 'historic' in front, as if that somehow improved the smell of it: 'the Quiroga House, the George House, the Favret House, the *historic* Boullet House,' he'd say. People like Maria-Louisa and me, like Harding—you too most likely—we, it seems, produce only carrion flowers to his nose. Frances Boullet sprouts.

"During the years when she was still alive it was as obvious as a natural cause that she had some kind of power over the Canes—Maria-Louisa says everybody said so, and I guess that's why James Stuart Hurd's mother finally went to her for help. It must have been like calling on the devil for financial advice, considering how people around here felt about Frances Boullet, absolutely a last resort. Anyway, Mrs. Hurd arrived at the house one morning with a stack of deeds and a story about how her poor James was getting no income from the Hernando—or any other place for that matter. Old and weak as she was by then Frances Boullet was still in full possession of her wits—this was in 1935 not long before she died on her ninetieth birthday—and Maria-Louisa, who seldom left her side by that time, says her grandmother saw in a flash that the Wentworths, both Jeremy and Annie, had been done in by the Hurd Trust, which had been funded by transferring nearly worthless properties to it from the old Wentworth Trust. Mrs. Hurd went on and on about how she'd been to Mr. Cane first and how he'd told her he'd recently been forced to auction off a couple of trust properties to cover debts due, and then she'd gone to young Mr. Randy, who was joint trustee with his father, but Randy claimed he was trustee in name only, so designated in case of his father's incapacity—he'd advise against selling any properties in the Hurd Trust, if that was what she had in mind, because the debt load on them would wipe out any proceeds of sale. He couldn't in good faith recommend liquidation at that time.

"What did Miss Boullet think? Well, Frances Boullet thought she might be able to do something if all the deeds were left with her. She then attached a letter to them that spelled out the evidence regarding transferals of the bulk of the Wentworth properties to the Hurd Trust, Maria-Louisa delivered the packet directly to Jeremy, and all hell broke loose. Jeremy demanded immediate distribution—directly to him—of any property left in either trust and threatened lawsuits all around. After a lot of wrangling there was a settlement, with the deed to the Hernando going to Annie's daughter Katherine, and Jeremy getting what was left of the old Wentworth properties—all in debt all right, and Jeremy was no manager. Lost the whole kit'n'caboodle in record time.

"And that wasn't the end of it. Frances Boullet and Zula were no sooner gone than Jake Landry set out to dispose of Maria-Louisa, the last of them—his way, I imagine, of showing how indispensable he was to the Canes—even threatened her with a police investigation for double murder of the old women and hauled out a search warrant. Jake always did work hand in glove with the law, his threats weren't idle, so Maria-Louisa made a deal with him. She signed over the Boullet House to the remnant of the Wentworth Trust in exchange for a clear title to her little cottage. More to the point, the police investigation was to be stopped then and there, which, given her color and her reputation—not to mention her dealings even back then in the thirties with back-door immigrants from occupied Haiti—was one thing she couldn't afford to let him get started on.

"The house was boarded up until Jeremy Wentworth married and took over the downstairs, where his new wife—poor family with social aspirations, from the next county over—delivered a daughter and kept him more or less in line until she died in the late forties. Maria-Louisa used the library for her own ends, with Jeremy's connivance. He'd come to regard her as an ally by then—the two of them cooked up all kinds of schemes for getting around Jake Landry, who lived for a few years at the back in that God-awful addition Harding finally tore off. Jeremy was convinced to the bitter end that the Boullet House belonged to him free and clear even though the Wentworth Trust had long ago been dissolved and the house put into something called the Old Tarragona Trust, of which Uncle Randy was—you guessed it—sole trustee. It was eventually donated to the Committee for the Preservation of Historic Tarragona, the legal owner when Harding bought it.

"Jeremy liked to lump all these different legal entities together under the name of 'trusses for the Cane fortune' and would pass the time brooding and ranting over evidence of deed-switching among them. What income the Wentworths subsequently received came from Jake Landry by way of what he called 'Dr. Cane's charity' and Jeremy referred to as 'hush money'—informed that the house had been sold to one Elizabeth Harding Dumot who was going to restore it as a home, he was dead sure she was the newest 'agent of chi-Cane-ry,' as he used to say, intent on dispossessing him. He called Maria-Louisa to his bedside early the very day in May of '77 when Harding took possession, and gave her all the old documents—the ones from Frances Boullet—and then he showed her his will, signed and sealed, leaving the house to her. Jeremy was madder than a hornet before he died— round midday according to the coroner's report—and Maria-Louisa says he practically made her swear to call up all the demons of hell, if necessary, to bring down the Cane family. All the dope and liquor Jake Landry poured into Jeremy through the years did nothing to break his determination to get even. 'That nut-case Shibbles has one thing straight,' he told Maria-Louisa. 'You're the last of the blood line and your blood calls for Cane's, take it and drink, or, like the one on the white horse, I'll never rest easy in the ground.' She promised she'd do it, in her own time and way.

"When all's said and done, though, it *was* Uncle Randy who arranged for the down-and-out Wentworths to move into the Boullet House and live there, rent-free, until Jeremy's death. Nobody could reasonably have expected to make the Wentworth estate solvent again after the huge debts Jordan racked up during all those years Jeremy and Annie were growing up. But Maria-Louisa heard a different story from Frances Boullet, who thought Randall Jr. had borrowed money on the Wentworth Trust properties to finance his own private investments. My own grandfather.

"Well, I don't know—maybe there was nothing against the letter of the law in anything the Canes did with all that deed-switching from trust to trust and, for sure, Jeremy had an income far beyond what he was worth to the Cane & Wentworth firm. I mean, for close to half a century he lived like an absentee landlord who never questions the source or conditions of cash flowing into his account year after year. Poor old Jeremy could never get it all together, because there was always a piece missing for him—you see, Frances Boullet never betrayed Miss Annie's secret and neither did Maria-Louisa, so he just grew more and more convinced over the years that a Cane conspiracy of some kind was functioning like common law in Tarragona. And Maria-Louisa has certainly become Uncle Randy's nemesis—what finally leveled the playing field was her knowledge of *the reason* behind the property switches, the secret identity of Jimmy Hurd's grandfather."

"So it took the sexual knowledge of kinship secrets to do it," I said.

"We met alone, Maria-Louisa and I, with Uncle Randy here in the house. We accused nobody of anything, merely showed him the documents Jeremy'd passed on to Maria-Louisa, all signed by his father, and let him understand that we knew all about the Wentworth-Hurd marriage deal and the two trusts. We'd gone to Miss Annie for back-up—Miss Annie who spent her own life keeping the truth from Jeremy, protecting both families, Wentworths *and* Canes, from public dishonor."

"But brother Jeremy was long dead by then and so was the old moral era, right?"

"Sure, and there was Jimmy, alive and needy. With his future as the issue, Miss Annie was ready and willing to swear to Uncle Randy's paternity in court if necessary."

"And what did you get from Dr. Cane?" I asked

"Three concessions. One, he would sponsor Maria-Louisa for the Preservation Board and make sure she succeeded him as chair. Two, he would find immediate ways and means for the Hernando to yield Miss Annie and Jimmy a reasonable income for life. And three, he'd take on the Preservation Board personally, which in this case meant Greeley Connor, and get him to approve my unorthodox remodeling plans. Maria-Louisa assured him our objective was not to ruin his standing in Tarragona or to strip him of power, but to control historic matters under the auspices of the Board with an authority equal to his own. He's met all three conditions down to locating a developer for the Hernando who's coughing up a sum that should keep Miss Annie and Jimmy Hurd in a style to which they're not accustomed.

"And that's the broad, messy compass of it, the answer to your question—the story of how Maria-Louisa and I managed to transform the original, mosquito-ridden back gallery of the Boullet House into this inauthentic interior/exterior space where I can vegetate with my plants."

"Have you managed to make peace with him yet, your Uncle Randy?"

"He's done all we asked of him but he never attended another meeting of the Board, and he's never visited me here or invited me to his home again or communicated with me in any way, and neither has Aunt Sophie. A shame," she smiled in ironic resignation, "my garden room would secretly delight him."

It's obvious; even this minute she'd like to frolic with Randy Cane again, tease and please him as she did before he cast her with the enemy. For him the enemy is not—as Harding realized—those who are different from him but those who share the secrets and don't keep them. The secrets hold everything together. They're the virtual collagen of his world, the ground of its flowering—without the secrets, all's pathological and broken.

"I take it your Uncle Randy has lived and will die protecting his wife and world from the odor of that knowledge. The polluting toxic secrets of personal life."

"He'll be eighty-one this year and until our . . . negotiations, he was still the old lion of Tarragona society. Since then he never leaves his grounds, receives no visitors. It's his way of refusing to share power—better the purity of staying in, and on. If you drive over there you may catch a glimpse of him hanging on his wife's arm like a blind man, frail and unsteady—they walk slowly back and forth together on that splendid veranda overlooking the Gulf, a dying king in his Hyacinth Garden with his hyacinth girl.

"Despite everything, though, I never think of him without grief. I'm like a buzzard circling over something dead and gone, forever hungry to peck at what I'm finally free of and no longer fear, scavenging the loss. That's how it is with us, and that's the price I pay for this." Aimée flung her arms wide to indicate the room—one of those clearings we live in that mark off our limits and tattoo us with the individualizing images and colors of our humanity.

The very feel of her in a place so unquestionably her own—the sweep of her energy—holds me still like a gift just opened, lost in its compass. Aimée with the garden outside beckoning through the darkness. Already, I'm eager for a daylight exploration of it, that collaborative space worked by Maria-Louisa and Aimée these fifteen years—and so many more years ago by Frances Boullet and Zula. To clear my head and remain centered on where I am and what I'm here for, I slide the glass balcony doors open all the way and maneuver a big armchair there to settle in, diary on my lap—plump, soft, much-handled, among others by me. I'm to return it to its place in the sanctuary before the opening tomorrow. But for this night—a Southern May night as balmy as any Harding could have wished for—its future is mine.

2
Bride of Freedom

T he sea, the sea—its vastness so usurps preoccupation with the particulars of life's dilemmas that I can only exult in its liberating détente. I'm as insatiable tonight, on my Island overlook, as a rat with hypothalamic lesions. The flat sheath of darkness across the Bay is dotted with the lights of Tarragona, setting a distance reminiscent of some astronomical moment in a museum display. A light breeze off the pewter depths of the Gulf whiffles the diary's filmy pages. Like Harding that night after her fall into the sanctuary, I smooth down the first one and trace Frances Boullet's clear old-fashioned cursive with my fingernail:

My Last Writing, wherein the years from December 24, 1860 to December 5, 1935 are recollected in decoupage.

As if I didn't know what was coming, practically word for word, I turn the page eagerly and begin.

March 3, 1935—Lately, the advent of my death has led me, not to set my affairs in order, for I did that long ago, but to hold our final hearing of time's patter in these our last months together. How grand, at the close of nine decades, to take survey from the certainty that the end is nigh! Not to be traded for all youth's energy or love's bliss, all promise of scientific progress, worldly success, excitement of discovery, pleasure in the beautiful moment, justice and its satisfactions. I have lived them all and pronounce them goods of a kind tied to time. Here at my journey's end I am rendered thankful to hold my peace. This peace that does indeed pass all understanding spreads from our sanctuary and I am resolved never to leave it, the very possibility of it having allowed for eighty-nine, soon to be ninety, years of visitation elsewhere. It lies about me, the stretch of this peace, home-like, the home I now move in at long last, where the final moment of life beatifies each passing second.

On with the disposal of my writing, thirty-nine volumes crammed to the margins. Here in this, the fortieth and last of them, as if willfully saved for the purpose, I open the moment to life's disempowerment of stories. Until now, I've added nothing to my diary since the hurricane of '28 in the autumn of my eighty-third year. Creation of an ending requires both sacrifice and sacrilege. One can begin over and over, but ending over and over clips away at finality.

March 4th—Away then with coquettish diffidence—this fading remnant of an apricot-colored skirt almost a century old. So long ago, and like so many others of my time—yet I cannot think they were of my kind—I wrapped it around the leather-bound set even before making my first entry but anticipating many, and attached the directive: "To be burned unopened in the event of my death." This note penned in girlhood survived as my diary grew through the years, from the time I began writing in it in emulation of my plantation-bred cousins and their friends, a few days before Florida seceded from the Union. Now that little passes unremarked in my sight (for clarity, not insight, sets in when so little matters) the archaic formula presses itself on my notice as a coy invitation to be violated. If few in the last century would have admitted to encroaching on the intimate space of a diary and might, indeed, have destroyed what they found there to hide their own perfidy, few in the present age would fail to seize the chance of publishing their very transgressions of another's privacy. Thus one becomes a "news item." The thought of public exposure sizes the rage, of no mean proportion, which has been my lot for a lifetime and has ballooned like the quiet of a hurricane, no longer able to destroy me but throwing the white pervasive light of its eye over my life.

Unfolded, the old silk yields proof of my existence: page after page of words, words, words. This large room, housing now as always only our books, the table and three chairs (Nongka's poteau mitan rolled away in the cupboard underneath the steps to our cushioned window seats) acquires the promise, with this little multitude of filled tomes spilling over the silk, of an infinite and indigenous luxury. And now the spine of the one I write in awaits the gold ink that has numbered each over the years—XL, the final volume. Begun yesterday, to be ended on December 5, 1935. Nine more months. I take note that it matters, in tending to the disposition of my writing, to look after such minutiae.

If I tremble somewhat before Volume I, it is not with trepidation, for youth and its secrets no longer touch me. Nor with anticipation— I've long forgotten what was committed to these thousands of pages and have little curiosity about the past. What vibrates through my hands is the play of final composition. I open it and scan the initial entry set down nearly seventy-five years ago—such energetic flourishes, especially on the capitals and the final d's and t's.

Christmas Eve, 1860. El Inglés—A diary of forty volumes, enough for a lifetime!—and bound in beautiful softest dark morocco, my most fervent wish fulfilled beyond all expectation. Had we stayed home for the Christmas season you would have been mine nearly three weeks ago, dear diary, in time for my fifteenth birthday as Papa intended. We were all at breakfast when the packet arrived, and as so often when my nearest feelings are touched, I expressed not my delight but my doubt—"How shall I ever fill so many volumes in a mere lifetime?"—for doubt capers in me like an escapade. Afraid that Papa might fail to sense my gratitude—and containing the shyness that makes me so unlike my society-loving cousins—I kissed him, with all eyes on us, and whispered that none might hear: "I mean to write in them throughout my whole life, Papa—and if nothing happens to set down, I'll make it up."

"You shall do no such thing, Françoise," he replied sternly, "all your writings must be true—la pure verité—no matter if you fill no more than a single volume." Perceiving my mortification, he softened his manner—"Never mind, Fan (his pet name for me), journals are for giving young ladies the leisure to ramble on, n'est-ce pas? You must write what you please, provided that you keep truth and fancy clearly apart. A journal is not for lying to yourself in private"—he finished to titters all around—"there are more than enough places for that!" My cousins believe they have more reason now than ever for teasing me with harboring "secret literary aspirations"—

As for the rest of that entry, we'll never know. Snipping this passage out of Volume I, the old Boullet pasted it here in the one I now hold, number XL, the paper so fine and the seal so smooth it hardly shows. All thirty-nine got the same ruthless cut-and-paste treatment. Dismembered, whole years shorn away—continuities severed, intimate revelations consigned to gaps like a graveyard for epiphanies. A resolute simplification. I think of Matisse going blind and his big colored paper cut-outs, childlike in their near organic rudiments but never really to be mistaken for the perceptual whimsy of a child. More like the residual exuberance of a lifetime of looking, making a virtue of the impatience and infirmity of age.

Below the salvaged scrap from her youthful entry, self-consciously fancy in the way of such occasions, the slower, plainer hand of the old Boullet resumes briefly:

Ah Papa, how I failed you on both counts, and having arrived where I am I feel neither shame nor guilt. Still, if I am lacking in these, I do experience something very like sorrow that my existence and your straightforward lucidity could not have been mutually preserved. Let me now transpose the whole of my next entry from that long ago visit at El Inglés, inasmuch as it does constitute an Aristotelian beginning of sorts.

Then another pasted snippet from the eager fifteen-year-old:

Christmas Day, 1860—Quiet at long last, everyone abed—have tried all day to find a time apart from holiday-making—only now am I free to put pen to these pages, while Cousin Julia sighs and moans as she turns in her bed, too wearied by the day's festivities to take notice of me scribbling away. How impatient I am to be home again! I should write whenever and however much I please. Though courtesy and delicacy legislate privacy, I fear there may be some in this house capable of setting such considerations aside, for the mere pleasure of spying others out—what I intend to confide to my journal touches upon this household—I must take care—or do these fears of mine rise from a guilty conscience?

For some time, I have been expected to pass a part of each year at El Inglés—but have never before come here with Papa, who has had no intercourse with the Howards, or they with him, since my mother died giving me birth and grand'maman assumed my care. Not even she accompanied me on my annual visits here, declaring always that her duties kept her in Tarragona with Papa. He harbors little love, I think, for my mother's very English family—who remain so, even after several generations on this side of the Atlantic. Three years ago, when grand'maman died, he received only the briefest of condolences from Aunt and Uncle, and I realized then how seldom anyone at El Inglés spoke of him—and how little notice was taken of any mention of him on my part; I became unable so much as to utter his name—among the grown-ups certainly—without some fleeting sense of indelicacy—from which I concluded that the Howards so thoroughly disapprove of his decision to dismiss the governess hired after grand'maman's death—and to bring Nongka from Hayti—that their former coolness opened to a breach.

Once, when Uncle Edward and Aunt Virginia were recounting how my cousins like to "hold school"—to teach the Negro children at El Inglés reading and writing—I began all unthinkingly to boast that I had brought Nongka's children, Zula and Ibo, to the proficiency of natives in the use of English, while they have taught me all I know of Spanish (their island patois, of course, does not count)—until I intercepted the look that passed between them. As I was leaving the room, I heard Aunt Virginia's soft, gentle voice address Uncle in troubled tones—"Surely Edward, no good can come of that situation." Since then, I studiously disguise my feelings for Zula and Ibo, and theirs for me, cognizant that both Aunt and Uncle manage to ask about them without appearing to put any weight on their queries—

With Nongka's help and the lessons Zula, Ibo, and I give one another, I have learned more in recent years than in the whole of my childhood—Fräulein added little to the French I had from grand'maman, and I was never fond of my governess (though I was sorry to give up our German, Latin, and Greek lessons); but neither she nor grand'maman had mastered many tongues, like Nongka. Languages excite me—the words, what they are able to express, and how their meanings change over time, and their music most of all—how and why these little concatenations of sound can exercise so great a power in our lives. Nongka says the human breed survives on the magic that draws breath in words, and the time to fall silent is when survival is no longer at issue.

Last year, toward the end of my visit, Aunt Virginia broke the ban against mentioning Papa—"Frances," she said, "now that you are growing up—even though, at fourteen, you and your cousin Lucinda are still our little girls—do you begin to take an interest in the management of your father's household? I do wish he would buy Jennie and Jackson from us—they are two of our very best and have been with us from birth, you know—we would never think of letting anyone outside the family have them, and you surely must be in need of trustworthy servants now." In reply, my voice held the quality of standoffishness suitable for discussing strangers, or any of doubtful position—"Oh, I think it unnecessary—I confess that since I give so much time to my studies, I attend little to how it happens that all at home is accomplished so simply and well—I suppose Ibo and Zula must help their mother with everything." How artless my voice sounded even to my own ears!

Dear, kind Aunt Virginia—said to be so like my dead mother, though not intimately related by blood—her brow cleared momentarily as she murmured: "Yes, I suppose they manage well enough." Soon the troubled note returned—"Nonetheless, dear Frances, it would do you good to enter society more, and to begin receiving guests when Captain Boullet is with you in Tarragona—not, of course, that your Nongka and her brood are not perfectly capable, as you say; but if our two trained servants were added to your household—" Aunt Virginia broke off uncertainly, it becoming evident that she felt the rightness of her proposal, while somehow unsure of the grounds for a proper defense of it.

Truly, I have all the society I could wish for at home; but what I did not tell Aunt Virginia is that Zula, Ibo, and I live as the sisters and brother we are (even if only half-so)—sharing everything, working and studying together, eating and playing together under the watchful eye of Nongka, with her passion for order and formality— sitting down to meals with as much elegance as may be seen in any great plantation house upon the visitation of foreign dignitaries. We must always disown our habitual way of life, Nongka cautions; and if anyone comes to call, we must be prepared to behave in an altogether different manner—one that Aunt Virginia and Uncle Edward would approve. I cannot think just when and how we came to practice such refinements of dissimulation with as much ease as others do their social graces.

Nongka once said—"Time spent without life's sweetness starves la liberté—we are the kind who know how to live well and stay free. The others would kill us for that, not because they want our knowledge, but because they fear its power—that is why we must dissemble. Even so, they will sniff us out—we trail the scent of what they hate and fear. We must be clever as the creatures of the earth are clever that escape their hunters—turn their attention away from us when possible, and when not possible, we must look more like their kind than they themselves. Never forget who the true deceivers are." In the grip of prophetic vision, she would add—"Take care, my children, take care."

Nongka's words make danger personal to me—yet try as I may, I can not grasp why anyone should trouble about us enough to do us harm—it seems to me that I injure no one, and am careful to avoid doing so. Still, even when her admonitions begin to sound excessively sibylline, I feel she speaks truth—the sense that I habitually live in a world of private joy enclosed in public danger has grown keener since our arrival here, three days ago, from Savannah and Charleston, where Papa had business. As ever, the hospitality of El Inglés, like that of other plantations hereabouts, envelops all in warmth and kindness, and I am lulled by what Nongka calls the First Seduction, that seeming offer of unending nourishment and safety—but lulled, this time, as a dose of strong spirits (I imagine) soothes and dulls the cut of the surgeon's knife.

Two days after the New Year commences, Papa is to attend the Secession Convention with Uncle Edward at Tallahassee. Public concerns now seemingly override personal animosities; there is perpetual talk of secession and the collapse of plantation life, which would follow upon emancipation of the slaves—Uncle Edward maintaining that the value of his land would plummet to little or nothing; freed slaves might be put to work on small parcels owned by farmers leading niggardly lives, yes, but he can conceive of no order under which freedmen could successfully cultivate a cleared acreage the size of his, not to mention the task of further clearing and support of the whole. Papa, as seemingly at his ease as if there had never been a rift between himself and the Howards, appears to agree. (All such talk—amidst the celebratory atmosphere of Christmas, with its continual feasting, and the smooth pace of daily life on the plantation—augments my wariness and fastens my thoughts ever more upon Nongka's warning.) Strange, I had been under the impression that Papa is a Unionist who, as far back as I can remember, has hoped for the expansion of the Union by annexation

of Cuba; but he used to say too that Florida belongs with the Spanish-
held islands—and that there has been a prolonged invasion of it by
Anglo-Saxon and other American pretenders. The Howard family,
who were among the original planters in Middle Florida during early
Territorial days, must be included in this description—has Papa now
joined the pretenders?

March 20, 1935—Such a girl's appetite had I for recording the fill of
my days I used up Volume I of my diary in little more than a month.
I have snipped from it my Christmas eve and Christmas day entries
of 1860 and bonded the pages here in this volume as if there from
the beginning—others already excised from that eager first tome
await their turn. As I took the ruined thing in hand to place it in our
iron zin, the feel of it so touched my love of objects I was moved to
set it afire. This seems right and well done. It burns still as I write,
the sting not unlike those sentiments confided to it, ardently and
copiously, so long ago. Their smothering vapor rises all about me. So
orchards fill with protective smoke from smudge pots.

The ashes shall be stored in my pot tête. Such simple acts etch
out rituals for joining the freedom of being with the happiness of
living. And having thus staged the source of my joy, I live and breathe
in this work of composing. May it deliver me from both mythos and
ethos in the months to come before celebration of my ninetieth
birthday. Thirty-nine volumes equal thirty-nine rituals for burning
up what matters. Incinerating all the faithless revelations to preserve
only this.

The fortieth, here in my hands. Which I've been nervously toting around
for two days like hot merchandise, wanting to be rid of it one minute,
caching it on and around my person the next—turning myself into a hideaway for Frances Boullet's nonagenarian cutouts. Anything that survives
so much destruction wants looking after.

Up here on the eighth floor on this moon-washed sea-enveloped balcony, a night clear and empty all the way up to the stars—infinitely suspended—it's just possible to feel that's what my mission amounts to: caring for this lone survivor. Here, now, no thought of tomorrow. Reading it
yet again, hearing it speak to me—for the time being.

Not yet daylight the morning after her fall into the sanctuary, Harding woke
up in a cold sweat, not even a sheet over her, motel air-conditioner grind-

ing away at top speed and her head full of dreams. Sergeant Peaden of the Tarragona Police Department heaving up the hatch, sticking his head in for a good look at her face streaked with plaster grit. One-way mirror glasses, bug-eyed, jaw clapping up and down like a ventriloquist's dummy. Only there's no sound. A whiff of spearmint gum shoots up her nostrils. She's struggling to pull the goose-down quilt over her so she won't be seen, but they're already lining up behind the Law, one by one, raising the hatch to look and sniff at her like bloodhounds, before letting it go with a thud. Up and thud. Up and thud. Last of all, Margaret Avery of Heritage Homes, Inc., dark blue butterflies hovering around her beauty parlor hairdo, whispering maliciously: "What did you expect?"

But it wasn't the musty chill that made Harding jump out of bed so much as the thought of Ware's crew punching holes in the plaster wall under the dormer windows. Headline: Wreckers Find Secret Voodoo Room in Historic Home.

Not a human in sight when she rolled into the rutted drive of the Boullet House fifteen minutes later, only the birds making their summery ruckus in Doc Shibbles's garden next door. Up in the library everything was as she'd left it, the plywood shoved over the hole in the plaster-strewn window seat, her tools on top for good measure—a cover so transparent anybody inclined to peep and probe could bring the sanctuary to light without even trying. It wouldn't take a demolition crew knocking out walls.

Shovel, bucket, broom. She threw herself into the clean-up, imagination running wild: a revitalized Boullet legend nesting in "Then & Now," the *Sentinel*'s popular Wednesday feature by Roland B. Markit, master of speculation-in-a-stew-of-facts—history as "heritage"—camera crews milling through the sanctuary, follow-ups and spin-offs in weekly installments. Local entrepreneurs lining up to make purchase offers, while the house became a prime attraction on the walking tour of Old Tarragona, aversion for its one-time occupants passing into romantic appropriation. Her big chance to escape risk and drudgery with something more than a whimper—a success story.

And it would spread; success feeds on itself. Interested faculty from the Community College dropping by for their piece of the action. Art historians from Tallahassee buzzing about the heretofore unknown "primitives." Would-bes from afar, in various fields, competing to edit the diary, seizing on the fad for women's life-writing and launching interdisciplinary projects—under the aegis of the newly founded Center for Southern Studies, most likely. Mad old Frances Boullet's diabolical way of life explored in all its sensory and theoretical deviations while, back up North, they'd repackage the legend as a mode of revolutionary survival in the secrecy of boundary-crossing creative space. Female occult practice as stratagem for political and aesthetic subversion.

Her purchase would take on the enviable status of a prescient investment turning up a pot of green.

No doubt about it, she could make a living (a career even) off Frances Boullet's private life. She could—it was hers now, this secret space that had come with the house. Hers to do with as she liked. And she did not like the feel of the public eye on it.

In the desolation of the ruined library, the sun just starting to peep slantwise through the dormer windows, Harding put hammer and chisel to work on the broken sill. But the question kept at her like a loose screen banging you into wakefulness on a windy night: who besides her might already know? Rumors there must have been from the start, as usual, but no observational proof either at street level or in the library—the four dormers perfectly in character inside and out, commodious perches for reading or surveying the neighborhood, with some fancy iron work along the front of each sill. Interesting ornamental touch. Identical, all four of them—except that the fretwork rim of the easternmost sill quite literally held the key to the sanctuary: a pair of hidden rods working others below. Out of sight, out of mind.

She ticked off names at first in no order, merely as a way of holding anxiety at bay.

Margaret Avery. Shrewd about real estate but definitely in the dark about the property's inner potential. Very Southern, would have grabbed it herself if she'd known. Ditto Greeley Connor—arrogating to himself the authority to decide on all matters architectural on behalf of the Preservation Board, rooting out anomalies and failures to perform in accordance with principles of historical authenticity—he of all people should have figured it out. Evidently he hadn't, so far. But as her consulting contractor, he'd have every opportunity from here on.

There should be a list of those who might suspect or come to suspect something out of bounds, something more than meets the eye, and Greeley belonged on that list. But didn't that apply as well to the other Board members? All just as compromised, she felt reasonably sure, though not clear about what specific slice of historic pie each might appropriate for personal use.

Above all: *Randall Cane III.* Not only because he was the Board's chair but because he (alias the Committee for the Preservation of Historic Tarragona) had sold her the house. As owners the Canes must have had the run of it.

She added the entire Board to the list, with question marks. Randy Cane and Greeley Connor at the top.

In less than an hour the ragged planks were cleanly pried out and disposed of. And she had a good hunch about where she'd find what was needed next. In the topsy-turvy wreckage of the add-on, a tangled mess of salvaged old flooring and other woodwork, she spotted them—odd lengths of random-width yellow pine. Grubby and, like every wall and ceiling of the Boullet House (along with the cypress woodwork she was pulling off piece by piece for refinishing), painted a sickly pea-green. The green of poverty, of tenements. Depression green they called it. Turned out to match the boards in the window seat as closely as if milled from the same timber stand more than a century before. Repair is a process of fitting on a mask. The patched sill must not stand out as unusual in any way—difference emerges, sameness recedes—and such bricolage is very much Harding's kind of thing. Its economies of improvisation, her body equipped with whatever likely tool comes to hand, concentrate and calm her. "There's such a thing as false economy, lady," a passing carpenter once yelled out as he watched her measure old decking saved from a near-by demolition and fit it piecemeal on the floor of her front porch in Athena, New York. He himself used only treated lumber fresh from the yard—a man had to learn how to value his time. Harding works at something and, in the fashioning, discovers whether or not it will do.

Life in the street was beginning to stir. Reluctantly, she unlocked the front door and left it ajar. After three weeks of doors and windows wide open from morning till night, a closed-up house would attract attention—difference emerges. Especially with her Chevy parked inside the carriage gate as usual. (Proposition: the only innocence that protects is a function of artifice.)

The Wentworths, speaking of people having had the run of the house. For thirty years or more, and running it down royally at the Canes' expense, she'd heard. What did the Wentworths know? Would they have kept silent all those years, then vacated the place just like that, without a word to anybody, if they'd been in on the sanctuary? Still, just in case, she made a place for Mr. and Mrs. Royal Wentworth, their son Billy and daughter Stephanie, on the list with their ex-landlord and his colleagues on the Preservation Board. Near the bottom. And the baby was still cutting his molars. The old man was a different story—those furious eyes facing her down that bright May afternoon of her arrival at the Boullet House to take possession, seemed to be mocking her with knowledge. Jeremy Wentworth, paterfamilias, dead as an Audubon bird—wouldn't budge from his bed when they trucked away the last load, the family said. Refused help and ordered them out, dying alone in the Captain's old bedroom shortly afterwards. Finding his corpse could not be said to have been arranged—but not entirely accidental either. Would it have made any difference if he'd still been alive?

Old Wentworth was bent on having something out with her, that she was sure of.

Fitting one plank at a time she took care to angle and finish each cut without saw marks to draw the eye. So too with hammering—driving in old cut nails set aside for reuse, steadying her hand for each blow to make it land head-on and come away clean. No telling dents in the grain of the wood. Intermittently, her saw paused in its track—she listened for footsteps, a voice calling out from below, ready on the instant to ease herself off the window seat, shut the library door and bolt downstairs, business as usual.

But no one stopped at the house that day, no tradesman presenting an estimate, no official to quibble about permits, not a single drifter or nosy snoop. Predictably, Ware's crew never materialized. For once she took comfort in her relegation to lowest priority, hugging to herself the safety of their contempt. Little thrills of smugness, more than the satisfaction of work well done, more like a sense—distinctly triumphal—of danger averted rippled at the margins of her concentration, the memory of her dream-self wrapped in goose down shimmering cheerily through it all. Up and thud. Up and thud. The virtual reality devised by dreamwork for experiencing what you're living.

Dead or alive, there was the *Female Relative* without a name. A version of the local lore had it that Frances Boullet was poisoned in her own home by a West Indian housekeeper—woman of mixed race whispered by some to be her half-sister, one of the Captain's bastards—or maybe by her granddaughter, who tried to get her hands on the house afterwards. The latter's disappearance, along with the bodies of the two old ones, fed rumors about a ghost—often in company with other unquiet dead. The granddaughter, or whatever, if alive, would herself be getting on in years, and, murderer or no, she'd have the secret for sure. That called for a new list, with this nameless woman—or her progeny—at the top.

And for more than one reason. Somebody had been in the sanctuary lately. Not over a couple of weeks ago by the look of things. Perfectly clean, perfectly kept, conditions there were in striking contrast to the rest of the house—the downstairs garbage dump and the putrescence of dead insects and vermin sealed in the empty rooms upstairs, and, throughout, that dense half-caked crust of dirt that forms in the South during any prolonged spell of humidity and neglect. Except in the sanctuary. Not so much as a speck of dust on the dark leather of Frances Boullet's diary, as if it were still being put to regular use.

Who else should go on her new list? What about *the Hurds*—didn't they pass by almost every day? Jimmy, eyes peeled and head screwed around in that unnatural way. Severely retarded, people said, didn't qualify for any of the special ed programs. What if that inarticulate spasm that sometimes broke from him was an effort to express something he knew? The old Dollman, too, hanging around at odd times—same leer as the boy, same twist of the neck. Same face despite the age difference. And the likeness of both to that delicate white mask of a face peering from the altar frescoes seemed more than chance. On the basis of this inscrutable correspondence, she decided to include the Hurds, migrating somewhere between her two lists.

In the same blink another face popped up like a jack-in-the-box emitting cigar smoke. What could he have been up to last night, making a beeline across her yard from the alley to Valencia Street in the dark? Definitely not just straggling through the alley gate like the old drunks from the Hernando. The alley gate—a gate not looking like one, blending chameleon-like into the fence it was part of—had been her first discovery of Boullet stratagems for concealment. The junked stove jammed up against it for some unknown number of years had gone off in Ware's truck, along with a galvanized tub, an old hand-cranked washing machine, and two toilets, lashed by masses of vines. *Jake.* Something was keeping the little snoop busy late at night on the grounds of the Boullet House. Almost as if he'd been waiting for her to come out—definitely one to watch for.

Likewise *the Police.* Sergeant Peaden in particular, who'd stepped in unannounced the previous afternoon, not long after the wreckers left her high and dry, hung around for a good half hour poking through the mess downstairs and asking questions—something about "old documents." Anything "suspicious" she might have spotted in old Wentworth's vicinity.

The police, she concluded, were on another trail. To be on the safe side she added both Jake and Peaden to her list of those who might suspect something.

By mid-afternoon the window seat was whole again, the twice-salvaged planks worked back into the house as naturally as the body using up its stores of excess. Unremarkable except to an eye with x-ray vision that could penetrate to the underside, detect the new brace there. Considering how many passersby thought nothing of wandering in now that the Boullet House was officially under restoration, building permits up to prove it, Harding added the *Public at Large* to her growing list of maybes. With any who entered at any time to be starred for surveillance. On her main list, only one candidate—the rumored relative without a name.

All signs of repair disposed of—wood scraps, nails, tools—she swept the sill clean of sawdust and the floor below it and, on second thought, swept off the other three dormers as well. All four exactly and innocently alike. Cross-legged on the repaired window seat, with a distant sense of the street and its life through the screen of leaves outside, she crunched her last Granny Smith apple down to the core.

That night: Tired as only an animal, even a human one, can be after fifteen hours of labor, Harding opened the diary and began reading. Slowly at first, like a barely literate person, deciphering the marks one by one until, gradually, sense began to flow in a living voice from the page.

Proposition: What a lover chooses to read mirrors the space of her passion. For close to a week, Harding resisted reading on in the diary but never failed daily to assure herself that it was still there. By then she'd formed the habit of browsing the morning paper (the *Sentinel* arrived at the house right about when she did) over a solitary fast-food breakfast in a spot of shade behind the house. A way of orienting herself, via Tarragona's daily news, to the day of labor in store for her.

On the seventh day, the demolition crew turning up unexpectedly for another round of interior bashing cut short Harding's morning ritual. She marched them promptly upstairs. Under no circumstances—no circumstances—was anybody to touch the window wall of the big front room. Indifference gave way to blank incredulity, she weakly explaining why it was of the essence to keep it intact—"aesthetic reasons, you know"—old-time thing about antebellum homes having special powers built into second-story north walls—their eyes sliding back and forth from her to the intact plaster till she gave in to her sense of having stepped too close to the truth and shifted gears.

"It's all superstition of course, I just like the look of that wall the way it is, so please . . . but you will of course be gutting the other three walls in here," she finished lamely. Willy and Mo and Scooter filed out the library door, body-language saying all. That New York honky bitch bad news, going through changes. Ranky dank.

That night, after beating plaster dust from her clothes and hair, she made her customary round of the sanctuary and stayed on—and most nights after that, no matter how tired and even if only for a little while. Quieting body and soul after the daily grind by losing herself in the diary.

December 27, 1860. El Inglés—A fever of excitement among
the Negroes for three days now, and almost ceaseless feasting.
The carnival procession of masked John Kunahs appeared early
Christmas morning—my cousins and I were awakened at first light
by the beat of their gumbo boxes and triangles, and raced down to

the veranda to watch them dance, and to enjoy the uproarious
songs always composed for this occasion. Uncle Edward, aided by
Papa and Jonathan, poured out West Indian rum until one would have
thought the well had run quite dry!—Aunt Virginia, striking the correct
balance between hostess and mistress, dipped into a basket of silver
coins set out for her by Jackson the butler. The domestic servants,
while performing their duties as usual—though with an air of being
above it all—appear to harbor expectations of some extraordinary
occurrence; when I said as much to Uncle Edward yesterday, during our
morning ride through the Negro settlements, he replied in his gently
knowledgeable manner that "it is always thus during the Christmas
season—come tomorrow, a Lenten quiet will prevail."

All the better for me—brain brimming with all I want to confide
to this journal about life on the plantation—as different from our
life at home in Tarragona as can be imagined. My lovely new gold
pen from New York, a birthday gift from Zula, itches for the next
opportunity—

December 28—Like Caesar's Gaul, El Inglés is divided into three
parts, with the cleared land in each worked by Negroes grouped into
their own settlements edging a large hammock of basswood and
beech, green dragon and parsley haw, oak and ironwood, hickory and
elm. This forest separates cropland and settlements from the Great
House. Except for the northwest tract, which is upland, all cleared
lands lie among swamp and pine flats and all manner of jungly
growth—passion flowers and other vines and grasses and orchids and
green eyes and hibiscus and butterwort and pitcher plants pushing
up among dogwood and black titi. About half a mile from the Great
House, in the large hammock, is a place known to all in the region
as Overseer Town, where the Negroes engage in diverse crafts of
manufacture; with its rows of shops and people passing in and out
of them all day long, Overseer Town has the lively bustling air of a
small center of commerce, the heart and soul of El Inglés and all who
belong to it. I once passed a whole afternoon there with Jonathan,
watching the work—shoe and boot makers, farriers, spinners,
weavers, coopers, tanners, seamstresses and lacemakers, tailors and
milliners, masons and carpenters, soap and candle makers—there is
even a shop with a great oven where two slaves do nothing but bake
bread—and pies and cakes on holidays—for their fellows.

It all began, in a clearing amid the forested hammock, with a trio
of dog-trot log houses, one quite large and two smaller ones behind it,
when Grandfather and Grandmother Howard moved south from their

native Virginia to the new Territory—"that perfect Canaan flowing with milk and honey"—bringing with them fifty-one slaves young and strong enough to live on the frontier, the rolling slopes and swamps of Middle Florida. The biggest of the log houses, situated at a convenient distance from a bountiful fresh water spring, was built for their own use, while a plantation was being established; then a second, smaller cabin was erected behind the first to house an overseer; but after more land was acquired and partially cleared for cultivation, Grandfather looked forward to a time when he would need a second overseer, and had still another log house built beside the second one. Meanwhile, settlements for field hands had sprung up here and there on cleared tracts, gradually consolidated to their present size and number. The family finding it advantageous to have certain crafts and other services at their beck and call, one white-washed cabin after another was added in a neat horseshoe back of the three log houses, until Grandfather was beset by daily problems more like those of governing a prospering village than of running a mere growing plantation. He was only too happy, therefore, to build a home more suitable to the master of such a domain, years before any other planter in Middle Florida—the Great House stands serenely among live oak and cedar, on a bluff overlooking the St. Marks River.

Life at El Inglés being now so well ordered that his personal supervision was no longer required, Grandfather Howard hired two apprentices to aid the overseer, Mr. Landry, in managing day-to-day affairs, establishing him in the big log house and the new men with their wives in the two smaller ones. With leisure of a kind the frontier had thus far denied him, Grandfather was now at liberty to indulge his taste for books. It was in those years of orderly prosperity that his custom of extended sojourns in England and Scotland, Italy and elsewhere on the Continent, or in other parts of the Union more congenial to his tastes, took hold (to this day, the Howards still migrate to the cool parts of Virginia during the summer months, while the cotton grows, renewing old ties with relatives and friends—they are especially fond of the springs, with the White Sulphur, their favorite, being always their last stop on the way North for a stint at Newport).

The dust had no sooner settled after the brothers Jonas and Bob Evans, the apprentice overseers, moved in than they began vying with each other to find reasons for employing ever more slaves as artisans, with ever more specialized skills. A certain Negro adept at making nails, for example, might be put to work at nothing but their manufacture; in consequence, there must be carpenters whose sole task was constructing workshops for the growing arts such as nail-making; in this manner, what had been a cluster of cabins expanded over the years to a small town, laid out with crude storefronts, in something like streets running behind and alongside the three log houses. Other plantations in the vicinity not being nearly as self-sufficient, their overseers found it convenient to make certain of their purchases in "the town" at El Inglés.

During that time, Uncle Edward—then a young man—was away at Merton College, Oxford, reading the Classics; returning home in the autumn of 1835, he remarked that life among the Negroes and overseers, although always materially plentiful compared with other plantations in those parts, had acquired a new splendor. Field hands had taken to carrying parcels of clean clothing to work with them, and, at day's end, after washing up in basins of water, brought by youths from nearby settlements and set behind white sheets hung over wooden frames—a supply for the males being placed at a decorous distance from the females—the hands changed into their fresh attire, which, although of the coarse, mostly grey, variety worn in the fields, was embellished with fine-spun cotton sashes of all hues, more often than not matched by a colorful kerchief or bandanna. The settlements themselves showed signs of a more than ordinary affluence, with each cabin now possessing a kitchen garden, as well as a fenced area in which either a cow or pig fed—not to speak of the veritable multitude of chickens, turkeys, guineas, and pheasants roaming freely around each dwelling. This air of plenty in the settlements, however, was trifling when compared with the magnificence of what Grandfather had now officially dubbed "Overseer Town." Chagrin, perplexity, and amusement play in equal parts over Uncle Edward's features when he tells of that time:

"It was the season of the harvest, the busiest time of year on any plantation, and I, knowing that my homecoming would have been noised about in all the negro settlements, paid my respects at each of them in turn before the week was out. As I was far from eager, however, to re-acquaint myself with the overseers—who were a rough lot in those days—I postponed my visit to Town until the last; and that only after daily encountering Mr. Landry, the head overseer, who never failed to assert that I would find the place 'much changed and growed.' Even so, I could not have been more surprised, on riding into Town, to see tables and chairs set out in an open piazza, with negro artisans—chiefly males, but not a few females and their older children—congregating in diverse states of semi-fashionable attire.

They were, I was respectfully informed by one of the blacksmiths at the head of the group that had come forward to greet me, 'taking morning tea.' Having been shown to a table at some distance from the others, beneath a great oak—from which station I could survey the entire scene—I too was offered refreshments. None of the artisans lingered over their chilled lemonades and mint teas, but duly resumed their employments; while others, upon issuing from workshops all around, greeted me with the most commendable courtesy and gravity before taking their turns at table.

"Males were, for the most part, attired in Cossack-style trousers and paletots sashed at the waist, while females sported colorful muslin day dresses with puffed sleeves, the children emulating their elders in both attire and manner. Negresses who did not wear caps of massed lacy frills, banded with taffeta, sported wide-brimmed satin bonnets set at an angle and tied below the chin with cherry red, orange, or yellow ribbons; one beauty had devised a most ingenious turban of purplish hue, with fringed streamers down one side to her waist. The most prized article among them, by far, was the parasol; no negress, young or old, plain or fetching, walking without one in the heat of the sun; and it was in part they—with their canopies of red, green, azure, rose, and yellow silk, edged with embroidery or tassels—that imparted to this novel scene the air of an exotic spa.

"With the approach of the noon hour, the field hands having leave to take early dinner under the shady brushwood of drainage ditches, the overseers found it convenient to ride into town for theirs; and thus it came about, as I still sat at 'morning tea,' that they entered the square on horseback accompanied by two similarly conveyed negroes, all five attired in trousers and morning coats of reasonably good cut. A trifle disconcerted at finding me there, the Evanses fumbled with their hats and, following their chief's lead, dismounted and hastened—as the negro artisans had done—to welcome me home. Curiosity overcoming my distaste for the man, I beckoned Mr. Landry to my table, where he was promptly served a dinner of soup, roast pig, cold beef and turkey, oysters and eggs, with greens, beets, hot breads, celery, and hominy—topped off with an orange punch and fresh peach tarts! The three negroes who served him appeared disappointed at my refusal to partake—I being distinctly of the impression that the sumptuousness of the chief overseer's dinner had been not a little curtailed by my presence.

"'Mr. Landry,' I commenced, making straight for the point, 'how have these new ways come about and at whose expense?'

"'Well sir, Mr. Edward,' he replied eagerly enough, 'like I said, you're bound to find Overseer Town much changed and growed— growed in ever way, sir. You see, sir, the best crop on this here plantation is slaves, Mr. Edward, when the most of 'em be still-born and dying on the other plantations. Why, in my time, I seen the number of our live homegrown nigras double—not counting the new ones bought at auction—and the handy crafts has more than doubled! We done cleared more virgin land ever year, Mr. Edward, until this here plantation is come to be known as the most prosperous in these parts, since being under my management these many years. Mr. Geoffrey—your father, sir—he don't never doubt me—wasn't I here with him in the Territory when El Inglés amounted to less'n a hundred cleared acres?'

"Knowing that Father did, indeed, hold his chief overseer in higher esteem than ever, I took a placating tone with him. 'Nor do I doubt you, Mr. Landry, but what I would know is how it came about that the negroes began . . . began—' being a trifle uncertain as to what precisely it was they had begun to do, I singled out the most visible of the changes—'began to deck themselves out as they do.'

"'Oh that,' he returned, scrutinizing the platter of meats set before him, 'that commenced some years back I reckon, when you was still a lad, but while you was abroad, sir, they's got fancier.' He paused as if to reconsider the size of his serving, then plunged into this tale:—

"'Here's how it come about, Mr. Edward. Jingo the shoemaker, he made several pair of pumps for Mr. Geoffrey, and none of 'em suited the master right well; now it happened that one of the milliners was parading around—for the fun of it, sir, no harm done—in a pair of these same pumps as Mr. Geoffrey didn't have no use for, when Jingo says, 'for fancy shoes I got to have me a fancy hat', and so the milliner made a top hat for Jingo from old surplus stock, and kept the pumps; but then one of the tailors wanted him some boots, and the boot-maker had to have him a waistcoat, and then all the other handy craft workers wanted pumps and boots and top hats and waistcoats; whatever one of 'em could make out of scrap and surplus and hand-me-downs, he did it for anybody as could make him something he wanted. Right there it come to me to devise a new rule for putting the situation to advantage, so to speak—you understand, Mr. Edward sir, how I always look to bring prosperity into my overseein by utilizing what comes natural—well, by this here new rule, sir, every nigra has to turn over to me an accountin of all his manufacture, and what he trades off ever week, and to who, and for what in return. I figured as how I could cross-check the overall inventory in that fashion, my principal object bein, sir, to insure they was turning out more than ten times as much for the plantation as for they own trading ends. Any nigra caught cheatin is forbidden to trade for six months. Now there ain't much I don't know about nigras, begging your pardon, sir, but I never knowed they could keep such fine records; and this here system has worked out better'n any yet devised for keeping them in line—why, these nigras is turning out more goods for the master and stirring up less trouble all the time, sir!

"'Now, you know good as anybody, Mr. Edward, sir, I ain't never been one for advocatin leniency in the handling of slaves; but this here system—which I put the name of 'Fancy System' to—meaning that those as turns out piecework over and beyond the usual—and I well nigh keep a record of what's usual for every male and female amongst 'em—those as goes beyond the usual, like I said, sir, they gits a chance at the fancy goods; and the more they goes over the usual, the more chance they gits at the fancies. Iff'n you come to Sunday preachin, sir, you'll spot in a jiffy those as stays over and beyond the usual: they be about as well turned out as you and Mr. Geoffrey, begging your pardon, sir—and the top ones, they sits with all they own kinfolk, specially if they got an ole pappy or mammy, and they kinfolk is spruced up to match them as is over and beyond the usual.'

"'But Mr. Landry,' I interposed, 'does not this prodigious flow of material goods create an inequality among the negroes, arousing envy and jealousy, and exciting ill feeling, discontent, and dissension amongst them?'

"'Just the opposite, sir,' was his spirited reply, 'I won't say as how there ain't no envy and jealousy and such amongst 'em; but I will say as how it don't lead to the fightin you might expect; fact of the matter is, sir, we been seein less and less in the way of fights, considering all hands. You take the case of Matador—I could see right off he meant trouble, the worst kinda trouble, and I reckoned we'd have to sell him off after the time he broke that one nigra's leg, and the arms of them other two; but this here same Matador, now, he riz right to the top of the Fancy System—why that buck outworks all the other field hands, and now he don't hold with fightin no more, in the usual run of things. You see, sir, it's his standing—he's got to uphold his standing with the others—and he can't do that no more by fightin. The proof of the puddin, like they say, sir, is the having of the fancy goods; you'll see yourself as how Matador and his kinfolk is better stocked-up than any as is over and beyond the usual.'

"'And are there some among our negroes, pray tell, who are not over and beyond the usual, Mr. Landry?' My faint irony appeared to escape him.

"'Now that there is very peculiar, Mr. Edward, most peculiar—because there ain't a one as don't move into the over-and-beyond now and then; but there be some it don't seem to come as natural to, and these is the very ones to keep a particular watch over as to fightin. You see, sir, it ain't those with the fancies that fights, but those that the Fancy System don't come natural to—if I put it plain enough, sir.'

"I replied that he had, indeed, but that I wished to hear more about one other innovation—that being the role of the two negroes, both evidently well-stocked in 'fancies,' whom I had seen riding into Town with the overseers.

"Here Mr. Landry's manner grew a trifle less assured, but, in short order, volubility restored self-possession. 'You be referring to Parson William and Parson James, sir, and you might say as how they be a part of the general progress and prosperity of this here plantation, where the need for all kinds has more than doubled, sir, more than doubled! Don't you recollect, sir, how your Pappy used to ride over to the slave quarters every Sunday when you was a boy after holding early mornin religious service in the big cabin—he'd stop at nine in the southeast quarter and ten-thirty in the west, and twelve noon would see him in the northwest quarter, readin out the Bible and prayin with the nigras at every stop? I reckon you know what a intolerable hardship this here Sunday schedule proved for Mr. Geoffrey, until he built the family chapel, 'piscopal-style, and turned over the handling of other Christian duties to me as part and parcel of the job of overseein. I divvied it up at first between the Evans boys that serves under me, with me having the main direction of it and reporting to Mr. Geoffrey like I do with all sides of overseein. We got busy picking out a nice spot on the west end of the hammock—where it wouldn't be no bother to Mr. Geoffrey—for building a Baptist-style church as was proper seemin to the plantation.

"'I'll say this about them two Evans boys, they do about as good a job, with me looking after them and setting the rules, as you can expect from any two brothers that always sees eye to eye, and not much else. They can read and write plain talk and hard figgers, you understand, sir, but when it come to readin out the Holy Bible, why any one of my own little 'uns could do better; so I had to admit that the handling of religion was not progressin any too satisfactory along natural lines, and I promised the nigras I would put Bob and Jonas to studying up on they Bible readin—maybe git a little instruction from Mr. Geoffrey. It warn't long though before the nigras put forward they own two, William and James, that come down with your Pappy from ole Virginny and studied readin-and-writin when they was little 'uns; and I looked up my records on them bucks—both was quartered in the northwest settlement, and neither of 'em much use for field work, or any other kind; but I had to admit they had a proper seemin manner about 'em, and when I opened a Bible and ordered them to read it out to me, well, William commenced in a calm-like manner— reminded me of your Pappy, Mr. Geoffrey, sir—never missed a word; but James took up readin even more to my liking—no disrespect to the Master, sir—in the manner of the Baptists, with a rise and a fall to every word, and a shoutin out to put the meaning of it square to your face. Twarn't nothin for it but to make parsons out of them two, which I done right then and there, and that has been they business ever since. Bob and Jonas was relieved in mind and soul to have the handling of the Christian religion took out of they hands entirely; and Mr. Geoffrey agreed with me that Parson William and Parson James—what everbody always calls them two—warn't no loss to the fields atall.'

"Mr. Landry had by now arrived at the peach tarts—his mien one of fastidious satisfaction, whether on their account or at his superior skill in the arts of overseeing, I could not discern—but I pressed him further. 'Most ingenious, Mr. Landry,' I said, 'and how does it come about that the Parsons, as you call them, ride about with the overseers, in full morning dress?'

"'Well, sir,' came the offhand rejoinder—as though he had already rehearsed all that might be of value, having made limitless survey of my question and leaving but trifles to be accounted for—'seein as how the Parsons can read and write so gentleman-like, they keeps the records for Bob and Jonas; and that's how it come about that they ride with the overseers like you say—over to market at Tallahassee some days, or even on up to Savannah—to supply the running of the plantation, sir, and all such.'

"And to supply your artisans with materials for manufacturing their fanciest goods—the odd length of fine English worsted, let us say—and perhaps even to transport those goods back to market, Mr. Landry, for cash?"

"'You know how it is, Mr. Edward—you cain't keep an eye on a body day and night; but t'aint nothin that comes out of the Master's pocket—I wouldn't never tolerate that, sir—every nigra man and woman on this here plantation knows that like they knows they own mammy. Why, Parson William and Parson James, they be as good Christian nigras as you can find, sir; and seeing as how it be such a benefit in the handling of religion for the shepherd to know they herd—so as to guide 'em right and proper—the Parsons have the daily overseein of the field work with Bob and Jonas directly over them— that's so any mischief stirred up amongst the hands can be set to rest right then and there; and seein as how the Parsons was one-time field hands, and knows they ways, them two has they own qualification for attending the overseers, you understand.' Here Mr. Landry directed a curt nod to the negro serving him and was promptly poured more orange punch. 'As for our attire,' he added offhandedly, 'it ain't that we sets out to rise above our station, sir; but the Fancy System brings up what you might call a new accountable for us as has to answer for the overseeing and guiding of the flock and such.'

"'Do you mean to say, Mr. Landry, that the overseers and the two parsons set the fashions for what the negroes endeavor to earn in the way of fancies?'

"My query must have betrayed some measure of disapproval, for he appeared to take offense from it, returning with severe dignity— 'Not so much that, Mr. Edward, as to draw the line, you might say.'

"'Arbiters of elegance,' I thought to myself, but held my peace. After a moment's reflection—and another generous draught of punch—Mr. Landry's usually stern visage was transformed by a curious smile, an expression both proud and sly: 'Next time you come to Town, Mr. Edward,' he said—after ascertaining that nobody else was within earshot—'I'd be honored to show you my private records, sir; you'll see I got my own handy craft for keepin account of what goes on—ain't a thing of any moment on this here plantation escapes my notice, sir.'

"And so he did—at my very next visit, having ushered me to the commodious log cabin of my youth, now his domicile as chief overseer—and laid before me some fifty or more account books, which I understood I was at leisure to examine. To my astonishment, I discovered therein detailed renderings of every individual man, woman, and child at El Inglés, not a few of whom I recognized as long deceased—every negro on the place, depicted from at least four different perspectives, while engaged in his characteristic occupation, such as churning or smithing; in the lower right corner, the subject's name was noted in Mr. Landry's neat hand, as were his approximate age and one or two distinguishing facts or marks, such as: 'bought for $1200 at auction, May 11th, 1825' or, 'good breeder' or, 'fastest cotton picker.' Even the members of my own family were amply catalogued, myself included—identified as 'heir to El Inglés'—lately caught astride my grey mare; descending the steps of the plantation house in formal attire; seated at my desk in the library; and sipping brandy on the verandah.

"'You have an undoubted talent,' I remarked, to which Mr. Landry replied with some pride that 'twere all in the particular manner of his overseeing,' and that his 'particular records'—as he always referred to the stack of oversized ledgers filled with his sketches—had 'come in handy' on more than one occasion, when all else failed to stand up to the accounting needful for his overseeing—there followed anecdotes about runaway and lost negroes apprehended in short order, thanks to his 'particular records.'

"While Mr. Landry's drawings could not have claimed the accuracy of modern photographs, nor even of Daguerreotypes, their resemblances to actual persons portrayed were nonetheless as immediately convincing—their detail sufficiently sharp to impart the sense of a relentless mechanical eye, devised to perceive only certain features and no others, etching its selective images patiently one after another. Some subtle disfigurement, perceptible not so much to the eye as to some spiritual organ within, marked the lot like a skewed signature; for, where a photograph of a man may be unflattering or grow dim with time, all the while preserving that individual's own being, Mr. Landry's 'records' conveyed to me the eerie sense that, however unmistakable his subject, I should not recognize in him the man I knew. Even many years later, my imagination is still haunted by these images—their impersonal, coldly vivid etching of living moments in hell; yet, I am certain that Mr. Landry would have been mortally offended by any such description. With the passage of time, I came to attribute their disturbing quality not to artistry per se, but to the use made of it—if the hand from which such likenesses flowed excised a man's very soul in the rendering, it must be, one could only conclude, because of the soul's superfluity in questions of mere identification."

Uncle Edward pauses here in telling his story, as if it had brought him to some abyss of perplexity—I think because he does not know how to judge his own actions during that long-ago time, when, in the face of ever-multiplying signs of affluence among the Negroes, and against the cautions of old household servants—intimating that they were afraid to tell all, but that the Fancy System was not what it appeared and was bound to come to a bad end—he submitted to his father's conviction that such systems of bartering among the Negroes not only encouraged industry, but prepared them for self-government; the inculcation of which—within the ambit and precepts of the Christian faith—Grandfather judged to be essential for repatriation to their native Africa. That his father could so idealize the benefits of the Fancy System was understandable, for he had turned over all association with the Negroes to his overseers and then to his heir—Uncle Edward himself having, from the time he returned home, taken up his father's custom of riding the plantation three or four days per week. His own propensity, as a young man, to view plantation life as a species of theatre—allowing himself to be amused by the colorful spectacle of slaves experimenting, under Christian oversight, with the perquisites of civilization—can be explained (he now believes) only by a fervent, if misguided, wish to see them progress, at an advanced rate, toward a state distinguishing the character of free Christian men. "I quite expected that—during my own lifetime—our negroes would realize their American destiny by pointing the direction to freedom for others of their race," he confesses in tones that expose his young man's folly—hastening to add, in his own defense, that such visionary hopes were not peculiar to himself and his father. Widely reputed the most forward-looking plantation in Middle Florida, El Inglés was without equal for crops produced, land cleared, and healthy slaves bred. Overseer Town had grown into a kind of regional center for finished goods of a quality often superior to those available in the shops at Tallahassee and attracted buyers of nearly every station in search of footwear, fitted apparel, and metal work of all kinds, from tools to precious ornaments.

Uncle Edward increasingly—and not without pride—assumed the hospitable role of guide for the many visitors who came to view the artisans "taking their tea." Not a few visitors objected that spoiling slaves in this fashion was certain to end in rebellion (the name "Nat Turner" falling darkly from their lips); or that such latitude of daily habits would dispose the Negroes to the incitements of abolitionists, from which they ought to be defended by a stricter enforcement of discipline; or, whispered by the wise, that so liberal a system of labor and barter was in flagrant violation of the Code Noir—those laws, written and unwritten, held as a sine qua non for proper regulation of black life and preservation of white property since the reign of Louis XIV. Uncle Edward recalls how one overseer from a neighboring plantation, having been pressed by his master to study the Negroes at

El Inglés under the Fancy System, made the bewildered determination that: "Something ain't right here"—all of them he knew "would find a way to git out of doing the master's work, and git the fancies too." Despite the evidence of his eyes, this man still held that "the only proper fancy for a nigger is the whip."

"In the year after my homecoming"—so Uncle's tale continues— "Overseer Town became a favored site for Saturday night merrymaking among the field hands, attendance being subject to certain rules promulgated by Mr. Landry: that no more than thirty-six hands, none under-age, be permitted to congregate in Town on any one occasion; that permission be granted to twelve adult males and females from each settlement every week, but no more than once per month for any hand; that a list of eligible names be read out at noon every Saturday; that all merrymaking be suspended for a period of three months, in the event that a field hand set foot in Town without permission; and that any negro indulging at any time in acts contrary to Christian precepts be denied the Saturday night privilege for a duration to be fixed by one of the overseers.

"The introduction of Saturday merrymaking into the Fancy System came about when a young negro couple from the southeast settlement—accompanied by eight or ten of their friends— approached Mr. Landry's domicile one Sunday to seek permission for a jump-the-broom party in Overseer Town the following Saturday, their pretext being that the best fiddle players were to be found among the artisans there. Uncertain as to what number might safely be allowed to congregate in the Town square for such a purpose, Mr. Landry sought my counsel on this point; I, deferring to his greater experience in managing slaves, merely offered the observation that, the three settlements, each averaging some three dozen souls (not counting children), and all remaining thus far untroubled by serious rebellion or conspiracy, that number would seem to have proven itself an acceptable limit. I thought it prudent, however, to put a concern of my own to Mr. Landry: namely, whether some special selection process should apply—whether, for instance, a quota ought to be imposed upon individuals to whom the Fancy System did not seem to 'come natural,' inasmuch as such slaves tended to be troublemakers." Uncle Edward owns he had fairly convinced himself that the healthy negro's native disposition leans toward material comforts and dandyism—"Even now," he avers, "I believe that inclination to be so strong in our negroes that, given the opportunity, it will triumph over more spiritual pursuits in the majority of them." Mr. Landry was of the opinion that the fewer the rules, the greater the scope for the exercise of judgment—that, in his opinion, being a good thing; for, as he explained to Uncle Edward, "these here Saturday night Town parties gives occasion for overseein that can't easily be had no other way." As a precaution, Mr. Landry made it his business to station himself and the Evans brothers at the long table reserved for them, beneath the central oak; the two Parsons—equipped with flintlocks— were assigned the task of patrolling the lanes hourly from one end of Town to the other.

Such consolidation of social life under the Fancy System seemed to bring it to perfection, according to Uncle Edward, all hands working diligently and with a happy air of expectation the whole week long. On Saturday nights, the atmosphere in Overseer Town was so jovial and peaceable—the Negroes being so wholly occupied with one another—that Mr. Landry reported, "us as does the overseein brings our missuses to set under the tree and look on—a feller would have to admit nigras have a way of lettin loose for a good time that's hard to beat."

Early February, a chill in the air—Saturday night merrymaking had been established in the Fancy System for nearly a year, when a petition from Matador, to be married in the Baptist meeting house, was conveyed with furrowed brow by Mr. Landry. (Of the two houses of worship at El Inglés, the Baptist was regarded by the field hands as theirs, while the domestic servants and some of the artisans laid claim to the Episcopal, originally constructed for the Howard family's religious observances, and looked with disdain on the Baptist meeting house.) Matador and Henrietta, having consorted together for some years, now had as many children, and, although the union of two slaves could have no standing under law, Uncle Edward was inclined to view Matador's desire for a proper Christian wedding as gratifying proof that slavery, rightly administered, not only served the White Man, but civilized even those negroes once considered lost to all save the lash. He was, thus, favorably disposed towards Matador's second petition: that the usual attendance limit for Saturday night merrymaking, having gradually risen without incurring disorder, be temporarily set aside in recognition of this unprecedented occasion, and that all who so wished might join the celebration in Overseer Town after the church ceremony. So strongly did Uncle Edward incline to make an exception in Matador's case, that he dismissed Mr. Landry's reservations about the party's size out of hand; the wedding being set for nine in the evening, he argued that none of the celebrants would likely appear in Town square 'till ten—a mere two hours before the midnight curfew—scarcely enough time for serious mischief.

As the day drew near, Uncle devised a scheme for partaking of the festivities from the vantage point of an old tree house in the great oak on the plaza, a lark much to Grandfather Howard's liking. Thus, by the stroke of nine, while the ceremony was in progress at the Baptist meeting house, the old and the young Master ensconced themselves in the leafy observation tower of the latter's boyhood, there to enjoy a comfortable and unimpeded view of the Town center; the foliage being dense, their presence in the dark need in no way inhibit their slaves' festivities. At the last moment, Uncle Edward fetched his fine inlaid dueling pistols, one of which he placed at the ready—not, he avers, in expectation of putting it to use, but with an instinctive desire to hold some badge of authority in hand.

So situated, they whiled away a pleasurable hour smoking and conversing, until they spied the three overseers, with torches aloft, escorting their wives to the table beneath their secret lookout. "Arrayed in their finest, the small party might—in torchlight—have passed for ladies and gentlemen," Uncle Edward declares. After the wives were seated and the torches staked out, he was about to make his presence known, when he heard a voice stiff with vexation say:— "Y'all will never git away with this, now that the young Master's in charge."

"Ain't no harm in it, Jack," the younger of the Evans brothers endeavored to placate their chief—"Jack" or "Jacob" being Mr. Landry's Christian name, according to Uncle Edward (who considers it overly familiar to address a white man thus, unless he be a relative or intimate friend). "And there ain't no call for you to lift so much as a finger," the elder brother remonstrated, "you can leave it to us—none of the niggers is gonna let on, you know that, Jack—why, you can trust a nigger better'n any white man, when it come to holding talk close to his chest to keep hisself outta trouble." The head overseer made no audible rejoinder, but Uncle supposed him to be glowering at his importunate underlings, there being a difference between them not only of station, but of age as well—Mr. Landry, nearing forty, had some fifteen years on the Evans brothers. Emboldened by their chief's silence, the younger brother, Bob, burst in fervently—"We was only lookin to make sure you and your missus come in for your part, Jack! These here niggers, they works their time for the master, and they works their time for their own selves—so it ain't but right they should work their time for us overseers too, specially seein as how they gits extra fancies into the bargain. I ain't heard them complain none, have you, Jack?"

Mr. Landry stood unbending, head held high.

"Why these here niggers is living like gentlemens," Jonas added hotly, his voice rising on a wheedling note, "and us overseers is goin down, and that ain't right Jack. The way me'n Bob figgers it, the fifty dollars you take this month will be comin to you ever month from here on—iff'n you jest say the word Jack, iff'n you puts the matter to your missus, just the two of you together—she'll speak for it, I don't doubt; a woman always understands the advantages and suchlike of bringing home every month more'n your wages for a full year!"

Uncle Edward reports he never learned Mr. Landry's reply; for, at that moment, a procession of some one hundred and fifty Negroes— including a few faces from a nearby plantation—whose clapping and singing had been audible in the distance, entered Overseer Town. At the head, a one-horse chaise driven by Matador in formal attire, flanked by the parsons holding torches aloft their steeds; behind them, a double row of torches, one on each side of the west lane winding into Town from the Baptist meeting house. As the procession neared, the torchbearers were seen to be boys and girls of an age not usually permitted at Saturday night entertainments—the lane between them filled with adult Negroes, four abreast, clapping and singing and half-dancing in rhythmic fashion through the Town.

Not until Matador, guiding Grandfather's white mare to a slow stately walk, had begun rounding the open plaza—about to pull to a halt under the oak—was Uncle Edward able to discern what it was he had sensed to be wholly amiss about this dignified, yet exuberant, procession at its very first appearance: namely, that the personage seated beside Matador was not Henrietta, the mother of his children, but a Seminole woman resplendent in the dress of the Creek nation.

Mr. Landry's indignant voice demanded to know on the instant the meaning of "this here Injun woman with Matador"—to which Bob Evans replied that she was Matador's new wife.

"But Henrietta—he was fixin to marry Henrietta!" Mr. Landry spluttered, making off at a run to the big log cabin—from which both Bob and Jonas doubtless understood that the new "fancy" that had engaged Matador's desire violated some undeclared rule of the System, and—Mr. Landry presently returning with one of his great books and pen in hand—that their judgment as overseers would forthwith be called to account. The next two hours were occupied by Mr. Landry in muttering to himself and sketching furiously; Uncle

Edward and his father, meanwhile, (their shock on several counts notwithstanding) determined that the most prudent course was to remain concealed in their tower, thence to observe how the wedding feast would unfold.

Never, declares Uncle Edward, had he witnessed such a ball, nor one where so much care and deliberation had been expended upon details of fashion. While some of the Negro ladies (for so they appeared to him) favored the Empire lines, most wore one or another of the newer fashions, with bell-shaped skirts above flat-soled satin slippers and silk stockings; dark shoulders gleamed over deep berthas covering short puffed sleeves or loose, lightly flowing ones edged with ruching and frills—some even sported the newest sleeve fitted below the elbow; taffeta and challis, cut into close-fitting bodices, with skirts of chiffon and gauze over silk, were principally of the tawny pale shades—blue, pink, yellow, orange, and violet; mantles and shawls were of patterned silk, and a few, worn by artisans' wives and daughters, had the softness of cashmere; coiffures were parted down the middle and brushed up the nape, with a velvet ribbon round the back, like a small cap, and curled or puffed out over the ears. Most opulent of all was the display of elbow-length white or honey-colored gloves of silk and kid, elaborately worked fans, velvet evening purses and fur muffs, gleaming bracelets and necklaces that looked to be of wrought gold and silver, along with resplendent ear hoops and drops inset with pearl, amethyst, agate, topaz, lapis lazuli—Uncle Edward insists to this day that his astonished eye even caught the glimmer of sapphire, ruby, and diamond adorning the earlobes and fingers of a few dark beauties. The gentlemen's attire was no less sumptuous, Matador setting the standard in a coat of maroon-faced cloth tailored with darts under the arms and cut away at the waist, its satin collar and lapels rolled for padding at the chest; the puffed sleeves emphasizing his shoulders' width tapered to a close fit at the wrist above the narrow band of his shirt-sleeve; and cream-colored trousers, finely patterned with dark maroon flowers—beneath a velvet cloak lined with satin over slippers of the finest, smoothest kind—matched the resplendent satin waistcoat. Indeed, the Negroes' general magnificence so overshadowed the faintly genteel costume of the Overseers and their wives, that they began to look positively dowdy to Uncle Edward.

What mainly astonished this invisible audience of two, however—once they had accommodated themselves to the high fashions of the Negroes—was, so Uncle Edward mused, their air of being quite at home amid so much splendor, while wholly absorbed in their savage style of dance. No less impressive was the Negroes' aptitude for a most cunning style of mimicry: as the musicians struck the opening chords of some dance or other, familiar from many a plantation ball, one of the celebrants would assume the pose of some member of the Howard family, and commence dancing in the manner of White society—little by little introducing his or her own style of movement, with the music changing in response—until, finally, all signs of mimicry gone, the dancer moved freely and ecstatically in his or her own native African style; the other Negroes watched closely, nodding and clapping their approval at a part well-played, then, leaving mimicry behind, joining the dancer, until the whole of the plaza was awhirl with finery, and the night air throbbed with rapturous movement. One after another stepped forward in this fashion, struck yet another English pose, and re-enacted the entire sequence in accordance with that performer's style. The women, Uncle Edward observed, appeared especially to relish the spontaneous theatricality of this entertainment.

A half-hour before midnight, crates of champagne were brought to the plaza and placed in rows on the ground—whereupon Matador invited every adult male to accept a bottle as a gift from the groom, with the reminder that no spirits were to be consumed in Town; the wedding guests, proclaimed Matador—after demonstrating how to pop the cork—were to go forth and enjoy themselves in their own dwellings. With that, he presented foaming glasses to the overseers and their wives, who promptly drained them—all save Mr. Landry (more intent on his sketching than ever). Clapping and beating time with his feet, Matador then initiated a ring-shout, clasped a bottle under one arm, the Seminole woman in the other, and struck off in a shout-step along the northwest lane to his settlement—the others followed his example, singing in unison and falling into the shuffling shout-step, in spontaneously formed circles, towards their own settlements. By the stroke of midnight, the artisans having retired, Overseer Town was once more deserted and dark, save for the bright moon overhead.

Mr. Landry, ledger clapped shut, addressed the Evans men in a cold rage:—"I hold you two idiots accountable for this predicament, from start to finish, hear? I'm talkin about reparations—reparations has got to be made afore the night's out; y'all git yourselves on over to my place, lickety-split!"

When the brothers defiantly refilled their goblets, Mr. Landry snatched away the bottles—one with each hand—dashed them

simultaneously to the ground, swept the bubbling glasses off the
table, and commanded in a low but dangerous voice:—"Git a move on,
you fools!" Whereupon Bob and Jonas Evans and the three women, all
for the first time visibly cowed, dashed after the chief overseer, to the
big log house.

No sooner had the door shut behind them than Uncle Edward
and Grandfather descended from their perch by means of the old
ladder still in situ; upon touching firm ground, and steadying himself
against one of the low, sweeping branches, the latter said with hushed
urgency: "Edward, my boy, we have much overestimated our negroes'
capacity for rightly assimilating the habits of civilized Christian
men. Steps must be taken at once to shield them from their own
waywardness, that they may be content to revert to their former
simple lives. Be so good as to have the Seminole woman brought to
me—without delay—until she can be removed to her people; permit
none to call on her—and warn the Evans trash to say nothing of this
so-called wedding.The Woman, Edward, look to the Woman!" And
without another word, Grandfather Howard disappeared into the
darkness.

"I understood perfectly what I must do," Uncle Edward recounts.
"I hastened to Mr. Landry's domicile, where the rough and jeering
voice of one of the Evans men accosted me through the open
casement:—'It's you as don't grasp the consequence, like you said, of
this here predicament, Jack; they say that Injun squaw is Osceola's
sister, come with a message for Chief Charley's tribe to burn up
every plantation in sight—like they done last year over 'round St.
Augustine—and they all better git theirselves ready to take up
the war. Any Injun figurin to give up and go out West will get his
comeuppance quicker'n Osceola kilt off Chief Charley. What I'm
saying Jack, is, we got us a squaw here that's wanted by the Gov'ment
and the Mikasuki both, and you mean to tell me we cain't put this
here situation to advantage, like you's always saying?'"

Uncle Edward's outrage—though having a different cause—was no
less than Bob's. Osceola's sister!—was it possible? Fiercely rapping on
the cabin door with the butt of his duelling pistol, he shouted "Open
the door at once!" Had matters been less grave, the stupefied faces
of the three men, at his sudden nocturnal appearance, might have
struck him as comical; in the event, they comprehended instantly
that he knew all. "Listen to me, and listen carefully," he commanded,
"the Seminole woman is to be presented at the Great House within
the hour and the Fancy System abolished without delay. I hold you,

Mr. Landry, accountable—should your men fail in delivering the Woman unharmed, they shall be turned over to General Jesup for harboring a dangerous Indian hostile." This last was thrown in to impress upon all three overseers the need for haste.

Mr. Landry and his subalterns hurried out the door with their firearms, patently relieved to be in possession of orders for a clear course of action. Nodding a curt goodnight to the women huddled by the hearth in their finery, Uncle Edward strode rapidly along the wooded trail to the Great House, where Grandfather awaited him with knitted brow and a flask of his rarest brandy.

In less than an hour, Mr. Landry arrived breathlessly with the Seminole woman, and a tale of how she had had to be prised away from Matador, who would not willingly yield his new "fancy." The overseers having spotted him and other Negroes outside their settlement in the northwest quarter—on the point of opening their champagne bottles—a few shots into the air sent all flying but for the bridegroom, who boasted he could protect his property as well as any man. Mr. Landry held a rifle to him, while Bob pinned his arms behind, and Jonas took charge of the woman—no sooner had Bob turned him loose, than Matador came out with a knife from somewhere in his sumptuous gear, slashed Bob's cheek from eyebrow to chin—gripped Jonas by the throat and threw him to the ground and would have stabbed him, had not Mr. Landry aimed at his head and fired. With Matador dead, the chief overseer advised the Evans brothers to make haste to leave the plantation before sunup, and forget all that had passed.

The Negroes of El Inglés were quick to apprehend that a slave's abduction of Osceola's sister, should the Indians ever have wind of it, was certain to provoke the fiercest reprisals—a threat which, in Mr. Landry's opinion—conveyed at length to Mr. Edward—was sufficient to keep them too frightened to protest the demise of the Fancy System, at the same time that it would encourage them to hold their tongues about anything to do with the Seminole woman. Parson William and Parson James—having been duly instructed to exhibit at all times, in both habit and demeanor, the modesty and humility befitting their spiritual office—were promoted to the rank of "overseeing foremen"; with the departed Evans men in disgrace, the Negro parsons would hereafter carry out all their tasks under Mr. Landry's personal supervision—inasmuch, he attested, as they had been doing the lion's share of the direct work of overseeing for a good long while anyway, along with keeping "good records." In short, the two parsons were entrusted henceforth with shepherding the slaves of El Inglés back to life as it had been in the days before the fancies.

Although signs of opulence persisted among the Negroes for some time (even, Jonathan says, down to the present day, if you know how to look for them) life in the settlements gradually returned to its old routines. The house servants, gratified to find themselves once more acknowledged social leaders among the Negroes—they and their kind having been vindicated—were heard to declare to artisans, carrying supplies to the Great House, that they had known for many a day what was coming—but nobody had wanted to listen.

Uncle Edward's account ends here. I flip back to the beginning— December 28—I have been at it for three nights running, neglecting even to record the days!

"Thought for a minute you was dead"—voice chattering inside her skull— "looked to me like something got hold of you and yanked you down." A hand on her arm and another one under her head, cradling it.

Harding tried to get up and went blank again.

"Just you lay there and draw up your knees—got to be higher'n the head I always heard." Reek of tobacco and syrupy after-shave.

"I'm all right"—struggling for self-possession, she was doing as told—"thank you, Mr.—"

"Jake, thass what everbody calls me, ma'am. Jake Landry." Could she be dreaming, not really blacking out on the floor of the back gallery in plain daylight, but nodding off over the diary?

Proposition: Time and place lose their social dimension under the power of passion.

She was far, now, from any vision of a future—the Boullet House as a home, a sometime space of beauty. Rations of future time drained away in routines of drudgery, under the steady goggle-gaze of Jimmy Hurd talking gibberish at her through the fingers of one hand as she dragged load after load of woodwork from the house to the shed out back. Or pressing his face through the iron palings with a mute primate gloom she experienced as her own, hauling bricks by the armful saved from Ware's dump truck—the old Spanish ones from the piers of the demolished addition. Stacks of them in rows along the fence on Shibbles's side—ten, twenty-five, fifty, a hundred, two hundred . . . a growing heap, too, of broken ones for patching. Her body, relentlessly driven, gathering here and there the leavings of her slavish exertions. The roughness of her own hands no longer startled her—mallets, not hands; chisels for splitting apart great hunks of cemented brick, machinery for rubbing brick-face against brick-face to meal away mortar.

Harding raised herself to a sitting position, slowly this time. There was a throbbing in her left foot. One of the heavy French doors that opened from old Wentworth's bedroom to the back gallery had slammed down on it as the hinges suddenly sprang loose. Reeling out to the gallery she'd crumpled and almost blacked out with the screech of winter pig-killing on the farm in her ears.

"What was that sound—like an animal being butchered?"

"Hurd boy, ma'am, he gets them whatchamacallits—tantrums, ain't that the word? Old hunchback musta tried to grab 'is radio, them two's always at each other's throats over one little thing or another—man cain't hardly get no sleep over there what with the hollerin and all. But you let folks like that breed and what can you expect?"

"What did you say your name was again?"

"Landry, ma'am, born and raised right here in this ole Quarter. Jake Landry at your service." He stooped as though to bow and plucked a large sketch pad off the floor beside her.

Harding pulled herself all the way up, unnerved, and leaned straight as a rail against a porch post, a good couple of inches taller than Jake.

"Hope you don't mind me coming up on your veranda, ma'am. Natchrally, I was real concerned, you workin away here in this heat since before six o'clock this mornin."

What else did Landry know? Impulsively, from a generalized uneasiness in his presence—tendrils of innuendo winding suspicion around her—she considered moving him to her main list, those with knowledge of the sanctuary's existence. Right after the nameless *Female Relative.*

"Say," he went on over his cigar, in the chit-chat of neighbors, "you ain't seen a certain individual nosing round here lately, have you, acting like she owns the place? Got a way a disappearin right in front a your eyes, you never know when or where."

Bumping the heavy door along in spurts Harding snapped, "Who?"

"Ole colored woman, wears one them turbans on her head, green most times. Sure you'll be all right by yourself, Miz Dumot, or should I say Professor?"

"Watch your foot Mr. Landry, you don't want to end up like me." She had the presence of mind to lean her load against the porch railing and pretend to have urgent business inside. A way of virtually, if not literally, shutting the back door in his face—a man, she figured, who knew how to take such moves. Who was himself a master of them. ("Jake and I had that in common," Harding once mused, "both of us being such self-made connoisseurs of the virtual image we could despise each other with understanding.")

But she was not up to any more heavy work that evening. After another couple of hours scrounging every last visible brick from the mountain of rubble out back she called it quits, drove to her motel earlier than usual with a roast beef sandwich from Roy Rogers and soaked her foot in Epsom salt. On further thought she decided to leave Jake in the company of Randall Cane and Greeley Connor—a threat only because he turned up all over the place and watched her. Watched everybody for that matter. Most of all because there was a Landry in the diary—a dead one who sketched people.

More than a century ago. When had she ever taken blood-guilt for anything more than a literary conceit?

Round about that time, Harding's diary readings began to function like a private calendar for organizing her experience of the restoration. Take the day she hired Tony Krasner—grizzled, curly-haired Gulf-coast cowboy ready for action and leisure, as compelled by his own romance of freedom as any patriot. He was lined up to install a cedar shingle roof on the cottage across the street, one of Randall Cane's properties. A trustworthy recommendation therefore. (Uncle Randy's favorite niece, Aimée Hulin, was at the tail end of a steamy flirtation with Krasner at the time, rendezvousing in plain sight of the front veranda one afternoon.) He seemed a godsend, her first solid contract, negotiated the day after she got to the end of the Fancy System—the killing of Matador as vivid before her as the mountain of woodwork piling up on the porch.

That night, she browsed back over it before turning to the next entry, and afterwards took a silk ribbon from a bowl on the altar filled with pens, needles, threads, odds and ends and slipped it carefully between the pages—to mark her place—as she would do for the remainder of that summer. A little stained and twisted, it now marks mine.

September 28, 1861—From Papa and Jonathan I learned that Matador had been an intractable field slave in his youth, running away from El Inglés and the overseer's lash at every opportunity; the last time, he found shelter in one of the small reservations on the

Apalachicola River. Chief Econchattemicco conceded readily enough that runaways lived among the Seminole, but refused to give them up and extended as much protection to them as to his own Negro slaves, who enjoyed much liberty. It so happened that Papa—who took a keen interest in finance from a young age—was in Tallahassee at that time to attend the chartering of the Central Bank of Florida (which absorbed the four-year-old Bank of Florida, the first in the Territory); it was there he made the acquaintance of Uncle Edward—about to embark for England—and Grandfather Howard, who despite his scholarly temperament, had a landowner's sense of what benefits a growing plantation, and understood the advantages of a railroad for transporting his cotton. Papa—ever eager to promote any venture that promised to lighten what he called "the travails of living"— introduced his new friends to the organizers of the future Tallahassee Railroad Company, builders of a railroad of sorts—a twenty-two mile stretch of rough track with wooden carts pulled by mules between the state capitol and Port Leon. (There was not much more of a railroad in the Territory when I was born in 1845, the very year Florida joined the Union—indeed, only two years before, a tidal wave ripped out much of it and destroyed the port.)

Discovering that Papa had some influence with the Seminole, and understood their speech, Grandfather charged him to negotiate for the return of his property; Papa accepted—on condition that Matador suffer no punishment. After long parley—and with Papa's personal guarantee that he would not be put to the lash, or otherwise punished on returning to El Inglés—the Indians assuring him that Papa's word was good—Matador agreed to submit once more to the yoke of slavery. What Grandfather never knew was that Papa consented to the mission only because he knew that the Chief's refusal to give up this Negro runaway, known to be harbored by his people, was certain to be used as an excuse for further raids on the Seminole, the true purpose of these raids being to appropriate this plentiful source of slaves. (The treaty the Indians called "the Trick of Payne's Landing" was negotiated about this time.) Likewise, it was the fear of causing harm to his Indian protectors which persuaded Matador to give up his asylum among them.

Thereafter, Papa became the Howards' trusted associate, never failing, in the course of his many journeys east or south by way of Tallahassee, to pay his respects at El Inglés. My mother was only fifteen, just my present age, when they met (I am said to bear a remarkable resemblance to her, though with some singularity of difference); but he says he loved her from the first, because she was so good, taking his love for her to be an innocent love for a child, even as he watched her mature into a comely young woman during the era of the Fancy System—his visits growing ever more frequent, and acquiring a character beyond that of mere social calls on business associates.

"El Inglés," he recalls with a wink, "was a moot court—comprends?—convened most especially on my behalf, by the entire Howard clan." As the son of trading people—and Gallic at that!—he was hardly "one of their circle"; but, would his counsels not save them from ruin to come in the financial panic of '37—had he not rung an early alarm at the impending failure of the Union Bank of Tallahassee? Allowances were made for so prescient and agreeable an associate. "Not that I lacked decorum," Papa explains; "the question was, did I possess the savoir faire for the qui vive such a family might wish to encourage? Tu vois, mon ange, as I was neither doctor, advocate, or landholder, there was some doubt as to what staked my prospects. Only the need for discretion prevented me from divulging certain expectations for an unparalleled future in finance—for even then, I had more in banks and railroads than high hopes, chérie."

Papa was well into his thirties by then, and prospering—still, could he have won the day at El Inglés but for Matador's doomed wedding, that night in early February of 1837? I have often pondered this question, most especially because it bears upon the fact of my own existence. Jonathan recently gave as his opinion that Grandfather Howard must have harbored more than one or two reservations about his congenial associate's suitability as a husband for his favorite, his prettiest daughter, Caroline—Papa's exemplary decorum during his courtship of my mother notwithstanding. He had made no secret of his ties to the Indians; but what Grandfather may only have suspected Jonathan claims to know with certainty—namely, that, during the wars with the Seminole, Papa supplied them with arms smuggled into the Everglades, via the Spanish islands—Papa, long known as the one man able to move by water from New Orleans, up and down the Gulf Coast, past the Everglades to Key West, weaving among isles where a White face had never been seen—even across Florida, out to the Spanish islands, and back again, using whatever transport suited his purpose. All this, without once being detected by the authorities! But if his treasonous relations with the Indians were at first a cause of Grandfather's reluctance to have Papa for a son-in-law, they were to become a compelling reason for accepting him after

the Seminole woman was wrested from Matador that night—a turn
of events to which Jonathan and I owe our coming into this world
(along with the bond of sympathy that has always existed between
us). Here is how Papa related the story to me not long ago, when
he entrusted to me, as a keepsake, a letter written by Grandfather
Howard:

"During his stay with the Indians, Matador conceived an idée
fixe—so the Negroes at El Inglés believed tous jusqu'au dernier—that
he must take no bride but a woman of Indian blood. This proud
African man felt most keenly that he had been born un esclave, and
would die un esclave; but he had known a free people—he had been
sheltered by them, and lived as one of them. In his way of thinking,
he alone had succeeded in escaping from El Inglés, and he alone
had thereby won the right to make freedom his own. Ecoute, Fan—
Matador's route to freedom was to make it his property—to possess
it, as surely as the planter possesses his land. Thus, in true Biblical
spirit, he labored five, if not seven, years for his Bride of Freedom.
The field hands say he strove always to have men report of him, at
the end of each day: tonight he goes to bed richer than yesternight,
and rises each morning encore plus riche. Proof of his wealth was to
be this woman, this Bride of Freedom. A Chief's blood must run in her
veins—mais écoute: she was not, as some said, Osceola's sister; mais
non, she was the sister of Coacoochee the Wildcat—I had parleyed
with this brave many times.

"Stolen from Matador, and conveyed against her will to the
Great House, the Woman was given to understand she would be held
there for her own protection and treated as an honored guest. I,
meanwhile, was operating my marine salvage business out of Indian
Key, and chartering my steamers to the government for transporting
troops and equipment. A message was sent from El Inglés: would I
act, once more, as Indian envoy for the Howard family?—but it failed
to reach me, and the Bride of Freedom continued in her exalted
position for nearly three months, until I—plein d'espérance comme
toujours—returned to pay court to your belle maman.

"How well I remember that bright blue morning in late April.
Jackson the butler, cautiously opening the door, informed me that the
family had made a riding party to Spanish Moss—then as now there
was much visiting back and forth among the plantations. I was on
the point of remounting pour donner la chasse—I knew they would
not return until the following day—when Jackson added: "All 'cept
Marster and the Indian Princess." Comment cela? It was not like him,

this correct and officious Jackson, to stall off visitors if his master was at home—and who might this Indian Princess be? Something to do with one of Edward's spectacles, no doubt.

"'Monsieur Howard wishes not to be disturbed?" I inquired.

"'Nawsuh,' came the swift reply, 'Marster Geoffrey been expecting you every day. If there's trouble with the Indians, Marster Claude, us house servants implores you to speak for us, now that Gen'l Jesup is bringing in Creek warriors to round up any negroes that's been associatin with the Seminole—and every negro a Creek catch a Creek can keep for his own slave or sell off if he don't want him."

"Voyons, said I to myself, il se prépare quelque chose—'Jackson,' I directed, 'announce me to your master.' Without further delay, I was admitted to the library, where your grand-père's reception of me was more than cordial—it had, if I may say so, a certain éffusion suspecte. For my part, I was speechless: there, by the fire, eyes sparkling and keen, sat Coacoochee's sister—it was she without doubt, she and none other, commanding and regal in Geoffrey's favorite wing-backed Chippendale chair—her crimson velvet gown cut Indian fashion to fall softly about her ankles, feet nearly touching, breast adorned with a gold-spangled necklace; one of her hands was lightly clasping the ends of her shawl, the other reposed in her lap—tout calme et tranquille. Some moments passed while I strove to comprehend—why had I been summoned, and at whose behest?

"I was to be entrusted with an embassy—plût à dieu if I do not receive two different sets of instructions. His first, while she listens as if to the chatter of an ignorant bébé: I must go to her people and let them know that Coacoochee's sister is safe and well-attended, and that her eminence is held in high regard; I must assure them that those who attempted to coerce her into their possession have been punished, and that she has suffered no abuse or indignity. These assurances made, I must say further that Geoffrey Morton Howard, Esquire, emissary of White civilization and a distinguished planter of English descent, is prepared to escort Coacoochee's sister home to her people, there to dwell with them under their protection—the be-all and end-all of his life being to lead Red men and White men to a peaceful accord. 'Say to them that these are my words,' he charges me, with his piercing gaze. 'You may rely on the probity and justice of my intentions, even as I rely on yours, Monsieur Boullet.'

"The Woman rises—'Now,' she declares, addressing me softly in her own tongue, 'go to Coacoochee—tell him his sister is of great worth here and must soon be in his plans.' I vowed to deliver their messages faithfully, but not before receiving from Geoffrey—can you guess what, mon petit chou?—his heartfelt blessing on my courtship of your maman—may she rest in peace with the angels. Before the day was out, I asked for her hand, and at my request a date for our wedding day was set in late June.

"I caught up with the Wildcat at Tampa Bay, where his people were waiting in camps to be sent West—this was before he put on his white-crane feather headdress and rode under a flag of truce into St. Augustine to meet with his father in the fort, and was locked up with him there. Coacoochee the Wildcat framed his reply after long deliberation: 'All plans shall be made by Chakaika.' This seemed to satisfy them both, parfaitement. Geoffrey understood that the Spanish Indians—who had taken refuge in the Glades during Spain's occupation—were to be the advance guard for resistance, and that he must henceforth transact with Chakaika, their leader; the Bride of Freedom, after a moment's reflection, declared with unassailable confidence—'Coacoochee has made his plans for me.' Allowing for some error, they were both right.

"In the weeks following, I had no moment to call my own. Was I not at once courier between El Inglés and the Glades, and husband-to-be, honoring the trust committed to me on both counts? What hectic preparations! She was the bien-aimée, remember, your maman, and the first to marry—no expense must be spared, nothing passed over for his adorable Caroline; the wedding would be the social event of the season. Imagine, Fan!—all the important planters of the region and their families, together with le beau monde of Tallahassee; not to mention friends and relatives from Virginia, and the Carolinas, arriving with such retinues of servants that carpenters were at work day and night building two enormous cabins to house them—and, in the Great House, quel remuement!—the ladies dared hardly look up from the secrets of the trousseau.

"Can you wonder that we paid scant attention to the father of the bride and his Seminole ward? We were conscious, bien sûr, that the Woman observed the preparations with keen interest—as if all were being done in her honor, and for her particular edification. One met her here, there, arms folded, regal in bearing—never without the splendid necklace—attended by Geoffrey, and listening gravely to his discourses. From this, we began to suspect that he was schooling her for his mission.

"Once again I was employed to convey a message from him to Chakaika: the White emissary, together with Coacoochee's sister, was preparing to bestow a great gift on the Chief of the Spanish Indians and his people—a gift beyond price that was the greatest delight of the English. On a previous embassy, Chakaika had shown himself little disposed in Geoffrey's favor, saying only—'Let him at once send Coacoochee's sister to me.' The new message appeared to soften him. He marked out a route in the sand, which I must commit to memory—the White emissary must travel by this route and none other; Chakaika himself would come from the Glades to receive his gift beyond price. Geoffrey—observing the Woman nod, when she heard Chakaika's instructions—declined my offer to guide them to the Glades by a more direct route, in a fraction of the time.

"What gift, you ask, is beyond price? Your maman and I alone knew the answer—no others were privy to Geoffrey's secret extraordinaire: that he was preparing an adaptation for the Indians, in their own tongue, of the great Shakespeare's tragédie of Othello the Moor. And it was the assistance of none other than Claude Boullet he sought in his theatrical project! This old head—filled, you say, with nothing but les affaires, le commerce, les comptes, l'argent—it labored day and night to translate Geoffrey's words into something approximating the Muskogee tongue!

"How clever your maman was with her pen!—sitting as still as the Indian woman herself, attending to my haltingly spoken translation, she set it all down in Latin letters, to enable Geoffrey to read and speak each part of his play in the Woman's alien tongue. He declared that no better means of instruction had ever been devised, or could be. Coacoochee's sister seemed never to tire of his orations, but refused all entreaties to speak the part of Desdemona. Your belle maman was charged with reading the lines out to her again and again—to no avail; and, because Geoffrey's command of the Woman's tongue did not suffice to communicate his wishes, he often summoned me to remonstrate with her. I must convey to her that the gold-spangled necklace she so esteemed— his gift to her—was an item of Shakespearean costume; I must persuade her that she who wore the necklace was obliged to speak the designated lines—rien de succès, not until I inquired if she understood the White emissary's mission. To this she replied—'Yes, he has made plans for me.' In that moment, I hit upon the point that won her over, tout court: the embassy, I said, could not advance without Desdemona's words; the mission was doomed— and she herself would not be free to leave El Inglés—unless she learned to speak the Venetian lady's part.

"Your grand-père had yet another secret—of which we knew nothing until afterwards—the old alligator, he had hired a theatrical troupe, which was to rendezvous with him in Tallahassee, on their way north from an engagement at Apalachicola. You may be certain that only the lure of a rich reward persuaded them to give a single performance in full Shakespearean dress for an Indian hostile— Chieftain or no—in the middle of the swamp!—and speaking only the minor parts, at that!

"But I leap ahead—you must hear what came to pass at the wedding feast. Ah, the round of felicitations, the music, the dancing!—all this held our attention, until shortly before we were to depart on our voyage de noces—at which time we discovered that Geoffrey and the Indian woman were nowhere to be found! It was so unlike him—he doted on his Caroline—where could they be? Cheers and applause soon interrupted our frenetic searches—here was our carriage, at the front steps, and Geoffrey in the coachman's place! Tenderly, he made his adieux to his beloved daughter, and helped her up into the carriage—I started in after her (thinking to myself, enfin, enfin!) when he gripped my arm, and with eyes curiously intense and bright, declaimed thus:

"'Your part in this great mystery of freedom, my son, has been a brave and necessary one, and now your marriage to my heart's treasure seals our two destinies. Matador's self-sacrifice has not been in vain. Dieu vous bénisse, mon frère!' All eyes fastened on our coach as we sped down the avenue—Geoffrey, we learned later from the servants, taking his seat beside the Wildcat's sister, in a second coach, and exiting by way of the back lane.

"Hélas! Our wedding journey was cut short by news of his untimely death. We returned to a house in mourning, and the letter now in your hands, Fan—all we had left of him. For the remainder of her own brief life, your maman retained it among her valuables."

El Inglés, 28. June, 1837.

Beloved Children, Friends, Servants:

Destiny called us to this land of Florida, Frontier of Flowers. Here, we have felled trees, cleared land, erected shelters for our bodies, and houses of worship for the safe-keeping of our immortal souls; we have laboured to build roads and bridges for our wagons and carriages, that they might speedily transport all we hold dear in this world; we have planted crops, established mills and workshops for our artisans, and perfected all things needful to the dispensation of hospitality; and we have triumphed in our Mission, my dearest ones: the joys of abundance being proof positive of our triumph. Not without sorrow, therefore, do I now take leave of you, in obedience to a new Calling that Grace Abounding may spread also to our Territory's aborigines. To this end, I take to wife her who rightly bears the name, Bride of Freedom: henceforth, her people shall be my people, and I shall lead them West. May the red suns of autumn usher into this world the fruit of our union, in whom the best of civilized and natural man conjoin; and may his life's actions evince the proper fit of these goods. Do not, I pray you, endeavor to seek me out among my chosen people; call upon your faith to grant you the patience to accept what Providence hath done, and men cannot undo. Let the envoy between my new people and you, who people the dear abode of my former Destiny, be Claude Francis Boullet, my esteemed son-in-law, whose life has truly prepared him for this task—and to him do I charge it. To my beloved son, Edward Hull Howard, I leave the dispensation of all my worldly goods. May God so shine His light before you that no doubts darken your way, no regrets or reproaches cast their shadow. Though I dwell no longer among you, my love and blessings shall ever be with you. Farewell and Godspeed.

Geoffrey Morton Howard

"We learned afterwards—from the youngest member of the theatrical troupe, a lad of sixteen—that they met up with Geoffrey at Tallahassee, as arranged, and traveled thence along the route described by Chakaika: 'Cross the St. Johns River, and proceed south by water. Turn inland to the Big Lake and follow the river to the Glades.' Now, according to this youth, Geoffrey gave orders to stoke the campfire after their meal each evening—for the light, tu comprends, to rehearse their drama. On the tenth day, as they lay encamped along the road from Picolata to St. Augustine, disaster struck—that night Geoffrey's Lady Providence granted him his final curtain call.

"Mais d'abord, ma petite Fannie, you must know why this famous tragédie of the great William Shakespeare so captured l'imagination de ton grand-père. What did he see in the character of Othello? He saw a man of true natural goodness, honest and honorable, innocent of all things ignoble and false. This good man is duped by Iago; and this Iago, he is no man, but a snake cast in the mold of Civilization's wiles. In Othello's fate, Geoffrey saw nothing less than 'the tragic plight of the Indian'—I give you his very words—the noble savage fashioned in Nature's own image, free until he becomes the White man's dupe: believing that Freedom has played him false, he betrays his own natural being, and is lost. In the role of Desdemona, the Seminole woman would portray none other than herself, the incarnation of the noble Indian's own sweet essence of natural freedom: la liberté. She, the unwitting instrument of his destruction. C'est une tragédie vraie—pitoyable et terrible, mon choux—mais aussi une vraie histoire.

"Let me recite for you, en anglais, the final words of Cassio. In Geoffrey's adaptation, he expressed his parable of Freedom endangered:

> Cas. (Pointing to Iago as he stands over the bed
> on which the lifeless Othello and Desdemona lie):
>   This Cuban bloodhound
> Hath put to chase a noble lord and his bride,
> With this effect: Freedom's own body doth
> On a couch of nuptial joy smotherèd lie!
> A grievous duty now befalls me—Enforce
> I must the daily lashing of the villain,
> And tell this Providence ordained for Man:
> Freedom, blood-reddened, never more can join
> With happy peace in striking coin.

"Oh how your maman and I struggled to render Geoffrey's English more or less comprehensible to Chakaika's people! Profoundly torn between the two principal roles—Othello and Iago—he decided in the end that, as a man of some years, he was better suited to portray Othello, the dignified and oh so foolish cacique; Chakaika and his band would more readily perceive the White emissary's true feeling for the plight of Florida's Indians—communicating to them en personne that which must awaken their wisdom and save them from ruin.

"On the fatal night, Geoffrey and his troupe were rehearsing the murder scene—they had arrived at the climax, where Othello speaks these lines over the lovely Desdemona on her death-bed:

> Oth. O Bride of Freedom, accursèd be thou, Wife,
> Whose promise follows not the path of sun
> Nor moon, but sets a course of no direction;
> For Chaos is thine acolyte;
>   (Smothers her) Die, then Sweet Bride.
> No cession to Chaos alters Death.

"Imagine: there stands the white-haired émissaire, reddened by the campfire, pressing a pillow over the face of Coacoochee's sister, and fervently declaiming these words. Shots ring out—he falls beside her, silenced—a band of warriors rush into the encampment, firing as they advance. They kill all but the Woman—she does not stir under her pillow. One other is spared—this garçon, from whom we heard the bloody tale, who, on account of his youth and slenderness, was assigned the role of Emilia. His costume, tu vois—his skirts—saved his life, despite the unladylike agility with which he fled into the woods!"

Papa says that Chakaika—for it was Chakaika and his band, moving under the very nose of General Jesup—had long distrusted the White emissary; deducing, rightly, that Grandfather would not expect to meet the hunted Spanish Indians until well beyond the settled areas of Florida, the wily Chakaika determined to outwit this White man by spying him out on his own ground—by which ruse he thought to gain foreknowledge of his designs. Not even Papa understood what the Bride of Freedom had grasped directly upon hearing her brother's decree: that, henceforth, all plans were to be made by Chakaika— namely, that she was to be betrothed to him, by which betrothal Coacoochee recognized the Chief of the Spanish Indians as his ally and equal in war against the Whites. That Grandfather should be delivering his Betrothed to him—along with White men's gifts—could signify to Chakaika only the thread of an uncommonly nefarious plot, a strategy to force the Indians out of Florida to those reservations in the West, where so many had preceded them.

It had not been in his plan to attack Grandfather. After initial astonishment at hearing White men declaim in their own tongue (however strangely), Chakaika's band huddled in the dark beyond the campfire, becoming wholly absorbed in the spectacle: what they beheld was an old white man arrayed as an Indian chieftain wedded to Chakaika's betrothed. Chakaika held himself in check, with the object of discovering this old one's plot—the same setting out to smother to death Coacoochee's sister, he interpreted this act as destruction of the very pledge that guaranteed his leadership of the Indians; the old man was impersonating him with the object of making it appear that he—Chakaika—was murdering the woman, thereby breaking trust with his own people. Moved by such an understanding, Chakaika opened fire and claimed his betrothed, together with a trunk full of theatrical costumes and trinkets— believing these to be the White man's gift beyond price.

February 14, 1868—Occasions of biology, says Nongka, offer a natural means for shaping what is to come. She reminds us of how Papa saved the Bride of Freedom and her newborn from certain ostracism, if not death, at the hands of Chakaika's people—the best example, to my mind, of the benefits of supplanting truth with a working lie. We heard the story from Jonathan, who pieced

it together out of what his mother and others among the Spanish
Indians told him.

A month before Jonathan's birth, the Bride of Freedom had sent
a message to Papa, at his trading post on Indian Key: the time for her
labor was drawing near. Not wishing to leave the Glades or lose her
place there, she awaited the guidance of the White Father's envoy.
From this Papa understood that, had the Spanish Indians known
the Woman was with child by a white man, she would not have been
welcomed as one of them—nor would the offspring of such a union
be allowed to live.

The Government's second war with Florida's Seminole was at
its peak, but Papa's reputation as a sense-bearer permitted him
to move safely among them, and more freely than others of his
skin. To add to the weight of his own word, he enlisted the help of
another sense-bearer and trusted friend, Abraham—an Indian Negro
held in high regard by the Seminoles in negotiations with Whites.
Together, Papa and Abraham sought out Chakaika's isle in the Glades,
the latter carrying a message from General Jesup, promising safe
conduct out to the reservations and death to any who refused to go.
(The numbers of Glades Indians had lately grown, after hundreds
waiting to be transported West slipped away into the swamp with
Coacoochee.) The General's message prompted Chakaika to send word
to Coacoochee to prepare for battle.

But Papa counseled patience: "Look to the child borne by the
Wildcat's sister—if he shows the light of great sense-bearing power,
victory will be yours." Chakaika was to wait first for a whitening in
himself, then in his newborn: a pallor akin to that of the white enemy
and as mighty as light shining with the force of sun and moon at
once. "This is the light of sense-bearing the child will bring to you,"
Papa declared. Skeptically, Chakaika examined his bronze skin, but
joined the two sense-bearers, the white and the black, in drinking
to the birth of his son as a sense-bearer of victory. Shortly, he fell
down senseless, while Papa proceeded to soak the Chieftain's hair
with a decoloring solution he had brought for that purpose. Abraham
summoned the Bride of Freedom, Papa apprising her of the whitening
to come and its significance.

By the time she gave birth (Jonathan came into this world—as
Grandfather Howard had foretold—in the late autumn of 1837,
eight years before me) Chakaika's hair was bleached to a whitish
gold—fair as the fuzz that covered the newborn's head. And Chakaika,
no longer skeptical, sent word to Coacoochee that the time for

battle and victory was at hand. The bloody Battle of Okeechobee, led by Coacoochee on Christmas Day 1837—in which many Whites were wounded and killed—was viewed by Chakaika as a turning point in the War. His own hair having grown in blacker than ever, he still pointed to little tow-headed Jonathan as undisputed sense-bearer of Indian victory.

Three years later, a detachment of soldiers disguised as Indians, having hunted Chakaika down on his hammock in the Everglades, shot him and dangled his huge body high, under the bright moon, between two of his warriors—in full view of his wife, mother, and sister. The Bride of Freedom, with Jonathan strapped to her back, together with other women and children of the tribe, escaped by hiding in mud up to the chin.

Harding switched off her spotlight and slumped against the altar amid fading afterimages. Dozed lightly for a while, mouth dry and bitter with plaster dust. She needed rest, a change of scene. Nights of deep sleep. Most of all she longed to be out of sight, to get on with the restoration but without being seen. Dissolution. A craving for a death of sorts—a suspension not of the faculties, physical or mental, but of the sense of self and its boundaries, the organization of memory and desire felt to specify one's own being. "Destiny," "personality," "identity," "subjectivity," "individuality"—that mode of existing which has somehow come to be ours alone, to belong to us like a possession. She yearned to crouch in the free mud of self-termination with others of like kind.

Proposition: Passion mirrors the prison of who you've become.

Not one to rehash her personal past, Harding hangs it in a corner like an object of little value laid by in case of some unforeseen need. What you're apt to get from her in the way of autobiography slides by coldly, like a sociological toboggan. But ask her a straight question about herself and you get a straight dose of her. "What," I once pressed her, "did it feel like to grow up in the Yazoo-Mississippi Delta? I'm not asking what it was like there but what you really felt."

"It felt like Judgment Day in Eden," she answered promptly, "Eden unrestored, gone to swamp in the interim, populated by émigrés existing in a deafening flow of final judgments, squirming incessantly to their vibrations, snaking through the bog of them, coiled in seats of opinion given and received in hisses, a webbed hierarchy of ever-tightening snake decisions to be escaped only momentarily by sliding to cover—cover, finding cover, was the name of the game for me. Not fight or flight, but judge or hide, rattle only when necessary, hide hide hide, go with the butterflies, the spiders, the crawfish, keep to earth out of striking distance, above all, out of sight of their food-hungry eyes, the whiplike squeeze of their suffocation, the dribble of poisonous stink, hide hide hide in mimicry of judgments, track their heat trails, one sidewinding wriggle could save you from a judicial fang, puff up, whip your tongue out, slither into a den but hide hide hide, or . . . or, blinded by the spit of venom, stand up in the dock for the passing of your snake-sentence. Slow death by paralysis. What's it like to grow up in Eden unrestored, the place of reckoning? It has the feeling-spread of neurotoxins piercing your boll of a body like cotton stainers."

October 3, 1861—The events leading up to Grandfather Howard's death were related by Papa with his customary ironical air—which often grows pronounced when he speaks of Mother's family, though never of her—but I don't doubt that he took seriously his charge as go-between for the Howards and the Indians.

    Less than a year after Chakaika's death, Coacoochee the Wildcat surrendered. He was waiting, with some two hundred of his followers, for transport to Oklahoma, when Papa succeeded in obtaining permission from the authorities to take the Bride of Freedom and her son under his protection at Indian Key, where—with her assent—he was christened Jonathan Redman Howard. When a temporary reservation, extending from Peaden River to Shark River, was set aside the following year for the remnant of Florida's Seminole, she disappeared promptly into the Glades. She would visit Indian Key at irregular intervals thereafter, giving every sign of appreciating the comforts of white civilization—leaving Jonathan behind for short periods at first, then for months at a time, after he reached the age of five or six. Papa retained a tutor for him at Indian Key, and often put him to work aboard his ships. "At fourteen," Papa was wont to say of him, "Jonathan Redman is the most skilled of all my men, lacking only the judgment that comes of long experience." The Bride of Freedom was adamant in her refusal to accept Uncle Edward's offer of adoption, giving as her reason only that "the White Father" had directed her people to consult with none but Claude Boullet—and that her brother Coacoochee had commanded that it be so.

Jonathan was eleven years old when Papa first brought him to us in Tarragona. The visit merges in my memory with later ones—for he stayed with us regularly thereafter, at least two months out of every year, until settling in at El Inglés two winters ago—but Jonathan remembers that first time well, when he came with his mother, who requested passage back to Indian Key after only four days. In my mind's eye, I see a Seminole woman sitting very erect, feet together—one hand clasps the ends of a shawl at her breast, on which are draped loops of magnificent gold spangles—while the other rests on one leg, palm up; her dark eyes sparkle with keen watchfulness. Is this the Bride of Freedom? Papa says that my memory-picture—all but the sumptuousness of the necklace, which Jonathan has often described in some detail—fits any of the half-dozen Indian women, who, having managed to escape Removal, used to wander in and out of Tarragona all during my childhood; as I was barely three years old on the single occasion of our meeting, it is likely to be a composite—but Papa's argument, though plausible, is not altogether convincing. Jonathan's wide face, with its high cheek bones and coppery tint, has just the contours of that memory-face, and his hair, originally golden white, has darkened to the pale copper hue of his skin; but the likeness ends there, for he has brilliant blue-green eyes, like Uncle Edward—Grandfather Howard's eyes, Papa says.

How I always looked forward to Jonathan's visits! He was as much my brother as any brother by blood could ever be—everything about him became proof of our kinship, including even the Indian quietness of his movements, cultivated, much like my own, to preserve the silence I so love—or his occasional droll lapses into French, in playful imitation of Papa. When he was a youth, and I only a little girl, Jonathan never teased or mocked—nor did he condescend to me, as older children are wont to do with their inferiors. He is the most unfailingly kind person in my acquaintance; and if, in consequence, I have adored him as only a younger sister could, he accepted grand'maman and me as a completely natural and integral part of the world he shared with Papa. Nothing has made it easier for me to discover countless likenesses between us than Papa's influence over him. And, truly, Jonathan is so like Papa in thought and manner—especially his reserve, at once courteous and ironical—that they might even now be mistaken for son and father.

When fighting with the Seminole broke out again for the last time, the Bride of Freedom and Jonathan—two hundred and fifty dollars being paid for each, this being the bounty for live Seminole—

were captured. Jonathan contrived to relay a message to Papa (who in turn bribed the stockade guards to connive at their escape). Papa was building our house on Valencia Street when he received the news that Billy Bow Legs (Alligator's brother) had given up the fight in the Big Cypress, after they took his little granddaughter. When the Bride of Freedom heard the old Chief had succumbed to the shame of exile, which had overtaken nearly all his tribesmen by that time, she again slipped away into the Glades; despite all efforts to locate her these three years, she has not been seen or heard of since.

Before her disappearance, she instructed Papa to "make plans for Jonathan Redman"—and Papa has: Jonathan having reached his twentieth year, it was high time for him to learn the ways of his father's family, the Howards, who were only too eager to receive him at El Inglés—and the more so when they discovered that Uncle Edward's handsome younger half-brother, with his gentle demeanor, was possessed of a keen practical intelligence, and might as effortlessly pass for one of the family as if he had been born and come of age on the plantation. My cousins Julia, Mary Elizabeth, Lucy, and even little Cathy look upon him as a brother—and for Aunt Virginia, and Uncle Edward, he surely fills the place of the son they always yearned for.

Jonathan appears to me to have learned all there is to know about life and work at El Inglés—still, he lately asserted, with a manly modesty that makes us both gay with mischief: "the tadpole cannot hop until he becomes a frog, ma chérie."

January 8, 1861—"My dear Frances," said Aunt Virginia to me after tea yesterday—I sensing something of moment in the air—"if I may be so open as to bring up a delicate matter, I wish you to understand that your Uncle Edward and I could not be more in sympathy with you than we are—I am certain, moreover, that dear Caroline would wish me to advise you in this fashion." I suffered my hand to be fondled—inwardly agitated over I knew not what— she continuing: "It is only natural that two young people, placed in proximity over the years, and growing into the handsome and refreshing—not to say 'original'—couple that you and Jonathan Redman make together, should develop tender feelings for each other."

Original couple? tender feelings? my mind was awhirl—could Jonathan have sat as still as I? In her kindly manner, and cradling both my hands in hers, she pressed on: "Be assured that, unlike some, your Uncle Edward and I have no objection to youthful marriages. And as you know, my dear, your Uncle and I are cousins and have always considered a touch of blood in common to be the most pleasing of bonds—I speak of this only to remind you of society's judgment in such matters, my dear, and to urge upon you the need for propriety and delicacy. WE believe, dear Frances, that some two or three years of enlarging your social circle would not be amiss, and might well conduce to your future happiness; in short, we wish you to know—your Uncle and I—that we would not stand in the way of a union between you and Jonathan—should it weather the interval of waiting, of course."

This last she added after watching the color rise in my face—not from delicacy of feeling (as she may have believed), but from the sheer astonishment that pulsed through me as her meaning grew plainer with every word—

"But Aunt Virginia," I protested, "Jonathan and I—we never speak of such things at all!" My reply must have been to her satisfaction, for she said with an air of closing our little talk: "My confidence could not be greater that you and Jonathan deport yourselves entirely as you should, my dear, and will continue in the same manner."

How has this come about?—no doubt because Jonathan and I like nothing better than to wander off together to the fields, woods, or mills, where he answers all my questions about how and by whom things are done on the plantation—all such operations as grinding cornmeal, keeping accounts, shoeing horses, making molasses, tending ditches, and the like. I have learned from these conversations that the loamy sand of Middle Florida—which has built many a fortune in the generation since the Territory was opened—is exhausted from too much cultivation of cotton; other crops must be tried to replenish the soil, Jonathan believes, and the local arts of manufacture encouraged and joined to the larger commercial system. In fine weather, we go riding after breakfast; and it is true that, when others ride with us, we find ways to leave them behind—or slip away somehow unnoticed, so that we may go and do as we please. (Not so much because we wish to be alone, as because we do not think they share our interests.) When we reappear, my cousins and their friends exchange mysterious glances—still, I do not think that either of us would have caught their true meaning—those exchanges of shared perception, as I now know them to be—had not Aunt Virginia broached the subject of marriage to me.

When I related her observations to Jonathan, he chuckled with no little incredulity, and continued so on and off the whole afternoon, even in company. This morning, he reverted to the matter rather more gravely—we ought to give it our thorough consideration before dismissing it outright, he said—to which I replied that the night had given me time for thought as well, and that, although I saw nothing in marriage for us, I did perceive that the prospect of it might confer a certain status which would induce others to leave us alone.

Harding has often reminded me that, on Frances Boullet's own account, she burned what matters and laid out in Volume XL the ordering of events to be heard, mute about the things that, one would think, meant most to her. It strikes me as I read—yet again—this, her "final composition" of salvaged entries and fragments of entries, that her thirty-nine rituals of incineration were acts of love. The blaze of the intimate stuff that smokes to the end and dies with us.

Received, in hand, what she chose to leave behind: this terminal register of passion "wherein the years from December 24, 1860 to December 5, 1935 are recollected in decoupage." Proposition: Passion leaves its remains in history. Restated: History is the coda of passion finishing itself off. And I—I've become remainderman of Frances Boullet's passion.

January 11, 1861—I shall not sleep tonight—have been tossing and turning a good hour and growing ever more wakeful—caught up in waves of energy, promising to take me to ever greater heights of invention and subtlety!—must try to calm myself by writing and let words break the frenzied spell of my own word-magic—

Papa and Uncle Edward having returned with news of Florida's secession from the Union yesterday, there have been murmurings all afternoon about holding our own intimate celebration (no visitors at El Inglés today, the first time since our arrival here before Christmas). Baby Cathy having been put to bed and kissed "goodnight" all around, my three older cousins—with the enthusiastic support of Aunt Virginia—proposed a cozy evening of "family chatter," meaning that even the gentlemen—Uncle Edward, Papa, and Jonathan—were seduced from their disquisitions upon the fate of nations, and other weighty cigar-smoking subjects, to indulge in—I knew not what, but prepared myself for the worst.

All made for the library with its blazing hearth—or were swept together, as it seemed to me, on currents of anticipation. "Finally—we can finally be ourselves!" whispered cousin Julia, preceding Jonathan and me, and joining Lucy on the hearth-rug; Mary Elizabeth came leading Papa by the hand, Aunt Virginia and Uncle Edward following behind. The "chatter" turned on the recent Christmas and New Year festivities, and our steady flow of visitors. Lucy—my favorite cousin, because of her gently inward nature—referred in her shy way to something she had written in her journal about the holidays— because, she said, "I wish never to forget even the least little thing."

"Surely the most complete account around here must come from cousin Frances!" Julia teased with her naughty, coquettish tilt of the head—"Few nights pass that she is not deep in her Dear Diary, until all hours; she imagines me asleep, and blissfully departed into Dreamland—little does she know! At your present rate, Fannie, you will fill up your forty volumes before the month is out!" Everyone laughed, as the color rose in my cheeks.

"I too love writing in my journal," confided Mary Elizabeth—ever more tactful than her older sister—"but how do you find so much to say, Fannie?"

"Not all of us have your penchant for economy, Mary Lizzie," Uncle Edward intervened.

"Oh—I know, I know!" exclaimed Julia, her naughtiness now irresistible—to all but myself—"Let's just this once share our secrets by reading aloud from our diaries!" There: it was uttered. Judgment Day.

Aunt Virginia professed herself charmed by this tribute to familial solidarity, as she looked for approval to Uncle Edward, who declared pensively: "In the ordinary course of things, the privacy of these writings is sacrosanct; but inasmuch as there is no public ear with us confederates tonight, I see no reason why we might not—this once—share our recorded mysteries. But only on condition that one, and only one, entry be chosen for reading aloud," he added, directing a kindly gaze at my abstracted person—"and, of course, that none shall feel obliged to enter into our foolishness."

By the time we reconvened in the library with all our volumes, I was in a highly agitated state—to say the least—and, recognizing through it all that Uncle Edward was offering me the big Chippendale chair, which has the best light beside it, and that hospitality dictated yielding first place to me, I fell into a veritable distraction of tremors and palpitations—limbs, tongue, and brain seeming no longer my own. "Oh no, please," I protested with as much equanimity as I could muster—which is to say almost none—"I much prefer to read last." ("Not at all," I yearned to say, feeling a shout of "No, never!" rise in my throat—but I dared not; Uncle's remark about not feeling obliged undone absolutely by the solidity of the waiting Chair.)

With characteristic delicacy, Aunt Virginia herself proceeded to Grandfather's place—evidently construing my plea as girlish diffidence. I confess I took in only that her entry turned upon the marital relationship—something about how it both contains and transforms the forces of nature—some elaborate conceit picturing the struggle between plants and the insects seeking to devour them, its artistry much admired by all, and the style of her little essay said to suffer not a whit by comparison with the best of Goldsmith and Irving. No doubt it would, in the normal course of things, have interested me as well, had I not been so hopelessly mired in my dilemma—letting a page of my diary fall from time to time as if by accident, and dropping my feverish eyes in a futile search for something suitable to be read aloud—anything.

Cousin Julia came next to the seat of majesty, with a lively rendition of whisperings overheard (purportedly!) at the Christmas ball—amorous badinage between certain ladies and gentlemen, sure to have consequences at this year's May party! Amusing enough— wickedly clever, at others' expense, as I perceived even in my distress. Mary Elizabeth's piece surprised and, therefore, held me: a vision of the future—a time when families such as ours must persevere amid forces set against our way of life and its material foundations. Our moral principles and the conduct of our lives, under the ideal conditions that now prevail, being what they are—here followed an apt précis of these principles and conditions—our conduct in adversity is predetermined. She glanced often at Uncle Edward, who nodded soberly as her earnest little treatise drew to a close with the proposal that a coat of arms, bearing the motto "aut nobilitas aut nihil," be crafted into an amulet, for the masters of all such families.

Lucy was so flushed by the fire, I could see little droplets forming along her rosy brow when she expressed her trepidation that—after Mary Lizzie—her own scribbling must appear jejune by comparison. Once in Grandfather's chair, however, she launched readily into her detailed, if—even to my half-listening ear—freely embellished, account of recent festivities at El Inglés—the Great House, and the settlements as well. I could not help being struck by the emphasis on all that was consumed and worn during the holidays—as if they had been an uninterrupted banquet feasted upon by lengths of satin, silk, and brocade!

It did not escape me either that, after each reading, Aunt or Uncle would pass judgment—gently critical and laudatory, all at once—on

the performance as well as the composition itself; but what had
been creeping into my consciousness at a sickening snail's pace—
preoccupied as I was with my own plight—and what suddenly hurtled
to the forefront, after Lucy's turn, was the recognition that both
Aunt and Uncle had perused—nay, were in the habit of perusing!—
my cousins' journals. These jottings of ours were not at all what
I had supposed! Not, I now understood, recorded for the writer's
eye alone—"private" only in the sense that, what the diarist made
of herself and the world would be put to the test—and brought to
correction!—in the intimacy of the family circle, before assuming
the form of a wider representation. Mine had been private in some
different sense entirely, I having no prefiguration of my public
appearance to offer.

I saw nothing for it but to feign the onset of a disabling illness—
sudden pallor, faintness, loss of voice. . . . Readying myself for the
event, I comprehended not a syllable of Uncle Edward's entry, deep
and fine though it must have been. My eyes caught those of Papa—
seemingly at home in this family gathering—and then of Jonathan,
bemused and inscrutable in their detachment. Desolate, I tried to
guess what either of them would do in my place—and then, just as
Uncle Edward closed his volume and vacated the big chair—amid
applause and praise for the wisdom of his exegesis—in that instant,
inspiration fell on me like rain: taking my place in the chair, I opened
my diary I know not where, and began to "read"—haltingly at first,
but gaining in confidence with each sentence—making up every word
I uttered as I went along:

"El Inglés is a theatre, for playing out the parts assigned to us
by the times we live in." I could see I had their attention. "Aunt
Virginia, as Mistress, sees to everything, never appearing to do
so—and Uncle Edward, as Master, sees to it that everything is seen to,
never appearing to do so either." Laughter from my audience. "The
colored folks see to it, that the Master sees to it, that the Mistress
sees to everything"—more laughter. "My cousins and I are seen to
by everyone at El Inglés"—still more laughter—"where hospitality
never fails, and guests are assigned parts akin to those my cousins
and I play, and, so, are seen to by one and all." Laughter takes on an
edge—something too much of this line of wit. "My own part is not to
question, but to take my place—to accept the honour of hospitality,
and to learn what it has to teach me. On my arrival here with Papa, I
was a child eager for merrymaking, for the special sights and sounds
of Christmas; soon, however, I apprehended that the times hang over

us like a cloud, beneath which everything becomes more itself than ever—" I fought off the urge to provoke more laughter, by saying that Papa and I had certainly been "seen to" as never before—and, most especially, so had Jonathan and I; but, having led my audience in another direction, I felt their push to go on.

"Uncle Edward's sweet anger shows itself for what it is—the heroic resolve of the master to give his life for his part; the covetousness of the house servants turns to desire of what is best for all, and envy becomes emulation"—now that I had got on the track of the Deadly Seven, nothing could stop me; it was sheer rhapsodizing! On to gluttony: "Elsewhere, Gluttony craves orgies to feed his gross appetites; but, here, on the plantation, he turns away from mere excess, and commands satisfaction of epicurean palates. Lust is gentled to loving-kindness, and Sloth to blissful ease and rest—even Pride alters her demeanor at El Inglés; neither puffed up nor contumelious, she is the quiet strength that upholds all." I had my momentum now, even though I had run out of Deadly Sins—no matter, I could invent more: all were attending to my words, all in my power—I could move them wherever I wished, and I knew just how to do it. They sat about the fire entranced, eyes fixed on me, awaiting the pleasures at my command.

I lowered my voice—a bit more husky, the better to veil my true intent: "Thus does our beloved plantation home adumbrate the Creator's own plan—we who see but shadows cannot encompass more. When God cast sinning Man from Paradise, the curse that toil and death would be our lot flowed from that same gracious hand as the great Creation itself—ah, Felix Culpa! How fortunate our Fall!—God's harsh gift teaching us to restore the bliss of Paradise Lost in the happy round of each day's work—each of us in his place here at El Inglés, in the daily revolution of that innocent ignorance which was ours before the Fall—for ignorance, here, is the greatest of all goods—Ignorance becomes more herself than ever—Ignorance becomes the Wisdom of Obedience; and if—" In the heat of ex tempore composition, I glanced at Papa—no longer at ease, but alert and imperceptibly shaking his head at me in warning.

I, sensing that my "reading" had best be brought to a speedy and resounding conclusion, regained perfect control: eyes lowered to the page—still as if seeking the words there—I carried on, in steady, level tones: "If El Inglés reflects, but dimly, the Eden whence we sprang, its diminished light still shows the way—still points to secession from that Union which blocks Florida's work; for, if Florida is to become more herself than ever, she too must join that happy revolution of labor and fulfill her promise of Paradise Regained—"

Beneath my outward calm, I was in a veritable creative fever, seeking something to bring it to just the right pitch—a turn that would combine patriotic fervor with prophetic vision in simple, homely, childlike fashion—a verse, of course, a verse! "And so, Dear Diary"—my voice grew breathy with emotion:—

> We who love El Inglés well
> Must forever toll the bell,
> Calling those prepared to fight—
> Each according to his delight—
> For all our goods, by the dozens,
> Encircling my sweet cousins;
> For Uncle, Aunt, and our yokes
> To our dear, dear Colored Folks.

The hush of something like awe, preceding the applause that followed my performance, did not escape me—nor did Papa's troubled face, and Jonathan's speechless, incredulous stare.

"This demolition is . . . is . . . I mean we just keep on smashing and shoving stuff around every which way and getting nowhere. It's . . . chaos." Every surface in sight, inside and out, piled with the tangled guts of the Boullet House. "I've got electricians and plumbers lined up ready to go—my roofer won't even set foot here until the last piece of this junk's gone to the dump."

Mr. Ware removed his hat, wordlessly mopped his dark brown face with a checkered hanky. At lunch, over his packed snack from the corner store, watching Harding unclog a passage down the stairway, he'd counseled with a more than ordinarily morose expression: "Best you go on about yo' business, Mizlizbit, drop by every now 'n nen. We gone git this job done for you."

She'd stayed, going about her business as she saw it, tiptoeing around them to avoid provocation—like disregarding the color line by making specific requests in line with their verbal contract, or showing real pleasure when pleased or real annoyance when crossed or disappointed, or any real feelings at all. A problem for her since childhood, when neither Oedipal tugs of sexuality nor the pressures of white Delta society (for whom, she says, "social distinctions were fine to the point of seeming cryptic") enmeshed her as the color line did. One of the tenant families on the plantation where she grew up was part African American and part Choctaw with straight black hair and bronze skin—closer in physical type to what she then thought she looked like than any other people she knew. Her own dark hair cut in Prince Valiant bangs hung flat and straight across the back, like theirs. And the fact that her body, instead of tanning in golden blond tones, turned the deep copper more common to brunettes tended, if not exactly to confirm, then at least not to belie her self-image. Not that she was unaware even then of being Caucasian; rather it was as if a social contract beyond her grasp, made without her consent and without reference to her essential being, had so classified her. But since she didn't experience her whiteness, she must be something other than white somehow. It could only be that something off-white coursed through her—"a raindrop of color was all it would take"—the task she was born to being not so much to hide it as to collaborate with the fraud of her whiteness.

Getting on the school bus with white children, riding into town to the brick schoolhouse where she saw only white faces, and sitting day after day in a whole room full of them was a perpetual trauma. After the first day she got off the bus at the commissary store and ran, as usual, to play with her friends shooting marbles in the dirt. As she dropped to her hands and knees to take her turn, a coal-black man in whose house she'd spent countless hours playing with these same children stopped beside her and inquired, "How you like yo' school, Miss 'lizabet?"—they'd never before called her anything but "Lizzie." Even as an adult she never forgot the pain and humiliation of that moment, her black playmates backing away from her and staring. Shortly, they all used the hated name, making it sound like "Mizlizbit" and, eventually, shame passed into the shadow of loneliness that comes from permanent and irredeemable separation from one's own kind.

Even in middle age, she was still dreaming of herself as colored but was fully aware of the white woman her demolition crew saw facing them. Mr. Ware adjusted his hat and spat smartly across the drive before crowding into the cab next to Scooter. "I got to check on this here truck fust thing in the morning, front wheels ain't looking none too good." And for sure they didn't. Not that he couldn't afford a better truck—rumor had it he owned a potential fortune in strategically located run-down rental properties all over DeLuna County.

Above the roar and sputter of the engine Harding shouted: "I'll expect you here no later than eight a.m. and I want the entire first floor and the stairway cleared out by the end of the day tomorrow."

"Yes'm, Mizlizbit," hat tipped in the gesture known as "respect." Willy balanced on the footboard inserting a blade of grass between impeccable teeth, in blasé detachment from the old minstrel show. Looking straight ahead, Mo put the engine in gear. Wheels spun and spit out soft blackened sand, and the truck heaved forward raining rubble down sides and back.

From Dr. Cane's property across the street, Bill Simmons, artist of Old Tarragona carpentry, called it a day and assessed the situation. "Relax," he said with arms akimbo, "relax. Ware's a good ole fellow." Could always be counted on to haul off mountains of historic garbage at a reasonable price—sooner or later, more or less.

January 12, 1861—Of two minds, I sank into a restless sleep as the sky began to brighten—in one mind, the wish to repeat my performance (for I feel that my "reading" was but an intimation—a mere shadow—of more subtle heights I might yet scale); in the other, relief and gratitude at having contrived a place for myself (if barely!—by means of the turn I gave to my perilous recitation) where I can move freely, unquestioned and unremarked, for the remainder of our visit here.

Not long now—two more days until we leave for home—Papa has arranged our travel by coach from Tallahassee to the steamer "Alice" going down the Apalachicola River to the Bay, where we are to board another ship home. Despite a certain flatness of spirits overall, I have a kind of hunger for Tarragona after these weeks of absence—although not grand like El Inglés, our house suits me; it is comfortable, with more than enough space for us all. From the time I first entered it—that brisk January day in 1858, after grand'maman's death, when I had scarcely ventured out for weeks, and Papa prevailed upon me to walk down the Alley with him to our new home on Valencia Street, then under construction—ever since that day, my favorite room has been the library upstairs, wide as the house itself, all across the front. It would have four great dormer windows so high up none would see inside, Papa said, not even from the upper balcony of the Acosta place across the way. "The better not to spy on us," he added with rare solemnity, followed by a sly smile—which, at the time, I thought was meant to cheer me up, nothing more.

So, too, the task he charged me with, of considering what furnishings we would require; but this had the unintended effect of throwing me into a quandary, from which I neither expected nor wished to escape: given a free hand to choose whatever I pleased, I found that I wanted both everything and nothing. In the end, except for some few necessities for the new kitchen, I refrained from adding anything to the handsome pieces accumulated by grand'maman, with the idea of waiting to see what the future would bring—a prescient decision, as it turned out, for it shortly brought an admirable collection of chests, tables, and chairs, along with boudoir accessories—Nongka's things from Hayti, mostly French of the last century. They give our house a look unlike any other I have visited. It was that same wintry morning, on our way back from Valencia Street, that Papa relayed the news that passage from the Islands was being arranged for Nongka and her children—to coincide with our move at the end of the year. The two downstairs bedrooms in the new house, at the back, would be his and Ibo's—Nongka and Zula and I should have the use of four commodious rooms upstairs as we pleased.

Would they be our servants, I inquired? Mais non—it was "nothing like that." Would Nongka, then, be a governess to me? That was "something like it," but I must not trouble the little head—was I not a mere innocent of twelve at the time? Nongka would make everything clear—"parfaitement, tu verras, ma petite fleur." All that was expected of me would be revealed soon enough; I could trust Nongka's judgment in all things, and I was to do her bidding—I must follow Ibo and Zula in this—and I was to remember, at all times, that Nongka and her children were free gens de couleur. Our conversation left me both dissatisfied and impatient for their arrival.

As for moving out of the Hernando Inn, I was not in the least sorry about that, even though my childhood there had been happy for the most part. While our apartments were remote enough—and, on the whole, much to my liking—I early discovered the delights of shutting the door upon that privacy for intervals, and dawdling— unobserved, as I imagined—in the foyer downstairs, with its busy comings and goings of visitors from near and far. Tarragona, according to grand'maman, has never attracted la crème of society, as does the much younger town of Tallahassee—"but persons of distinction do have business here occasionally"; in consequence, I had been introduced to as many of the "socially desirable" as had my Howard cousins. True, she hastened to add, mine had been the questionable advantage of a far broader range of introductions. Even before grand'maman died, however, Papa began to admonish me—in a voice wholly devoid of levity—that, inasmuch as I was growing into a "young lady" (said emphatically en anglais, to dispel all risk of ambiguity) I was no longer to stop in the foyer—only pass through it.

The doom, alas, of ladyhood seems in these latter days definitively upon me—irrevocably!—Et maintenant, Papa?

Time for this night owl to find a roosting place too? Perched here and there on the posts of the hotel pier down below my balcony, birds hunch like drunks on bar stools. Pelicans, a few cormorants, one night heron keeping its distance from the others, obviously an habitué. "Time to *do* something with yourself," parents used to tell us as teenagers. Find a suitable post for yourself. Being a woman who doesn't quite act her age, I've managed to avoid it longer than most. Perpetual part-timer.

"It's a headache—getting yourself set up—but the boat sails on without you if you don't," Sam lingered in the airport departure lane, engine running, when he dropped me off this morning.

"Ah well, Sam, maybe one of those old freighters will happen along."

"Give me a call if you see one on the horizon, I'll jump ship and join you. Guess my paternal side's coming out here, but I really feel you, of all people, ought to be enjoying the fruit of your . . . what with so many others chomping on plums they don't deserve."

"You mean I'm due for a makeover—should I become somebody else or just make a better packaging job of it?"

"I'm only reminding you of the internet of possible connections, Jael. And it's not too late to plug into my port if you're having access problems . . . how's that for Bessie Smith in computer garble?" And he was off with a parting honk.

More than one of my cronies has been sending out signals lately— some version of Sam's advice, if less friendly. Like last Saturday, at the farmers' market, a colleague about to undergo a tenure review shaking an accusatory finger at me over my carefully selected vegetables and fresh herbs: "You adjuncts don't know *beans* about what it means to risk yourself—you're not expected to be on the cutting edge of your *field* . . . there's no pressure on you to *cultivate* your prospects, *produce* . . . you go home after your class and forget it."

Or the reunion of Marshall Scholars at the Waldorf a few weeks ago. My college roommate, Marilyn, big buyer for Sotheby's now—haven't seen her over two or three times in nearly twenty years—after inspecting me from various vantage points in the room and, finally, face to face, with eyes skilled in minute shades of class distinction American-style, declared (impulse could safely be allowed to take over now), "I do wish you'd come to the city more often, Jay."

"Actually, I was looking at a place in Murray Hill just this morning. Easy walk to the Public Library and the airport express. Not to mention that little French patisserie with the steamed eggs, corner of 38th and Madison, is it?"

"Murray Hill—hmm—call me as soon as you settle in, we'll arrange something, you'll be so busy meeting people you should know you won't have time to fade out again. If you're up for the scene, kiddo, it's all out there. *Carpe diem!*"

Filtering out the noise what I hear is that I should take immediate steps to *be* somebody—cut more of a figure, as they used to say. Carry my weight in society. Overall message: this thing about positioning myself has become critical, shape up and open up, or. . . " Or what? Time's running out, can't go any place on the information highway with an empty tank of time. As if a person of no position, having a history of what could be perceived—is perceived—as wasted time, cannot but be (oh, the shame and pity of it) a waste of time for others and run the risk of a personal isolation she cannot foresee. Oh the senselessness and pathos of it. Lost human resource. Self-loss.

None of them seriously yields me the *distinction* of no position (which would suggest—wouldn't it?—a dispossession beyond my control and shift the critique from my person to society, or the times we live in: had to play the cards dealt her, not much you can do about that). Already part of my problem—this not being sufficiently subject to the personal judgments of others—how, after all, can you judge someone with no position except to say she should have one? It's a quantitative problem, in a sense. I don't have *enough* of a position: too little too late.

Let me posthaste consider how far I'm willing to go with this. After all, more-than-enough fails to satisfy public demands as drastically as not-enough. Take Marilyn's hand and scale the social ladder? Could be pleasant, easy—considered strictly as a project. I'm generally comfortable with such people and their concerns. My past correctly packaged—Eastern European roots with Ivy education *sans* pedantry, writer-refugee, freelance this-and-that—an asset. But if time's the issue, there's no reason scintillating enough to while away any portion of mine on any step of the social ladder, despite numerous incidental rewards at upper rungs I would gladly accept. Money, for one, and a little respect. Not fame, though. Money and respect can be used and concealed, fame sucks. Literally sucks its figures into the public domain for exhibition. Performance obligatory, no choice about it. Granted, I both admire and appreciate great performances and love to perform myself—in fact, I spend most of my time (like everybody else) performing. What I refuse to give up is the privacy of my own performances.

And you can't live blissfully unaware on the social ladder, it's not blissful. Always too many on every rung rushing to drag you to this or that, and after so many polite refusals, lack of reciprocity, broken promises, insincere expressions of interest and outright lies fail to keep them at bay, comes the shakedown—people can get mean. Make direct personal attacks. More typically, they exercise their absolute power to withdraw their concern to the point where you survive only at a lowly level, if at all. Clearly, the enough-line in social life absolutely necessitates a degree of engagement that keeps key members on various keyways satisfied.

Make a lunch date with Marilyn when I get back. Better, I'll plan out a whole social calendar—pragmatism of self-protective positioning (on a trial basis). Sam's right.

The thin pages of the diary flutter at me in the night breeze like wings—if only I could fly on its hard reality to the line of enough position. An unhailed place of social and political usefulness? *Et maintenant!*

3
Heroes and Refugees

January 20, 1861—Homeward bound—aboard a cargo ship on its way to New Orleans. By order of the captain, Papa's old friend, she will make a special call at Tarragona; until then, we shall once more be looked after—and royally on all counts, judging by this evening's repast and society. Our quarters are tight, but comfortably outfitted— one little cabin for Papa, and an adjoining one for me, stocked with interesting old maps and books about seafaring. Papa says we must enjoy it all while we can—while there is still peace.

Time alone with him, finally, this evening—to inquire why he now supports Florida's secession, when formerly he was a Unionist. His curt reply was that the Boullets have always been traders—as though that explained all there is to know. I said nothing, for silence is Papa's favorite inducement to carry on. And carry on he did—while we walked the deck under a bright moon: he has never—à vrai dire—been a staunch advocate of federalism—he had hoped that expansion of the Union would promote trade, while holding foreign powers under control; from this standpoint, the Union was a failure—he would have preferred Florida to go her own way, a nation among similarly autonomous Caribbean states—Hayti, a free Santo Domingo, Cuba—all seeking alliances with one or more of the foreign powers; as things stand now, he must accept her entry into some new confederation of Southern States as all but inevitable—il n'y a point à choisir. "La Florida, chérie, is a lily floating in a grand sea of promise," he sighed— "always plucked, she always withers." (Always plucked . . . always withers—what could have led him to confer my middle name on me? My mother—her life sapped by giving me birth—died with the request that I be called "Frances" in Papa's honor, and he had me christened "Frances Florida.")

His optimism about commerce remains undiminished. Provided a confederacy of Southern States can prove itself a power—other conditions being what they are—the times could not be more propitious for the businessman able to establish a community of interest with the region's landholders. "They need a good trader like me," he boasts—more than he needs them; a good trader knows how to transport any commodity to and from any place in the world, and how to obtain the best price for his goods. Above all, a good trader understands how to keep the advantage—and when to let it go.

April 9, 1935—My middle name did not suit me and I've always been grateful that none but Zula, careless of pomp and propriety, intelligent, graceful, tender, was disposed to use it. Grasping its purport, she so alters it that the flower cannot but bloom. Maria-Louisa follows her example. But in the world at large I am the namesake—if only a Frances—of one Claude Francis Boullet, ship's captain, entrepreneur, champion of independence.

January 24, 1861—Home at long last—the familiar sandy mud lanes of Tarragona, with their lowly rows of clapboard cottages, that now look so undisguisedly shabby to my eyes! The waterfront, with its

lively shipping, behind us, I noticed—as never before—how different
Tarragona is from Tallahassee; and saw, ever so clearly, the basis for
my feeling that, despite the unfailingly warm reception accorded to
me at El Inglés, I must always bear the stamp of "cousin from the
provinces." On circling the Plaza—to which the Hernando Inn lends
a rather more prosperous air—I had the impression of an earnest
attempt to reproduce the bare rudiments of civilized life in an aspiring
frontier outpost. Truly, Tarragona is Florida's harbor for the world's
discharge (and yet, as such, a less limiting province than Tallahassee).

Our home on Valencia Street, though not grand, is a little off
the beaten path and has the dignity of being among the best houses
hereabouts. The gate opened for our carriage, Nongka waiting within,
Zula and Ibo behind her, like proper servants in a receiving line—the
constraints of El Inglés, and of our journey, to which I had adapted so
readily as to be scarcely conscious of their grip, fell away as I threw
myself in laughter upon them; then Papa, with Nongka on his arm, and
I, with Ibo and Zula to either side of me, proceeded jauntily upstairs—
to a feast of boiled crabs, fruits, cakes, and an excellent Rhenish wine,
awaiting us around the blazing hearth of the library. Whatever manner
of thing the world outside the gates of this house, my home lies here
within it, and I eagerly await tomorrow. Already the perpetual holiday
of life at El Inglés recedes and dims, like infancy; for Nongka allows
nothing—not even Papa's business—to interfere with the vigor and
excitement of choring—kept to the service, as Ibo says, of the rhythm
and reach of things—

April 3rd, 1862—Tarragona has been placed under martial law and
daily grows emptier—munitions, men, and all else of any military value
having been gradually removed these past weeks. In February, the fort
was fired, along with the hospital, barracks, and other installations of
possible value to the Union side. Official eyes are reported to be falling
with suspicion on "certain lounging worthless persons, white as well
as black," suspected of harboring inimical designs. The gallows (we are
informed by circular) will be in frequent use henceforth.

Some weeks ago, learning through Jonathan's connections that our
house might be requisitioned for the Confederate cause, Nongka took
swift action—and it has turned out well for us that she did. Supported
by a letter from Captain Boullet—stating that, as political exiles, she
and her children had been offered sanctuary in his home on Valencia
Street—she presented herself with Ibo and Zula before Colonel Jones,
as unfortunate neutrals caught in hostilities of no interest to them;
they had, she averred—displaying Papa's letter (along with testimonials

of her conspicuous role in effecting the overthrow of General Soulouque, self-proclaimed Emperor of Hayti, and the restoration of the Republic)—been on the point of returning to their own country, when the War between the States broke out, and all egress was blocked; once safe passage could be assured, Captain Boullet was of course prepared to supply vessel and crew for transporting her family back to the Islands; meanwhile, the Union government having undertaken diplomatic negotiations with the Republic of Hayti—which there was reason to expect would shortly lead to long overdue recognition of her country's independence—the good gentlemen on the Confederate side could surely be relied on to refrain from interfering with the extension of hospitality, by one of their own, to free and independent Haytians, who were, in any case, without allegiances in the present conflict—all this in rapid-fire French, after a brief preface in carefully parsed English, to the effect that she had no choice but to employ her country's official tongue on an official diplomatic occasion. The Colonel endured her Gallic expostulations with the dignified silence of an officer and a gentleman, and, upon their cessation, turned to me for a rendering into English—which I provided to the best of my ability, while Nongka stood by with her foreigner's air of comprehending little or nothing of this barbarous interchange.

After some moments of astonished silence—during which the Colonel's eyes flitted uneasily back and forth between Nongka and myself—he requested me to oblige him with a private audience. Door firmly shut, he beckoned me to a settee and took a chair opposite. I explained that, while my position as hostess to political exiles of color, prolonged as it had been by the war, must needs be an embarrassment to one of Southern birth, I was nonetheless duty-bound to uphold my family's honor; personal allegiances notwithstanding—here I paused with a telling emphasis—my father, the Captain, had admonished me to preserve the neutrality of our home on Valencia Street during his absence, as befitted Florida's tradition of giving safe harbor to all in need. Perceiving that my words aroused little sympathy, I closed on a decidedly ominous note by confiding to him that Captain Boullet had warned against precipitating an international incident, the consequences of which might harm the Southern cause.

That evening, Colonel Jones posted a guard on our verandah, who, brandishing a rusty musket, relayed to all comers that, "any fooling with these foreign niggers could stir up trouble." Orders were to shoot on sight "any looking like they might be bent on precipitating international incidents." This went on about a fortnight, at which time—the Colonel having evidently judged our neutrality a matter of record, and no longer in need of fortification—since no guard was any longer mounted for us—our home once again became no man's land; nor has any soldier, of whom fewer and fewer are to be seen about town each day, so much as peeped through our fence. With martial law in effect—and the remnant force concentrated at the harbor—not a soul passes by the whole day long. We stay indoors, awaiting the final exodus—and what is certain to follow in its wake, at least for a time: the precarious freedom, Nongka says, of the abandoned and forgotten.

In the peace of this quiet about us, removed as we are from the war—and having undergone a long proof of my capacity and endurance under hostile, as well as joyful, circumstances—for, Nongka says the extremes of living, not sought out but imposed on us, are the key to our powers—I shall be allowed to enter the vodun sanctum tonight—our hounfor, in Nongka's Kreyòl—and there, we shall celebrate my lave-tête.

May 5, 1862—Only once, that instance being her agreement to oversee my education here in Tarragona, did Nongka allow Papa to impose his will upon her. The impending overthrow of General Soulouque (who had honored her with a second noble title after himself becoming Emperor Faustin I) made it convenient to absent herself from Hayti at that time. She intended to return to Hayti after restoration of the Republic there but Papa's importunities gave her no respite; and so she consented to stay in the house devised by her for my education until she—and only she—deemed it complete. I used to wish that Papa had brought them all to Tarragona when I was little so that Zula could grow up here with me—but I dismissed the thought for fear that, had they come earlier, she would not be as she now is—wiser and stronger in so many things than I, despite being nearly two years younger. With Zula, even Papa eases into repose. Ibo, being already a youth when she was born, looked to her with the unquestioning trust of one who loves in himself the child he is expected to put behind him; as she grew, so did the intimacy of their understanding—and this, I suppose, makes it only natural for him to place that same trust in me. Still, if all be told, I do envy them their early years together in Hayti, that gathering of a past not to be unsettled by others—

My past, Harding once said of herself, is an unsettled issue. So, I feel, is mine. But then, nobody's past reaches stability—a platitude young Frances Boullet seemed to resist. Still it's possible, as Harding and I do, to connect with another as if sharing a past, calling up a lost time for each other. In the dark luxury of an uninterrupted night on this balcony, the coming and going of her voice so accompanies my reading of the diary that each summons the other like taste and smell joined in perception of their object.

The primitive link between us has nothing to do with experience or knowledge, nor with beliefs or principles of behavior or social ties. It's an intellectual process of sorts—one as unlearned and involuntary as the workings of the autonomic nervous system. You find yourself forming a sort of imaginary *oikos,* a habitat that concretely unfolds, like an ambiance in which to locate yourself, what's desirable and undesirable in any situation—Harding calls these projections "world-visions." It's these world-visions that give our relationship its uncommon ease and naturalness. I've been at it for as long as I can remember, though with no particular consciousness of what I was doing till I met Harding, whose capacity for world-visions was so well-developed it seemed uniquely hers. Formed under the force of feeling, world-visions orient you in the moment by bringing into view vividly—almost palpably—the future or past you're projecting. Harding refers to this as a "self-world" laying out the temporal geography she's moving in. Hers is the talk of time passing and the distances it marks off.

She lives in her self-world, and I in mine, the way an animal inhabits its territory. Except that ours is a human terrain with a flowchart revealing its nonspatial dimension. They're never wrong, these world-visions, despite always undergoing modification. The world projected may have a falsity in it—a distortion or ugliness that some new·act or thought may correct—but what's never wrong, never false for either of us, is the sense of existing within its bounds. She as herself, I as myself. And so we've come to suspect that in the concrete ambiance of world-visions you enter the only area of fundamental certainties human beings can experience first hand (rather than merely embrace through faith or tradition, or affirm by reasoned effort).

For all I know others also spin them out, but they don't seem, like Harding and me, to depend on them so habitually. They look "into" themselves for the source of knowledge about how to act, how to live. They undergo analysis or work on self-development, self-realization, self-construction, a socially constructed self—even, still, "my real self." Harding and I always look to the world. Not to others, not to the unities arising from "only connect," but to that larger, more extended dimension of a fictional self that orients bodily movement. From there, you can see what it is you want and do not want.

You'd think, with access to such rock-bottom certitude, Harding could simply have consulted her world-visions *before* entering into her affair with the Boullet House. But that misses the point—we're not visionaries of personal life in the prophetic sense. Our scenarios don't rest on prescience but entirely on projection of a world immediately present for our action—a world-vision reveals a possible play of desire merely. Past experience marks off limits and shades the range of that world, but the Boullet House had promised an experience so different from the usual infatuation, you see . . .

June 16, 1862—The St. Mark's Lighthouse, scene of childhood outings with my cousins at El Inglés, was shelled and fired yesterday—
March 30, 1863—How happily the days pass! Union troops have evacuated Tarragona, not a year since the surrender—a ghost of a town then, and so it is again. We are among the fewer than one hundred—thirty, maybe forty?—souls left behind, nearly all women and children. Papa maintains that there is no safer place in the South for the duration of this war than Tarragona; we live well, nay sumptuously, on his provisions, even to the latest publications from Europe. We are not to let it be known that he is in Cuba—"the mouse, Fan, plays in the world's beautiful trading crossroad, while the lion beards himself in his own den"—his message of safe arrival delivered by courier not long after he left us.

Ibo, too, is absent for days at a time—once home, he regales us with anecdotes of what he has seen and heard abroad. He and Jonathan keep Papa apprised of the deployments of both Unionists and Confederates—they boast that Papa, by splitting his cargo among small vessels designed expressly for swift movement, can run whatever he wishes through the blockade. The Unionists have their suspicions, but, as he so conveniently (and dependably) supplies them with necessities—food, ammunitions, clothing, medicines (Zula and I pass the early evening hours preparing all manner of packets, tinctures, salves, tonics, and poultices, under Nongka's direction)—they look the other way; indeed, both sides have too great an interest in his fleet to inspect cargoes, or inquire about their destinations. Nightly, we are all busy devising a machine to be used for so quieting Union distrust of Papa that he can move like one of their own through the blockade.

I daresay we may grow rich if this war continues long enough, but there is no time for idling. The hours of gardening lengthen daily, and, still, we are able to grow only a fraction of what is needed, much of it used for our weed salves. Papa keeps calling for more paregoric elixir and morphine. Once each week, we wheel our remedies to the harbor, where Jonathan boats them, and conveys materials to us for opium tinctures. More than ever, the war centers our days on the right ordering of life—balancing the work of alleviating suffering with the play of beauty's creation. We hold these—the only poles of action that stand the test of time, Nongka says—in tension in our own lives; and, as the war demands, work with Jonathan and Ibo, under Papa's direction, to bring what we can to others.

Strangely, it is Ibo who, of us all, frets most under the pull of this tension—Ibo, who once seemed the very spirit of careless freedom, and now, cannot remove himself from the pain he sees all around him, and the urgent need to relieve it—

19th November, 1863—Success! Two of Papa's ships having been caught behind the Union blockade, our storm machine was put to its ultimate test last night. A nimble vessel (manned by Papa and Ibo and a crew of three) was launched into darkness—and with a life-or-death air of urgency, steered among the six blockading ships, with dire reports of its own narrow escape from a tempest of unimaginable ferocity—such as had never before been witnessed!—that approached in a cloud of blackness with the roaring voice of a cyclone! Scarcely had Papa cried out to the captain of each ship, and implored the last to take him aboard, when there appeared just such a terrible dark cloud, and just such a shrieking wind as he had described. All six ships set about, at full speed, to move out of the storm's path, but one failed to escape—as the cloud approached, towers of water broke over her decks and men were swept overboard and tossed about by great roiling waves. They were to report later that a whirlwind from hell had enveloped their vessel and exploded over them with a force so tremendous it blew them out to sea.

Nongka had planned and organized all. As winter passed into earliest spring, Zula was already designing machinery that could rhythmically spew volumes of water some sixty feet into the air— thereby simulating a tidal wave—as well as a device for expelling smoke to disguise the source of the upheaval; meanwhile, Nongka herself, with Ibo, began building a great set of pipes and bellows for emitting sounds such as occur naturally in storms throughout the Caribbean and Florida seas. The secret, she maintains, lies in perfecting one's knowledge of perceptual differences, from large to minute, within our immediate surroundings—in the case of the storm machine, success would depend upon mastery of aural discrimination. My part was to train myself to listen—listen in a special way, for every shading of difference in sound—thus helping to perfect our device. For weeks on end, I did nothing but hone my hearing, as Nongka made patterns by sorting and mingling a vast palette of sound variations—in which all discord was scrupulously aligned to our purpose—then composed these patterns into sequences of repetition, always with me saying back to her precisely what my ears perceived. Ibo learned to play her composition on the pipes with faultless hand-and-foot coordination; his virtuoso performance—of necessity muted—clearly sounded the initial unison of winds breaking apart as the east wind split off and, circled by the north wind, rushed toward the southwest wind, furiously menacing, while the south wind danced tauntingly apart from the others, then roared just as unexpectedly back into their midst. "Maintenant!" Nongka cried ecstatically, facing Ibo, "Tout ensemble!" Here Ibo's body seemed to spring into motion at an all-defying speed, leaping from pedal to pedal, pulling and pushing faster than eyes could follow, as the winds surged in a shrieking alliance of destruction.

It was a vessel rigged with such water-spewing, smoke-belching, tempest-tossed machinery that bore down on the easternmost of the blockading Union ships, sinking it in a matter of minutes—then menacing the other five, which made their way to safety, upon the instant, at this horrific display of nature's violence inhabiting the Florida night. From his asylum, Papa looked on with captain and crew as the terrible black cloud seemed to draw their companion vessel to its doom, and, with the unpredictability of a wild force, rolled slowly out to sea. (Meanwhile, two small craft in Papa's fleet were already unloading a cache of supplies from Europe and the Union for Confederate sympathizers.)

"Quel triomphe!" Papa exclaimed, upon concluding his tale of this latest exploit—"the key, you see, is timing, and the timing, it was perfect! Even Louis the Last would concede as much." My grandfather Louis—of whom grand'maman, an avid storyteller otherwise, rarely spoke, and then with the formality of one keeping to herself the better part of an intimacy concerning only herself and the dead.

All doubts about Papa's loyalty to the Union have been dispelled; he is credited with wresting the blockade from the jaws of ruin—Papa has become its savior!

May 3, 1935—He was born to be a hero, I suppose. Even in death, he couldn't elude his fate. What was different about Papa—different from his Boullet ancestors—was not that he enjoyed being a hero—everything points to the conclusion they all did—but that he enjoyed being one under the conviction that he was not one. In his own eyes he was a failure. And if much of what he did was intended to conceal, and to transform, what he took as the fact of his failure, he steadfastly recognized and accepted it. How desperately he must have longed for failure! And never any way to satisfy his longing—he couldn't be merely a failed man, and thus one among his fellows, but must always be a tragic failure.

November 25, 1863—On the rare occasions when they are both here with us, as they have been these past days, Papa and Jonathan carry on their running dialogue—what is best for trade?—Jonathan holding that war is an unparalleled stimulus, and Papa that his is a young man's view—experience shows that, over time, the risks of war offset its possible short-term advantages. His favorite store of examples is the Boullet lore, to which he alludes as casually, and regularly, as other people advert to the weather. I first heard the tales from grand'maman, whose method for teaching me to compose in French was to go on at length about one or another of Papa's ancestors, then instruct me to write out a coherent and, above all, accurate "histoire" as my devoir of the day. With this, she would invariably find fault: "Chouchou, you cannot embroider as you please—you must write down only what I say—exactement—what actually happened! The way to listen is with the ears, child!" And I would heed her—obedient girl that I was, wishing to please those I loved, I learned my lesson well.

I do not know whether the histoire I am moved to commence writing today, under Nongka's tutelage—the tale of the first of Papa's ancestors to reach these shores—would please you, grand'maman. The ears hear differently at a distance.

How the Line Began
or,
A Chronicle of Early America

Once, in the long ago, when this land had only lately assumed the name "Florida" (though not in the tongues of its native population, whom history would quickly teach how ungentle were the donors of that gentle name), there sailed into the mouth of a great river a party of French Huguenots, under Jean Ribaut, seeking to found a colony and refuge. The year, to be precise, was 1562, and the river—wild, placid, majestical—was the St. Johns, which the French named "rivière de mai," because it was on the first of that month they sighted it. Among them was a young man who, if not wholly unmindful of things spiritual, understood only too well (as events would prove) how worldly affairs bend not to the pure of heart but to the keen of eye and quick of hand. This nameless man is known to us only as the progenitor of the Boullet line in the New World: the First Boullet.

The chief of the Timucuans, at that time, was called Saturiba; and this Chief being favorably inclined to trade, our enterprising Ancestor parted ways with his compatriots when they continued north. He was found, two years later, by René de Laudonnière and his French colonists, come to raise Fort Caroline, near the mouth of the St. Johns—a lone European among aborigines, at home in their savage customs and language. Success seemed assured by his new role as interpreter and go-between; but history intervened in the shape of Spaniards from St. Augustine, who, finding Fort Caroline poorly manned (Ribaut's reinforcements having, meanwhile, been shipwrecked in a storm) attacked it, slaughtered the Huguenots, and hung over them this sign: "I do this not as to Frenchmen but as to heretics."

By some unrecorded tilt of fortune, the Ancestor was among a very few—some say no more than five—who escaped the massacre and sailed back to France, where an expedition under Dominique de Gourgues promptly sought him out to act as their envoy to the Indians. With Saturiba's aid, the French attacked Fort San Mateo, formerly Caroline, hanged its Spanish garrison and sailed away; but not before our Boullet survivor burned this message on the trees from which the Spanish corpses swung: "Done not as to Spaniards but as to liars, thieves, and murderers"—clear proof of how a man's character acquires gravity through shaping, and being shaped by, the times.

Taking stock of his adventures in the New World, the First Boullet perceived that he was now in a position to render some service to his country, while simultaneously advancing his own interests. Trade, he counseled, could be rendered more efficient—and immeasurably more profitable—by leaving the accumulation and loading of goods in the New World to the Spaniards, then lying in wait for their galleons, relieving these of their cargoes—chiefly gold, gems, and silver—and conveying them to the Old World, with no inconsiderable prospects of further trading. The scheme's bold simplicity found willing purses in the home country. Accordingly, with eighteen of his compatriots, pledges of financial backing, and a woman from a Florida settlement, heavy with his first child, he established a rapidly growing population of corsairs on La Tortue, off the coast of Hispaniola. These Boullet traders—bound into a community of like kind and interests by the rule requiring plunder to be shared among all—now plied their skills in launching a fleet whose capacity for ensemble action in the apprehension, loading, and transport of pirated goods was without equal. Each vessel—some small enough to be manned by a single hand—was devised with an eye to doing only what it could do best; none was expected to perform tasks at a distance from its fellows; and all were built to make concealment, when expedient, both swift and sure. This motley fleet, its small craft housed within larger ones, lay hidden in Florida's Gulf, awaiting the home-bound galleons (with their New World cargo of bullion and gems), which, once sighted, were swarmed by the Boullet fleet in elaborate stratagems of distraction and seizure—the great armed ships lured into false chase and battle, while those bearing cargo were plundered almost before the alarm could be sounded.

But the Boullet woman, having borne sixteen sons and daughters in fourteen years, was dissatisfied; two of her offspring perished in raids, and although she could still bear more, and did, something about the fleet's modus operandi seemed amiss. She said as much to her spouse, who, preoccupied with the quotidian management of a rapidly growing maritime commercial venture, was inclined to leave strategic concerns to his brooding better half. Caution became her watchword, tactical foresight her guide. The Boullet traders, she recognized, had been childish in their single-mindedness: attending exclusively to superior mobility, they had all but ignored a fundamental requisite of success, namely, the mastery of routes. To correct this deficiency, she set experienced navigators to the task of mapping out all shipping in the region, together with winds and currents (a task expedited by absconding nautical charts and logs from the Spaniards). Understanding that superior mobility at sea must be joined to the same advantages on land, the Boullet woman proceeded to devise amphibious tactics which eventually thrust her into fame throughout New Spain.

Meanwhile, convinced that none were worthy of trust but her own flesh and blood, she had a craft fashioned, solely for observation—and christened "Elle"—in whose stern was a circular stair narrowing, at the top, to a seat made to swivel 360 degrees, on which mobile lookout the woman planted herself. Always with child, she reposed her youngest in the arms of her eldest on the bottommost step, while the rest crowded between. From her high seat, she gave staccato orders to a select crew charged with maneuvering the vessel precisely as instructed—not an instant too late and not a span too far; and from here, she supplied her offspring with a running commentary on transactions over booty within view, which pedagogy of experience would inculcate a knowledge of survival understood as the life of the trading unit.

The culmination of the Boullet woman's career was a three-pronged attack by land and sea, a feat that depended critically upon knowledge of the watercourses of Nicaragua, its many rivers and great inland lake. Her scheme called for a part of the Boullet fleet to be dismantled and transported from the shore of the Great Northern Sea to the Great Southern Sea, whence it would sail up the coast to the Gulf of California, there to lie in wait for galleons from Manila. Their fleet anchored and hidden, the men would join a contingent of their swiftest vessels stowed in the Gulf of Mexico, watch for galleons approaching Vera Cruz from Nombre de Dios, relieve them of gold and silver mined by the Incas, cache their takings, and proceed overland to their ships in the Gulf of California to capture the Far Eastern cargoes of porcelains, brocades, and Oriental silks; these treasures, transferred to a party of men waiting with mules, would then be hauled to the Nicaragua River, where nimble vessels, designed to convey precious cargo along waterways to the North Sea, and home to La Tortue, lay moored.

The enterprise entailed such numbers that the majority of La Tortue's corsairs were needed to carry it out. Boldness, swift movement, surprise (the Manila galleons had never before come under attack by small craft on the Pacific coast), brilliance of planning and organization—add to these a boundless patience (the arrival of the galleons being impossible to time, those lying in wait might continue so for many months)—such qualities, exacted from all under her command, proved crucial to the woman's daring scheme. The third prong was the riskiest. The Boullet corsairs must sail down the west coast to the Isthmus of Panama and intercept a heavily guarded cargo of gold and silver being transported by mule to the east coast. It was here that the First Boullet was killed in a skirmish with the Spaniards. Among the crew were all the Boullet children above ten years old (including, at the woman's behest, her daughters); seeing their father killed, they promptly took charge with the unquestioning fearlessness of children, the oldest of whom was but seventeen years of age.

Resounding success established the Boullet woman as uncontested Queen of a growing empire of privateers. Living in great splendor, she and her young came to accept the spoils of trade casually, like daily bread. As much from a desire to dazzle their mother as from youthful high spirits, the Boullet offspring began making raids on their own initiative, bringing them to conclusion with such unerring finesse that the woman openly boasted of having borne a race of minds all functioning exactly like her own.

The downfall of this familial trading unit followed directly from its triumphs. It happened that the Boullet woman expressed displeasure, one day, at the quality of gems taken in the latest raid. To vindicate themselves—and add even more lustre to the family name—the most ambitious of her children plotted a lightning attack in complete secret; scattering Spaniards to all four winds, they brought home a glittering hoard finer than any that had ever been seen in the New World. In the midst of celebrating their exploit—regaling their mother with Epicurean dishes and baskets of emeralds, rubies, and pearls—they were treasonously attacked by members of their own crew under the captaincy of an English buccaneer, leader of a recent influx on La Tortue, who charged the Boullet faction with violating the custom of distributing booty equitably among all.

May 29, 1935—If possessions chart the circulation of power, history's substance, then the acid of power etches in time the status of all that is, one etching after another, each thing's official existence defined by where it hangs in the museum of the moment—nation or individual, from beginning (am I not Captain Boullet's daughter and the fairest of the Howard cousins?) to end (soon now, the tryst of self-possession with its enemy). As history's subjects, we are already both horse and rider, power-possessed possessions.

And there lies the problem; not in the slipperiness of facts or the incompleteness of records or the inevitability of bias. No, the problem of history is the force, never summoned and always present, of possessions. Land or lover, name or nature, car or culture, person or place, home or hoax—if ours, it becomes a possession in the dual sense:

we claim it and it claims us in slavery's symbiosis. Tales of possessions
given to us as our due, possessions we are privileged to receive and
call "history"—these come to possess us on and on through time.
(How they function as a prerogative in the lives of cultivated men is
not even now adequately appreciated.) What Zula and I make here is a
very monument to history, one that would deny history its power but
affirm time. This home of denial drawn about us like an old serviceable
cloak, we live in joy. Such a home I prepare to leave forever rather
than be put to the knife of undenied power.

How now, even as history digs our grave, to talk to the Silence
framed there, waiting? Say, "I'm on Your side, Death, I rage not against
You but against the history that only You can end, and not against
life but against its enslavement to history and vice versa?" Or else, in
half-elegy, half-epos recite over and over how power, however paltry
and of whatever kind, accumulates—how an ever-rousing spring gushes
from the primordial thrill of the ultimate crisis? Better yet, why not
talk the truth-telling language of concession? Airy flights and mincing
steps, twisted windings and ever-shifting camouflage, hands shaping
whatever they touch into my own agonistic likeness, the lifts in a pas
de deux defying gravity and the proneness of the body succumbing to
its earthiness in the repetitive ritualistic teasing of another blink of
time, another hair of space, out of death's hold. This, my exploratory,
organic accumulation of power's modes—knowledge, riches, strength,
love, and their contraries: ignorance, etc., and so on ad infinitum et
nauseam—the true-story tale of life to be enjoyed only in a home such
as ours, ensuring in the round of the clock ticking that I claim no
power and that none claims me, neither in the passing Now nor the
coming one—here, where the cock always crows, Friend Death.

You, Friend, who have no history, are the future I welcome in the
closure of my official existence, whose remains I leave to be disposed of
by history.

Chronicle (continued)—As it was plainly the case that they
were all about to die, the Boullet woman made a sporting proposal
to their attackers. "Give me three of my children," she said, "and
let us go. Wait a quarter of an hour. The night is clear, the sea
calm; if you catch us, you shall hear my scheme for taking more
cargo than is carried by the entire Spanish fleet. Afterwards,
you can kill us." She then selected the loveliest of her daughters,
sixteen years old, as well as a strapping youth of eighteen, and
her youngest, a lad not yet ten, and looked on as her other
children were slaughtered. Their captors, in a jolly mood, escorted

the woman and her chosen three to a vessel, helped them cast off, and cheered wildly when she shouted, "catch us if you can!" After ten minutes, she directed her daughter to sail back to the waiting men, while she and her two sons—stripped naked—began the long swim to Hispaniola. Found by Spaniards on a beach next morning, she gave out that they were French Catholics come to save the souls of Indians; Huguenot privateers had attacked them in the straits of Florida, and cast them overboard to drown. The Spaniards expressing disbelief, she offered them her elder son as a hostage until such time as her tale could be verified. In this wise, the Boullet woman gained passage for herself and the lad to St. Augustine, where she promptly told something like the truth to the friar from whom she sought sanctuary, thus saving an only child—the strongest, albeit the youngest of them all.

May 31, 1935—Not an iota of my rage has diminished. Age may attenuate the skeleton that props this body up, but not much else. Age abstracts from the blood-flow and the diffuseness of life's yearnings and brings their distillates to the surface, no more meanings to be sifted or facts to be ascertained, all the endless formation of intangible and invisible hazes under the sweep of a befuddling light, and I—always a lone image of humankind, writhing hopelessly through haze and light to escape understanding, sunk into the whirl of absurdly unequal struggle, or plunged eroticized into the thrill and risk of twisting roller coasters, yielding to the clutch of infantile delight in swift and unpredictable motion and mistaking it for proof of a head-on encounter with hard reality, evidence of a purely personal power—I, sickened beyond all measure, knowing I bear (without strength or reason) what cannot be borne and ought not be borne, revealing thereby the godly in the human and despising it to the depths of my non-existent soul! With an effort amounting to no more than the flick of an eye I could step into the old frame, the past that is mine now.

But it would take an effort, if infinitesimal, to take that step back. The spirit rides me now with a light loose hold and I can scarcely refrain from paeans of gratitude that I am where I am, while death crouches and waits, courteous, undemanding, dutiful, the friend always at hand, as unsentimental and unintrusive as a cup of water.

Rage on Maria-Louisa, rage on.

If, during work hours, Harding was a thing existing more brazenly than others and therefore never escaping notice, by day's end, after the professionals fled to greener pastures, she became merely another existing thing—this, generally, being her preferred mode of living. Bent over baseboards, cupping out plaster leavings with bare hands (work gloves too full of rips by then to do any good), ignoring insect husks, mouse skeletons, moldering bits and pieces beyond identification—so mesmerized, at last, by a catlike cadaver, hide stretched over bone and strangely elongated as though by hanging, that her sense of herself as human and other seemed to dissolve in the accumulated heat of yet another lost day. Eyeless, owning nothing, living nowhere, humping in corners harboring lumps of multi-mattered past so sticky they had to be plucked away with an old pair of tweezers and, when those gave out, with fingernails—so much for the epiphanies of passion.

Proposition: On the dunghill of passion dung is the only sustenance, mindlessness the only bliss. Hadn't she been famed among family and friends, since childhood, for sheer endurance? A workhorse, but one that never went out to pasture.

Gutting over, the house stood buried in its own viscera, the restoration at a standstill. "I sure would like to get the plumbing roughed in next week, Mr. Evans, while the roof's going up," said with the smile he always waited for. Tom Evans of Evans & Son, Plumbers; salt of the earth, everybody said so the minute his name was mentioned.

"Just dropping by to check on you, young lady, make sure you're not in any trouble. No point getting ahead of yourself," as he squeezed her arm, looking sorrowfully at the mess. Nongka's voice came back to Harding in the context of danger she always sensed under the animal eye of paternalistic vision: "Take care, my children, take care."

No roof about to go up either—and without a roof, no electrical wiring, no sheetrockers. And so on down to carpenters and painters. None of them had a truck for hauling and nobody knew anyone who did. By midafternoon, Martin Kingston, Krasner's West Indian helper, pulled off with his final load from the stripped roof across the street—Randall Cane's property. Not the least interest in trucking her junk away over the long holiday weekend, not at any price. What, on Independence Day?

Outbound traffic on Cadiz Boulevard surged to a roar—on to the suburbs, the beaches—then slowed almost to silence. Old dead-white derelicts came stumbling along the alley from their rooms at the Hernando rented by the week or the month. Sketchbook under one arm, Jake Landry (another one just dropping by), sidled off after ranting about this and that in the old Quarter and boasting how the Canes and the Howards before them, way back in Injun days, had always relied on his folks, the Landrys—starting with Grandpa Jacob, rest his soul, who'd worked up to, he bet, three or four hunnerd head in his day over on the old Howard plantation. Affirming Semiramian intimacy with her—like having an unsavory family member rattling old skeletons.

In the muted light of the doorway, sun sliding out of sight, Harding picked deeply buried splinters out of her puffy hands. Pulled at her coarse hair, ratty as old furniture stuffing. The daily grind of her passion had worn through sweet affirmation to the keening yes of resignation. No longer the breathless yes-yes of surrender.

A paper-thin phantom of a fighter plane soundlessly approached vanishing point in the azure-blue dome of the sky, as if to demonstrate the off-limits of the local air base. And overhead, a string of white ibis pointing down-turned bills toward their nightly perch on Segovia Crescent, where generations of Canes, all the way back to the Judge and Cousin Lucy of El Inglés, lived in waterfront seclusion.

March 14, 1865—I had thought to get through this war untouched by personal loss. Among the aging men and boys left to defend Tallahassee Uncle Edward took his stand; and Jonathan, loyalty to the Howards overcoming all other considerations, fought by his side at the Natural Bridge but failed to save him. Aunt Virginia writes that both "acquitted themselves with all the courage and honor of Confederate gentlemen." We are much relieved that Jonathan suffered only a minor arm wound; he now takes his place as protector of the Howard belles and their property.

December 8th, 1865—"When you need to see, do not go where all is the same—there you see nothing, and for that you're not yet ready—" thus said Nongka, examining one of Zula's pencil sketches. These mornings—Papa away on business, Ibo already out among the people—we rise early to marshal time into the day's chores; then late in the morning, coffee, with books and paper and conversation—Zula forever drawing, I forever writing. Afternoons, when dusk settles early on the town, the lights of ships making for harbor beckon at a mournful distance, as if confirming the last leg of their journey, the homecoming, to be the least assured; we often work late into the night,

the call for our potions now even more urgent since the war's end—
but the mornings come always on this long, slow swell of excitement
akin to discovery, a paring down of life to its daily return of joy.

Zula looks up from her sketches of Nongka—Nongka warming her
hands at the fire, Nongka pensively stirring her coffee, Nongka seated
at the library table inspecting these very sketches.

"But where there is little difference, isn't there much sameness?"

"I'm talking about seeing, Zula, seeing —what you see is only
difference, however small, not a big sameness."

"Even if a thing could be repeated in exactly the same way," I
venture, "you can't copy time—it would be at least the second time
around, not the first, and that would make the difference. No moment
of time can be duplicated." Time has been much on my mind of
late, another birthday having just passed. Twenty: a round sobering
number.

"Then," says Zula, undaunted and quite unperturbed, "I'll mix the
colors of time to create sameness—I'll paint past the differences."

"Alchemy, Zula, alchemy."

Zula falls silently to her drawing—Nongka and I talk of politics,
war's surrogate, and of the multifarious stratagems by which nations
and persons attempt to perpetuate themselves; and as is often the
case, whenever we speak of such things, we come back to Papa's
ancestors—"the Fathers," Zula called them once, and the name has
fastened to them like skin.

"When you unexpectedly glimpse yourself in a glass," I say, "it is
as if the features were not yours—momentarily, you don't recognize
yourself. That is how the tales of the Fathers are for me—I'm like a
stranger blocking out my own image—but, in Papa's eyes, they end in
himself, along with whatever wisdom or folly accrues in them."

"Because," Nongka agrees, "in his eyes, the real world and its
actions flow from the tales—whereas for you, tales are what it all
comes to."

"Telling the past makes a real presence of it, lets it lodge and live
inside us—"

"And stiffen and die," she finishes, collecting our empty cups on
a tray— "after a time," glancing at me, "you grasp how not to tell a
thing"—to which Zula adds, "and how not to go where that hearing
would take you."

I hasten to write it all down. Nongka has shown us how to hold
hearings for the love of it—the body trained to oppose the signings
and sayings that move it away from itself. How slow mine has been

to learn, as though teaching itself, after a crippling accident, to walk again, step by unnatural step.

June 2, 1935—Composing the past by cut and burn obliges immediate recognition of what begs for restoration to a lasting moment. As those deceptive simplicities—tap-taps long ago on window or wall—burn, I carefully paste what does not matter into this final volume wherein its distance from my person can be heard. Mine is a memoir of the fulsome play of stories and images teeming at life's end.

    Chronicle of the Fathers (continued)—The Second Boullet, Christian name unknown, was even more prolific than his sire (he who perished on the Isthmus of Panama with offspring looking on). He proved himself the true heir of his mother, former Queen of Privateers and mistress of strategy. In middle age, he took five wives, on whom it is said he fathered thirty-four sons and daughters—a state of affairs owing as much, one supposes, to his vision of the human panorama—which, though it might extend its horizon by the daring of a few, drew its lifeblood from the many— as to the irresistible promptings of Nature. Grown to manhood in the Franciscan mission at St. Augustine where, at his mother's prodding (here history has finished with the Boullet woman) he mastered the Spanish and Timucuan languages, he became a kind of self-appointed messenger for the Florida missions, welcomed by all and moving freely amongst them. To the siting of new missions he devoted all his ingenuity and care, the missions being, for him, extensions of his own capacity for unhampered movement. Schooled from infancy in the strategic arts, and seeing the possibilities of missions as Indian forts, he allied himself with Timucuan chieftains in a revolt; which revolt coming to naught, he was betrayed by the Apalachee to the Spanish, by whom he was summarily shot.

    And what of his wives with their burgeoning charges? Them he left scattered at strategic distances from one another throughout the spreading missions.

Philippe

    Undaunted—if anything, spurred—by this turn of events (nota bene: suffering actuates), the oldest son, Philippe Boullet, assumed guardianship over the five groups of siblings, oblates one and all. In emulation of the paternal method—and in revenge on the Spaniards who had murdered his father—Philippe devoted himself to ever-expanding proliferation of missions, whose territorial domains he regarded as the Boullet progeny's rightful legacy.

A perspicuous, almost uncanny, grasp of circumstance so often met with in men of ambition led him to establish his headquarters at Charleston, a thriving settlement in the last decades of the seventeenth century; there, he ingratiated himself with the English and created a network of alliances with the Indians of North Florida for purposes of trade. Success seemed assured when he stumbled on a remnant of the old Boullet privateering empire in the Islands (where the family name was legend), which had operated under the leadership, tenuously maintained until her death, of his Aunt, that lovely eldest daughter of the First Boullet who had (through stratagems not to be imagined) escaped massacre after all. Philippe set out to coordinate richly profitable maritime raids by these island-based privateers, with attacks on the Spanish missions by Indians bearing English firearms. In 1702, when South Carolina's Governor Moore invaded Florida and laid siege to St. Augustine, Philippe was able to swell the Governor's ranks with no fewer than one thousand Creek warriors. As the Carolinians withdrew, they fired as much of the old town as they could, including the wooden Friary, leaving the Franciscans to squat in hastily built straw shelters in the streets among other survivors.

Spanish Florida—the Boullet half-brothers and sisters living here and there throughout its missions believed—was about to be theirs. Heartened by this same faith, and having tutored his oldest son Raoul (a mere youth, who fought manfully at his side) to take his place in furtherance of the family enterprise, Philippe Boullet, too, met a precipitate bloody end.

Raoul the Twice-Born

Thanks to young Raoul's brilliant coordination of Indians, Boullet pirates, and les Anglais, the remaining Spanish missions were soon destroyed; but now, seeing the only home—and the only world—they had ever known in ruins about them, the Boullet offspring grew dispirited: the very realm they were to possess having been razed in the attempt, such devastation must be God's judgment on dynastic ambition. As an unforeseen corollary of the ancestral design, they had become more Franciscan than the Franciscans; thus, by way of penance, they dedicated themselves to the construction of a new stone friary at St. Augustine—the same for which the English later found a new use expressed in its name: "St. Francis Barracks."

All but the doughty Raoul. Embittered by the double loss of legacy and sibling loyalty, he journeyed—tout seul—to New Orleans, there to renew connections with others of French allegiance, and strengthen these with a French consort. Accordingly, when Austria, Holland, and France joined in the war against Spain, he followed Le Moyne and Bienville to Tarragona: a rough settlement, already old in those days, of palmetto huts behind a wooden Spanish fort overlooking—across its magnificent Bay—that blaze of white sand which lured the first conquistadors to their doom. When Tarragona reverted to Spain by treaty, Raoul Boullet, unlike most of his compatriots, did not give up his claims there; instead, he sent to New Orleans for possessions and wife, and stayed on. The pious siblings' betrayal of the Boullet destiny had left its mark on him, the marriage (by all accounts satisfactory) producing an only child.

In the skirmishes of the period, when possession of Tarragona passed dizzingly back and forth between the Spanish and French, the latter burned all but two or three of its dwellings to the ground, leaving what remained of the inhabitants to the fury of Indian tomahawks. The conflagration of Tarragona was Raoul's *sursum corda*: what his meek mission-bred kinfolk saw as divine retribution, he grasped as opportunity. Tarragona in ashes— reduced to a bare site for a town—became, for him, the soil of all his ancestral hopes, clear ground for reaping the riches of what a Spaniard, nearly a half century before, had praised as "the best harbor I have yet beheld." Was he not, now, in an ideal position to take advantage of the contest of nations through his own vibrant attunement to it? Tarragona thus became a laboratory for proving his schemes, through the slow circumspection of a man of science: the play of power in the New World was to be experienced, observed, and turned to good account, much as the elements of matter may be studied and put to use. Calculation and patience were Raoul's method; wars—Jenkins Ear, King George's War in America—and Indian intermediaries his opportune instruments.

Chronicle (continued)—When the balance of power was tested once more in the French and Indian War, Raoul—having established trade relations with the French to one side of him, and the English to the other—was prepared to accept either side as victor. Still, he must have been gratified when victory fell to the English. Had he not made a point of warning them of the dangers to be met with in Florida?—the difficulty of access to fresh water; the risk of maintaining settlements without ample reserves of food;

the seasons of heavy rain, and the hurricanes and other storms even more violent; the long coast's vulnerability to piratical raids; the threat of dysentery; the ever-present menace of Indian hostiles to be placated only with continual gifts? The perils of the land were legion, and well he knew how to paint and enumerate them. And, when the English arrived at the start of hurricane season to take possession of their American prize—and their exploring parties brought back tales of harassment by savage natives—Raoul's alarms became fact; henceforth, the English authorities found his knowledge of Florida indispensable to their dominion. (The predictability with which epidemics of dysentery on the high seas followed the outfitting of ships from Tarragona, and only from there, escaped notice.) Their patience sorely tried by the "Florida problem," a number of small settlements and negligible forts were gladly relinquished to their man, Raoul Boullet, it being understood that he was to maintain them as trading posts for English goods. This he did, with the result that increasingly lucrative trade among these posts proceeded with little impediment on through the eighteenth century. On his deathbed, Raoul bequeathed to his only son, my Grandfather Louis Joseph Boullet—known as Louis the Last—what he believed to be the articles of his success, repeated to my father by his:

1) Never tell your business to anyone. Wear the wrap of success at all times, but style the drop of it, and never allow signs of weakness or failure to outweigh signs of strength.

2) To increase success, augment the range of your movements, and remember that your base must both protect your movements and facilitate them.

3) Negotiation is the enemy of freedom; freedom of movement is won only in victories over negotiation, never by means of negotiation.

In sum: Know your enemy, Stake out your Place, and Move without interference.

June 10, 1935—Ah, but Raoul, knowing your enemy matters only when the goal is victory; but if you consider that the scramble for victory not only vitalizes the opposition and converges on false enemies but may itself be hostile to our interests, what then? Surely, no trope erects more barricades against reality than warfare. You seek strategic locations, places that insure invulnerability, even for battles so small as to be negligible. Always you go into action with this prospect—and here lies the confusion spread by war without its tropological antithesis. None of life's activities that I know of—except war—require such protection of vulnerability when the question is considered practically. Do not all our doings pull us to those very chinks in the fortress of our invulnerability that propel us into the open—the unlimited? And from that deep the delights of this place framed in horror make their chamber of love. But the Boullet formula always rouses a guiding purpose for many and Louis the Last attributed his success to it.

November 2, 1873—To whom, dear Papa, did your dying lips whisper the formula of which Raoul's life was the testament? It tells nothing either of the price of success or its reward, the price being life's energy and the reward death.

December 5th, 1873—Papa was a child of Louis' senescence, come into the world when he was nearing seventy years of age. If he alluded easily to the early Boullet Fathers—now with pride, now with some mischievous caveat—when he spoke of Louis, it was as though to ponder some lingering paradox. The disparity between the power of the old man's knowledge and the weakness of his declining flesh would not be reconciled; to his boy's eyes, the body of this father whom he adored was a failing body. His presence, being one of assured success, belonged not to his flesh and blood, but to some other body—unknown and unknowable, a mystery truly his.

Louis died when Papa was twelve, an ancient remembered in his coffin as fragile and unguarded. "Old Louis," Papa would say pensively, "he really was the last somehow, the last of the kind who live with certitude. Not because he had all the answers, but because he knew— sans réfléchir, tu comprends? He knew where he was going and how to arrive there."

June 20, 1935—Ah Papa, how deeply and distantly I loved you, and do so still. How knowingly—a love which would not touch or charm you, but neither would it bind you. A harder love, this.

Harding was thinking of taking off a few minutes to finish reading the Chronicles of the Boullet Fathers in the sanctuary, when her roofer, Tony Krasner, turned up. She'd lingered over breakfast on the cracked stone garden seat by the fence on Doc Shibbles's side, back resolutely turned to the wreckage, browsing the remainder of the morning *Sentinel*. Piecemeal unfoldings of the local drama overlooked on first reading. Founders' Day Committee in disagreement about what to call their annual antique auction benefit; rash of downtown break-ins and knifings in Segovia Villas, the work of an "alarming new criminal element in the community"; local chapter of Ku Klux Klan making arrangements to rent the Community College's auditorium for a "teach-in" in late August.

"Hiding out, are we?" Krasner leaned over her from behind and wiped his damp forehead with a dark, muscular arm above her head. Swirls of smoke. "This, I'll have you know, lazybones, ain't the first time I've been here today looking for you—didn't even have to climb through a window, with all your doors gone. Not that I couldn't still make that kind of entry, easy as *l'amour* . . ." two smart slaps at the bulge of his midriff—"Booze, can't live without it."

Harding folded the newspaper and finished her coffee.

"Went up in your attic and the bad news is I should've done it before I gave you that price."

"Oh?"

"I do mean *gave*. You got four fuckin layers to come off, starting with two sheets of asphalt, then some nasty old tin on top of wood shingles— probably oh-riginal."

"All that on my roof?"

"Almost killed myself on your wobbly excuse for a ladder in there, ough- ta get yourself a real one if you're gonna do this kind of shit for a living."

"I'm not doing it for a living—that's Ware's ladder, which I guess means he'll be back. You ordered the cedar shingles?"

"Sure, sure." A deep final drag before flicking his stub at the nearest pile of broken laths.

"Step on it."

"What?"

"I can't afford a fire here."

He toyed ostentatiously with the thick silver chain on his damp neck. "Taking off all that mess ain't gonna be easy, sweetiepie."

"Any worse than other old houses around here?"

"You ever tried tearing off old tin with asphalt falling apart in your nose? And that oh-riginal cedar's as rotten as rat turds. Rafters could be going too, never know for sure till you peel away all the other crap."

"This place will do me in for sure." Nothing in their contract about re- placing rafters—another possible expensive extra.

Krasner sprang one of his open winning smiles. "Hey now, chick, I made you an offer you couldn't refuse, right? These other turkeys down here can't come close—too dumb to buy at the right price and get a full day's work out of their help. You get a good man you give him good pay. Did you check out my roof across the street?"

"Did I!" The good man to whom Krasner was giving good pay was Martin Kingston, his West Indian helper. No one in the Quarter as steady on a roof and as fast—the deep mahogany body straddling the ridge, like a statue on a great pedestal, as sure-footed moving along the incline as on a run down the beach, dropping to a half-crouch, a twist here and a flip there in perfect rhythmic accord as he stripped off the layers, first one knee bent for leverage then the other in a swirl to the half-crouch of a new position. And he kept it up for hours at a time. Krasner'd been able to hire the man and, even after several tries—so she had to admit—*she* hadn't.

"OK," he let go of his chain, seeming to resolve some doubt, "so I didn't just pop by in the wee hours on business—came looking for *you*, knowing how you usually whip in here at sunup. Had a late night?"

"So what's up?"

"Been thinking," Krasner flipped a bit of tobacco off his lip, "these crackers don't know the first thing about how to deal with a woman like you, know what I mean?"

Taken off-guard, she dropped her eyes to the folded *Sentinel,* refolded it.

"Oh-ho-o, didn't think I'd caught on, did you? Fact is, I've had my bellyful of baby dolls, enough for this life and the next. Look here, Elizabeth—that's your name, right?—I'm just about to blank out on the old game, wouldn't mind a real woman friend. F-R-I-E-N-D, no strings. Woman that can handle a boat or a gun, machinery, tools . . . no fuss, not always reminding a man with every little fanny twitch that he's supposed to keep an eye on her in case she needs a hand for one thing or another. Make sense?"

He removed his dark glasses. Big brown eyes faded to a mossy green at the outer edge of the iris, softened by the tanned crinkle of his smile, communicating simply this: no need between us two for self-protective gimmicks.

From time to time, she'd received other such invitations to join the special, the free, the beautiful people and couldn't, she says, altogether rid herself of a secret modicum of pride in her unequivocal lack of any temptation to yield to the call. Now Krasner's working man's version of this mode of seduction—she took the quick way out with the plain truth, ignoring his new rules for old gaming.

"Sure, perfectly. But where do you expect to find such a woman? I, for one, need help all the time—like right now, I need you to help me with my roof."

The expected contempt was a relief. "Easy, baby, no need to beg, but like I said before, no hassles. Better call up your Uncle-crew and keep 'em hauling day and night, clean up the place. One thing I ain't is an ass-wiper.

Come Wednesday and this shit's still here, deal's off. Kaput." Dark glasses back in place.

"I get the picture." Not a guy to be jerked around—nor one to acknowledge the leveling effects of sheer time, the biological weakness that gets everybody in the end. It lent him the dangerous air of a faintly heroic character even as it rendered him absurd.

"Make Uncle get his mess outta my way on schedule and you got your man. Deal's on and I'm off to du-wah-diddy-do"—he beat out the rhythm on his chest. Strutted off with a flirty wave, whistling softly.

Chronicle of the Fathers (continued)—Louis Joseph Boullet was but two years old when Spanish privateers abducted him, one sunny morning, while he was playing alone on DeLuna Beach. They did him no harm—his kidnapping intended merely as an exhortation to local traders for more favorable treatment of Spanish goods. Discovering certain propensities in the boy, his captors set out to train him as their pet for sighting enemies and sniffing out danger; to that end, little Louis learned to move through the spreading maze of inlets and channels of the Florida coast with an unerring ease possessed only by creatures of the wild. Seven years later, he was released to his father as a token of Spanish defeat at Bloody Marsh, his captors having bestowed on him the sobriquet "Louis the Last": he would be the last of his kind, they said—the last to possess a knowledge of Florida's coastal labyrinth so instinctual he could calculate, as effortlessly and accurately as a hound tracking scent, the direction and duration of any movement within it.

Quick to recognize his restored son as an asset, Raoul Boullet continued where his Spanish trainers left off: on the boy's sensorial mastery of coastal regions, he would map the trails and waterways that linked the scattered English trading posts in his charge. During the next fourteen years, as Louis passed from boyhood to manhood, his labyrinthine knowledge of terrains joined with his father's strategic and organizational skills to build success upon success: Louis was like the woof shuttling across the warp of Raoul's posts, weaving the threads of his movements into an ever-expanding network of trade.

December 10, 1873—"I failed old Louis," Papa used to say, "because I learned from him by thinking. Mine was the wrong way. I can only think my way to where I am going—I lost the knowledge. N'importe, to a thinking man of action like myself, what counts is getting there with or without the knowledge."

July 4th, 1935—Papa's skeptical assessment passed into Jonathan and Ibo as a sense of the absurd—for Jonathan, inescapable in the nature of things, and to be met on its own ground like all else. But Ibo . . . Ibo revelled in the whirl of a groundless dance.

November 21, 1864—Not long before she died, I asked grand'maman how she had come to take Louis the Last as husband. To my surprise, she replied readily—as if no longer constrained by the past and its entangling obligations—that the marriage had been part of a trade. "I was lynchpin and crown of all his schemes," she recalled wistfully—"in me Louis saw life's seal for them." Her Huguenot refugee family settled inland, at Campbell Town, where at sixteen, she was fervently courted by Alexander McGillivray, a young Charlestonian born of a Creek mother and a loyalist Scotsman, and educated after the English fashion. Assuming leadership of the Creek, Seminole, Chickasaw, and Choctaw Indians, he became their liaison with the European powers and the emergent American nation. Louis shrewdly foresaw that marriage into a Huguenot family would serve no useful purpose for this ambitious Charlestonian; and, with the trader's acuity that was so natural to him, he persuaded Alexander (whose health, grand'maman said, was always delicate) that he could ill afford—either for his own sake or that of the young woman with whom he had lately formed an attachment—to make a conjugal alliance of no value; given his friend's regard for her, Louis himself would gladly take this lady to wife—with the understanding that Alexander would be welcome as a partner in the Panton Leslie Company (with which, it so happened, Louis was affiliated) if consolidation of Indian trade, under the said firm's auspices, were assured.

"I was said to be a beauty then," she conceded with a small flush of pride, "thirty years younger than Louis, and I was to be the living pledge that their compact would neither be broken nor dishonored." And it never was; both men remained loyal, until Alexander's death, to the trading firm that linked them. The stratagem by which Louis made grand'maman his wife was both the warrant of his success and proof positive—if any were needed—of his capacity for untrammeled movement in the world of affairs. Had she not been wounded by her separation from Alexander? I wished to know. To this she replied that, yes, it had troubled her—for some years; but, with his premature death, she recognized that all had come about for the best. Alexander

McGillivray was rumored to have taken several wives—meaning, in her view, that the one in need of consolation had been Alexander himself.

Unlike Papa, grand'maman never regarded Louis' advanced age as a failing—finding him to be vibrant with enterprise and intelligence until the day of his death. "Although not given to dotage, Louis did dote on me—un peu," she confessed. "He liked to say our marriage had been a happy fusion of opportunity with purpose—but I was no mere tool for his ends. He let me have my way with the many I took in for refuge." And it was in carrying out grand'maman's wishes that Papa first began to devise ways to hide people—

July 16, 1935—Being a refugee was, for grand'maman, an unalterable condition like a biological strain passed on to one's children. And Florida was never the territory of any national power, nor even a state of the Union, but the place where all in need of refuge came—the great influx during and after the Revolution, all of them looking, she firmly believed, for safe haven. To these, a motley crew of loyalists, runaway slaves, deserters, convicts, and renegades of every complexion, she would give shelter. That Florida might fail in its offer of sanctuary (as it had in its prospect of untold wealth) could never have occurred to grand'maman—the spring of promise becoming the grave of defeated hopes was a contradiction she could not encompass.

To this day, when Zula, Maria-Louisa, and I designate ourselves as a group, the three of us together, it is still in grand'maman's words: nous les refugiées.

January 15, 1874—During Louis the Last's final years it appeared that Florida might be wrenched apart, and Papa grew up amid this turbulence, a child apprentice in the old Boullet art of profiting from the conflict of nations—just ten years old when Congress declared war on England in 1812. Louis had placed all his confidence in an old Indian named Snakefoot (the only man Papa would trust after his father's death). Snakefoot helped Louis carry out his scheme of keeping up trade with the Indians, and of collaborating with them—and with fugitive Negroes—to support English attempts at thwarting territorial encroachments by the United States in pursuit of its "manifest destiny." Use power against power to keep the balance; for balance promotes non-interference with trade. (Still, Jackson invaded Florida, and grand'maman ever after referred to anyone she considered an enemy of her Florida refuge as "a General Jackson.") Thrust into early manhood by Louis' death, Papa developed something of his Grandfather Raoul's ear for modulations in the concert of power, forging trade agreements with Spanish privateers, while shifting the center of his enterprise to the Caribbean—there, the weakening of European dominion facilitated the transport of goods.

Ah the advantage of unhampered movement! The old Formula at work once again, turning Papa into a champion of independence for the Islands. Hayti above all, the first of them to achieve it, called to him with abiding force. He was only eighteen when Nongka took him to her bed, she already a veteran of the bloody turmoils spawned by Hayti's revolution—she, with her beauty and her knowledge, incarnated for him all the best to be won through independence.

First of May, 1866—"She stole my soul," Papa reminisced this morning as we strolled through the Plaza, "and put it into our son Ibo." Papa's slight physique has a musculature so tightly drawn he appears even now unceasingly prepared for movement at critical speed—and Ibo, Ibo is both remarkably like him, and remarkably different: wiry strength and dexterity translated into the dark grace of a manly loveliness.

Ibo was a planned child, born the year Papa began to court my mother. Would he have married Caroline Howard, I once inquired half in jest, if Nongka had objected? Entertaining the question with unexpected gravity, he replied at long last: "Non . . . non, that would have wronged your maman." As a matter of fact, Nongka heartily approved the marriage—regarding it as a way to strengthen his position among the landholders of Florida, thereby mitigating hostility to trade with her country.

January 17, 1874—Within days of their first meeting, Nongka used to say, she was able to follow the operations of his mind like a part of herself. He belonged to her, this young American—not yet a man, no longer a mere boy—coming and going among her people, on business, always business. As much as their goals differed, she saw from the first how joining forces with him politically would bring about an alignment of economic interests, and he understood that Ibo was to be hers—that he would, in deference to her intentions, play no part in their alliance. Yet Ibo was to mark its existence like some beautiful soul-wrenching emblem—

C'est trop, Papa. Enough.

July 18, 1935—Nongka and Papa were proud to live on a frontier. He, taking no pleasure in the fray as such, thought it right to be at its forefront, with no goal other than that of clearing new paths by means of victory. She had a certain fierce delight in the contest for power. It was ground to be plowed, sowed, and laid by with the expectation that the twin crops of victory and defeat would yield in equal measure—

this, even as she strove always to set aside both crops, to lay by both victory and defeat for the pursuits of a private peace. We three refugees learned from Nongka what to do with the knowledge that descended to us from Papa's line. Both the heroic formulation of it, how to wrest meaning from life, and our own inversion—how to wrest life from meaning.

April 25, 1898—A fine morning's walk with a latish breath of cold in its brilliance. As I rounded the bend along the water towards Segovia Crescent, out strolled Lucy and Randall Cane with Randall Jr., who must be all of nineteen by now. No escape, not without some ostentation (worse in its aftermath than the encounter itself). I've become an embarrassment to them—young Randall, scarcely able to contain his impatience, appearing to fight an inclination to shrink from me; Randall Senior all ramrod dignity and paterfamilias. Poor Lucy. Despite her unchallenged standing here, she keenly feels her remove from Tallahassee, and remains, at fifty-two, one of the Howard belles of El Inglés.

They were radiant with the excitement of this new war. Quoth young Randall in the spirit of Teddy Roosevelt's Rough Riders: "I am ready at a moment's notice to volunteer for the liberation of Cuba!" Twenty-five years after Papa's death the United States is about to intervene in that island's fight for independence from Spain, with Florida as the base for invasion. Independence was much in the air in Papa's time—"Hayti, a new Hayti!" ran the whisper—and it is said of Papa that he died for the Cuban cause. Events might therefore be expected to touch me more nearly—but just for that reason they do only to the extent I can't ignore them in the round of my daily life.

"You must know, Miss Boullet," added Randall Sr. (the testiness in his voice somehow belying the purport of the words), "that we have always admired the Captain's championship of freedom for Cuban landowners. At the decisive moment he made clear, against his own interest and prospects, which side he was on."

There was a time when I would have felt called on to set the record straight—explain that Papa neither opposed nor favored a mercantile system per se, that the word "trade" held its root meaning for him: paths, or courses, for moving through the world. Obstacles to trade— such as friction between Cuban merchants and landowners—were a kind of traffic problem. All during those years of insurgency Papa would grumble, "These belligerents, they interfere with my plans!" War got in the way of building railroads, and railroads were indispensable for the transport of goods. So the landowners make their own paths for commerce, and the merchants claim their interests are harmed—

the solution lies not in destroying the former to please the latter, but in making it possible for each to travel without trampling on the path of the other. "Eh bien, Randall, it's not a matter of principle—merely that the easement of the Cuban traffic problem requires a trader like me to support the landowners in their struggle for independence."

But what are traffic problems to the Randall Canes of this world? And who am I to instruct them? How long it has taken me to understand, not knowing Papa as Nongka knew him—without the slightest effort; hers an easy, intuitive understanding. Never one to turn his back on a winner, Papa used to say about the Cuban rebels: "Ecoute, they have no distance to travel. They have the numbers, and time is on their side!" He kept quiet his association with Antonio Maceo, of the Cuban branch of Nongka's family in Santiago de Cuba (as uncompromising about independence as Nongka herself), through whom Papa sold guns to the rebels, concealed amidst machinery for sugar production. Antonio was killed in battle three years ago— whether Pinar del Rio or Havana Province I am not sure—the same year as José Martí, who wrote: "Cuba wishes to be free in order that here Man may fully realize his destiny, that everyone may work, and that her hidden riches may be sold in the natural markets of America."

A trader to the end, Papa would have had no quarrel with the last bit of Martí's manifesto. He spent his final years strengthening commercial interests in Cuba, where, having acquired a sugar mill, along with its contingent of slaves (through the failure of a landowner to pay interest on a debt), he had it equipped with the latest machinery and hired a small number of skilled workers to run it. The slaves he freed, having no use for them—an act that earned him the reputation of abolitionist. Which, in the absolute sense he was. "A trading world, Fan, has no room for labor that cannot be freely traded," he would say. Still, he might not have passed muster when all's said and done ("were I a slave in Cuba under Spanish dominion, chérie, I might settle for a royalist master"). By 1873, the year he died, Europe was close to satisfying demand with her own beet sugar, and he could declare: "My feet, they are Cuban-planted now, both of them. Jonathan and I, we steal a march on the American Sugar Refining Company. The time has come, you see, to free Cuban traffic of Spanish interference—in the interest of trade, mon ami!"

I contented myself with murmuring that freedom-fighting and trading are not so very different for some—a remark that evidently failed to gratify. Or merely rendered my unreliable person the more suspect in Randall's eyes.

Lucy, anxiously clasping her son's arm, sought my opinion: "Fannie, should he go?" By virtue of bearing my father's blood, I must have a more than ordinary understanding of this war, it seems.

"Spain will do battle chiefly by water, son," Randall averred, "our first duty must be defending Tarragona's harbor. The naval yard is already fitting out our boats with guns, mark that."

I offering no advice, Lucy caught my hand in hers and, gazing deep into my eyes, remarked that the trials of war let none of us escape. She was certain—utterly convinced, for her part—that if either of us were in need, the other would open her arms. Dear Lucy, she would rather that I simply not exist; still, she never fails to let me know that I have only to return to the fold and all will be forgiven, all will be delicately— very delicately—forgotten. I regret that I cannot, conscious that I must appear obtuse for failing to apprehend how easy the cure—all I need do is take my place beside her. Having the door to all that is Good, True, and Beautiful opened for my entry, I blindly walk past it toward some chimera vouchsafed to my eyes alone.

Captain Boullet winds a thread of respectability between us, and Randall père took it up again, with some warmth this time: "Your father gave his life for his convictions. No more can be asked of any man and now we—all of us—must vindicate his death." (The penetration of those grey eyes, I observed, has been bestowed by the Cane lineage on his patriotic son.)

There remained the awkward business of leave-taking, when young Randall, eyeing me with rising passion, broke in with "Boullet is the name of a hero!" Whereupon the paternal grip on his shoulder made as though to steady him. Holding back my antipathy for the sake of a courteous farewell, I said, "Captain Boullet was as fond as I of Voltaire's maxim, 'Ce qui fait le héros degrade souvent l'homme.'"

Initial reports of his death made it out to be an execution, but by whom and to what end? By the captain-general of the then newly declared Spanish Republic of Cuba—on account of Papa's trade in contraband? By Cuban rebels who took him for a traitor because he was heard to remark that autonomy had many advantages over independence? ("Better to stand with Spain, weakening on the other side of the ocean, with no time for the capers of a growing young giant.") By Cuban slave-owners, who took him for an abolitionist? By discontented Negroes displaced by machinery Papa had shipped into Cuba? Killing to settle accounts had become common practice on all sides. Then, in the year after his death, a story circulated so persistently it acquired the aura of authority. Captain Boullet, on this account, had arranged illegal registry in the United States of the steamer "Virginius," with a cargo of men and supplies bound for the rebels; but the Spaniards captured her in Santiago flying the U.S. flag, and shot her captain and fifty-three others on board. One of her surviving passengers (never identified by name) pointed Papa out to his chief competitor, a Creole sugar-mill owner, who charged Papa with being a member of the Cuban junta in New York and promptly had him assassinated. The story was padded by rumors that Papa had for some time been in the habit of conveying Cuban refugees to Jamaica.

This last, says Jonathan, is true enough. As for the Virginius connection, he claims Papa's death had nothing to do with any illegal registry, that he was murdered because the Creole "discovered horns growing on his own head—which he kept, but minus his sugar mills. All four of them, up in flames, not a day after the Captain died—a misfortune of political confusion, you think maybe?"

Jonathan has made a great success of the trading life he took up from Papa. I too share Papa's delight in arrangements that make intercourse among human beings easy, comfortable, safe. A good trade is above all a safe transaction. But I am no trader, I have never been reconciled to the ways of trade, though—as Jonathan says—it yields "the best of goods from all worlds." For me, there's only a Faustian bargain of my own making.

They went, Lucy with tears pooling in her round blue eyes, as though she'd been unduly chastised. I would have preferred not to wound her, but I lose patience with simple faith and simple good will. As for père et fils, neither manages to notice me on the street as a rule, and neither would have done so today, I'm sure, had not Lucy made it impossible for them to direct their attentions elsewhere. May the scenery beyond me long continue to hold their eyes.

Ah Papa, how amused you would have been with their magnification of you, to oh such heroic proportions! "It makes the strategic mask par excellence for a trading man such as myself," you might have said.

July 31, 1935—The innocence of my mother's family found its consummate expression in the women. Lucy, Mary Elizabeth, Cathy. Even Julia, for all her clever stings and barbs, never lost it. In this as in much else Aunt Virginia made Uncle Edward a perfect wife. And it is for this they should be held accountable—refusal to give up their innocence. Only my young mother surrendered hers, when she gave birth to me and died.

August 15th, 1898—So the war is over—the Spanish are to evacuate Cuba. (One power the less to sidetrack, Papa would have said.) I hear on all sides laments for the passing of their influence, and every other family in Tarragona lays vociferous claim to formerly despised "Spanish origins." So the present recolors the past. Florida could never have been anything but a frontier for Spain, a temporary convenience (or a necessary aggravation) in hegemonic struggles with the other European powers. There always was too little here. Yet the era of possession by Spain seems now to have left Florida gilded—some aureate haze lingering still from the bullion stowed in those greedy God-fearing galleons.

Life has returned to what counts as normal. This morning, Randall Cane's new associate, Jordan Wentworth, paid me the unsolicited honor of a visit; now that Randall has achieved his ambition of becoming Judge Cane—and is, as he puts it, "ethically bound to withdraw from other pursuits"—Mr. Wentworth will represent the Canes in the daily conduct of their business. It appears, too, that Zula and I have a new calling. We possess, according to Mr. Wentworth (with whom I've never before this day so much as exchanged a greeting, and who, despite reeking of spirits, has not yet lost the appeal of a thriving dissipation), "a rare knowledge of the arts of natural healing." Our services are much needed—Zula's as my trusty retainer—on behalf of the First Florida Regiment encamped at Tampa, where the typhoid epidemic rages out of control. Reservations for two, by steamer, have already been made, and we're to enjoy privileged (which is to say, quarantined) accommodations in Henry Plant's new Tampa Bay Inn on the water, courtesy of the U.S. Government.

A moot bargain has been struck: if we undertake this mission (and survive it) an aura of respectability—perhaps even a faintly dangerous dignity—will for a time ring our persons and activities. Under the aegis of risking our lives for Florida's sick heroes of the late war, we purchase a spell of peace. The more lives we save, the longer the spell.

August 7, 1935—Today a young man from the university sought an audience with me as "the sole survivor of the Boullet line." He believes me to be in possession of lore pertaining to his doctoral research on commerce in Territorial Florida. So invaluable an oral history resource, he said, must not be lost to posterity.

He'd come forewarned, prepared to meet resistance and striking what I believe is regarded as a diffident pose—a little awkward and thus bound to be sincere. I was assured that my opinions commanded the greatest respect, that he wished in no way to invade my privacy, would talk with me only at my convenience for as short or as long a time as I preferred, and that nothing I chose to tell him would be used without my approval and with appropriate acknowledgments once his work reached print. I replied that it was neither here nor there to me whether I commanded respect, that I had nothing whatever to tell him, that there was no time convenient for me to see him either now or later, short or long, that I was going on ninety and every second he continued to stand in the doorway constituted an invasion of my privacy.

"Furthermore," I said, "the 'line' to which you refer is not mine, and the posterity that so concerns you holds no interest for me."

"Ma'am"—he tried again, on a more personal note—"the truth is I need your help in ascertaining some facts that could be crucial to my argument. I'm just asking you—please—as one human being to another."

Energized momentarily by the inhumanity of youth's vitality projecting its hopes and goals, I leaned closer and hissed loudly, strongly, before shutting the door on him: "Never!"

"Got to e-lim-i-nate the neg-a-tiff," Harding once sang to me in parody of Norman Vincent Peale's stroke of populist genius—in the fifties, was it? Gained a huge following and fortune with little more than the repeated injunction to "think positively." Overnight, people discovered a powerful inner technology for position-finding, free of charge, available to all and offering immediate access: thinking.

Kept to the right one-track mood-track, no doubt about it, thinking yielded the positive, decade after decade. All sufferers of the negative— racial minorities, ethnics of all kinds, Vietnam vets, gays and lesbians, Weight Watchers, the disabled, and especially those avatars of the negative, the mentally ill—group after group gaining instant position by regulating thought about themselves with use of affirmative labels. Sure, the seventies had their lapses (bra-burning, secular humanism, performance art, Darth Vader / Sid Vicious types, etc., all stimulated by negative infiltrations) and skills in policing the negative became all the rage. Thus, the Moral Majority, the election of President Ronald Reagan, and the Soviet Union as Evil Empire.

Nobody respects the positive more than I do and what characterizes respect for the positive is that four-letter word FEAR. Like Harding and

Frances Boullet's crowd I fear the positive, meaning the positings of position in all its forms. All wars have been fought on the side of one positive or another. All positives exact their toll in time, like HIV. Has anyone ever been known to give up a life for a negative? Somewhere here the power of positive thinking comes to a dead end.

Still, the need for positive action remains, right? A plan, a policy. What are think tanks for if not to take aim? And if they say "hold your fire," then who am I to opt for an interventionist position? So far, "Containment" has still been the word for the nineties. Entering my own think tank, I'll start with the fallacy that what's good for our nation should be good for me: any plan of action must be a plan of containment. Act in such a way as not to get involved in any violence unless necessary for my immediate self-interest—a policy not without an ongoing risk, but it appeals to those, like me, opposed to violence. That said, it does not follow—I know from experience—that I won't under any circumstances commit a violent act. Push me *enough* and I will, depend on it—self-interest or no. So will anybody else. Murder or suicide or, for the more moderate, something in between. (I lean toward suicide myself and incline toward others of that persuasion—whatever else, they're less likely to murder me.) But to extend the argument to a more inclusive range, let's apply the diplomacy of the times equitably to everything: subject each and all, collective entities included, to Containment. Think ecologically—whatever's within the reach of thought. Animals, plants.

Well, that does it—that's how easy this policy fails to draw a line. I mean I can stop eating meat, but fruits and vegetables? A ripe tomato, a few herbs, a mess of beans and greens fresh from my garden—just start with the tomato alone, it was about to fall off the vine and would probably have rotted on the ground if I hadn't picked it.

A weird thing is happening in my think tank: I can't get Raskolnikov's murder of the old pawnbroker off my mind. I want to say that I, picking that tomato, ripe and about to fall off anyway, am like Raskolnikov killing that old woman (useless and without much life left in her anyway) and that just as his situation led to the unplanned murder of her sister, so mine, ripe tomato in hand, leads to oregano and—but so it goes in think tanks, there's no analogy behind this persistent association, motivated merely by a sense of the blind kinetics at work in both cases. A presumption of violence as it were—entropy or the Big Bang, always back to physics sooner or later.

Still, to stop there—to say, thing of nature that I am, I can't help it, violence is in the very material of being—may, like stoicism, be a wise position but you don't have to be a Chekhovian patient in Ward No. 6 to see it isn't altogether practical. Think-tank questions are meaningless to an old-time positivist like me—no answers to them. The century winds down in daily reenactments of the Holocaust and we tend to our business like ordinary, more or less well-meaning, citizens of the Third Reich, our power to intervene diminished and understanding only too well at last why, even knowing the score, there's no putting a stop to it (except, at best, in thought). And those citizens understood, too, what it is to live with it—as we continue to live with it, only a few feet away, for a sharper image. Easier on the eyes. Today it's ethnic cleansing in Bosnia with CNN ratings in the stratosphere.

Well then, given that the world can't seem to run without violence, suppose we go for absolutely the least possible amount of it. A scarcity of violence, forget justification by self-interest. Call it the new economics of violence on a trickle-down basis. And how little violence is little enough? In the time it takes, with minimal understanding, to process the media's unending serial of violence—the daily news—my body screams stop, stop, stop! I can't carry on the simplest conversation without these silent cries interrupting, making for chasmy communication.

A body can only take so much. When scouting out the range of positions rather than listening to my body-cries, I *feel* free to choose what sides to come down on, what to reject, condemn with faint praise—all the positions I move around in daily, all the little political actlets that engage my imagination. But let me *do* anything political and my body outs with its cries of stop, stop, stop! The bottom line is I have a problem with political acts.

So I swallow my privilege while I still can and proceed with a radical skepticism. Holding my tone of doubt as long as I can hang on in the suspension . . . perceived to be nonpolitical or, if political, perceived to be ineffectual. Perception problem or performance problem? Might be both. Sam and Marilyn are telling me I could use a makeover and they're offering opportunities. I can become sought after. Somebody, that is, with a solidly grounded future. If I hurry up—please! They're prepared to put themselves—their positions—in the line of fire for me if I, in turn, perform in such a way as to enhance my own position (and theirs by association). Have to enter the fray and—last call—am I up to it? Good players always wanted; race, religion, ethnicity, class, gender, sexual preference— all those differences—are counters you bring to the table now open to full-scale participation for mutual enhancement of position in the global village.

Sorry, Sam, all this will have to be adjudicated by my body and its cries, a matter of the action that follows from arousal. You're always welcome to call, machine stays on around the clock, but I'll be making other arrangements for lifts to the airport. When I took off with the diary, Harding's last words to me were, "If you don't want to break its hold on you, put it to use." It should follow that if I don't use it, I want to break its hold . . . a good instance of how one of a pair of logical equivalents can be true and the other false.

Early morning on the Fourth of July, Harding, dragging Ware's sorry ladder over mounds of rubble from stud to stud, yanked out old nails by the hundreds to make ready for walls she now felt she wouldn't be around to see. Time to consider going to Randall Cane: confess her mistake, suggest that the Committee for the Preservation of Old Tarragona, previous owner of the Boullet House, buy it back at a bargain (loss kept to 40 percent, say, no more than 50)? Fooled by a home-mirage, dream of a final resting place, dupe of her own élan and dunce for the painted luxuriance of a sanctuary and its patchwork diary—now that she'd almost certainly lost, she could think such thoughts.

But as I've been unable to give up the diary, so she, without a shred of illusion or hope left, heavy with the sense of her own enslavement, could not bring herself to leave off the restoration.

"Do we begin at the back and work forward—what do you think?"

The musical West Indian inflection of his voice wrenched a gasp from Harding as poignant—salvation and doom traveling the same psychic pathway—as Butterfly's farewell to her little boy. "Martin Kingston! I . . . I didn't expect *you*."

Plaster crunched underfoot as he maneuvered a large wheelbarrow down the central hall. "Didn't think I'd manage it, eh? Independence Day and all that. Well, you have my aunt to thank for it—she made me cut short my long weekend at the seashore." A truck with a roomy bed for hauling stood in the drive behind her Chevy.

"Your aunt? Sure you're talking to the right person?"

"Miss Mary Louise, and she's sure. Know the name?"

Harding has a policy, when confused, of denying what she knows until more fully informed. "Can't say I do."

"You will, you will—but let's get on with it, I've brought extra shovels."

And about noon, another pair of hands—a young man introduced as "Christophe," swapping occasional pleasantries in Kreyòl with Martin Kingston, while they worked steadily and efficiently until dark.

And again from dawn Tuesday morning. Fifteen hours later, the three of them had emptied out the Boullet House, upstairs and down, and cleared the yard of rubble. Alone again, in semi-darkness, Harding marveled at what was left of the shattered insides—that this was all—the fine trails of grit leading mazelike through the house and out back, marking the spill of the wheelbarrow's coming and going.

4

Of Legacy and Dispossession

"Bee-eep! Bee-eep!"

Sledgehammer in full swing over her head, Harding barely registered the teasing, attention-grabbing honks at her back. Another carload of half-drunk Alabama hoodlums most likely, across the state line for their weekend of fun. The previous Saturday, on the way back to her motel, a gang of them in an old Buick convertible had played road-rage games with her, tail-gating with staccato blasts of their horn then hot-rodding alongside, whistling Dixie and squeezing her off the road. "Git yo tail back to Noo Yawk, cock-suckin bitch," frolicked the driver. A couple of his pals stood up and chimed in through cupped hands, like an old-style public announcement, "Pussy-feedin time down on the plantation, milky-tail-honey-pie."

Crash! A single chip split off the last and ugliest of the ugly concrete steps, the extra-wide bottom one. Another swing and another, head aimed at the same spot. The step cracked in two.

Aimée Hulin was making an exit from the air-conditioned comfort of her creamy white Jag parked carelessly wide of the curb—not another car in sight. No Alabama drivebys had a horn like that either. At the gate, Aimée hesitated, staring through the iron pales for some moments as if forgetful of where or who she was until Harding put down the sledgehammer and invited her in.

"It takes *some* nerve to handle one of those things. . . . I'd probably smash my foot with it, or worse." Aimée had it all just right, a tad too right—the intimate, lightly self-deprecating voice and manner called for by her class, female line; the special flair of her very straight, really quite ordinary honey-blonde hair; the gangly frame made svelte by carriage and dress. She was two or three years shy of thirty that summer, still married to an up-and-coming young oncologist from an old Maryland family. And carrying on a not-so-clandestine affair with Tony Krasner, roofer and would-be man-about-town.

"Brawn is what it takes," Harding said, "a trifle more than my birthright." She knocked the dust out of her work hat and ruffled her hair. "Remarkable conditioner, plaster dust, not to mention the benefits to the skin of the daily sauna," plucking her work shirt an inch or more from her bosom and letting it sink back in sweaty adhesion. Only nine-thirty and already the fierce noon heat of high summer in the deep South.

"You should hire a couple of strong backs for this"—the elegant fawn sandal nudged a broken-off hunk—"what about Tony's guys? I see your roof's ready for shingling."

"And I'm to see that nobody gets in his way . . . or else."

Krasner was really moving now (or Martin Kingston was). On the promised Wednesday, while he kept stalling her, two alternative fantasies showed him who was boss. Fantasy one, affording the crude pleasure of revenge killing: beat him to a pulp with a blunt instrument—the biggest of Ware's crowbars, left behind with the sledgehammer, would do—then gouge him, surgically and repeatedly, with the two-pronged straight end and watch terror replace laughter in those mocking dark eyes. Fantasy two lingered more sweetly in the imagination: she's a kind of female Randall

Cane, laying it on with ironic self-assurance. "Tell you what, Krasner old fellow, this draggy business with Ware has been a damned nuisance for us both. You're not a man to let things slide, I know, you'll get in there, rip off ye olde roof and there'll be an extra couple hundred in it for you if the new shingles go up pronto. No need to change the bottom line for tax snoopers, hmm? Just a little personal token of my appreciation."

Aimée was giving her an idea. She could sneak these last hunks of concrete (demo rubble and therefore "Ware's shit") into her own roofing trash, Krasner's mess yet to be hauled off.

"Tony likes his independence," said Aimée, in a artful conversational turn that put Harding on the alert, she didn't yet know for what. "One hot stormy night a month before he was born, his daddy took off with some floozy and never came back. He says it doesn't take a male authority figure to know how to be a man."

"Yeah. Guess it comes natural to some." They had a good laugh and retreated from the bright sun to the canopy of the old tree.

Sunglasses cocked atop her hair, Aimée gave the Boullet House an appraising once-over. "Your restoration will probably win some kind of award."

"For unprecedented nerve and backbone?" Surely not for her age-old mistake of taking the past too seriously. Margaret Avery—and Aimée too, no doubt—would have known better. "Tradition, that's what sells," her agent advised, "make it *believable*. Nobody'll ask how you pulled it apart room by room or what's under the cedar shingle roof, just as long as it's got that look of heritage. *Make people remember.* And stay on the right side of the Board."

"Tell you what," Aimée's smile turned naughty, "I'll just instruct Uncle Randy to make sure." The thought of pulling that particular string seemed to leave her very quiet, as though plotting in detail how to raise Harding's ante on a restored Boullet House.

But no, Aimée was otherwise preoccupied. "Don't you think people have gotten just too class-conscious," she ventured, "or ethnic-conscious or whatever—and right when it's all changing a million miles a minute? Makes things so unnecessarily complicated." Sighs, all ten fingers running through her perfectly styled hair, French cut.

"Rather like trying to make something up from a mere idea."

"You're so right, instead of starting with the real thing."

Here it comes, thought Harding, and decided she might as well relax into the pleasure of lounging in the deep shade of the great live oak after three hours battering concrete, weekend at a standstill, house stripped bare, waiting again—and still, incredibly, after weeks of misery, this tiny surge of the original promise.

"Sorry I can't offer you a cup." Harding poured coffee into her red thermos top, spread a napkin over her lap and laid out crackers, cheese, and an apple. "Do nibble with me if you like."

"Can I drag you to lunch later—there's this new little shrimp and oyster bar—"

"Not until the restoration's done, thanks anyway."

"What were we talking about?"

"How things *really* are . . ."

"Right . . . Tony's mother died when he was only two, something gruesome . . . peritonitis, I think. The Sicilian strain's from her side, one of those huge families with no money, came to Florida looking for the realms of gold, but things stopped booming about that time."

"An old story, the same as far back as you can go—Ponce de León got an Indian arrow for his trouble, and take Tristán de Luna's big discovery, after the first hurricane blew his ships and supplies away, that the noble savages' plans didn't include him nor"—flicking a gnat from her cheese—"were the sugar-white sands edible."

"Terrible—even that far back . . . and it's no better today. Tony was raised by his oldest sister and the juvenile courts, in just the worst squalor—had to fight his way out of it by sheer guts and brains. . . . Underneath all that blustering vulgarity he's as sensitive as a little child, he'd die before he'd let on though."

Ah yes, the tough façade concealing the wounded inner life. And Aimée still prey to it, not seeing through the heart made tender by damage claims. Still the Southern lady in her closely tended ignorance of the deceptions and self-deceptions she moved in—even as intelligence and natural vitality chafed at the feminine bit.

"I may be catching just a glimpse of what goes on underneath," said Harding, "but I don't seem to reach your ease with him."

Aimée watched the green apple peelings fall into the napkin on Harding's lap, as if they were deciding something for her.

Hesitantly: "You want to know how I got to understand Tony so well? I would *never ever* tell anybody here about it but I bet it'll tickle *you* . . . happened about a year ago at this old plantation near Tallahassee—El Inglés—been in the Howard side of our family as far back as the Indians. Where I used to spend summers before I was good out of diapers."

"El Inglés? What happened there?" Harding asked innocently and leaned back into the firm sweep of the tree trunk.

"James is so jealous it's the only place he'll *let* me go on my own—relatives, he figures, parties. But that's truly not what I go for, I mean it.

This time last summer not a soul at the big house would have dreamed I was miles around!"

"So where were you?"

"There's this little two-room log cabin from territorial times—Uncle Randy keeps the keys—wide plank pine floors, really rustic, though not as primitive as it sounds. He's fixed it up with a little cooking area and a tiny bathroom, all furnished in old iron and cypress pieces made in slave work-shops on the plantation almost a 150 years ago and never ever touched by a smidgeon of finish. Adorable, the whole thing. Originally, there was another cabin just like it and a bigger one with slave quarters and work-shops around a town square, but the Negroes burned most of it up during Reconstruction, and now all that's left is fenced off from the woods—just one little cabin, the old blacksmith shop and two run-down tenant houses somebody threw together sometime or other from scraps of the old slave quarters. Nobody's lived in them for years and years. After the colored people all moved to town and got brick FHA houses, they were used for storing cotton—that didn't last long either because they couldn't get hands to strip after the picking machines, so they're just a place for field mice now. Uncle Randy feels he owes it to the family to preserve the log cabin and the blacksmith shop in their original state. Sure you want to listen to this?"

"Absolutely sure."

"Well, last summer when it all happened, it started with one of James's old professors from Johns Hopkins, who wanted him to fly up there for three or four weeks to help with their cancer research. First thing that popped into my head was, here comes the perfect chance to get away by myself.

"That was the easy part, with James's mind set on this Big Opportuni-ty to get back into some genuine lab work. I said it looked to me like I was going to be tied down Lord knows where in Baltimore nursing two Basenji puppies, waiting and fretting every minute for him to turn off all that DNA and do something interesting with *me*, so I might as well stay home where it would be a lot easier to look after my babies because I won't stick a foot outside Tarragona without them—as soon as I got to the part about stay-ing home, he was nodding and agreeing with me and I said we would just have to be satisfied with talking on the phone and should set a time for it, like every Sunday morning.

"Uncle Randy was trickier, he's nobody's fool. I begged James to let me be the one to surprise him and Aunt Sophie with the news about the research opportunity, 'but I'll wait,' I said, 'until you're sure when you're actually going, so nobody will have their expectations disappointed.'

James thought that made a lot of sense and I was handling the whole thing
with maturity and tact.

"The very night he was leaving I invited them over for drinks, about
an hour or so before James had to be at the airport. As soon as they arrived
I started in on how I couldn't wait to tell them the big news and what a surprise it was for us and how that was why we were all excited and rushing
around—in fact James was still packing his briefcase and running every
two seconds to his study to pull another file.

"Every time they came up with suggestions about what to do and who
to look up in Baltimore and Washington, I leaped in with every syllable
about cancer research that had ever come my way—breast and uterine and
prostatic cancer, and how excess secretion of hormones can cause them to
grow—I got some of that straight out of the blurb that comes with birth
control pills—then about how just a tiny surface growth no bigger than a
pimple between vagina and anus (Aunt Sophie didn't want to hear about it,
I could tell) can spread unseen so that a woman's entire superficial space
has to be surgically removed, then on to lung cancer and the simian virus-
es. And E. coli—I carried on at length about splicing out what you don't
want and putting in DNA segments from cancer cells, even down to one
gene. And fluorescent experiments showing the difference in antibody re-
ceptors between malignants and normals, and I got off from there on the
technique of Southern blots and how important it is to isolate DNA so you
can see little two-stranded strings of it, and threw in as much as I could remember about technology—like how electrons instead of light hit the object in an electron microscope and how long it takes to make microtomes,
and that got me into cutting a sample, exposing it to chemicals, embed-
ding it in a hard surface like paraffin, slicing it with the diamond knife,
putting it on the wire grid and shadowing with electron-dense material and
so on—and when I ran out, I would carry on about how much it meant to
James and me to be in on the frontline of this new medical research and
how we expected a breakthrough just any time.

"You've got to remember Uncle Randy is a doctor himself, but by the
time James and I climbed in the Jag, he was looking at me with a new
respect and telling James he'd never realized how much of an inspiration
I must be to his work. James looked a little puzzled, he's *such* a baby—I
could see he thought this sudden to-do was how people act when a man
gets a big break. At the last minute James dashed back into the house for
something he'd forgotten and Uncle Randy offered to follow and drive my
Jag home from the airport, but I told him I'd arranged for a mechanic to
pick it up and do some work on it while I wasn't using it, and started emot-
ing about what a privilege it was to chauffeur a great research scientist

around and telling them not to worry about the house or me or anything, no need to run over and check, we'd taken care of every little thing. 'I promise to call the minute we're home and let you know what happened,' I said, 'there's a busy, busy time ahead.' I was in a regular tailspin by the time they shook hands and James kissed Aunt Sophie good-bye, and I hugged and kissed both of them from the car window. Then I pulled off real fast and waved like the American flag in a gale wind. I wanted to see that plane in the air with my *own* eyes—with James on it, and Uncle Randy and Aunt Sophie absolutely convinced I was up there with him.

"I just adore James, I really do, but you know how you want to go off by yourself once in a while? Well, that's how I got away. Imagine, a whole month and nobody in Tarragona had any idea where I was, and they still don't because every time the subject has ever come up I talk cancer research. Once, right after James got back, somebody at a party asked straight out, 'Aimée, what did you do all that time in Baltimore while James was slaving away in his lab?' 'Me? Why, you know, I was just waiting around for him to come in so I could hear the latest about the breakthrough,' and I launched into cancer research.

"It was no time before people stopped mentioning it and if they did, they would ask about the progress of James's research in that polite way you know all they want is about a three-word answer. After a while it was like having the Nobel Prize winner never leave town, and everybody was glad to forget scientific progress and just have James be James again, and James most of all—everybody just plain tired of living up to it . . . now, where was I?"

"The plane—in the air."

"No more than an hour after James took off, my baby pups and I were sailing along on Highway 10 East and it was close to eleven when we turned in the back way at El Inglés and pulled up by the cabin. See, I'd been to the big house for a visit early on that summer, and that's when I got this idea of going back when nobody would know about it, so I had a set of keys to the cabin made for myself unbeknownst to Uncle Randy or anybody else.

"That place is unreal—three or four hundred acres never cleared, still one hundred percent virgin, a forest of hardwoods along with smaller ones like wax myrtles, wild olives, willows, buck thorns, chinkapins, cabbage palms, on down to the plum bushes, elderberries, possumhaw and saltbrush, with wild vegetable climbing to the tallest of them. There's a little half-moon bay with a spring feeding into it—like a sink coming off the creek that winds back to the river. I had a mind to walk there and sit on the limestone boulder by the spring—it was one of those clear summer nights when all the stars are out and close. I headed toward the woods but the puppies were excited and something a little scary about it too, so I turned back at the fence. Figured I had about as much chance of finding my way to the bay in the dark as my saintly great-grandmother Lucy would have getting to hell and back, so I picked an armload of oranges and plugged in my phone and called James.

"He'd just arrived at his apartment in Baltimore and was obviously relieved when I insisted he should get a good night's sleep and not bother about ever calling me while he was there doing research because I would be keeping everything safe and sound at home and would report to him once a week. And I meant it, I didn't want him to think about me or worry about a thing.

"Before sunup next morning I was walking my puppies around the square in the dew. Nobody ever goes there anymore except Uncle Randy when he spends a weekend in the cabin once every year on a retreat—he says it's important to go back to the beginning—but I realized if anybody even got close, my Jag would be a sure giveaway.

"The first thing that didn't seem just right was finding the heavy old plank doors to the blacksmith shop closed—I had to drag them open. There, ready to move out any time, was one of those little El Camino pickups and my first thought was, my God, John Howard's on the loose again—John Howard's a scream, he's Aunt May Julie's sixteen-year-old. She married one of the Georgia Tates, not a lick of sense but luck pours down on them no matter what they get in their heads to do, and John Howard is just like the rest of them except he's heard so much about the Tate luck he got the idea early on of doing something with it. Taking the initiative. Well, he started slipping out to gamble when he turned fourteen and fast got himself such a reputation they set up special sessions, until John Howard was winning double and triple and all kind of stakes because he didn't play just to win a hand—he made bets with any taker on what he stood to win. And he'd accept just about anything for payment, didn't matter to John Howard. Before long he had the blacksmith shop piled up with two boats, a sporty little classic MG, estate silver and jewelry from all over, TVs and enough VCRs and audio equipment to open a store—nobody ever looked in there.

"No telling how rich he'd be by now if it hadn't been for the electrical storm. It'd been a bad rainy season and turned squally, all thunder and lightning, early one morning before daylight when John Howard bumped along the dirt road through the woods and stopped outside the cross-gate to the square. He says he didn't want to take a chance getting stuck in the muddy lane to the blacksmith shop with the storm getting worse, so he swung his thirty-gallon plastic garbage bag of loot over his shoulder and climbed over the gate. The gate has a rusty barbed wire running along the top of it and, when he jumped down, a barb hooked the plastic bag and ripped it wide open. He'd thrown a dozen—a good dozen—handfuls of fifty dollar bills among fives and tens and other winnings into that bag and bills went flying through the air, thick as bats leaving the roost—they claim a fifty got as far as Spanish Moss five or six miles away at least and God knows they could use a few, run-down as it is—but John Howard grabbed his bag tight in his arms to save it best he could and streaked down the lane losing some all the way. He made it to within a hundred yards or so of the blacksmith shop before a dragging arm of that gigantic old oak— it spreads out over a quarter of an acre—caught his foot and brought him down, and his loot spilled in the mud. The wind got the bag and took what was left in it.

"He still made it back home and to bed before daylight, and his luck would have held even then if it hadn't been for Mary Lucy—she's one of my cousins in the big house, Mary Lucille L'Angeles, old Spanish Florida family Aunt Peggy married into. Mary Lucy is smart, graduated early from high school and put up a fuss to go to the University of Mexico so she could live in a real Spanish culture and learn to speak the language naturally, she said. She was just back from a year of that, and from there of all places she picked up some notion about women having the right and the obligation to take care of the land—that mostly means about six-thirty every morning, right after the hands drive out to the place from the black subdivision and get the machines going, Mary Lucy jumps on her horse and rides half the morning along the turn-rows of all the fields.

"Well, she was up on her horse as usual, and all the machines were in the field and making a big racket as usual, except they were all empty and standing stock-still, idling away. I guess this was her first real challenge in handling problems of land management, so she set about it at a trot and trotted straight on into the woods where she had to rein her horse to a slow walk to keep an eye on all the fresh tracks she was following down the lane. Mary Lucy says you could hear the hootin-n-hollerin a mile away before she rode up on them—nearly a dozen hands, three or four supposed to be driving in the big south field—she never did find out how they got the word—hanging in that huge tree half-way to the top of it and so strung up with gray moss she said they looked like the tree's own knights charging through it in their hauberks and yelling out to each other, 'Pick 'em, niggers, pick them greens!' Because there were fifty dollar bills flattening themselves as pretty as you please all over that big old tree. Some others, all moss-matted, scrambled under it and all over the long arms dragging the ground, catching anything that came drifting on down and hollering, 'Shake it, dude, shake that thing!'

"You might know it would have to be her—John Howard and Mary Lucille just can't stand the sight of each other. Well, she investigated some more, and she sure found some more: John Howard's whole cache. He owned up to it right away—John Howard's just that open and honest when he's found out—and his papa was as proud as could be, said it was 'clear material evidence for the genetic grace of God being passed on in the Tate men.' He put the proceeds, a clean hundred thousand from goods and packets of bills stuffed all over the blacksmith shop, in a trust fund for John Howard, but Aunt Peggy convinced Aunt May Julie he had to be kept under guard every night to keep the Tate blood from overcoming him until he's responsible enough to carry the family name. They've had so many shifts of sentries guarding John Howard after he got caught you'd think Aunt May Julie's house was Buckingham Palace.

"It's become a real problem since he turned full-time on to girls, dating and running around every chance he gets, so they hired Pépé, the son of one of the tractor drivers—he grew up in town and never did a thing until he got this job following John Howard around all over the county. Pépé has this little souped-up VW bug. Imagine parking to make out with your girl and having somebody in a bug a few yards away watching all the time, but John Howard just laughs it off, says all the girls love to be with him because they feel so safe. My suspicion is that he's got a partnership going with Pépé and the Tate fate is back in operation—that's what I meant when I said my first thought, when I saw the El Camino in the blacksmith shop, was 'John Howard's loose again.'

"I climbed in to see what might be stashed in it, thinking he was dumber than I gave him credit for, with Mary Lucy due home again from college in another month and bound to be on his tail—I'll have to tell you all about *her* sometime, but right now, I have to finish about how I got to know Tony. You tired of this subject?"

Harding, who'd been nodding at the right places and encouraging Aimée to go on, shook her head, "On the contrary, I'm dying to hear more."

"Well, I'm dying to tell it. Like I said, I wouldn't dare breathe a word of this to anybody from around here—it would get back to Uncle Randy for sure, but as soon as I heard about you being a literature professor doing all this work by yourself, not talking to a soul and never sticking your nose outside the Boullet House, I had an idea you would be just the kind of friend I've been dreaming of."

"You can depend on it, I'm not from around here."

"Well, the key to the pickup was hanging in the switch so I started it up and worked it over to one side to make room for the Jag. As soon as I cut the motor I saw him—my puppies squooshed under his arm—standing in the doorway with one hand on his hip and his legs apart and naked as a jaybird. Not a strip on him except that silver St. Christopher he always wears around his neck, and with the light of dawn just breaking between his legs he looked so enormous and sca-a-ry!

"I had that El Camino out of there before you could blink twice, just barely missed the Jag but there it stood blocking the lane, so I swerved and took off into the clearing over by the big live oak, and raced around it three or four times like a stock-car driver before I saw him sitting on the Jag, waving every time I passed and doubled up he was laughing so hard, and the puppies running in circles at his feet. I saw I needed a plan, and fast, so next time around I slowed and yelled, 'Want a ride?' He took off after me and when he was about to catch up, I said, 'Are you going to behave yourself if I stop?' and he says, 'Behave myself?! I'm going to haul you to the sheriff's office for ripping off my truck!'

"That did put the situation in a new light—I mean how was I to know it was *his* truck—but I wasn't taking any chances with a stark naked man, so when I got a little more than half way around the tree again, I slammed on the brakes, jumped out and threw his keys under the tree and made a dash for the Jag. As soon as I got in I knew I'd lost but I locked the doors and just sat there. He calmly picked up his keys from under the tree and strolled over to the Jag, dangling mine in his other hand. When he opened the door, he said, 'Even-Steven swap.' I was scrambling to get out the other side but he was already sliding into the driver's seat and had a convincing grip on my arm.

"'Now,' he said, 'just what in the name of holy Jesus do you think you're doing?'

"I started up a babble about how my puppies had whined for attention so bad last night and woke me up so early this morning that my *husband* had told me to bring them on down to the cabin—they could use a little country air—and my *husband* had stayed behind to close the house and get in touch with Uncle Randy and they both—*both of them*—both of them were due to arrive any minute, just any minute . . .

"'Hold it right there, babe. Like they used to say when I was a kid and they caught me, you got chiggers in your hair piles. For starters, you and your pups pulled up at that cabin at 10:52 p.m. last night, and at crack of dawn you were in my El Camino. If you want me to help you out—and I just might—you got to be a touch more careful about the order of events. Who you running from, honey?'

"'Don't you have any clothes?' I asked. I mean how can you tell a man without any clothes on the truth?

"He looked down at himself then as if he'd just noticed for the first time. 'Damned if I'm not so used to it I clean forgot how women get the wrong idea the minute a man takes off his pants. Relax, babe, sex is the wrong place for force in my book—I like my women to beg for it.'

"I did relax some, at least to the extent of proposing that we park the Jag and the pickup in the blacksmith shop, out of sight. He had no problem with that and we walked over to the cabin and had breakfast together, wolfed it down—I gave him a towel to wrap around himself—he said it'd been a while since he'd eaten bacon and French toast with cinnamon and grated lemon peel and real maple syrup."

She stopped and smiled as if she'd come to the end of the story. Harding waited, and Aimée waited.

"You have a month or so to go yet," Harding said.

Aimée took a deep breath then and leaned forward to gaze with beseeching intensity into her eyes.

"I wouldn't say he exactly ever used force, but I was like . . . like a kind of hostage for that whole time. I mean I was free to do anything I wanted except leave, but when it was time for James to come home from Baltimore he let me go.

"After breakfast he took all my clothes, including the ones I had on, locked them in the trunk of the Jag and put the keys on the chain around his neck with St. Christopher. 'Sorry, babe,' he said, 'but you moved in on me so you'll just have to take up my way of life—besides, weren't you looking to hide out? I'll teach you how.'

"Of course he took control of the phone right off and would only let me make my Sunday calls to James, and I couldn't very well run over to the big house or anywhere else without a stitch of clothes on when I was supposed to be in Baltimore, now could I? I had to make the best of it."

She stopped again, her eyes demanding an equal intensity from Harding, who nodded and said, "You're a survivor, who can knock that?"

"That's it, I knew you'd see how I got into it and why I had to do what I had to do. I just knew you'd understand how it was."

"And how was it, Aimée?" Harding returned her look now.

"A new kind of night life, he called it. Real night life. We'd rise before sunset and go to sleep about nine or ten in the morning when the day was just getting off to a good start. Thank God I'm a fast learner—you have to know how to see and move in the dark. There were two hard and fast rules, one was you never switch on the light in the cabin—you want to always be where you can see them first and not the other way around, he said, not that we spent much time in the cabin except to cook. What we spent our time doing was looking for food—I had only brought a few items I'd picked up at the last minute—and we had to find it in the woods because that was the other rule: never leave the woods. When we got up he usually gigged a bream or trout in the bay and we had that with a salad of scurvy grass and purslane and wild lettuce, or with boiled groundnut and hog peanut seeds we pulled out of the ground. Three or four times a week there'd be a rabbit or squirrel and once even a bobwhite in the traps he set—he could make the most fantastic game stew with water parsnip and wild carrot and ginseng roots, with a few duck potatoes thrown in, flavored with redbay leaves and peppergrass.

"One of the first things I did when I got up was to pick camphor tree leaves and twigs with lavender and lemongrass, for replenishing our supply of insect repellent. I made a fresh batch every day mixed with a little juice from bloodroot stems; you had to keep putting it on all during the night. Between that and the sassafras stalks stuck in my mouth off and on all the time—he even locked my toothbrush away, said I wouldn't ever need anything but sassafras twigs to clean my teeth where we were—we smelled like an outdoor herb and spice cabinet.

"He reset the traps and we'd get our flashlights—that's all we ever took with us at night—and lazed around watching the last rays of the sun disappear. We knew the real night life would be starting in about an hour when the little pink-winged and white-lined sphinxes whirred past. Gradually, the lightning bugs start flicking on and off, and the walking sticks parade up and down tree trunks and limbs with their long-legged, skinny tremble—when you shine a light on them, they stop and sway like twigs— the weavers get busy on their webs and the brown and black huntsmen go after their prey the night long. At first the masses come out, the little ones—fruit moths, fairies, pusses and tiger moths, and then—then, the beauties—O, the beauties—we tied our flashlights to shrubs and saplings, no more than six inches or so from the ground, then spread a white sheet dabbed with honey beneath the light, and the first night, that very first night, a Luna settled in the little circle of light. In my excitement—I didn't know how to act in the night world yet—I frightened it away, but later on other beauties would flutter into the spotlight, sometimes just for a little. They'd light and shy off abruptly, almost like they sensed the violation, and sometimes they'd head straight for the light as though they'd been looking for it. They had this desperate need for it. Cecropia, with Oriental slits in that dragon face across its span, comes early on—then the Regal, and the Imperial, lingering the night long in yellow gown splashed with muted lavender, and Polyphemus and Io with those great eyes, and little

Rosy Maple along with Promethea showing her subtle finery only in the darkest hours. They're all there, it just takes time and patience to . . . to learn to move in their glory. But as he said, can you think of better company to hide away with for a time? And the Black Witch, always coming back with the beauties. . . .

"The name of the night game, he said, is Hunger and you eat, like the others coming out, whatever you can lay your hands on, whenever it serves itself up. Hardly more than a few minutes ever passed without something for the purpose—Solomon's seal rootstalks and lily roots, or the inner bark of slippery elm, berries, sunflower seeds, old fruit trees planted around the cabin by Uncle Randy: peaches, plums, grapefruits, little bananas just getting ripe.

"And the night world passes, the creature hunger gets subdued by the coming of light. At dawn, from the shallow edges of the sink, millions of ephemera crawl out for their few hours in the sun and then dive back into their birth-water to die in delivering more millions—that's the day game, he said, mating, producing, dying. After our morning dip in the little bay, we'd picnic on the rocks with boiled cattail on the cob and lie in a little hidden nook with the early morning sun on us and snake-doctors and dragonflies and bluets flitting above us until it seemed like the mad heat of the sun had snapped up the whole world. We'd be sleepy and relaxed, and we'd blink out the strong light and walk yawning down the path we made to one of the old tenant houses he'd cleaned up. We slept in it instead of on the bed in the cabin because Tony said if any of the family came over, they would only go there. Our old tenant house was empty except for the pallet of cotton and Spanish moss he'd laid in the middle of the floor, and our insect repellent and a bucket of our toilet water made from witch hazel leaves. We'd use that to splash and cool ourselves, and then sleep."

So that's how it was, how she'd gotten to know Tony. Aimée gazed at Harding, not for understanding or approval, or even assurance that her confidence would be kept, but asking a kind of question.

Harding poured out the last of her cold coffee and screwed the cup back on the thermos. The sun's glare oozed along the rim of their shady oasis.

"I see why you need to tell it," she said and stood up.

"You've been trying to get back to work and I've been jabbering on for"—she glanced at Harding's wrist watch—"my God! way over an hour."

"You may be getting mixed messages; I can't afford to interrupt my work, it's true, but a real break—I'm grateful for that."

"I never got around to the reason I barged in on you," Aimée said in a fast recovery of self-possession. "I really only wanted to ask if you'll be around tomorrow, late afternoonish—which is ridiculous, because of course you will. I thought maybe we'd stop by, Uncle Randy and I, on our way back from the . . . tennis club." A hint of apology in the slight pause.

"I'll be around," Harding cast a sour look over the broken concrete hunks and the gutted wreck of a house, "but I should probably have my head examined for being here at all."

"Uncle Randy admires women who *do* things—well, anyway I'm sure he'll admire what *you're* doing. I can't wait for you two to get to know each other." As though the subject called for irony but feeling demanded a deeper truth behind the irony, she added self-consciously, "There really *is* a difference, you know, between members of the 'old families' around here and the rest, whatever they say. Uncle Randy's grandmother was a Howard from the old plantation I was telling you about, and his granddaddy practically kept Tarragona from being taken over during Reconstruction. Judge Cane and his wife, my great-grandparents," she added archly, "but I've heard their praises sung so often I'm a wee bit weary of them. They must have been saints back in those days from what I've heard, I don't seem to be able to live up to my blood. Strain of the wrong color sheep somewhere, I guess."

"Lucy and Randall!" Familiar figures from the diary, their given names popped out of Harding's mouth as if she too had long heard of them.

"What?"

"Your great-grandmother, she must have been the Lucy Howard who married the first Randall Cane," said in a deliberate move to the more public and socially acceptable use of surnames.

"How in the world did you know that?"

Harding didn't miss a beat. "Can't possibly go to a new town and meet anybody without a little advance information about family lines—I mean, how else would we Southerners know how to talk to each other?"

Warm laughter from Aimée. "I keep forgetting you're really one of us—and remember, Uncle Randy can be *very* useful to you." This last said with all earnestness as Harding saw her out the gate.

Wouldn't Dr. Cane be put off by her grungy condition? Aimée assured her she looked like one of those revolutionary women so full of ardor for their cause they had no time for vanity, and Harding offered to donate her work clothes to the historic society when she was done with the Boullet House—"not an iota of ardor washed out of them." "I can already see the exhibit caption," said Aimée, *"Authentic uniform worn by a stalwart renegade daughter of the Confederacy."*

The visit increased Harding's sense of swimming in deeps neither anticipated nor chosen, looking into the town's face half-sunk in the ocean floor like some bottom-living fish. "I'd long ago seen knowledge for what it is," she says, "a predator, invisible to most, waiting in the depths, recessive and patient for the quick kill." Too much, too much—too late to surface now.

The weight of the sledgehammer rent a hairline fracture in the last big chunk of concrete and some kind of insight into why it was she had never been able—and would never be able—to throw in her lot with the survivors came clear for Harding.

Dr. Cane lived up to those flattering personals in the daily paper, had he been moved to write one: *Eminent psychiatrist, mid-sixties, handsome, athletic, impeccable taste, breeding, education, appreciates the fine things of life, intelligence, wit. . . .* When he extended his welcoming hand of introduction she'd checked an impulse to say: "Yes, of course, I remember your father at nineteen, all fired up about Cuban independence." Soothed by the feel of civilization in casual Western dress, Harding stood mute with him about Frances Boullet, acquiescing in the sanction against any recognition of her.

The tour of the Boullet House, more strained on her part than his, was as brief as she could decently make it. No innocent ambles around the premises—and no peace for her in the sanctuary that night either. Her joy in it collapsed as willy-nilly as walls under the onslaught of Ware's demolition crew—images seeming to fly at her in bits and pieces, or, just as wildly, melting into a horizon so flat, so hopeless, so poignant with absence she could distinguish neither form nor color. Like engaging in an act of pleasure without the experience of it.

But she stayed, tending to herself in the way now open to her, sinking to the floor with diary in hand, braced by the altar—on with her reading.

June 18, 1863—Am I really Moundong's "horse"—a chwal? Was I "possessed" by a spirit? Never wholly forgetting myself—even when Moundong took control and spoke through my mouth—I knew he would leave me and I could quit the absurdity of this concealment, ascend into the light of the library, never to return. Yet in all truth, it was not I who spoke thus; and I begin to see how it is that, through the discipline of being not myself—but something other than myself—I cannot avoid becoming what I am being—I become Moundong, drinker of blood and eater of flesh, all the while knowing myself for what I am.

I do not feel the same. Nor even after five years under Nongka's tutelage was I prepared for the rudeness of it—I am in some way angry—or would be angry—if I did not accept that the shock cannot be softened. Moundong is a special loa for Nongka and it is she who brought me to him; he rarely associates with Legba or Erzilie Freda, who have mounted Zula and Ibo from their earliest years. For the first time, I grasp why it is that, while playing with the freedom of children, they never seemed so—and understand, at last, how far from the guilelessness of childhood Zula and Ibo have always been. How artlessly I have loved and prized my studies! Shall I ever, again? Nongka says yes, but henceforth, love will root in this condition of being entered by another—of not being myself, but Moundong, drinker of blood and eater of flesh. Submitting to possession makes knowledge what it is— drinking from the primordial welling of things into being quenches my thirst to become what enters me. I have no regret even as I feel a loss of something, or some way of being myself, that is forever behind me— the way of an animal, a kitten or a kid. Or a baby, that unnaturally and precociously masters a great range of physical and mental aptitudes, and romps in vigorous exercise of them. I have lost the ignorance that enabled me to frolic in this fashion but was unsecured—not ill-judged, but unjudged, like the actions of an idiot. Nongka says my capacity for the animality of happy idiocy has not been lost, only schooled to undergo transformation; the passing of such delights—however much they may depend on ignorance—is never to be dismissed lightly.

From now on, whenever I wish to write in my diary, I am under command to come to our sanctum—here, where all gods enter, writing is to be my practice for receiving them. As I stand in the lamplight of our altar, Nongka's paintings of the loas—interwined among the eaves and rafters, and streaming out of every corner—wrap me in their wholly animated space. Like Nongka and Zula and Ibo, I shall be visited often now, and must train my capacity to let myself be taken fully, and forget—learn to forget, for I cannot do so naturally. I am not afraid, as long as Nongka is here with her mambo knowledge of Moundong, the only spirit I fear—that power to intervene and force me from all I love.

At sixteen, Zula has a natural control that promises, in time, to be the equal of Nongka's; but in Ibo there has always been something like a longing for possession, that makes him depend on help from others. For two days he was wholly possessed by Erzilie Freda, remembering nothing afterwards. This morning, in his gentle fortitude and agile beauty, I see him again as she mounted him—alternately lovely, with an aura of refined mystery, and openly sensual in the slightest movement of limbs under the shimmering pallor of her dress, with its silver skirt and fringed chiffon shawl fading into panels of palest blue. Had Nongka not lured the loa from him, he could not have put her aside, freed to be his usual self. Dear and beautiful Ibo—how willingly all of us would stand watch to ensure that you come back to us!

July 21, 1867—Last night after kanzo, a new loa took possession of us all. Under the guidance of her gros-bon-ange Zula designed the vèvè—pulsating parts of animals and plants, through which tentacle-like chains loop and converge upon two raised arms, crossed so that each hand at once winds and unwinds the chains around the wrist of the other. This loa, whose name is Vò—the very spirit of vodu—is mine. Mine as no other, even Moundong, is mine: my own image transformed by the harrowing of our sanctum. After chanting and singing in the library (our peristyle), we had just begun to dance when Nongka—all marks of age shed in both voice and gesture—began speaking langage in an ecstatic timbre:

From the first, yé!   Through all time, yé!
        I listen, oh!   And wait, oh!
            For your summons!
    I am the spirit, yé!   Slavery in all things, yé!

Dirt my food, yé!   Florida water my drink, oh!
        Vò my life my love, yé!

    I Vò-Frances, oh!   Spirit of all color, yé!
    No jealous god, She!   As old as all things, yé!
                She comes not forth, She!
    Nongka first I mount, oh!   Vò-Frances rides, oh!
                Only the free in their slavery, yé!
                She rides, yé!

Only these, oh! God-ridden, yé!   Bear me, oh!
            Taken by all, oh!   Enslaved, yé!
            All things subject, yé!
                I touch, oh!
                I smell, oh!

                She ties all things, She!
    To eyes to ears tied, oh!   I round the living circle, yé!
    The dead reach out, oh!I ride on and on, yé!
                From the heads of my horses, yé!
                I Vò-Nongka-Frances, yé!
                Come to you, oh!

Take me and eat, yé!
Deny me this, oh!   Earn my revenge, yé!
Through all time, yé!

Let those who can, oh! Dispossess me, yé!
To you Florida-Vò all that is, yé!
And is not, yé! Surrenders hé!
No harness, hé!
Zula-Florida-Vò tops a wild one, yé!

Sing now the catalogue of kinds! Chant, yé!
Yé, I belong now to my-kind
The kind of my-kind is no-kind
I belong now to the woman-kind
Woman-kind not my-kind
I belong now to the white-kind
White-kind not my-kind
I belong now to the strong-kind
Strong-kind not my-kind
Name it! Name it! Chant, yé!
I belong now to the African-kind
African-kind not my-kind
I belong now to the man-kind
Man-kind not my-kind
I belong now to the human-kind
Human-kind not my-kind
Yé, I belong now, etc.

I Zula-Florida-Vò-Nongka, yé, answer your call!
Yé! Yé! Yé!
Hé! Hé! Hé!

We turned to Ibo intently tapping out the new rhythms on the bébé,
and motioned him to join us. He took down the manman—which we
have never before done without muffling its sound—nor has Ibo ever
before been allowed to horse a spirit while drumming. Zula took the
bébé, and Nongka the moyen, and placed the ogan into my hands—
and for a time, the rhythm of our new spirit resounded clear and
unforgettable around us:

Look look! Quick now the tree there and there see me see!
Quack and roar and hiss oh hear oh see!
Squirm there the worm—see me see!

Breathe the vapor of slavery in all things!
I boil I fluff I flurry I glide!
Hear the roll of my silence in all things!
Frances-Florida-Vò spirit of slavery!
See me hear me!
Along the shore of human eyes and ears I gallop!
Unseat me not feel me feel!
Mine no beast of burden's feet!
Who weakens under excess I mount not!
No human I mount not human!
No tree not a tree holds me!

Ignored not forgot I never leave!
Today opens tomorrow me on your back!
I Frances-Ibo-Vò yé hear and see!
The spirit of slavery in all things!
I double I serve all things!
Ibo-Zula-Frances-Florida-Vò-Nongka!
Rein in spur on ride ride ride!

April 2nd, 1872—Without Nongka the spirits would never have known me nor I them. And now she is leaving us—she says her work here is done and unfinished odds and ends beckon her to Hayti. Papa will take her there, where a band of friends wait to sail with her among the Islands, Cuba and Jamaica to start with, on through the Antilles and up through the Windwards and the Leewards, then back to Hayti and the new Liberal Party's welcome. She smiles at our tears and our fears for her safety. None of us, she says—not even Papa, who ought to know better—comprehends the freedom of old age. She leaves us in her seventy-ninth year.

Last night Papa and Jonathan smoked and drank their brandy downstairs while we celebrated together for the last time. I received the asson. The loas come often now and I am taken without fear for myself or others. Laughingly, Nongka has vowed to provide for me after death: if I am overpowered, her strength shall be mine. Nine years have passed bringing my capacity for enthusiasm under the harness of control, years of apprenticeship in horsing the powers hunting materialization here.

At breakfast this morning Jonathan asked—with an amused concern I no longer find lovable—whether Zula and I "really believe in" what he likes to call "that spirit-twaddle." I took his question seriously this once and replied that belief is irrelevant to the practice of vodu.

In our sanctuary, we celebrate the undeniable repetition in experience, we enact this opening—our performance comes to each of us in bodily form, we repeat ourselves and create rituals that stretch us to our limits. Where we are going and what we are becoming emerge in their movements and rhythms—it is thus, I said, we learn to have some voice in the matter. "When I speak as Vò-Frances," I finished, "I see myself passing over a frontier of the unknown—horse and rider in the precarious unity of our existence."

At this, Jonathan turned thoughtful and said, "What you're describing sounds like a rite of intellectual discovery. You take such pleasure in the intellect, but—tiens!—I cannot imagine how something so barbarous in appearance could serve so high a purpose."

Zula threw up her hands in a merry pique. Touched by his earnest bewilderment, I reminded him that the world's religions all have an air of barbarism about them—and all lay claim to some more or less highly developed mode of insight. "What is it about vodu," I put it to him, "that provokes so much superstitious fear?"

"Surely, the practices of some give ground for such fears," he retorted, and Zula returned smartly that these were the very ones who proved the need for a longer apprenticeship. "Apprenticeship in what?" he wished to know. "In the pleasures and responsibilities of hosting spirits for the right practice of vodu," she shrugged, and wandered off into the garden.

Could I deny, he persisted, that the "mumbo jumbo of vodu" was the very language of superstition? As patiently and plainly as I could, I then tried again to make him understand that our sanctum is a place we go to not for magical power or esoteric knowledge, but for sounding the distances: drastic actions opening views from where we watch and hear ourselves in progress. The sanctuary is our scene for rehearsals of tomorrow, for what can be freely done only in its privacy—a panopticon of practices for living.

He questions no further, but treats us like votaries of some exotic, though not wholly discreditable, secret society with a penchant for busk-like rituals—he has begun calling us his three "buskers."

On our walk this afternoon Zula—à propos of my remark that our sanctuary provides escape from the evolutionary dilemma by opening a social time apart from the human hive—initiated a conversation much to his liking—about a primitivism in Darwin's theories that both makes our continuity with nature evident, and reveals how we humans actualize an impetus in nature toward self-transcendence by re-presenting ourselves: a renewal in the form of another. Given our accord on this point, Jonathan again expressed amazement that a woman of Zula's warmth and ways with children would choose to have none of her own. In response, Zula pointed to a kitten cavorting among the butterflies and, dropping her usual womanly manner, stalked and leapt about in kittenish mime.

Late Sunday it rained, hard lashing rain until well after midnight. Next morning at dawn, clear and fresh, Harding raced to the Boullet House to check on the library wall and the sanctuary behind it. All dry, safe under a layer of tarpaper newly tacked over the roof—Miss Mary Louise, who had sent Martin Kingston around with his wheelbarrow and dump truck the previous weekend, had seen to that too, she was sure. Shortly, Krasner, Kingston, and a third man were up on ladders in the first sparkle of daylight, preparing to shingle.

She pieced together a garden hose long enough to flush out the house, upstairs and down. The three on the roof sawed and hammered straight through lunch and into the hottest part of afternoon as the house gradually dried out, bare gutted interiors really clean for the first time. Purged of grit clinging to wooden wall studs, of putrefied matter crunching underfoot.

But outside, scraps of rotten cedar and asphalt, scraggy slivers of tin, and generations of tacks and nails still clung to every ledge and crevice. Fine particles of old debris drifted in, along with fresh sawdust. She shut the windows and, despite temperature readings in the high nineties all that week, blistered tenement-green oil paint off sashes with a rented torch, scraping and cleaning up after herself as she went. Fumes of old lead paint burning off, lingering.

Proposition: Comes a time when passion survives in the toxin of its bitter end.

The owner of the Strip Joint stopped by mid-week: doors, moldings, window frames ready for delivery. The sooner the better, they were not in the storage business. When was she planning to have a phone installed? It would make it easier to do business with her.

Close to four on Friday, Krasner whistled for her at the bottom of the stairs.

"OK, prof, get out your checkbook." They'd worked an hour past their usual quitting time.

"All done?"

"Done up and done in and waitin on my ree-muneration, babe." Crinkles around his eyes darkly precise with grime, a film of dust dulling the silver St. Christopher.

At the bottom of the check, taking care to make it clearly legible, she wrote: "For completed roof job at 321 Valencia." He sauntered off with it but swung back around in the doorway. "Party time—how about it? Last chance." A quick study of her—eyes dropped to stubs of checkbook, putty knife stuck in shorts pocket—then with the objectivity of one recording a pointer reading, "didn't think so."

Gone, all of them for now, and the stink, the rot, the sheer ugliness disposed of finally—rite of exorcism complete. The specters of Frances Boullet and her associates, along with the Wentworths in their decline and degeneracy, evicted—for all to witness—her shell of a house scrubbed clean inside and out, fresh patch of cedar on its back. ("Lifetime roof," he'd bragged—giving his word and refusing a written guarantee—"the kind that weathers through the years to a gorgeous gray like your own momma's hair.") It was easy, now, to imagine the sales pitch at Heritage Properties:

> Structurally perfect, historically significant residence in the heart of the Old Quarter. New cedar shingle roof. Plumbers, plasterers, electricians, painters can move right in. Original woodwork stripped for remounting. Ready in no time for those personal touches that make a one-of-a-kind home of distinction.

Margaret Avery would know just how to market it to buyers of history's upscale side, with money and a taste for the old and genuine, who'd never dream of grubbing in corners for rot and remains—it's elementary, every hour spent on your knees, whether literally or metaphorically, diminishes your effectiveness as a transactor of human affairs at a rate so astronomical no one has yet managed to devise an accurate measure.

But Harding's conclusion that the dirty phase of the work was over proved—very shortly—to be a fallacy of unexamined heights.

January 3, 1923—You, too, Jonathan? Days long gone revived this morning with the visit of Mary Elizabeth and Cathy, brought together in their gentle concern for me. And young Randall with them—no longer young, but as deferential to his aunts, in that imperiously formal manner of his, as ever he was to his dead mother. Mary Elizabeth, always small and delicate, looking very frail. With Julia's reign as Tallahassee's social luminary prematurely ended three decades ago now, she's done her best to keep up the family tradition at El Inglés, where Cathy joined her for Randall's reading of the will. (Cathy's husband, we've heard, is prospering beyond measure with his new hotels in Miami.)

Randall broke the news (his first words to me since Lucy and the Judge succumbed to influenza near the end of the Great War—"Charlatanism!" had been his reply to our offer of help). The sisters looked on with their familiar self-effacing solicitude, and when he was done, embroidered his dry report of Jonathan's death with a tale that delicately avoids putting him in a bad light. It seems that Jonathan's love of the sea and rambling in the islands, a love he never lost, led him to gather a party of young people (one of whom was Julia's grandson, an up-and-coming member of the state legislature) on an outing to Cuba in a convoy of his small speed boats. The authorities, on the lookout for vessels running rum cargoes from Havana, fired on and overturned some of them on the homeward stretch. All managed to swim safely ashore—all but Jonathan, whose eighty-five year-old bones put to the test among the treacherous coral reefs failed him at last. They recovered his body and brought him to El Inglés for burial as he wished.

Nothing has changed. No reproaches or hints of censure. The two belles (as I still think of them) appeared animated as ever by the sincere and magnanimous wish to embrace me, their quaint cousin Fannie of old, in the warm oblivion of feeling.

Randall's presence gave me strength. Executor of Jonathan's considerable estate, he was in my house in that capacity alone. Inasmuch as I, the will reads, had expressed my intention to lay no claim to Jonathan's material possessions (mainly lands acquired in South Florida), he wished these to be divided equally among his surviving Howard cousins—Mary Elizabeth Howard Brooks and Catherine Howard Stein. Having so informed me, Randall produced a small leather trunk, padlocked and tagged: "To be delivered unopened, by Randall Cane Jr. to Frances Florida Boullet, who possesses the key to this lock." The sisters were of the opinion that it must contain papers relating to some old business between Jonathan and Captain Boullet, possibly to do with the latter's adventures abroad (Papa having entered the annals of legend since his death). "Whatever the contents," I said, "they can be of no interest to anyone but Jonathan and myself." I meant to deflect their curiosity—amazed to see them exchange glances with all the coyness of our young days!—in truth, I had not the slightest idea what was in the trunk and possessed no such thing as a key. Quit of his obligation, Randall mentioned in an off-handed manner, as they were going out, that Jonathan had added an "eccentric" codicil to the effect that Miss Boullet could, if she so chose, lay claim to any or all of his estate at any time. "A legal absurdity, I believe," he opined, "in which Uncle Jonathan betrays his descent from that old mountebank Geoffrey Howard." How well Jonathan learned the art of trading from Papa! I recognized his stratagem for leaving the door ajar to my mother's family, should I ever want to have dealings with them.

I think that none of them (Randall least of all) would wish to see this "legal absurdity" put to the test. For me, it brings respite from their lifelong pressure to be one of them, a kinswoman in some sense that is not possible; and my cousins seem to share my relief, thankful that Jonathan's will somehow releases them from further solicitude for my welfare. Should I want anything, it is now plainly up to me to claim what is theirs. They're not in the least apprehensive, believing that, if I did, I would as a matter of course share all with them as they would with me, if only I let them. It doesn't occur to them that their beliefs and wishes might not coincide with mine.

Not a word about what I'm sure Randall knows as well as I (and what even his ingenuous aunts must have some inkling of), namely, that the coastal authorities were not mistaken in their identification of Jonathan's convoy. I doubt that any of the Howard belles or their husbands (except for Lucy's—the Judge always did keep a cool distance from Jonathan and asked no questions) ever recognized that the generous incomes they all enjoyed under his management of El Inglés, after Uncle Edward was killed in the war, could not possibly have derived from land worked by freed slaves. Even that would have been lost to them but for Jonathan's providence—and Papa's shipping business too, no doubt, revived by Jonathan in the early '80s with benefit to all of us. Since Prohibition went into effect statewide, he has conducted a smuggling operation of liquors and rums on the Florida coast, and the great fortune amassed thereby he converted into the only form of riches with which any Howard could ever feel wholly at ease: property. Acres and acres of land. The legacy insures that they'll go on prospering.

August 30, 1935—Jonathan wagered that I would never exercise my power to cancel that insurance. And as far as that goes he was right. But like Papa, he never understood the nature of my relations with the Howard belles, that I had no stake in either destroying or protecting them personally. What I hesitate to destroy is innocence, the innocence that made their happiness possible and for which they alone must be held accountable. (With Maria-Louisa, that responsibility became a necessity for Zula and me as it was for Nongka in my case.) And now that I have outlived all four of Uncle Edward's daughters, they rest in my memory like dead children.

January 4, 1923—The padlock resisted our combined efforts to undo it, and we went to bed in something of a pique at Jonathan's little masquerade. This morning, Zula put our sharpest kitchen knife to work on the leather straps girding the trunk, and it opened without further ado. Neatly packed inside were two hundred bundles of a thousand dollars each and the "Shakespearean" necklace—finely beaten gold spangles strung from tiny hooks in the upper compartment— intended, we supposed, for Zula, who promptly wound it about her neck. With head back and arms folded, face poised so as to set off her wide cheek bones, she caught the look of an Indian matriarch grown old and strong in the preservation of cultural integrity. Jonathan's passion for her never waned.

Under the bundles of money Maria-Louisa found an envelope addressed "To my Three Buskers Whose Spell Renews Life." She opened it and proceeded to read aloud his letter, which I paste here into my composition of this, our book.

My Darlings,

One last effort to capture what it is I yet want from you. Even as I begin I see you, Zula, clamp your slender wrists together and shuffle your feet in imitation of a chained prisoner. You, Frances, you dart behind her to peer out at me in impish mockery of fear. And Maria-Louisa, with your sharp young eyes, you make as if to blow a kiss at a foolish old uncle who cannot think or write but by rendering his own thoughts captive. But I am not so utterly blind to my manly dotage as you suppose, my bewitching ones, for I understand that your failure to host the prisoner is one with your refusal to play the role of hostages, like the Howard "belles"—your name for them, Frances; for me they have always been "sisters," and they are pleased to call me "brother." I confess I love them all the more for their captivity. With my mother, the Bride of Freedom, I experienced the terror of natural forces. I came to accept terror as natural. From the Captain I learned how a man can harness and extend the forces of nature, mechanize them and turn them into instruments of terror, making terror acquire purpose. Victory sides with the Master of the Terrible. And the necessary consequence of necessary terrorism: the Horror? The very being of my sisters depends on it. It was love that compelled me, I tell you, love of them; but love too—if you like, Zula—of Culture in all its refinement and delicacy, love of Culture at its purest. As the Captain adored your mother, Frances, so do I pay homage to the goodness of that innocent beauty which cannot be mine, but to which I may return in my sisters. And if their existence is made possible by a man's acts, I put it to you, Frances, who know so well both their life and the Horror: is the one not worth the other? You, Zula, your wisdom so like my mother's, the fruit of Nature's terrors without purpose, is there not in you a cry to have plans made for you before disappearing into the wilderness? And you, Maria-Louisa, as you grow in knowledge, would you not reclaim your childhood if you could, to rest your eyes in its simplicities again?

There you have it. I have done what was necessary to accomplish a man's purpose, striving to divest horror of its ugliness. I have met my mother's mute reach. But oh my darlings, when you read this, how glad I'll be to finish with it! Ours has been a raging alliance, my captivating buskers, against all that kills and mutilates and defiles. And yet I feel that I lose you, and always have. Your incantations issue from a place I know nothing of. I find no meaning there, no power to mean, and this estrangement is something I cannot bear. I do not ask that you come to me—have I ever?—but only that you let me cross over to you. Nothing more, only to be with you now and again. But this, of course, is the greatest of all that can be given.

How I go on and on in my dotage, knowing that you wait for a story and understanding that this has always been my bridge to you. Let it be told in your busk for me. Begin, then, the púskita, prepare the tobacco, brew the black drink of the yaupon holly, dance the turkey dance—be my tadpoles, chant my old life in the fire of your memories, let all injuries I have done burn there and leave me as clean and pure as the new harvest. Dance the mad dance and let me come to you shrouded in the new form you give me. Hear, then, the last of my tales: how my mother became an alligator spirit.

Many years ago, when she was dying, the Bride of Freedom gave the gold-spangled necklace to a one-footed Indian named Iste. Her instructions were to deliver it to me with these words: "Let the necklace be wound three times thrice around the neck of the woman of your choice and the spirit of an alligator shall enter her. Choose carefully."

As a youth, Iste set out to become leader of a little band, no more than a half-dozen in number, calling themselves the Last of the Colusa. He determined to find a place for his people, somewhere safe from the white man. One wintry day, he came to a beautiful little lake fed at one end by a spring. At the other end the lake narrowed into a spreading marsh where green-yellow and gray moss gathered over fallen limbs and logs jutting from mush and saw grass. Young Iste walked in high spirits around the lake, back and forth. Three times he rounded it in each direction, counting the varieties of fish and smelling the freshness of the air. A good place for his band to finish out the winter. Pleased with himself, he dropped down with his back against a tree and, idly stretching his legs, tapped a foot on one of the mossy logs protruding from the narrow channel to the marsh. The fierce grip of pain around his ankle told him, too late, the truth as he was thrashed about in the slush with such might his foot was torn from his body. He never lost consciousness, and he escaped to lead his people back to the beautiful spring-fed lake.

The stump healed cleanly and fast. Iste used his arms and hands for balance so that he could hop about on his one sound foot. Daily he studied the ways of the alligator that had attacked him. All its needs were satisfied with a perfect economy of movement; alone and undisputed master of its terrain, the alligator never moved over a few inches in any direction. Its head stayed under water with only the top showing like a submerged log. It had even formed the habit of opening only one eye whenever any disturbance was near and seldom opened the inner shutters of its eyes at all. Once a week, it fastened one goggled eye on something edible and, in a quick sideways dart, clamped the intruder between its jaws. After a head-back gulp, it sank back into its place without disturbing the moss gathered in the narrows where it was passing the winter. Nothing escaped the grip of this alligator, and it never left the warm shallow channel.

Meanwhile Iste learned to leap about on one foot at astonishing speeds. He also mastered the art of lying on his belly for long hours, as motionless as the alligator he watched from a distance, eyes, mouth, and muscles working in perfect synchrony with those of his greening enemy. The day came when, covered with moss and mud, he lay so still a bird lit on his back. He knew, then, he was ready and called together the Last of the Colusa. As the alligator had caught him and devoured his foot, so would he in turn master the alligator and take its powers into himself for the benefit of his people. It had downed him with an old, old trick; he must prove himself worthy of becoming their leader by out-guessing it, head on, alligator to alligator.

Spring came and Iste's battle plan lacked only one particular: a decoy. The alligator's repertoire of habits enabled it to dispose with lightning speed of any commonplace object approaching it. The ideal lure, therefore, must be wholly unfamiliar, yet emblematic of an ultimate and intimate satisfaction. Now it so happened that the Bride of Freedom, travelling alone through the swamp with the gold necklace twined three times thrice around her neck, came upon Iste's band. She had them test the strength of the gut on which the spangles were strung and admire their soft luster and the musical tinkle they made in the breeze. As the necklace passed from hand to hand for all to marvel at, all agreed that the white man's gift was the perfect decoy. Its round spangles glinted like the night shine of a swamp full of alligator eyes.

Iste's enemy had by this time put aside its winter habits and was floating about freely, darting with an undisputed sovereign's ease and speed to snap up fish, turtle, water fowl, or young deer or muskrat on the lake bank, the full spread of its pewter hide flashing through the water. Its mighty jaws clapped over all manner of snakes with special gusto. Iste—his eyes always on his enemy—would thrust his head back when eating, extend his neck, and feel his chest flex upward like the alligator rising to swallow its prey.

On the day appointed for battle—a warm, bright day in April—Iste's adversary was nowhere to be seen. A fierce roaring and bellowing of alligators in combat could be heard from the swamp where they were making ready for mating. On the evening of the fourth day all grew still. Soon Iste spied his enemy squeezing through the channel in the company of a female. A single great roar broke the silence, and jets of potent musk steamed over the lake as he patted and nudged and circled her. Night fell and deepened, and still he circled her, faster and faster, in perfect silence under the bright moon and stars. Iste waited. Towards midnight, the female lifted her tail and was mounted, then floated to the channel and crawled into the marsh as the male lazily moored himself in the moon-washed shallows of the lake bank.

The Colusa, meanwhile, finished greening Iste's body with moss and bathed the necklace in alligator musk. From a distance, they watched as Iste dropped to the ground and, holding aloft a cane pole—the necklace looped along its whole length with one large loop at the front—squirmed toward his enemy resting motionless in its satisfaction. It turned one eye, inner lid still shut, on the tinkling glitter of alligator eyes approaching in the moonlight, and at that precise moment, Iste lowered the pole. The spangles quieted and Iste too lay unmoving with one eye open. When it drooped shut and he felt his own body slacken into somnolence, he knew the alligator had done likewise. Iste now raised the decoy and inched forward and let the glinting spangles swing back and forth. Again, one eye opened. Closer, still closer, slowly lowering the spangles near the alligator's head until he felt the sidewise dart of his own head and simultaneously jerked the necklace from his enemy's reach. Again and yet again it grazed the alligator's snout until Iste, bounding forward on one foot, pulled the cane toward himself even as his enemy heaved out of the water.

On dry land, the necklace tinkled softly between them. Iste drew the cane all the way back to himself and crouched low, eye to eye with his enemy, and wriggled his fingers through the forward loop. The instant the alligator's head thrust forward, Iste pulled the loop into a noose around the jaws as they snapped shut, and wound the powerful gut over the snout and head in a tight harness. Two of his band sprang forward, one to each side of the alligator, and gripped its front legs and dragged it to the pen Iste had built. There, throughout the morning, it twisted and rolled and thrashed its tail. Smeared with earth, the gold spangles could no longer be distinguished from the alligator's bony scales. But the great jaws remained muzzled. His enemy drained of strength at last, Iste himself killed and skinned it.

The Shakespearean necklace, washed in the lake and spread over a cypress limb to dry, tinkled and glittered while the Colusa ate their enemy and Iste tanned the hide. Every spring thereafter, he would wrap it around himself and vanish into the swamp for four days, where his fierce bellows merged with those of other male alligators. He never failed to attract a female, whom he would nudge back into the little lake for his band to capture and feast upon. They became known as Alligator Indians and Iste was called Champion of Alligators. As part of their annual rite, they dipped the necklace into the lake and wound it three times thrice around the Bride of Freedom's neck. Settled with them there by the bountiful lake in the wilderness, where they were much feared and left to their own ways, my mother basked and gathered moss like an old alligator and died.

Jonathan Redman Howard

January 6, 1923—Sacrificed a fat capon today, stewed it in herbs and wine surrounded by rice and vegetables. Succulent. Accompanied by fresh fruits and a chilled bottle of Jonathan's favorite sauterne, it was carried to our hounfor to satisfy the spirits in proper enjoyment.

Later, as I lightly drummed and Maria-Louisa danced for Papa Legba to open us to the spirit of Jonathan, Zula wound the Shakespearean necklace three times thrice around her own neck. The spangles had hardly settled into place when she dropped prone to the floor, arms and legs crimped in alligator fashion. By a wonder-work of reptilian squirms she raised herself on bent knees, feet splayed outward and palms upward at shoulder level, fingers flexed in alligatorish extremities, in which extraordinary posture she swayed hypnotically to and fro, sliding the lids up and down over her eyes like nictating membranes—before me was a somnolent alligator-woman. Age has done little to diminish Zula's natural capacity for control.

"Jonathan-Iste, come to me," she said.

Maria-Louisa's dancing passed into Jonathan's alert rapid movements so reminiscent of Papa. Tensely balanced on one foot in front of the alligator-woman, she answered: "I, Jonathan-Iste, hear you."

Alligator-woman: "As ever, you make plans for me, my son, because I am of great worth. Hear me: it is not the way of the women to satisfy your desire."

Jonathan-Iste: "Are they not my own three buskers, my allies in the struggle against the waning of our bodily powers?"

Alligator-woman: "Yours is the satisfaction of winning once and winning again, but I am she who stays the hand. The women are mine."

Jonathan-Iste: "What I would have from them, my mother, is the peace of their death."

Alligator-woman: "Your peace is in the long-seeing eye of the lover, my son, and the long-seeing eye knows no end of victory."

Jonathan-Iste: "I would have the beauty of their living and the flow of their joy, my mother."

Alligator-woman: "You desire more than my peace then. Hear the women, my son."

Jonathan-Iste (leaping gracefully on one foot beside the Alligator-woman and facing me) "Speak and I shall obey."

Alligator-woman (facing me): "Yes, speak now in the voice of the god Vò."

Vò-Frances: "I the god Vò-yes!". . (the oracular voice comes slowly now). . . "I Vò possessed-yes . . . a woman's rage, no hero's anger here-yes/the madness of peace-yes/I the mad Vò-yes . . . I embrace death-yes/the lonely, the crippled-yes/the humbled, the shamed-yes/the mutilated-yes/the sick and powerless-yes/the weak and defiled-yes/I Vò now take these-yes/for mine-yes/to have and hold-yes/in the passion-yes/of horror closed-yes/from beauty's space-yes/forever and ever-yes/ I Vò now come/cancel the Terrible/still the Power-yes—"

Here Jonathan-Iste broke in imploringly: "Take me O Lord and Friend, lead me into your sanctum. Take me, sicken and terrify me, shame me and blind me, humble me and madden me, corral me in the bonds of slavery, wrest my powers from me, have and hold me forever, make the many one-less, embrace me for all time! The beast has devoured my foot, I am entitled!"

Zula looked at me nonplussed and slumped to the floor rolling in laughter. Maria-Louisa has a good ear but it happens sometimes that she loses control and follows the lure of her own emerging desire before the passage has opened—this time it was the old pathos of transcendent reunion with Jonathan through eternity. We sometimes follow her detours to show where they lead; but the time has come for her to put aside her child's wish to find satisfaction in victimage and sacrifice, and so we talked with her of why it was that Jonathan could never quite grasp what we do here in our sanctuary—or, more precisely, do not do—how ours is neither the cut and thrust of struggle—the thrill of the fight—nor the peace of meditation, how we pit no power against power, have no need of either victory or reconciliation. Release from all that eroticizes the world—makes it seem grander, richer, and so hides the nature of the terrifying—would have sabotaged Jonathan's very reason for living. He "lost" us and could not find his way to us because there was no satisfaction for him in a beauty free of terribilitas—done with it but not unmindful of it, not innocent of it. In the face of his worldly knowledge, he could not shut out the beat at the heart of things and listened, like a medical man with his stethoscope, to its irregularities. We are a blot on the meaning of his life's work. We are the nemesis of the brother we so loved.

She is a quick learner and ever increases our delight in this, our sanctuary for drastic action. "What I hear you saying, she concluded in her admirably terse fashion, "is that Jonathan wanted most what he could never value."

August 14, 1935—To the end, Jonathan confused love of the terrified Howard belles with the mercy he extended to them. Mistook his gift of grace as proof of a natural justice due to them. But no power terrifies that does not bring, or signal, sharp loss—terrifying with the threat of losing all. A simpler passion infuses the weakening of our bodies since terror lost its power over us—the joy of living with neither Idea nor Agency to rule it. Nor tales to transform it into the agon of Civilization beating off the forces of Nature.

No, Jonathan, you were no refugee. Yours was a brave response to horror's clutch, but not, as you thought, one we shared. You could not escape repetition of nature's cruelties—you refused even to entertain the possibility of such escape. "The truth of things must be faced," you would say, never for an instant questioning your belief in nature's ultimate triumph, nor your resolution to take your stand there. That a truth can masquerade in lies you knew as well as any, but not that such a change of face can—like old age—reflect a change in character, and the masquerade become truth.

The space of beauty grows and the time for it dwindles daily as Zula and I approach death. The only answer from me even now, Jonathan, is that we can give you no help with your last request because for us, dear kinsman, there is no crossing over—nowhere to go and nothing to be. There is not now and never has been. So close— and so infinitely far from us!—is Shelley's "how terrorless the triumph of the grave." Oh brave solitary Jonathan, bent on bridling nature's power to horse Truth, if we charm you at such distance it is only the passing of life without antagonism that charms, singing its endless refrain of creation, its repetitive rounds lived out. Your dialectic of power-possession has no place for our truth. Even Zula was unable to persuade you that it cannot be possessed or shared but works merely to drain the power of whatever goes on. How could you, dear brother of old, have entered our sanctum, this place where what goes on is disempowered by its own truth? Could you have lived with us on those terms? The humdrum of our life, dear Jonathan—such drastic action freed by imagination of all heroism would have wearied you. We pass our days now like butterflies, their adult missions accomplished, folding and unfolding the full expanse of our wings in the sampling of nectars.

Six-thirty a.m., the face of DeLuna Bay flat as despair. And still no rain to dispel the heat, no nightly Gulf breezes working their cleansing ritual on the bloated air of the day before. Trees hunched motionless in Hernando Plaza and moss from the oak by the Boullet House drooped down the face of the dormers like the grizzled mop said to grow on a corpse's head.

Someone had hauled away Harding's improvised breakfast spot—the hunk of stone under the hibiscus by the fence. She gripped one of the iron palings to steady herself and took a swallow of tepid Gatorade, sickened by the rank mix of metal on her palms with old plaster-grit and dank de- caying leaves under her—no heart, this morning, for the worldly hodge- podge of the morning paper.

How to go beyond the synopsis, the mere pointers, to the arduous immensity of her weekend in the attic? The record heat, the brutalizing of herself—her strength finally at an end, even her endurance. Even that famous stubborn will of hers. Nothing that had come before could have prepared her for it. She'd forgotten all about the attic until after the roofers left and she went up to check on the new shingles. Her contract with Krasner nowhere mentioned who would clean up the debris collecting there—moldering wood, hunks of asbestos, shards of tin vicious as razors tangled up with splinters of fresh-smelling cedar. And nails beyond counting, old rusty ones and just-bought galvanized ones. An oversight, the junk that would fall through the rafters during days of ripping and re-roofing—whose shit was that?

She slumped sideways against the fence, condemned, it seemed, to fix these pointers eternally in their immense directions, reading them over and over again for the rest of her days. Telling no one.

Proposition: Passion guts like a mortician and leaves us in the finalities of silence on the other side of excess.

Seven a.m. Salt depletion, she reminded herself, and swallowed the last sour trickle of Gatorade, head sunk between knees. A pair of dainty scuffed ballet slippers stepped toward her on the other side of the fence—cotton skirt soft with countless washings and ironings, faded undulations of trumpeter vine on a ground pale as the green of midges' wings. Maria Zamora's wide black eyes looking down at her, hands pressed lightly together over her breasts, fingers pointed upward in an unconscious pose of reverence. A listening pose.

But telling what had happened—what had to be done—how to do that? How she'd hauled down bucket after bucket of toxic jumble, each descent from the attic a brief escape from hell into clean-picked ruin below. And back up into hell. No time to rest after the hauling—who knew how many buckets of the stuff, the numbers numbed with false difference—on without pause to the omnipresent black dust that was nothing like ordinary dust, so talcum-fine, so thickly matted and packed it should have been possible to roll back whole like a blanket of countless tiny skeletal remains—mice, was it? insects, baby squirrels, bats, birds?

"Dr. Shibbles says not to worry," Maria Zamora said softly, "rain's on the way."

Harding leaned into the fence for balance, legs trembling under her. The skin of her hands and forearms had the look of smoky crackle glaze.

Twenty-five hundred square feet of attic, top to bottom, two inches at a time through the sucking steel cylinder of the vacuum hose, a slide into nightmare taking on the feel of movement in an everyday world—how to explain that, once certain limits are crossed and the body has strained beyond those limits and then beyond, you can still go on. Without being anyone in particular, without a single thought or impetus beyond the next movement of a finger or foot. You can, it's true—done and proven—you simply keep going like a machine. But never mindlessly, not even when the mind is reduced to the mere transmission of motor impulses. Degraded, unrecognizable. Even when it splits off and hovers over the pain and sweat and weariness in voyeuristic separation, even then the relief of mindlessness is never within reach because you always know, for instance (as Harding knew without thinking), the danger of breathing in asbestos particles for hours on end.

Slowly she pulled herself up to face Maria Zamora. Someone ought to be told. Someone should be made to see that now, her ninth week in Tarragona, the house was in truth, and without media spin, ready for restoration in the proper sense—what everybody meant by restoration: new plumbing, wiring, walls, paint, floors, finishing touches. The harrowing done and she herself living proof of it, harrowed and mad—the ultimate null and void of the market.

Maria Zamora's slow-moving, frizzled salt-and-pepper head turned to gaze past the new cedar roof of the Boullet House. Perfectly compliant, receptive. Like the peasant girl in a classical ballet entering the village square early one morning, when the young prince is about to pass through on his hunt, she the cup that will slake his thirst.

Harding's right hand lost its grip, slipped away from her through the fence at nothing, and Maria Zamora took three quick steps back. A brilliant smile spread over her face. "You'll feel fine soon, when it rains," and her back receded into mazy green growth. Doc Shibbles came out his back door in a white cotton shirt clinging damply as he bent over to gather up the morning's trespassers: twigs, leaves, a feather dropped by a carelessly molting bird.

Harding drew back her hand and straightened, reorienting herself as though after an optical illusion. And with the sense that her neighbors watched from beyond the fence, where their meandering fifties rancher spread its mossy unrehabilitated safety about them, she swayed, wobbled, and rolled like an old drunk toward the back porch of the Boullet House, let the new handrail take her weight and stumbled slowly up.

Five minutes past seven: open the windows—stopping to breathe deeply and rest after each one—check the gutted house for anything that might have gone amiss in the night, gather tools for the day's work. Unbidden, there returned to her a glimpse of herself, that morning before driving to

Valencia Street, in the full-length mirror of the bathroom door: tired hag in a cheap motel room, crackled skin, lifeless hair, smudge-rimmed blood-shot eyes—one of those. The kind who, always overworked, grows old early and recedes into silent enervation.

"I am . . ." she sought the precise word for what she'd seen in the mirror, "pitiful." It was a truth that had the effect of bringing her back to herself—and to the darkness of the sanctuary, feeling her way till roughened fingers groping at the dress closed over the soft leather binding, the ribbon holding her place.

January 10, 1923—How this new wealth of ours raises the spirits! Papa's money gone so many years ago, already before Toussaint brought Maria-Louisa to us, that we've forgotten what it was like to have it, used as we were to living so long under the financial onus of satisfying our mere daily needs. The freedom to travel, of sheer physical movement in the world, gone for good, we thought. Now this release wrought by Jonathan's legacy fans the fire of our old passion.

A letter from cousin Cathy, wondering whether Zula—with her "exuberant imagination"—might be persuaded to design a mansion for her so unusual it would startle even Palm Beach sophisticates? A tempting proposition. But in truth we see no way to take it on, for any such design, Zula says, would have to be made on the spot, in harmony with the site, and under conditions suitable to our solitary way of life—this in a city where no Negro is allowed on the streets after dark, unless in the employ of some white resident (there's not even a Colored settlement in Palm Beach), and where all venues for gleaning experience necessary for such an undertaking are closed off to all but members and their guests. To Zula's brief account of these obstacles, I added a postscript—to the effect that I too regretted missing out on such a once in a lifetime opportunity.

But our imaginations are already otherwise employed; we spend the evenings surrounded by atlases and train and ship schedules and travel memoirs, plotting out journeys, always taking into account the climate at this or that time of year and how well we're likely to be treated—meaning, how truly we can achieve something like invisibility. We are old but strong enough, and Maria-Louisa, approaching her sixteenth birthday, must know the world before we die.

August 17, 1935—And she has. For the next seven years, as she grew to womanhood, we lived quietly and fully a few months here, a few there, with a stop every year or so in Tarragona, usually late spring when the garden was in bloom. We would do a little pruning and harvesting, and let the rest go. It was Maria-Louisa who insisted finally that we come back for good, to the comfort and privacy of our own house. The world no longer mattered as it once had. And I no longer worry about her. She has learned how to move with ease from place to place with the assurance that comes from never belonging to any place, her mulatto beauty worn like a prophetic ecstasy.

In the years since coming home we've been left to ourselves, tending our garden and keeping house. The right to solitude, and the extension of that right to Maria-Louisa, is one of the perquisites of advanced old age, and, in the dailiness of bliss, Zula and I make our plans. Would we have found our way so unerringly here without Jonathan's money? Zula and I, yes, but perhaps not the child, not Maria-Louisa. Money bought time that enabled us to bring her early, and more surely, into this home we have made—to live with us as we once lived with Nongka.

May 9th, 1927—Tarragona again, the garden running wild and the house as if struck dumb by another long absence, but all well, all undisturbed. Our "urgent business"—a Cane-ish exigency transmitted by telegram—concluded before the morning was half over, and Maria-Louisa and I impatient to be back with Zula at Trinidad in southern Cuba, where time passes much to our liking.

As for the urgent business, it concerned the Hernando and was hardly urgent and no surprise; the place has yielded nothing since the turn of the century, long enough that I've all but forgotten it was ever otherwise. There's not the money now, says Randall, to pay off debts that have accumulated on it—or rather, his agent says so, young Jeremy Wentworth, who recently entered the firm, after his father Jordan died in a drunken coma. Again, no surprise on both counts.

And so they've "taken it off my hands," that's to say they've assumed the debt in return for a deed made out to the Wentworth Trust. (Randall, it seems, cannot abide having the Cane name linked with the Hernando, although there's doubtless some scheme afoot for sharing any future profits from it.) Jeremy had with him one James Stuart Hurd, not much over twenty years old, if that, and looking perfectly phthisic, so pallid and bloodless he might well be the progeny, purified to the point of mortal remains, of some ancient Gaelic lineage. Maria-Louisa was so fascinated by his whiteness she seated herself behind a screen within earshot and proceeded to model his head in clay. He is to marry Jeremy's little sister Anne and take over management of the Hernando, where they'll have the rooms grand'maman and I lived in.

I feel a kind of pity for them. Hurd fretted about the condition of the building—with a shrill, distinctly ill-suited, husbandry—swearing he will not set foot in it until it is made fit for rearing his children. As for the Hernando—site of my mother's death, my first home—I feel no attachment to the place. Am relieved to be rid of it; another piece of baggage from the past now to be borne by others.

Labor Day, 1935—There's news that the Overseas Railroad to Key West was destroyed in today's hurricane. Along with sorrow for the injured and homeless, I experience, as Papa and Jonathan might have done, a savage pleasure—in mindless natural power periodically enforcing a levelling of mankind's unbridled strivings and dreams. If Florida beckons to the vicious, the sycophants, the parasites, the rapacious, the symbionts, but most of all—and most dangerous of all—the narcissists, to perpetrate all manner of exploitation in the name of growth and development, then the eye of the hurricane can be trusted to return again and again with its indiscriminate survey. Nature's violence taking its indigenous vengeance. Some say—I think they will prove right—that this land of flowers is destined to become so scarred by over-building it will no longer support human life, or any worth living.

So much for the old dream. There never was and never will be any gold here, as the line of Spanish questers discovered—Ponce de León, Narváez, de Soto, de Luna, Villafañe—ceding both life and fortune to the lure of Florida's false promise. Defeat and humiliation time after time. Of them all, Brother Luis Cáncer remains vivid in my imagination from childhood—seeking to save the souls of Spanish Florida's savages he tried, heedless of warnings, to approach them and the moment he stepped on dry land, alone, was clubbed to death. The prototype. His death a refutation of solipsistic projections as openings for movement through the world.

September 17, 1928—Last night Palm Beach took a direct hit from the hurricane before it moved inland, leaving nearly two thousand laborers, mostly Negro, dead. Cousin Cathy's life among the richest of the rich—her fondest dream realized by Jonathan's legacy, to own a home so splendid it would have no match anywhere in Florida, surpassing even the architectural refinements of Addison Mizner and Joseph Urban, even the Stotesbury "cottage" itself, with its forty-car garage and zoo—that dream may be at an end. Her "Minoan palace" sustained heavy water damage, and that probably means the frescoes are ruined.

We didn't expect to hear from Cathy again after Zula wrote back declining her proposal to design a mansion for her, but shortly a second, more urgent letter came. Understood—what she wanted could not be conceived in a vacuum. As for "obstacles," she had ideas about how to circumvent these and was taking steps towards that end; the three of us would, in a manner of speaking, be her "employees" after all—no questions asked. We could be entirely at ease on that head. I spelled out terms—dashing her fancy with a dose of my unreasonable nature, I supposed—we must be left entirely to ourselves if we came, never asked to lunch, tea, or dinner, or out into society for any purpose whatsoever. Was she in a position to provide the three of us with absolutely private living quarters? Within the week we received this telegram: "Have leased sixteen-room cottage with separate wing for you three. Own entrance and all facilities, walled courtyard. No social obligations. Please, please come at once."

And so we went, after all, the first of our journeys after Jonathan's death in '23, and stayed over a year in Palm Beach with its extravagant mélange of architectural fashions and styles to be studied—Spanish, Moorish, Italianate, neo-Gothic, latter-day Romanesque, Greek Revival, Algerian, Renaissance, even Turkish and Oriental. With no less deliberation (and the incomparable zest of senescence) we observed the town's seasonal habitués. What brought them to Palm Beach winter after winter? We started paying regular visits to the grandest hotels and clubs, all whose doors Cathy's "ideas" had somehow opened to us—on our own and, as we thought, incognito—hypothesizing that the pulse of Palm Beach life beat most strongly and clearly wherever games of chance were in progress, where the imminence of money cascaded into unspeakable fortunes vitalizes its own world of meaning. Once, when the doorman of a beach club announced curtly that unescorted ladies were not permitted in the gambling casino, I replied, taking hold of Zula's hand: "Young man, for what purpose would we at our age require an escort? No such rule applies to us. As for the young lady, we ourselves are her escorts, and I assure you she could wish for no more careful guidance, protection, or honor than we accord her." I then closed on him with an amiable but steely determination (what Maria-Louisa snidely calls "the Howard prerogative") not to be put off. He fell silent and, as we went in, ran off to consult with his manager who, proving to be an engaging young fellow, escorted us into the casino with amused courtliness, declaring himself privileged to welcome "Mrs. Stein's prodigies" (our first indication that we passed far from unnoticed). I can still savor the privilege of connections and the warmth of such encounters with those ignorant of our history.

Maria-Louisa seemed at first troubled by our gusto for gambling— and appalled, I think, at how Zula and I could so relish a world wherein suspense narrows life to the risk of losing everything that may be possible for oneself, or of winning all at a single throw. To her patent relief, she soon discovered the limits of our play and realized we were not putting at risk the freedom bequeathed to us by Jonathan's money. What, we asked ourselves, what in the midst of such daring to have all at one roll of the dice—and thereby to memorialize oneself as having taken the supreme risk and succeeded beyond measure—what, amid such frenzy of hazard and excess, would have the power to startle and intrigue? Zula concluded only that which was least like the prevailing spirit of the place could exercise such power.

By the time the season wound down—the glamorous winter guests departing like birds—she had conceived her architectural plan down to minute details. The Stein mansion would be built of irregular coquina blocks around a large central courtyard, with inner courts and light-wells from one to three stories deep—a marvel in channelling sea breezes and light. She alone must oversee its construction. Working with an architect, several contractors and crews, she soon earned the name "slave driver"—the building itself done in a record twelve months. No sooner were walls in place than she had scaffolds erected for frescoing the interiors, with Maria-Louisa assisting (any room where they were at work was off-limits to the crews). My role was to provide the presence of constant critical evaluation, to insure the desired balance between tropical exuberance and the effortless sensuous grace characteristic—or so one likes to imagine—of peaceable Minoan civilization.

Such days those were of uninterrupted sheer delight! I remember one scene in particular with deer, panther, black bear and king snake among windy palmettos, live oak, and hickory thickening into jungle-like growth, and opening into an orange grove with a life-size Nongka, in all her African strength and beauty, plucking fruit from branches. Female figures were everywhere represented by Nongka and males by Ibo, at times reduplicated with the stylized effect of Caribbean and Minoan group scenes, as in the great fresco of the main foyer—a steamer's decks crammed with Ibos and Nongkas in rapt concentration, all gazing down through the crystalline waters at the marine life of the great coral reef. But many of the frescoes were unpeopled, mere skies full of birds—storks and snakebirds, white ibis and egrets, herons, pelicans, magnificent frigate birds—masters of flight—kingfishers with their crested heads, and roseate spoonbills; or winding rivers banked with cypress and mangrove, threaded trumpeter vine, morning glory and jessamine, alligators gliding into brown ponds from slopes of wild blue iris, white callas, orange lilies, mimosa and orchids, and crimson-spiked air plants. Such was the Florida of our pristine play, a lost Guinée of undiminished beauty.

Word of the frescoes spread despite our efforts to guard them from public view. Workmen were bribed with phenomenal sums to arrange sneak previews for the curious (back in town for the seasonal whirl by then) until Cathy began to complain that the whole of Palm Beach knew more about what was going on in her new home than she did, her spirits, as anyone could see, soaring. Triumph was already hers—whatever was there to be seen had achieved the effect for which she was risking a fortune. Hardly an hour passed without some billet of introduction (purporting to honor our reclusive habits!) or flattering request for our appearance, all subtly or openly commanding our attention. Daily we rose with or before the sun to begin work in the earliest light, and the watch outside our apartments started at daybreak. The midday meal was a trial. It happened repeatedly that those serving our dinner were not who they seemed, but members of some family or other, or their surrogates, set on being the first to win a favorable response from the unbending female trio of "prodigies." One lady offered us a lifetime annuity for laying out her swimming pool in an original mosaic, to be followed by a single appearance at a pool party. A wealthy octogenarian promised to marry either Zula or me if our talents were put at his sole disposal, making evident that, although he somewhat preferred Zula by temperament, his bias towards whiteness was such that I came off as well. If the law permitted, he would willingly marry us both!

We felt ourselves enmeshed in some monstrously merry struggle with the whole of Palm Beach, everyone trying to cajole or purchase our appearance in the certainty that we must be playing some coquettish game of false scruples, to endow ourselves with potent mystery before finally yielding. A piece ostensibly about the Steins' "unique Minoan Palace," appearing on the society page of the newspaper, was abuzz with references to "enigmatic guests" and "undivulged names." Only then did we comprehend how it had come about that we'd enjoyed not merely an ordinary freedom of movement but the license flowing from expectation of some great feat—an authorization for inspired doings. Mention was made of a certain "Queen Zula," aided in the expression of "talented eminence" by her "exquisite daughter" and a Creole "lady-in-waiting." Queen Zula and her daughter were reputed to be the last scions of a West African dynasty transplanted to the Indies in colonial days and (with an extravagant disregard of differences among tropical islands) to be members of a noble family group portrayed by the French painter Paul Gauguin.

Cathy blushed to admit that even before our coming she'd planted hints about the "aristocratic lineage" of certain "exotic artists" about to appear on the scene to build her dream house. Later on she might have suggested—to this one or that one—how our seclusion from society was owing to the "secret of royal blood," our dignified ways being perfectly natural to us—always said with genuine distress to be discussing us at all. Other than that, she assured us, she'd always made a special point of declining comment—except to confirm that the queenly Zula was of island origin and I partly of French Colonial descent . . . also that our nobility was such that no one could confuse us with mere negroes. Wasn't that all right?

The scramble for recognition gradually undermined our joy in the work by destroying our freedom to continue it. As usual, our own struggle was for the power to maintain our privacy against pressures to set it aside for the sake of membership in the community. The struggle itself was now at the center of life, and the frescoes were turning into a grim task, no more than proof that we still possessed sufficient strength to go on. Cathy understood perfectly and, with that combination of acceptance and sorrow long ago adopted towards me by the Howard belles, did not press us to stay. If she had seemed to possess what others were seeking—our presence—we ourselves had become encumbrances to her and she was relieved, I think, to see us go.

We slipped away like wrong-doers, quietly, stealthily, in the night. Zula left a portfolio of studies for frescoes to adorn the unfinished walls, with the understanding that she would send an artist of her choice to complete them—we went straight on to Haiti and found a talented young man, the first of the long line of refugees we continue to harbor.

The Minoan Palace and Palm Beach life brought Cathy all she could hope for. A belle to the last. Her whole being answers to the capitalist tune of a call for public, communal ways of seeing and living in the manner of the rich. That we were instrumental in providing her with the final peg needed to establish herself in that life during the last few years is all to the good—the frescoes have served their purpose, and well, no matter how defaced by last night's hurricane.

September 8, 1935—A bit of conversation the night we left drifts back to me—Cathy, perplexed and as if she'd somehow failed with us, saying plaintively, "I feel I can never make you understand how loved you are here, and accepted. Truly accepted. These people want to honor, not harass you. Being either fantastically wealthy, or of good families, or unusually interesting in some way, or all three, they ask nothing but that you let yourselves be seen and admired. Yet it seems to me that you will not allow others to honor you—you don't . . . don't give yourselves to the love and acceptance they offer." Her voice had the old hurt in it, that always permeated my relations with my mother's family, and I, in turn, felt the familiar sting that always followed the perception of how my own being—my mere presence—pains them. I had no answer for her and gave none but redoubled my determination to be gone as swiftly as possible—remove myself and minimize the hurt, which can only be done by anticipating its rebound.

Zula's outburst took me aback. "Give ourselves? What, pray tell, do you think we've been doing here these many months? They have the frescoes and we gave ourselves to them. Gave ourselves—do you understand?—we gave ourselves to Palm Beach in the frescoes. We held back nothing. All we ask is to be left with something to give. It is not us people want but precisely not us. They want us to be one of them and that is precisely not to be ourselves. Oh yes, they would love and accept us as one of them, but we are not one of them, and I ask you: do they love and accept us as not one of them?"

Poor chastened Cathy, spirit of El Inglés, heard only that she'd been somehow inhospitable. "I don't know, Zula," she said with that troubled sincerity of hers, which was like a door opening to our childhood, "I do love you and accept you three as not of my kind, and I do deeply thank you for all you've done, and for the months and months you've spent creating the home of my dreams for me. I was just wishing . . . ," here her voice faltered in recognition of the distance between us, and Zula replied with equal sincerity, tinged with perhaps just a bit of irony, "as for that, it has been a privilege to give ourselves."

May 10, 1924—Maria-Louisa's body exudes the pain of erotic suffering, but of us three she is the most relieved to be gone from Palm Beach.

Surely no future lover could be any more dashing or handsome or brilliant than Ishmael Miller (or any more eligible—not yet thirty years old and sole heir to a vast New York family fortune). And unfailingly sensitive, in his passionate courtship of her, to our wish for privacy. He seemed to view it at first as the charming idiosyncrasy of privilege and talent, affected as a shield against the more vulgar stratum of the rich. (Also quick to grasp the advantage of paying court in the confines of our apartment, once he'd concluded that Zula and I gave them no mind.) Maria-Louisa retains the inflexible morality of the young, and Zula and I knew we could trust her not to endanger the life we have made—she would above all be fair to us, and that she has been.

It seemed too early to put her to the test, and he seemed too much of one, but we had no choice about it. They were in love. To our surprise he didn't reject her when she told him the truth about who we were—not royalty flitting about incognito, nor aspiring to that state. Initially, he appeared not to believe we were free of social ambition, though later on he came to view our lack of it as something he thought we had in common with him—a contempt for the self-appointed Palm Beach élite—persuading Maria-Louisa that he cared nothing for how others viewed her. In point of fact, given her beauty, intelligence, poise, talents, the protection and glamor of his money would virtually assure that anyone anywhere would find her more than socially acceptable—indeed desirable.

What Zula and I underestimated was not Ishmael but the influence that possession of Maria-Louisa would exercise over him. She said nothing, but it became clear from the change in his treatment of us—all three of us—that he had taken her. Courteous and considerate as ever on the face of it, his manner lacked respect in the etymological sense: to look back, look again. He no longer bothered to take another look at us because he now took for granted that he knew us essentially for what we were. A faint touch of camaraderie crept into his treatment of Zula and me—aging madams who, realizing they cannot attain to respectability themselves, have made the best of their misfortune by resolving to ensure that it does not befall their lovely young charge. That we should have left her alone with him for entire days, and with increasing frequency, could mean to him only our complicity in his possession of her—convinced that its price is marriage. Like a couple of crafty old sorcerers we've foreseen the potency of our bait and the trap into which he must fall. His very passion for her is evidence to him of its efficacy and he's prepared, even eager—if a bit rueful—to pay up.

Little by little a new "respect" for us began forming, respect of the more common kind: the esteem of one who has been had for those who have managed to bring it off. Through all his treatment of us now ran the scarcely veiled bitterness of one who, feeling he's fallen into the hands of others, anticipates a time when the power will lie in his hands once more. Maria-Louisa understands little of this yet. She suffers dumbly the transformation of an original opening on boundless warmth and satisfaction into the closure of abandonment to nightmarish compulsion. She cannot yet conceive, but feels, the threat of a future in which pain materializes like gangrenous tissue. Pain opens only one book of knowledge, and that of a very specific kind—of what we specifically cannot bear—and what she could not bear, and cannot bear right now, is her powerlessness to bring back the original thrill of simple mutual attraction. She cannot bear the fact that her own being is already such that she is unfit either to merge into his wealthy Jewish family or to join with him in rebellion against them so as to establish a separate unitary ground for their love.

Her judgment is proving sound. She makes no attempt to ignore, dismiss, deny, or distort this knowledge of what is for her an unendurable situation. She has resolved to be quit of it and has written him a letter to say they must never see each other again. Already her loss gapes like a wound. Zula and I suffer her passion silently and helplessly, aware and relieved that her seventeen-year innocence has passed. There will be other such experiences, for she is still only a girl. But none will take her by surprise now and none will hold her in this pain again. We leave for Italy within the week.

Nine a.m., on Harding's way back from the rental equipment store, outdoor thermometer at the bank drive-in above ninety in the shade. Barometer pressure holding steady, no forecast of rain, and back at the house still no sign of the blue truck, "T. Evans & Son, Master Plumbers" in shiny red letters across the immaculate cab door. Never mind that he'd promised, "Monday morning on the dot, shuga, just let us know if there's any change, hear?" and that she'd phoned daily for the past week to assure him there was no change, she was expecting them Monday first thing.

Harding stomped aimlessly through the clean-picked skeleton of the Boullet House, upstairs and down, then out the back gallery for a look around. Maria Zamora and Doc Shibbles had disappeared back into the cool safety of their cottage. Could be the Evans & Son truck was parked somewhere on the Plaza, Aubrey sidling down the alley to hang out in the shade for his nicotine fix, killing time before the old man showed.

No presage of father or son anywhere. She turned a bleary-eyed face toward the lush sequestering garden next door, where the distant flash of DeLuna Bay—a mirage of tranquility at the periphery of concentrated energy—sparkled through sunlight and foliage.

5

Blood Washes Blood

O save me from its inescapable wrench! Recessed in the wall, a pewter half-moon made for cupped fingers winked at me. On my way back from the bathroom just now, happily steeped in the security you sometimes feel when nobody knows where you are, I noticed for the first time—had been assuming I'd lucked up on some stronghold of progressive minimalism on Tarragona Beach, stripped of incursions by the world, present or past: externals like TV, wet bar, chocolate on pillow, bible, etc. only on request—but then, there it was.

I knew instantly and my fingers cupped without resistance. A slight tug and the boldly contemporary geometry of charcoal black on creamy white slid into the adjacent wall as smoothly as the sanctuary hatches on their tracks. And lo, it stands revealed: thirty-two inch Mitsubishi with remote, discreetly cached to accommodate a shelf-bar above. Singles of champagne, liqueur, a fifth of Jack Daniels Black Label, each in its own cage rigged to log what you take out.

Watch, watch, watch—I snap on CNN with a totally false nonchalance; I need to be sure I can never say I didn't know. Save our children from media violence, it's said on all sides—movies, cartoons, music videos, video games, porn. Not to be dismissive about it, but such images flipped off impatiently with a thumb tap simply aren't the kind I feel compelled to watch. It's the news—save me from the news. I live in the gap between common reader and news scavenger, somewhere between understanding and this screened take on the banality and blood of our daily leavings snugly fitted in their box like garbage readied for pickup.

Out of that limbo came this parable dashed off one sleepless night—I keep it in the diary after Harding's entry, for reading when the news crowds out everything else.

> Once there were three women, all Scorpios born the same month and year, who became inseparable playmates in childhood. During adolescence these three swore lifetime allegiance to one another and formed the Society for Elevation of Loving Friendship (SELF) dedicated to the ideal of realizing the best possible life within the limits of their ambit. An open-ended project. Each would find her own way and agree to mark the turns she took in proceeding toward the best possible life. At a SELF meeting in their eighteenth year, preparing to leave their childhood homes, they vowed to meet for a final say on the last day of the month of their eightieth birthday. On that occasion, sixty-two years hence, each would report on her success and her findings.

> The years swept by. In the twenty-fourth a tombstone was erected in the local cemetery, with this epigraph: *"She died, as she lived, for SELF."* Thirty-four more years passed and a second tombstone turned up close to the first, inscribed: *"She loved, as she lived, for SELF."* The seasons came and went four more times and the last day of the month of their eightieth birthday rolled around. None came forward to make a report but late that afternoon there was a funeral. When the earth settled, a stone appeared on the grave with this inscription:

Silence writes no ending
Ecstasy feeds on flesh and bone
Life opens death's scent-bag
Feeling seeds no sequel.

How, Sam, does one take a position in such ignorance? I refold my parable and, as Harding used to do, in her exhaustion and need, throw myself back into the diary.

March 14, 1880—Toussaint came home late last night with word of Nongka's death. His devotion to her has been single-minded—he talks of nothing but going to study in France, as "grand'maman wished." In the world's eyes he's still a boy, not yet twelve years old, but in Nongka's company our son has seen and understood more than others twice his age. Joined in our grief, Zula and I cannot assuage his.

They had joined a canboulay band of revelers at the Carnival of Trinidad, Nongka as a harlequin, a costume he chose for her because of its ancient demonic lineage. She was her band's leading chantwell, her sharp wit finding its consummate expression in the customary taunts exchanged with singers of rival bands, her mental faculties undiminished. Only her voice, at the advanced age of eighty-seven, had lost its resonant timbre—at moments, Toussaint says, it rose scarcely above a whisper—and for a time, friends were able to shield her from the violence that tends to erupt during Carnival season by closing about and echoing her muted repartee with their own booming choruses. They were thus engaged in rhythmic rounds of insult, shaking their six-foot long staves in accompaniment, when one of the other bands suddenly surged forward to reach the weak-voiced chantwell and Nongka became the center of a great mêlée—shouting and crowding from all sides, her companions determined to protect their voice from the eyes and hands of their rivals. The gendarmes arrived and, in their dispersal of the crowds, Nongka was struck on the head and fell dazed and bleeding to the ground. The revelers then turned in a body on the gendarmes and drove them off. Many suffered injuries. Nongka regained consciousness but was too weak to rise. They settled her as comfortably as they could and, in a mournful cortège, carried her aboard ship, where she died the next day. Toussaint saw to it that she was buried in her own compound in Hayti, and that all was done as she would have wished. He brought her govi here and placed it on our altar.

Reluctantly, we've agreed to see him off to France as soon as the journey, and his accommodations there, can be arranged to our satisfaction. His boyhood sense of himself as a child-god of dangerous powers (his very presence commands the respect that gathers about the person of born leaders) has settled into the conviction that his father, Ibo speaking through Nongka at the last, urges him to complete his education without delay. Toussaint caught only a few words here and there of a message from Ibo trailing between her soft gasps of effort—pwomes . . . zozo . . . mete po . . . té . . . machann . . . chache . . . givo chemen . . . ouvri . . . ayibobo . . . and then faintly but clearly in a final expulsion of breath: se Kreyòl nou ye. Her eyes fixed on him, he nodded to set her mind at rest. She died believing he had heard his father's message.

December 22—Another missive from Paris this morning. How he never tires of reading and learning—he's full of the excitement of books and new ways, but does not think it his vocation in life to be a man of letters. During his singularly passionate apprenticeship, Nongka transmitted to him—as she did to us all—the lore she had from her mother, and she from her grandmother, a fabled beauty whom senile old age shrank to an obsessional voice telling its unvarying tales. For Toussaint, these tales are like stones of blood chipped from the aggregate of life under slavery in the New World, now his to hold and ponder and guard with his own body and being. He broods over what has been lost of his African forebears' history and vows they shall not be forgotten. And so they bleed forever through his young memory as he works to recollect them, drop by fateful drop. And as I think of Nongka, always present for me here in this sanctum of our freedom—and now so finally and irretrievably gone from us—they bleed through mine.

Christmas Day 1880—The first of them, shipped in chains to Hispaniola some three hundred years ago to toil in the sugar mills, escaped to the mountains and joined a band of cimarrones (the English later called these fugitives "maroons"). He fathered a child—at least one, as we've heard—who grew to manhood as a runaway and was betrayed by a maroon leader, formerly held in Spanish captivity, and sold down the mountain along with his pregnant woman—to an Englishman, who had them sent to estates on the South American coast (in Surinam, or perhaps the shore of Guiana) and thence to Barbados. So it begins.

Descendants of this pair, some two or three generations on, were among Africans brought to Jamaica to clear land for vast new sugar plantations. The lucky ones, survivors. Prior to their removal from Barbados, slaves suspected of having played a part in a conspiracy to

murder all the whites and make an African named Cuffee king, were
roasted alive on turning spits and fed to hounds, with the entire white
Barbadian population in attendance: English gentlemen and their ladies,
and the little ones in whom they reposed all their care and hope for the
New World, all watching the spits turn and the dogs feed. Only by such
horrific example could the dark races be brought to see the barbarism
of their ways, they said.

The public record shows that the uprising occurred in 1675,
and Toussaint calculates thereby that his ancestral kin (any whom
clemency, or oversight, or greed, or some mix thereof brought alive to
Jamaica the following year) must have passed at least the remainder
of the century on that island—those who managed to escape the
common tropical fevers, and the wrath of their new masters. If
rebellious, you were butchered in some one of the ways deemed
instructive for black slaves—the more fortunate hanged, shot, or left
to perish from starvation and thirst; others drawn and quartered,
bones broken one by one, chained till their limbs rotted, or put to the
slow fire, starting at the feet and moving up—a means of inducing
death said to take about three hours before it reaches the heart; or
they might put you to the slow burial, sunk alive up to the neck with
sugar smeared around the head, most copiously over the orifices, as a
feast for swarms of ants and bees. Small wonder that Nongka's great-
grandmother, the legendary tale-bearer, ran off to the mountains as
soon as she could—at fifteen—where she fared little better than her
Hispaniolan ancestor; the maroons, always in need of arms to carry
on their warfare with the whites, traded her to a Cuban sugar planter
for munitions. Her body, she was informed while being delivered to her
new owner, had purchased the deaths of a thousand whites.

Truly a great beauty, she was the first among Nongka's people
of whom it was said that, if royal blood did not run in her veins she
bore herself like a queen nonetheless, strong and graceful of limb with
skin of finest ebony. Her Cuban master took her to his bed, where
she obtained his favor and convinced him she must learn to read and
write so as to become a fit companion for a man of his tastes and
accomplishments. Wit and beauty were hers by nature, and these she
cultivated and crowned with letters. All, so it seemed, to please her
master—to converse and sport with him across the ever-narrowing gulf
between them. She bore him several children, all schooled abroad at
her request; and as proof of her success, all were freed at his death.

The oldest, her favorite, a handsome black-haired boy of darkly
olive hue (the first bearer of mixed blood among Nongka's people) was

named Carlos, after his Cuban father. Toussaint bears a striking facial resemblance to him, Nongka used to say, although fairer and slighter of build. When this Carlos, who was Nongka's grandfather, concluded his studies in France and England, his mind a very edifice of the new European learning, he signed on as crewman on a Spanish merchant ship with the object of seeing the world. But his roving days were to be short-lived; not three or four months at sea, his vessel took anchor in New York harbor, where all aboard of Negro blood were put out to be sold by order of the British Admiralty Court in the year 1741.

Carlos was promptly bought by a New York family of Dutch extraction. Unaccustomed to being ordered about as a slave, he steadfastly and courteously refused—in several languages—to obey all such commands on the grounds that, having been educated as a free man he could never act otherwise. The Dutchman decided to take a personal hand in "seasoning" his new property—make a proper slave of Carlos, by means of daily beatings; he succeeded only at inscribing his back with the cockatrice of the lash. Tending to his own wounds, Carlos persisted in asserting that a free man cannot but act as a free man; whereupon he was put in chains, relieved of them once a day to be given some trivial command, and again refusing, was immediately chained more closely and for longer periods.

The Dutchman, hell-bent on showing who was master, repented his clemency and issued new orders—his expensive unruly property was to be shackled to insure complete immobility, and restricted to a half ration of bread and water per day, until said property chose to perform such tasks as he had been acquired to do, at which time he was to be unshackled and fed. Carlos was no nearer to submission when news of the so-called Negro Plot swept through New York. Perjured testimony obtained from a sixteen-year-old white indentured servant girl, charging certain Negro slaves and poor whites with hatching a conspiracy to burn everything down, murder all leading families, and take over the city, mobilized the public outrage and stimulated the ever-ready appetite for vengeance in the name of justice. Here was the Dutchman's chance to bring his seasoning to a grand finale. On five consecutive days, Carlos was led in chains to witness the executions of Negroes judged to be implicated in the Plot. Nongka remembers the proud old man describing—in cruel detail—slow roastings that lasted upward of eight or ten hours, the reek still pungent to his senses after half a century, and the taste of charred human flesh forced between his teeth.

Still Carlos refused to obey. His would-be master (no wealthy man as wealth was reckoned in those days) decided to rid himself of a useless chattel he could ill afford to keep and had little hope of selling, so he accused Carlos of having had a hand in the Negro Plot. While Carlos was in prison awaiting trial, full pardon was offered to all who freely confessed their guilt; this he promptly did and, along with scores of other shackled beings, was conveyed on a slaver to the Caribbees, where most were sold in the English sugar islands. Some, Carlos among them, ended up in Hayti, then known as Saint Domingue. A young French widow lately left in possession of a great plantation there was much taken with his nobility of mien and command of the French language, and acquired Carlos for her house servant. She was no worse than others of her kind (one of whom reportedly caused her cook to be thrown into the oven when his soufflé failed thrice in succession) and Carlos, having conceived a lifelong antipathy to being roasted alive, became the very model of a punctilious domestic.

The Creole widow, he discovered, had her kind's insatiable hunger for the mother country's cultural bounty—she would know what styles of apparel and coiffure were certain to be in vogue among the beau monde of Paris, burned with curiosity to learn what books and feuilletons were stirring French intellectual life, and had, therefore, to be sent for without delay. Carlos placed all his considerable charm and worldliness at her service, advising and—ever so discreetly—schooling her in matters of fashion and taste. As the young widow grew ever more dependent on him, his household duties declined proportionally and in time ceased altogether. Meanwhile, her home began to take on something of the air of a Parisian salon, attracting the notice of Saint Domingue's fashionable circles—she confiding to Carlos that she had never been so happy; never, while her husband was alive, had her sensibilities been so stirred, her capacities so gratifyingly exercised. In the seclusion of the library, while they read the great works of Greek and Roman antiquity together, she began to address him as "mon ami," he to exchange "*maîtresse*" for "madame." He took no small pains to impress on her the preeminence of certain moral precepts expounded in these works, and—by exempla of slaves who, on account of their nobility of character, were placed in positions of great trust by their masters—recommended to her particular attention the ancient Greek idea of the Good and of ἀρετή.

It proved a brilliant pedagogy, directed entirely towards implanting, nurturing, and defining the standpoint from which the lady must come to regard her teacher. She was eager, indeed greedy, for what Carlos knew, and his lessons were a banquet of just such delicacies as his own fastidious inclinations decreed. He had her partake of Newton on physics, Locke on the theory of sensation, Shaftesbury on sensibility—none in the raw but seasoned à la française with the piquancies of Montaigne, Rabelais, Bayle, Montesquieu, Voltaire. Above all, he bade her drink deep from those springs of thought and feeling that were to make Liberté, Egalité, Fraternité a revolutionary cry both in monarchial France and among the black chattel of Saint Domingue. In short, Carlos taught his mistress to understand all history, all human intellection and endeavor, as an upward striving towards reason and enlightenment.

The part of apprentice suited her well, though she was his senior by nine years. And, as she grew ever more accomplished, Carlos conceived a certain affection for this woman who was, after all, a thing of his own making. His public manner with her—even at their much sought-after soirées—remained that of the dignified house servant, reticent in the humility of his station; but in the intimacy of their learned pursuits, he assumed the demeanor more natural to him, of one who viewed the circumstances which had brought him into slavery not as the consequence of any defect in himself, but as the workings of an impersonal fate. And she—in the manner of apt pupils who mistake the warmth of gratitude for the ardor of love (and intellectual arousal for desire of an altogether different kind)—became immoderately enamored of him. Deeming it the less risky course to include her bed in his round of duties, Carlos consented—as a slave of great virtue—to gratify madame's passion.

Twelve more years went by agreeably enough—until a turn of events on the plantation roused his nearly extinct hunger for freedom. Carlos had long been in the habit of advising his mistress on the purchase of slaves, and in this capacity, urged her to acquire a newly arrived African female, some thirty years of age, in whom he perceived—so he put it to madame—all the virtues of an elegant fille de chambre. Tall, soft-haired, dark as night, the woman reminded him of his own mother. She was reputed to be in communion with the gods of Guinée, and her knowledge of healing herbs and roots shortly earned her the regard of the other slaves. Carlos fell with such gusto to his task of seasoning her that they were soon conversing together in her own tongue, and when madame happened to overhear their alien chatter, he explained that he'd found it necessary to acquaint himself with the woman's native speech in order to teach her the Island patois—without which she would be of little use as a lady's maid.

Truth was that, at thirty-five, Carlos longed for a family of his own and had chosen this African woman, Noemia, for his wife. But marry he could not—his mistress had not expressly forbidden it, but in her extreme possessiveness of him had come to take his personal allegiance for granted. Unexpectedly, she found herself with child—being then in her middle forties—and Carlos seized this circumstance to argue, with characteristic charm and vigor, that madame's dream of one day returning to France was now on the point of realization; clearly, too, it was the path of duty to their child, who would be born abroad, in secret, free of the stigma of slavery. Afterwards, it could be given out that he was an adopted foundling—he would flourish among friends and pursuits congenial to his undoubted gifts (it turned out to be a girl child, Justine Marie, of whom nothing further is known). Meanwhile, the loyal steward would be in a position to devote himself entirely to safeguarding madame's interests in St. Domingue, a task greatly facilitated in the eyes of the law if she were to grant him his freedom. How could an independent lady of means, with a hunger for the refinements of the Old World, which, heretofore, she'd tasted only in books, resist such blandishments? Solemn vows were sworn, necessary legal arrangements made—all in the name of the child to come.

And so it was that Carlos became a free man and the master of a great sugar plantation at a single blow. He managed it so ably that production quickly doubled; more lands were cleared—for growing sugar, cotton, coffee, indigo—more slaves acquired. Carlos knew that good harvests depended on good labor (he chose shrewdly among the Africans as they emerged, stunned, from the slaving ships) and that good labor flowed from good health, stability, and a certain modicum of well-being. As a result of his husbandry, both mistress and steward enjoyed handsome revenues even in years counted as "bad" by other planters.

Noemia bore three children, sons first, then the girl who would become Nongka's mother. Her given name was Delphine—"petite Delphine" to her adoring father and known among the slaves as "ti Fina." Carlos was by now a rich and respected planter; but an Island law forbidding persons of color to travel to France denied his children the schooling he himself had enjoyed. He resolved, therefore, to educate them at home in the traditions of liberal European thought—but first, he set them to learning some half dozen African tongues in which he himself had by then acquired some facility. So remarkable an aptitude did the girl exhibit that, in any dispute or misunderstanding among the slaves, it was always ti Fina they called on to act as interpreter. Though she learned to speak, read, and write fluent French from her father (acquiring, too, the rudiments of Latin and Greek) Fina was more drawn to the knowledge possessed by her mother and by other slaves, listening intently and stocking her own memory with theirs, and with that of her paternal grandmother (whom, at about this time, Carlos brought over from Cuba, where her beauty and fortunes had sadly declined after her master died).

In the years while Nongka's mother Fina was growing into womanhood, thousands upon thousands more were imported in chains from Africa, to slave and die in the rich fields of Saint Domingue. During that time, she travelled throughout the Island—conversing with newcomers in their own tongues and studying the conditions of bondage wherever she went. By her twentieth year, Fina was equally at home in all the regions, and renowned for her knowledge and wisdom, which were said to be sent her by the loa of Guinée. Carlos indulged her wish for a hûnfor. She officiated there as high priestess, appearing at ceremonies far and wide to propitiate the many spirits of her people's clans, and seeking to bring these spirits—previously unknown to one another—into harmonious diversity. "Let the unity of the loa be known to all," became her incantation.

On one of her forays into the mountains to recruit runaways for her father's domains (where conditions of daily life were reputed better for slaves than elsewhere) Fina encountered a powerfully built black man with both ears cut off—half-starved and intent on a scheme to return in stealth to the plantation from which he'd escaped, to murder his master and other whites on the place. She fed him and listened, and told him he would find others willing to join in his plot if he would follow her. This man became her husband, Nongka's father—"Bouc" to his compeers, for the goat's foot he never failed to carry into battle with him.

For six years Bouc followed Fina while she sought out among African tongues the signs of Liberté. She found suicide to be rife among the slaves, as was the all too common "jawsickness," not a disease of nature but an operation performed by African midwives on newborn infants to prevent their jaws from opening: better they should starve to death than grow into bondage. Fina urged that all such practices be set aside, henceforth, as means of escaping the hateful condition of slavery. The old gods in their unity, she proclaimed, had other ways. And so her hûnfor became a gathering place for all who aspired to another way.

January 2nd, 1881—In 1791 it began, the signals of Liberté transmitted by vodu to inspire the slaves to rise—the swift, merciless destruction of property and its owners. Above all, the sugar plantations and their masters. Nongka was born when the Revolution was two years old, only days before France decreed the abolition of slavery in her colonies. Her earliest memory was of her father, a giant of a man leaping here and there, the earless head ever in motion, eyes like fiery coals scanning all—never a laugh or a smile, scarcely a word and then only in his native African tongue. His sudden appearances and disappearances earned him a near mythic reputation for legerdemain. He destroyed the enemies of the Revolution with a fearless singleness of purpose, his talisman the goat's hoof; but unlike some who took pleasure in vengeance, by subjecting whites to maniacal tortures like those formerly inflicted on themselves, Bouc had no taste for the refinements of cruelty and concentrated wholly on destroying as much property and as many whites as he could. He wanted only to rid the land of them and their belongings.

Nongka was four years old when he was killed in battle. She used to say that her father was the slave par excellence: fierce with an animal's quickness, and unremittingly possessed. All of her life she was to carry within her a sense of his protective presence—held in his arms, folded to the blackness of his chest, where the feel, taste, and smell of moving muscle impressed upon her child's sensibility the very image of untamed power. But it was her mother who formed Nongka's way of thinking, and her grandfather Carlos, the French-educated mulatto. They bequeathed to her the profound conviction—which seemed at times the bedrock of Nongka's being—that to escape from slavery you must have knowledge of it rooted in the intimacies of oppression; never a knowledge to rest in, but to be cultivated day by day for the strange harvest that gives life to freedom.

This explains why Nongka was always in full accord with the judgment of many, that Toussaint L'Ouverture was the most remarkable of all the remarkable figures in the Haytian struggle for Liberté. A slave for nearly half a century, Toussaint assumed the leadership of his people's struggle, time and again putting a stop to massacre and reprisal, not from delicacy or pity but because he understood that freedom calls for a distinctive kind of conduct. His was a character formed, Nongka believed, through the wisdom and practicality of attaining personal joy even under slavery; having learned to master the excesses of feeling and action which are the bonded lot of the slave, Toussaint L'Ouverture opened the path of personal joy to freedom. The allegiance of Carlos to Toussaint L'Ouverture—he became one of the general's secretaries, penning correspondence with Napoleon Bonaparte during the struggle for autonomy—knew no bounds. He never tired of impressing on his children and grandchildren that the slave's rage for blood can be sated only in the freedom to drink of it and, blood-drunk, to refrain from further bloodshed. The free man knows the taste of blood, and the free man is known by his action when blood is his to let. But Nongka never forgot two incidents involving Toussaint L'Ouverture and, by association with him, her beloved grandfather Carlos.

The first was her mother's imprisonment, by order of Toussaint, for the practice of vodu, which—so Carlos sombrely explained to little Nongka at the tender age of six—was contrary to the French Republic's enlightened spirit, which spirit, he maintained, must be defended at all cost. In its service, Nongka was duly sent to France (just as the Republic was expiring in the last gasp of the Directoire) to join Isaac and Placide, the sons of Toussaint, in their studies. She became a great favorite of the future Empress Josephine, who rapidly concluded that, given some direction in the wiles of woman and world, the child would, like herself, find a place in expanding circles of power and be much sought after. Nongka was to hold Josephine in memory ever after with a child's affection for the trick well played. All the while, the Consular—soon to be Imperial—estates in Hayti were diligently maintained, and their revenues scrupulously forwarded by Carlos, under direct order from General L'Ouverture. (At the same time, being now in possession of all his former mistress's lands, Carlos continued his generous annual recompense to her.) But Fina was made to pay the price—exacted from her by the self-same spirit she and her work had helped to awaken.

And so, in turn, was the man who put Nongka's mother in prison betrayed by the very Revolution that had spawned him—the second truth about Toussaint L'Ouverture that impressed itself indelibly on young Nongka's conscience. Arrested and brought to France, Toussaint was incarcerated at the Fort-de-Joux in the Jura mountains, where his dying was prolonged for nearly a year by deliberate neglect, hunger, cold, and isolation—such were the facts. When the news of his end spread throughout France, little Nongka grieved for the man she had been taught to regard, above all others, as the very incarnation of Liberté. That this slave who had mastered freedom could be betrayed thus—that the life which opened the way should end thus—was a reality she would never lose sight of.

December 29, 1915—At eight years old, going on nine, Maria-Louisa is consumed by a fascination with names. How they roll on the tongue, their meanings, histories, their fit to the individuals who bear them. This morning it was: "Who gave Papa the name Toussaint?" Told that we all did—Nongka, Ibo, Zula and I—she wanted to know more, and still more. "But if. . . ? And why. . . ?" we are queried all day long. Why was General L'Ouverture called "Liberator of His People"? Was he a good and gentle man, then, like her Papa? And if Toussaint L'Ouverture freed Haiti from slavery, why do the people need her Papa to help them, why aren't they getting help now that our soldiers are there? Why are they so poor?

The rough complexity of lived experience wears away with the years, and it becomes plainer how and why her grandson's name functioned for Nongka as a memorial, one in which all of us granted due recognition to the African opening of European learning's enlightening power—a power, like all power, not to be taken at face value. Toussaint himself thought his given name to be no worse than many, and better than some. "Better," he used to say, as a mere boy— with that strangely unchildlike sorrow that surfaced in him as mirth and high spirits do in other children—"yes, better 'Toussaint' than 'Jean Jacques,' whether Rousseau or Dessalines."

January 23, 1881—Jean Jacques Dessalines was the most feared man in Hayti. Fina and her brothers had been among the thousands of mulattoes murdered in the south by Dessalines' blacks—blood required to wipe out the white strain, however mixed. The first year of Independence, 1804—which would see Dessalines crowned Jean Jacques the First, Emperor of Hayti—was inaugurated by his decree to massacre all whites remaining in the land. His followers set to the task with an ardor worthy of their erstwhile masters—a party of them slashing open the belly of a white woman, ripping out her seven-month-old infant and slicing it to shreds before her eyes and those of her husband, then chopping off the man's head and sewing it into her belly. Carlos was no match for Dessalines. Even so, he was able, on at least one occasion, to make good use of this man he regarded as a brutish fanatic. Through Josephine he prevailed on Dessalines, then still Governor-general of the newly independent nation of Hayti, to facilitate the return of his grandchild (in whom the wily Josephine discerned a talent for intrigue); and so it was that, as Napoleon warred once again with England, Nongka's five-year exile—nearly half her young life—came to an end.

No sooner had she set foot on free Haytian soil than Dessalines ordered her brought to him. She was a comely child who, when questioned, divulged what she had been instructed at the French court to say: namely, that the Governor-general could prevent another French invasion, and save himself and his wayward countrymen from certain retribution only by renouncing Independence. Pressed further, she reported things she had overheard. They were saying in Paris, she whispered in her scowling inquisitor's ear, that civilized negotiation with Jean Jacques Dessalines was as inconceivable as parley with a wild beast. At this, Dessalines set one hand lightly on the table between them, leapt over it—landing in a crouch—and thundered, "I shall ride horses through their blood and swim in it before any white man calling himself 'master' and 'owner' walks again on the soil of Hayti." Then he had tea and cakes brought in, and commanded his charming young Parisian envoy to eat her fill. Nongka, who never felt any personal fear of Dessalines, always said she understood him as naturally as she had her silent father.

At his coronation ball in October of that year, Dessalines had occasion to admire Nongka's aptitude, always remarkable, for the art of dance; child though she was, he professed himself enamored of her. Carlos, however, discouraged the Emperor's courtship and insulted his emissaries by refusing to recognize their claim to titles and offices of recent Imperial manufacture. He returned an Imperial sum of money untouched. In short order, Carlos was shot for plotting with Pétion, the mulatto general, to overthrow Jean Jacques the First. Nongka, now an orphan, was placed in the custody of Défilée, a black woman said to be of unsound mind, who peddled provisions to the Emperor's soldiers. Thus, at twelve, Nongka became her own charge and the sutler's apprentice in her dealings with men.

February 1, 1881—Dessalines sent messages. Nongka (who, having reached the age of thirteen, determined that alignment with Dessalines' enemy, Pétion, was the best available course) was to prepare to receive him. She agreed to a meeting at the Port-au-Prince garrison, where troops awaited his arrival to put down the army rebellion at Les Cayes; but at Pont-Rouge, he was ambushed and assassinated. Dragged to the Place d'Armes, mutilated and filled with shot, his corpse was subjected to further insults by the populace. Défilée alone crept close to collect the severed parts as Nongka watched from a distance and wept for the man she had deemed it necessary to betray. From Défilée she had learned that the triumph of independence flourishes on the growth of such monsters even as the preservation of liberty demands their death.

Not two years later, Défilée died by self-imposed starvation, and Nongka went north to Le Cap, where she passed the next four years in the secret employ of General Christophe during his struggles against Pétion for control of a factious, independent Hayti. Her youth and sex were a distinct advantage in the profession of espionage.

Enjoying from all parties the trust adults place in a clever child (which she was no longer) she learned to put to use whatever facts came her way with the shrewdness of a grown woman (which she certainly was not yet). Seasoned by her apprenticeship with Defilée, but pretending ignorance of politics and diplomacy—gifted, to all appearances, only with a facile turn in half a dozen European languages—Nongka made a place for herself in those years as a kind of unofficial go-between in the competition for trading privileges in Hayti. Her French and Spanish, along with the Creole patois, were those of a native, and her command of English, Dutch, and Portuguese (acquired early from tutors, and through reading) passable. Languages became her stock-in-trade in Christophe's service. Moving freely and easily among them—purportedly engaged in nothing more weighty than conveying messages back and forth between commanders of LeCap's international shipping—she was able to make close survey of all who passed in and out of the port.

Her intelligence-gathering was nothing if not artful. Once she'd delivered some message—always as if, ignorant of its true import, she were taking pains only to recite it in precisely its given form—she would promptly appear to lose all further interest in her commission. Fingers would busy themselves with loosening the drawstrings of her silken pouch and extract, in ritualistic sequence, a variety of mirrors, creams, scents, and other paraphernalia for enhancing the beauty of her person—which, with an air of entire self-absorption, she would then fall to inspecting, dabbing and perfuming, making minute corrections to the state of her dress or hair, perhaps changing some item of jewelry a number of times before evincing satisfaction. Thus did she acquire a reputation for so exclusive a concern with her own appearance that her name became famous in Le Cap through the epithet "vain as Nongka"; and in this fashion, she became privy to no small portion of the designs and schemes of Europeans and Americans alike—not one of whom hesitated to discuss his business in her presence, under the heedless conviction that this clever young mulătresse's fluency in his tongue was of a parrotlike nature and did not extend to a true grasp of its meanings. What could such a creature possibly know of affairs of state and deliberations among aristocrats of the skin? About the niceties of effecting diplomatic and commercial arrangements with ex-slaves pretending to statecraft?

The English, above all, were blind to her stratagems. Not infrequently, while the ship's commander to whom she'd delivered some message or other framed his response—or recorded particulars in his private log—Nongka would seem to fall ever more deeply to arranging and re-arranging her mirrors on the table beside him, breathing upon and polishing this or that favorite as a prelude to inspecting the charmed image it gave back to her. By this subterfuge she was perfecting her mastery of mirror-reading—to peruse everything in her vicinity, whether the gentleman's jottings or some document left lying about on the table. (French, English, Spanish, and Portuguese all came to her with ease, but to her disappointment, she never became really proficient in mirror-reading either Dutch or German.) All intelligence collected in this manner went straight to General Christophe, along with her own shrewd analysis and counsel.

It was thus in plying her trade as Christophe's spy that Nongka began to amass her store of gold; for, besides being in his generous pay, she contrived ways of dawdling over the business of replacing her creams, scents, and mirrors in their silken repository—all for the purpose of inviting plump little money-purses to slip in among her coquettish trappings, it being understood that, if the dawdling continued, said purses had been judged insufficient and further considerations were in order.

February 19th—Nongka never wearied of reciting the roster of achievements in the kingdom of Hayti under Henri Christophe, whom she judged the best of autocrats, for the rise, under his reign, of trade and agricultural production, the range of architectural achievements and the phenomenal strides in education. (The standard of morals and manners under a regime that punished stealing by death was, on the whole, also to her liking.) Christophe recognized, nurtured, and knew how to put to use the individual's pride in being part of a nation and its destiny; his shortsightedness, in Nongka's view, lay in failure to comprehend that such pride cannot replace—and may not match—the gratification of belonging to groups that more intimately support one's personal interests. It was this that Alexandre Pétion, the rival of Dessalines and then of Christophe, understood so well; by distributing small plots of land, moreover, Pétion made all men owners. Hayti would reap the harvest of its independence only, Nongka believed, when Pétion's determined nurturance of Liberté was joined with Christophe's enforcement of the discipline necessary for attaining the knowledge and wealth that make Egalité real.

And what if forced to a final choice between Christophe and Pétion? Pétion, she answered immediately; the Christophes of the world always fail to see how they themselves become the problem. "But," she said, "I speak now of absolute choices, ultimate allegiances. One ought to be thankful that choices are seldom if ever final and must be left to the dictates of prevailing conditions." The term of her loyalty to Christophe, I suspect, was due to her out-and-out abhorrence of the license under Pétion's rule in the South. "License," she would proclaim, "is slavery under the guise of perfect freedom."

When General Christophe had himself crowned Henri I, King of Hayti, she was eighteen years old; in recognition of her service, the new King adopted Nongka and made her a member of the hereditary nobility he had lately created. As "Princesse du Cap," she was appointed second in command, after the Queen, of the Royal Amazons who, although not expected to engage in combat, wore sabres and carried bows, weapons Nongka learned to wield with exemplary skill, as if executing some precise and dangerous dance. Such trappings were ill-matched with those of her earlier office, and so la princesse put an end to la coquette.

Nongka now turned her energies to establishing schools throughout the Kingdom and forging links among Africans of the New World. As her schemes grew ever more ambitious, she enlisted the help of an American noir named Prince Sanders. On the eve of completing their accord for provisioning a ship to transport American Negroes to Hayti (it awaited only the royal signature), Christophe the ex-slave shot himself. Nongka thought it a great misfortune when the King's death brought an abrupt end to her enterprise of resettlement; for despite differences of region and language, she always maintained, people of the dark colors in this hemisphere are bonded more surely by their shared centuries of subjection to Europeans than by their African origins. The Americans ended up sailing to Africa, where they were joined by others in founding the Liberian Republic.

As it happened, it was Prince Sanders who introduced Nongka to Papa, and the ship that was to bring the Africans of North America to a home in Hayti was a large seaworthy vessel inherited from Louis the Last. **January 16, 1874**—"I espied her in a royal procession from one of the King's palaces to another. She rode alone in a six-horse carriage, behind the eight-horse carriages conveying King Henri and members of the royal family. Évidemment, this was a person of distinction. I was some years short of twenty at the time, but no stranger to the world's ports and capitals. What I mean to say is that if my eye still had the freshness of youth when it gazed upon le beau sexe, it had seen enough to recognize une femme nonpareille—and that is what I saw in Her Royal Highness Mademoiselle la Princesse Nongka. I joined her retinue and drank toasts to her, to the Royal Family and the Royal Amazons, to Liberté and Egalité. I followed her to the King's reception for foreign merchants, to a ball at the Palace—and when the King was no longer, to the opera and to mass on Sunday. And I am still following her. Imagine my green jealousy when I thought I saw her looking with favor upon Prince Eugène, commander of the Chasseurs de la Garde! This company had three maxims, said to have been bestowed on it by Her Royal Highness: 'Quick as Lightning,' 'I Disperse Darkness,' and 'I Sound Terror.'" So Papa reminisced about Nongka not long before he left us for the last time.

March 16, 1911—Can it be so, Nongka—dead now these thirty-one years? Toussaint always remembers, writing to us this time from Le Cap on her death day. His first letter since he left us last summer.

September 19, 1915—Word of him at last, safe in Trinidad. He slipped away as the United States Army was occupying Haiti.

October 23, 1935—If a favored tradition teaches "Know Thyself," we—les refugiées—hold to Nongka's more practical maxim: "Know Power." This has been our work. Look away and you fall into that ignorance where slavery breeds like maggots and fear takes root. Fear, the risk of having nothing in a world where nothing is freely given—fear makes submission to slavery not only possible but, under some conditions, certain. We have never courted poverty, never sought it out as some do in quest of purification; but we have lived in poverty when necessary—when there was no better way. With the Depression and returns on Jonathan's money dwindling, the work of living has again brought us closer to the condition of slavery and the savagely intimate value of that experience. If we have striven to realize the right relation of freedom and constraint in our lives—of Liberté and Egalité—we have done so out of the discovery that our sanctum emerges from the safeguarding of that order. The power of poverty and pain and death dispelled in our mirroring of their horror, we are capsuled by the free flow of moments from the beauty of things.

The wrack and ruin of demolition starting to pay off, with restoration now well into its "creative" phase, so-called, and the worst supposed to be over—but Harding woke up dazed and trembling under the weight of some awful certainty, like a diagnosis of terminal cancer, or a loved one dead or lost. Dulled by five or six hours of near-comatose sleep full of dream-faces shoved up close. Generic faces, ashen and ageless. Like Doc Shibbles, her neighbor—or was it Jeremy Wentworth again, the cold sweat of death still on him? Or one of the Hurds, young Jimmy maybe, that stare of mindlessness older than the species? Among them, too, a Cane-ish face with a fine old-fashioned cravat at the throat, alternately stern and judicial, or smiling with beneficent irony. And polished spyglass faces—all eyes— riveted here there and everywhere. Or menacingly blank stocking-mask faces. Two, then many, then one, then two again, dividing and coalescing amoeba-like, rogue percepts engorged with unprocessed scraps of feeling. In a full-blown nightmare, a blank face attached itself to a fat man with an avuncular way about him and a tattoo on his rosy forearms, Greeley Connor in profile with eyes shut fast gliding along in front of him like a card over a full deck, bearing the legend: HATRED. Without pausing, he slid back the other way, profile reversed: TERROR. Three shots rang out with machine-gun rapidity, rat-a-tat. And again, rat-a-tat.

The shooting woke her up. She drove to a little Cuban bakery down-town, a place frequented by none in the restoration trade, and in the black shine of strong bitter coffee recollected them all again with the fullness of knowledge: the whole of Old Tarragona marshaling its communal claims. And she, in her bondage, pushing herself past what was reasonable.

October 27, 1935—The greatest horror has been our daily awareness of the ugly powers. Hatred, terror—these above all others. And if the beauty of our world reveals itself only in the space from which they've crawled to a distance where their blind eyes hold us forever in focus, this knowledge of our captivity to their presence has shown us the finality of our slavery. Forbidden the relief of escaping them—not seeing, not knowing—through innocence. Live with them we must, as with the elements. The nightmare rides us and we it in great free leaps each to the other.

Time flogged Harding, lashed her on from job to job. She could hardly get through a phone call to her daughters back in Athena without some ques-tion coming up about when she expected to return, Helen alleging they didn't need an answer right off, and Vanessa hinting that she'd better get on with it and be back before her school started. Three weeks? Four, at the outside. Where you spend your time in the cleanliness of restoration proper (the "creative" phase) becomes all-important—not letting others make a mess, which they're sure to do the moment your back is turned and the work takes on the air of being unsupervised. (Mantra: "What you need is a general contractor, lady.")

So the day Evans & Son installed a working toilet and sink in the Boullet House, Harding bought a foam mat from Woolworth's and moved into the library, as if determined not to be sold off from her master, not to forfeit the grim security of the infatuation that had brought her to this pass and left her destitute, anybody's prey. Errand-girl, mother confessor, troubleshooter, on-the-spot crony, cleaner-upper at large. Do what you have to do. Flatter, wheedle, beg, pacify, second-guess, just don't rattle your chains. Check and double-check on everything and everybody; scheme, organize, protect, cut corners where necessary (but don't let it show) and never ever complain. Complaining personalizes, stirs up the sadistic response—and it takes up time. Watch the time. Act as if we're all just one big happy family, all doing our thing together. What the others want to do and when is exactly the way you would like things to go if it were up to you.

January 2nd, 1868—Nongka reminds us, almost daily, that her bargain to stay in Florida with us is past expiring; but Ibo refuses to leave, and his resolute bearing harbors an intuition of possibilities near enough to close us in with reality. In a festive mood, he asserts that the coming of his child outweighs all odds—our presence here in Tarragona feeds into the stream of burgeoning Negro independence: "Here we shall remain," he declares, "until none dare violate us." Papa fears for our safety. Nongka prepares for the birth; to conceal the baby's growth, I'm to wear a loose cloak when we go out—a simple ruse in cold weather—and Zula is to pad herself, adding to the stuffing little by little in simulation of the female condition, that the child may pass as hers. Just another colored girl with child. "Call me Anonyma," she teases daily to rouse my envy, ". . . one of the advantages of color, my dear Florida."
November 2, 1935—Our safety—the very existence of the likes of us—calls for control of fictional truth. We lost it here and depended (as one often must when subjected to the excesses of others) on the poor expedient of clothing fact with falsehood, pitting fiction against fiction.
May 10th, 1868—Submitted our names at Tallahassee last week, to obtain teaching certificates. The list of applicants for our freedmen's

school lengthens by the day—all ages and colors represented. Many express a particular interest in Nongka's arts of healing.

Ibo has a new and altogether unfamiliar look about him now—a look that somehow commands fear, and somehow makes us one in feeling. He says what he wishes to convey to our pupils, above all else, is how to live without fear. Nongka, believing that such fearlessness inspires fear in others, seldom takes her eyes from him. "My father comes back in my son," she murmurs and her face sets into a weary mask. She has taken Bouc's battle talisman—the goat's foot—from among her valuables and hung it around Ibo's neck. They are called out more than ever now to treat the sick, and wherever Ibo goes the people of color walk with him, consult with him, put questions to him. He moves with Ogou's ardor, and often wields Ogou's sword while mounted by Erzilie. Nongka warns that Erzilie will not suffer Ibo's faithlessness and will have her way with him before it is over.

Although past seven months with child, I am not yet big but keep a loose shawl at hand, to wrap around me if someone calls. When we are out walking, Zula positively waddles beside me.

May 30, 1868—Surprise visit from Randall Cane this morning, Lucy's husband-to-be—in the company of Tarragona's new federal marshals, Jonas and Bob Evans. Only a matter bearing urgently upon my welfare could occasion so untimely a call; he would be as brief as was consonant with the exigency of his mission—quoth Randall. I sat draped under my shawl the whole time, leaning forward tentatively— taking him at his word.

"I come to you today," he commenced, "not in any official capacity devolving upon me as a leading Democrat of our city, but out of the regard and solicitude of a future kinsman—your Cousin Lucy's loyalties and affections, my dear Frances—if I may so address you—are about to become mine. Once Lucy has settled in Tarragona as Mrs. Cane, we shall endeavor to tempt you from your seclusion from time to time, that you may take up your rightful place among friends." During this curious peroration, the brothers Evans were all smiles, twirling small star-shapes from one hand to the other in perfect unison, like a pair of juggling automata. I could not help but watch—listening with one ear to Randall—spellbound by these twinkly tokens spinning across their fingers without any perceptible break in speed, mirror images of one another, the intermittent flick of palms and wrists creating the impression of machinery marvelously contrived to do only this one thing—keeping these small, flat, pointed objects unerringly in motion.

"Me and Brother Bob here," Jonas ventured, never once interrupting his handiwork, "we been athinkin how it used to be before you come into the world, Miss Frances, when we was your grandpappy Geoffrey's overseers—till the niggers riz up against us. And we want you to know we ain't never forgot the family what gave us our start in life, and has helped us time and again since. Yore folks is our folks, Miss Frances, and that's the spirit we come to you in this mornin." Brother Bob, nodding and twirling away like his elder's shadow—one cheek scarred by the thirty-year-old gash of Matador's knife—made a great point of emphasizing that "nary one of us is here in a official capacity, like Mr. Randall done explained." The perpetual motion of their hands, seemingly independent of the two before me with their weathered faces, could not have had less bearing on the visit's stated purpose than the clatter of carriage wheels outside. Jonas resumed: "And so's we could get this here point over to you, Miss Frances, me and Bob took it on ourselves to remove these here emblems of office"— whereupon, forearm extended, he brought the shiny twirling star to a clean halt between thumb and forefinger, Bob executing the movement in replica: a double image of the law appeared before me. I had no sooner identified these "emblems of office" as U.S. marshals' badges than they were released and permitted to glide into the brothers' palms, where supple fingers closed over them. Throughout most of the visit, the two fists guarding their "emblems" remained identically at rest, knuckles up, on their respective owners' knees.

Bob ran a thumb along the length of his scar—as though subduing a chronic itch—and mused: "There's some as say me'n Jonas ain't no better'n scalawags—promoting ourselves by 'sociation with niggers and standing for the Radical party; but Mr. Randall here, he'll tell you straight out—him bein a regglar Democrat and us bein Radicals—there ain't a hair a difference between us."

"Not a hair," agreed Jonas.

"Ain't but one side to be on, Miss Frances," Bob explained. "Like I said to Jonas yestiddy, 'the Cap'n—Miss Frances's Pappy—bein as he's always away some place on business,' I said, 'and her bein alone so much and living so independent-like, me and you owes it to her, brother,' I said, 'to put this here matter to her face to face.'" Jonas confirmed this tale of fraternal concern with a searching look around the room and out into the hall: "Me 'n Bob we figured there ain't nobody in these parts what's better qualified than you, Miss Frances, to appreciate how our way of life just cain't be preserved, here in Tarragona, without some associatin with the niggers." Whereupon Bob nodded thoughtfully, adding, "'but there's a line,' I said to Jonas—didn't I, brother?—a fine line, and it's high time the young lady gits on our side and comes in with us white members of this here community, dedicated to the public tranquillity and order, like Mr. Randall here can verify."

"Is it the relation between the races you have come to discuss with me, Mr. Cane?" I inquired of Randall, whose habitual stiffness was growing more pronounced by the moment, as his throat became suffused with a strange rosiness.

Here Bob would have intervened hotly, with a harangue about life "before the niggers was set free"—had Jonas not cut him off with the reminder that they, being federal marshals now, stood for the Law, and the Law applied to everybody, "niggers same as others."

Color was distinctly rising now in Randall's lean, smooth-shaven face. "Miss Boullet," he said, averting his gaze from the Evans men, "I must state unequivocally that our city is under serious threat from unruly elements, believed to have been incited by outside influences, and instructed in practices contrary to law and morality alike."

"And what has this to do with me, Mr. Cane?" I asked.

"It is your . . ." he hesitated, "your servants"—at which word the Evans men resumed their twirling more energetically than ever—"who are suspected of instilling ambitions that cannot fail to stir up discontent in our Negroes. I understand that Captain Boullet is away on business—I must warn you that, upon his return, he will be requested to remove these foreign influences at once from the territorial boundaries of the State of Florida. Until such time, you Miss Boullet are advised to insure that these incitements cease." In a softer tone he added, "After the departure of these aliens, I am prepared to discuss the schooling of our Negroes—in which you have lately evinced an interest—and to offer both my professional and personal services in directing your endeavors towards a useful end."

Gathering my shawl around me, I stood up, saying, "I shall take your advice under consideration, gentlemen." I then opened the parlor door, and Zula—puffed out to nearly twice her normal girth—showed them out.

June 2nd—Ibo has finally agreed—we must all go to Hayti and remain there, at least in the early years of our child's life. But until Papa's ship returns, and our journey can be arranged, he is resolved to work more tirelessly than ever to spread his message.

For an old house to be a desirable property it should have that fine vintage air of tradition about it, Harding repeated to herself. The immaculate look. And her resolution fixed like fate on that injunction.

June 16, 1868—Ibo dead and our child born within half an hour—the body rests in the vestments of Erzilie on the altar amid candles and I here with him. I must write my way beyond the spectacle, somewhere to live without him—

We were at supper and heard a furious knocking. Nongka went to the door. Two armed hooded men with torches pushed their way in and ordered us out to the veranda—five more of them on the steps with torches aloft and firearms pointed at us, all in white calico and hoods trimmed with red stars—all but the one at the front with his red robe and white mask and a tall white pointed hat with a red cross. Nongka hurled herself past them down the steps until a rifle butt stopped her. The fierce movements of my baby within me brought me back from a sickening reel into unconsciousness and I heard Zula gasp "NO!" Beneath the oak the flare of torches fell on Ibo, slumped forward, hands tied behind, blood streaming from nose and mouth over the mane of Papa's white mare—eyes raised ever so slightly at two hooded men tossing a coil of rope between them. One looped it over a branch and wound it around as the second fashioned a noose from the opposite end, the first man meanwhile already untying the reins of Ibo's mare and flipping them into the waiting hands of the other— four hands and a single will pulling the mare into place, twirling the noose in the air, tossing it over Ibo's head and jerking it tight. In that moment Ibo saw Nongka straining toward him—his eyes ablaze with the look I have come to know these last months. "Maman!" he cried out even as the executioners' hands whipped across the mare's flanks— "Les mains! Regarde les mains!"

My head flung back in the agony of beginning labor—was it the mare's shrill neigh or my own scream I was hearing?—the pain seemed to whirl me into the scene of Ibo's murder as into a mad and ghastly carnival tableau. Someone shouted "It's done!" the air acrid, thick. A thudding and thundering of horses' hoofs down the alley, then silence as in a dream, and all afire with pain. Zula was half-supporting me in

the doorway and I looked up—Ibo! flaming torches to either side of
him, hanging lifeless from the tree. There is no mistaking the dead.

From somewhere in that lurid night Nongka commanded: "Zula,
the mare ran back of the house, find her, bring her to me at once.
You Frances, fetch your father's gun and the robe of Erzilie. Move!"
Her violent push gave me a running start into the hall. I stumbled
into Ibo's room for the robe that hangs beside his bed—found the
gun in Papa's desk and was out the front door in time to see Nongka's
hands extending the crystal goblet the spirits drink from in our
sanctuary—catching the crimson ooze from an incision in Ibo's neck.
"Bring water," she ordered and had me fill the goblet. How bright the
mix of water with Ibo's blood! Zula came leading the frightened mare
and fixed her saddle, and Nongka mounted and placed the gun in the
right saddle holster. She maneuvered the horse under Ibo's body and
we settled him in a riding posture before her. Then Zula cut the noose
and lashed Nongka's body to his and both in turn to the mount. Over
this coupled body Nongka slipped Erzilie's silk robe, head low against
the nape of his neck, and covered all with the hood and tied it under
his chin. Before us on the white mount, face set in the commanding
urgency turned on Nongka as the noose tightened, rode Ibo in the
billowing raiment of the goddess.

In corroboration of this fiction Nongka addressed us with Ibo's
voice: "The goblet, Frances, hand it up to me"—and then to Zula:
"Look to your sister." Sweeping a torch up out of the ground, she fixed
it in her left saddle holster—this counterfeit of an apparition then
proceeded regally out the carriage gate into Valencia Street, one hand
on the reins, the other bearing the goblet aloft with ceremonial care.

I collapsed into my pains. Time no longer passed but froze into
a repetition of agony broken at last by a terrible explosion. This,
I thought, this is what giving birth is—this baptismal sweat in the
element of uncontrolled violence—and then, lying there in the peaceful
satisfaction that follows relief from unbearable pain, I heard a cry and
Zula saying, "We have a male child."

She had no sooner settled him on my bed than Ibo's voice
summoned us from outside, and answering the summons, she cut
him apart from Nongka and hid the rope remnants under the house.
I could hear them carrying him inside. Nongka strode into my room,
glanced at the baby, tossed me a gown and said in her own peremptory
voice, "Get up and put this on, your sister will take your place now."
Limp and weak, I had scarcely struggled into my dress when the front
door burst open and two men came bounding up the stairs, throwing

open doors, searching everywhere. The scene of recent delivery in my room surprised them—our dusky newborn nestled in Zula's arm on the bed—and they stamped out in a seeming confusion of purpose.

"He's not up here!" one of them shouted.

"Here, in here," a voice replied from below, "we found him."

With Nongka half-pushing and half-carrying me downstairs, I entered the sitting room behind the men. Randall Cane, already there, had lit a lamp and stood blinking in its light.

"Speak," Nongka whispered fiercely in my ear.

"Mr. Cane," I began—in a voice plaintive and alien to my ears—"my servant Ibo was murdered before my eyes tonight, and now you and your friends have forced your way into my home. I must ask you to explain these actions."

"A short while ago, Miss Boullet," came the cold reply, "two federal marshals, Jonas and Bob Evans, were shot dead. We know the deed was done by the hand of this man Ibo whom you call your servant."

"Impossible," I returned, "I myself helped take down his corpse and watched his mother and sister shroud it."

"I tell you this murderer could not have been dead when you cut him down."

"See for yourself, Mr. Cane," I said wearily. Ibo lay on the sofa— arms still tied behind, knees bent and legs thrust apart under Erzilie's robe, head thrown back with iron stiffness on the cushion, the cut noose still hanging above Bouc's goat's foot around his neck—eyes fixed in their gleam of polished stone.

One of the men whispered something to Randall Cane, who, examining Ibo's face under the lamplight, caught his breath and exclaimed "It's him!" The others pressed closer in to see—I too leaned forward, following their eyes to the small sooty hole in Ibo's right temple.

Ashen-faced, Cane turned away. "Burn him," he ordered, "burn him at once."

"In my country, those who are unjustly put to death are not quiet," Nongka said in her most stately manner. "My son Ibo has the knowledge. Set fire to him and he will rise from the flames and take vengeance on you and your children. Beware!"

The men looked to Randall Cane, but he stood like a statue, ghastly pale and deprived of speech. "Let's go," said the youngest (whom I recognized, from years ago, as a victorious knight of the annual Tallahassee joust) "he's dead now for sure." The others hesitated, looking still to Cane who shuffled out as if shackled.

It was the darkest, deadest hour of night when Zula and Nongka brought Ibo into our sanctuary—I so utterly drained of strength I lay here unmoving for some immeasurable time while they worked, neither feeling nor thinking. They are preparing a sarcophagus for him, to fit under our altar—but sleep denies me and if day has broken I know nothing of it, care nothing.

Afternoon in early August, a real scorcher. Doc Shibbles, periodically pushed off the deep end by demons of his own making (a farrago of phobia, memory, and misconception) prophesies that the return of the Boullet House to its original condition will unleash all kinds of hell. The hell of the past, he means, quite incidentally confirming what Harding already believes to be the case: that Miss Mary Louise of Valencia Street, four-hundred block, and the "female relative" linked to the mystery of the house in local lore (the only one living, on Harding's list, who would know about the sanctuary) are one and the same person. And that person is Maria-Louisa. Her dark beauty on the other side of the massive iron fence forbidden to him, she's part and parcel of the old violence whose return Doc Shibbles believes to be both inexorable and imminent.

Oh but the dead stay dead, Harding tries to tell him—the revenant past is a thing of nightmare and fantasy, no more. But the restoration was so far along by then that the house taking on its original hue and form, day by day, contradicted her. And Doc Shibbles, like all paranoids, was nothing if not logical.

August 18, 1868—Tonight we placed our son on the altar, Ibo's tomb, and baptized him in his dead father's name. Ibo once remarked that it was the black ex-slave Toussaint L'Ouverture who carried within him all the best of European civilization, to which I added that the white man deserving that distinction had lived long ago, near that civilization's dawning; and from this, Nongka playfully fashioned the binomen "Toussaint Platon." Zula says a male child bearing two faces of so much that is best must bear a double burden—so grave a lineage for so fragile a being, lighter in my arms than my shawl and steadily fired with life like Ibo.

In celebration, Nongka summoned Ibo's spirit and, in his Ogou-voice, recited the tale of justice administered upon his killers:

"My sister cut me down from the tree. My mother bade me mount and use her as my horse, and I spurred her to the crescent gates where the Canes live. Under a bright moon Randall Cane, one arm raised in a sign to the shadowy man-shapes behind him, squinted hard to discern whether he faced friend or foe. No servant came bearing a torch; but for this, he might have been bidding a party of dinner guests good night. My killers, seven in all. Without their robes and firearms, they had the air of parvenus consorting in stealth with a more securely established member of their kind.

"I held the goblet in my left hand—the bloody water shone like wine—and with my right I drew forth my father's weapon. 'Stand in line before me, side by side,' I commanded. 'Do not attempt to escape the justice of death.'

"'Who are you? What do you want?' asked Randall Cane, in his face the shock of recognition.

"'You know me well,' said I, 'and what it is I want from you.'

"'It's a trick!' one of them cried.

"'Yes,' I replied, 'Death is a trick, and I am the trickster you have made of me, brothers.' The line of men surged toward me. 'Stop where you are!' I commanded. 'Look on me and believe. I am Ibo, murdered by the hands of two among you acting for all. You shall bear witness that I who speak to you am dead, and that the dead cannot die twice.' With that, I, using the motion of my mother's arm, pointed the weapon at my right temple and fired, saying: 'Look for the mark of this bullet whenever I come before you, that you may always remember the trick of Death that lets none rest until the blood he shed lives in his brothers.'

"'You,' I addressed the man at the head of the line, 'Robert Simmons, whom I know to be a pattern of success in Tarragona and an honorable man, step forward and do as I say. Take this vessel with both hands, turn it half the distance of a circle with your right, and let it rest on your left palm. Do this twice. Then turn the vessel half the distance of a circle with your left hand and rest it on your right palm, and do this twice. On pain of your life spill not a drop of my blood.'

"He took the goblet and held it before him and did as I had bidden. 'Now,' I commanded, 'drink from the vessel of my blood.' He raised it to his lips. 'Drink!' I cried, 'do this in remembrance of my death.' His lips touched the liquor and recoiled. 'Drink!' When he had drunk, I commanded: 'Now step back and pass the cup to the next of my brothers.'

"The three next in line did as I bade, and the cup passed to Bob Evans who, having four times heard my instruction, came forward and twice turned it both ways, with speed and skill. There they were: the hands of one of my killers.

"'Stop!' I cried, 'you shall not drink of my blood. Let this testament to my murder pass to the next of you.' Jonas Evans stepped up beside him and took the cup with both hands. 'You,' I addressed Bob Evans, 'Kneel.' He did as I commanded. Now I addressed Jonas, 'Turn the vessel twice in each hand as your brother has done.' He did likewise, and I knew that I saw before me the second of my killers. 'Stop!' I cried. 'Neither shall you drink from the cup, but let it pass to the last of my brothers.' Then Randall Cane came forward and took the goblet, and Jonas Evans knelt at his brother's side as I commanded.

"'The cup refuses itself to these two among you,' I said, positioning my mount squarely in front of the Evans men. 'Your death is the price of my life's blood.' Then I shot both of them pointblank through the head.

"The others made as if to apprehend me. 'Be still!' I commanded, pointing my father's weapon at each in turn, 'there yet remains one who must drink his fill.'

"Randall Cane stood with the goblet in both hands, ready to turn it. 'You, sir,' I said, 'shall drain all that is contained therein. In you, above all, shall my blood live. Drink, sir, drink to the last drop!' Gagging and heaving, he drained all that was left. 'Now bring it to me, brother,' I commanded. He did so and backed away quickly, clutching his throat.

"Then I called them blood-brothers and addressed these words to them all: 'Henceforth my blood shall speak to me from your bodies and of me in your bodies every day of your lives. Let my blood hold the memory of me before you and in you that you may do no further harm to me or my kind, for you are now become of my kind and will be so bound through all time.'

"Thus saying, I dashed the goblet to the ground and drew forth the torch from my left saddle holster and thrust it into Randall Cane's hand with these words: 'May your memory burn like this torch.' And I directed my mount into the darkness. A few moments later I was home, unhorsed."

Taking Ogou's sword in hand, Nongka dropped her head and bent over it with twisted fingers measuring its length. She hobbled toward the altar and spit out a hoot of laughter before the spirit left her. In that instant, Zula and I saw Erzilie maddened and the dreaded Marinèt, killer and cannibal, join us.

243

Out of habit Harding reached for the spotlight (forgetting all about the lamp plugged in beside her sleeping mat) and made her way downstairs in the dark without switching it on—restless as a lover yearning for a relationship's earlier, less complicated urges, pacing the rooms silvery with moonlight. Walls and ceilings freshly painted, every last piece of woodwork back in place, wide pine floors burnished to a dark satin luster under her bare feet—cataloguing and reckoning. Grilles for heat and air vents stacked in corners, ready for installation. Boxed electrical fixtures waiting to be hung; cabinets and marble countertops in place throughout the kitchen. Out back, a final coat of paint to go on shutters and trim, veranda and wooden steps rebuilt at last (with strict attention to authenticity by Bill Simmons, the Quarter's master carpenter borrowed for the event from Dr. Cane's restoration). Shortly, a deep bed of oyster shells would cover the drive (and crunch underfoot for weeks to come). And out front, her own satisfyingly inauthentic handiwork: old Spanish bricks, slave-made, recycled into porch steps and winding in a walk to the gate—under the shade of the old tree where Ibo's body once hung.

Ahead of her now: all the correcting and revising, and touching up, hers alone once the last workman was paid and gone. The finish-work—what it would take to restore her own projection of the past without incurring the wrath of the Preservation Board. All the little odd jobs, so many it took her breath way. Windowpanes to be scraped and washed, switch plates and doorknobs to be mounted, old locks repaired, oiled, tested, refitted. The last things that would give the Boullet House its cachet—historic property, restored.

A public property. Already people off the street, not just workmen and inspectors and Board members with business there but anybody who felt like it, wandered in through the gates and across the yard to look and pass judgment. Some even barged inside for a sneak preview if doors happened to be unlocked. Caught, they'd mutter something about thinking it was "on the market," that indisputable opening for public inspection. The house was entering history. "Not I," Harding would say now, "but my work"— her enslavement's last gasp, the determination to finish it right. Though not in order to claim it for the privacy of a long life as once envisioned, but simply to work her way out of the situation she'd bought into. A trade-off: the Boullet House for her freedom.

June 16, 1878—Ten years ago today Ibo was murdered and Toussaint born. He goes to Nongka now, she has called for him. During these years of his childhood, Tarragona has been for us a place of perfect security and freedom. Shunned and feared we move where and how we please—like untouchables who have, in defiance of human standards, attained an ambiguous deity. We accept the place accorded us as our due and neither want nor ask for more.

Toussaint's fair complexion all but denies his African lineage, even if in features and stature he is so like Ibo that no one can fail to recognize his father in him. People take him for "Cap'n Boullet's bastard," borne by Zula—his movements have the controlled rapidity of the Boullets—but thanks to the heritage of Ibo horsed by Nongka, he escapes taunting and walks as if the space around him were charged with power. None dare enter it. Wherever we go, a wide path opens for us; eyes are averted, silence descends. We respect this ritual of avoidance and act in deference to its codes. Should some errand require us to share any public enclosure with others, I go in first to announce our business, Zula and Toussaint a little behind in the tabooed space encircling him. All but the most intrepid souls will make a hasty exit, and more often than not the three of us find ourselves sole occupants of premises only moments before bustling with customers.

Once, at Barrett's store, when Toussaint was not yet six, having made our entrance as usual—I a little ahead and to his left, Zula to the right, while the two or three remaining patrons slipped out without glancing our way—we placed our order at the counter as Mr. Barrett stood in strained attendance upon us. I neither saw, heard, nor in any other way sensed the presence of anyone else in the store; but Toussaint, so used to his inviolate space that the slightest trespass attracts his notice, darted to a far corner and pointed his finger at a mound of assorted provisions in sacks. "You," he said, "You are not to spy on me." His voice carried the force of conviction often heard in children who know that a code of behavior has been broken by those whom they presume to be its authors. A man staggered backwards into my view—Randall Cane—and reeled to the door and out into the street, clutching his throat as though in an effort to control the involuntary gasps which escaped him. In Hayti, Toussaint will learn to walk as a human being among others of his kind.

February 12, 1879—Nongka speaks for the spirits throughout Hayti now. She writes that age has opened her to all the loa, who chant of a time when the soil will horse them and the land give voice to their desires, and the people will dance to the rhythms of earth's language. Toussaint is at her side wherever she goes.

November 23, 1935—Nongka was a great serviteur. Zula and I have followed her fetishistic way of life and Maria-Louisa follows us. A hard discipline that came slowly, demanding as it does absolute concentration on any ordinary object in the act of materializing its power. Nongka used to call it "loosing the machine." The science of her time was, to her mind, a supreme fetishism, and she deplored the blindness of scientists to its import. But religion she always distrusted—was she not a child of the Enlightenment?—viewing it as the inevitable growth of doctrinal belief from cultism. An aberration of the spirit. The people's opiate indeed: shared addiction to a closed fetishism at once overvalued and underestimated; errors of spirit-measurement making for a leakage of magical power into the syntheses of religion. Nongka feared cultish mythmaking with its inexorable self-justification, the taking for granted of its own magic ritual-hardened into sanctified articles of faith.

We have used the leakage of magic from our lives to protect ourselves. Never aspired to religion's communal power, however, even as a religious admission is exacted from us by vodu announcing itself in the power of bonds among things, and this has been enough. May it serve you too, Maria-Louisa, may it give you the means to maintain your freedom as a solitary being.

April 19, 1888—Toussaint has adopted the surname of the family with whom he lived in France after Nongka's death. He is now Toussaint Platon Bernard and seems in no hurry to leave his adopted country.

June 6, 1903—For some months we have been expecting him but never the turn his life has now taken. He surprised us today with his Mexican bride, whom he met aboard ship. An orphan (the last of a criollo family) and protégée of associates of the late opera singer Angela Peralta, she was returning to the Conservatorio Nacional from a season of minor stage roles in Italy and France. They have known each other scarcely three weeks. Theirs is a marriage of passion, and Toussaint experiences it like a shower of salvation. He says Mexico will now be as much his home as hers and his strength will bolster the sound of her voice which, beguiling though it is as she sings old Mexican songs for us, loses resonance too easily—she is pale and overly delicate.

May 2, 1907—We have a grandchild, Maria-Louisa Bernard.

July 7, 1910—Toussaint's grief for the loss of his wife can find no expression or consolation. He brought Maria-Louisa to us and left after little more than an embrace, and this: "The child is yours. Revolution in her country cannot be stopped now—long and bloody, I fear—and it's time for me to go back to mine, back to Hayti as Nongka planned."

She is beautiful, sinewy and curious as a kitten, her chatter moving precociously between Spanish and French, and increasingly English. We have seen her only once before in her short life, but she appears at ease with us here—the ease of affection held in reserve, by one who has very early learned to be vigilant but unafraid.

"Anybody home?" Someone in the hall downstairs—front door left open again. Workmen never shut it even when leaving for the day. "Elizabeth?" No mistaking Dr. Cane's voice. Aimée's charming Uncle Randy. Voice of the Preservation Board, of finality about all that goes on in the Historic Quarter.

But how changed Harding's hearing since that late afternoon visit in July! And how altered by the image of grandfather Randall Cane, judge-to-be, gagging on Ibo's blood as his two henchmen expired at his feet. Evanses and Canes—still the old alliance more than a century later, maintaining their mutual interest in preserving shared ways of life despite irreconcilable class differences. Just that morning, Evans & Son (whom she believed to have more than a drop of Bob and Jonas in them) had put the last touches—the very last, they said—on her plumbing, proud as peacocks. Their pricey miracle of an up-to-date alimentary system of copper and plastic and enamel-clad steel was affirmed to be gurgling and flushing and disposing as it should, doing its part to revive yet another of Tarragona's landmark properties.

He was starting up the stairs. "Elizabeth?" Library door wide open—at the top landing he had only to turn and she'd be in his direct line of vision, in the hatch to the sanctuary. And why not? Let him think it a storage space under the dormer sill, one of those interesting nineteenth-century shipshape features in need of a little clean-up. But why should he be in on even a part of the secret? Best to shut the hatch, climb down and stand idly making a list of things to be finished in the library when he walked in.

But she didn't. On a split-second decision she sank down and softly pulled the hatch over her.

A pause at the top of the stairs—then he strolled along the hall from room to room, calling out her name with increasing confidence that the house was unoccupied. At the library door he paused again.

"Hmm . . ." The broken-backed, paint-spattered chair. A Wentworth legacy. She'd kept it for climbing up and down from the window seats until something like a wry affection for its usefulness tinged this emblem of her imperfect exorcism. To him it would look merely shoddy, as would her dime-store mat on the refinished floor of the handsomely proportioned historic room. "Hmm . . ."—a sense of discovery in the well-bred voice now as he tipped the chair back and forth.

Ironic detachment? Benign contempt? She looked through *his* eyes. Grey, steady, knowing eyes: the mat under its rumpled cotton spread, old *Sentinel*s stacked casually beside it, the junk-shop cloisonné lamp battered beyond rescue and lacking a shade. Evidently in use. One who truly belonged in a restored home of some importance would not be living, even temporarily, like this, and would under no circumstances incline to do so. Not his Sophie, certainly, nor any of her circle, even those of a more bohemian bent. Not, surely, his elegant, if occasionally wayward, Aimée—but, now, hadn't the Sixties and their aftermath wrought changes even among the best families, a certain testing of social boundaries along with challenges to the old ways? Not necessarily a bad thing, but not to be encouraged. Not to be taken too far—this far. Some excess here. Still—reasoning in his exemplary and, above all, tolerant and flexible fashion—our system does give all kinds the opportunity to cash in and move up, and this one sleeping on the floor, and who knew what else, did at least evince a modicum of know-how and discernment, he had to hand her that. Aimée could do a great deal worse in her democratic sallies for unusual friends. Any little help he might be able to offer—and gladly if it came to that—was no more than she deserved.

Harding moved along with him through the steps of this exposure of herself, this rummaging through scraps of her humiliation—an experience that cannot, of course, derive from him. She, not belonging here, cannot see as he sees. Such feeling must therefore be her own doing (or undoing): the self-consciousness of a brainy woman who can neither quite hide what she is nor own up to it.

Back in the hall now, done with her. And then calling down the staircase with warm good humor, "Is that you, Elizabeth? It's Randy Cane up here." The sound of another pair of footsteps on the way up—astonishing how they waltzed in as if the idea from the start had been to put the house on the walking tour . . . but this voice wasn't just anybody's voice. It was Jake Landry, loud and clear, remarking that "the professor's" Chevy was gone (it was, in fact, being serviced for her trip north) and that he'd just happened to spot Dr. Cane's Austen-Healey in the drive, apparently sufficient reason to make the library their rendezvous while he finished his cigar (whiffs of which seeped into the cedar hold through the crack she'd left) and made his evidently regular and no doubt well-paid report to Dr. Cane. Carrying on the family vocation of right-hand man to the higher-ups—in the surveillance business now, keeping watch on whatever needed watching in the Historic Quarter.

And *whoever*. Tony Krasner, roofer, for one. As for the Doctor's niece—sweet on the rascal, no doubt about that, something about the way they acted together—*she* was clean though, definitely not mixed up in Krasner's dirt. Now about that colored granddaughter of Frances Boullet's, he was making progress on a plan to put her away permanently. Had to do with those old legal documents that disappeared when Jeremy Wentworth died—

"No point stirring up imaginary problems," Dr. Cane cut him off, already back out in the hall. Then down the stairs with Old Faithful's chatter floating behind him along the brick walk and through the gate.

Harding rolled the hatch back and sat bolt upright in the hold, breathing deeply and expelling each breath with special force. This knowledge of the townspeople reaching her in the secret recesses of the Boullet House, unasked for and unwanted, seemed finally more than she could stand and she resolved simply to ignore it. Get on with her finish-work. She made a cautious survey of street and alley and, seeing no one about, locked up for the night.

Proposition: Passion brings us to the collaborative pit of the world and leaves us there, solitary, abandoned to our own base devices.

Toward the end of the restoration, Harding, I note, chose to recede from the world of Old Tarragona not from indifference or lack of understanding, but simply because she was no longer attracted to it—no longer a carrier of that pathology mistaken for the source of self-knowledge: time's brimming deep of others around us.

And I, shall I quietly withdraw now or make my place in that pit? Which?

December 5, 1935—On this, my last morning, images of my son fill my head. My love for Toussaint has all the comfortable familiarity of a daily walk, with its seasonal revelations of the same mysteries year upon year, his life a movement to and between the poles of nihilism and the sheared ethics of decency—but I grow restless in this my final venture and leave its conclusion to you Zula, freed of all sacrifice. And you Maria-Louisa, freed of our death.

NOON—Florida's end accomplished, her ninetieth birthday and the machinery of our burial in place. A fungal odor rises from our tomb with the pungency of a world long dead. The altar top ready to seal us in. We worked in unison these last months as in all our happiest times, Florida deep in her composition, I adorning our final home. Once, when I was sketching her at rest, she asked "will I ever be as still as that?" There now, she lies on our bier in perfect mimesis of herself and as I consider what we have done it seems to me good that this is all. Our death belongs to you, Child, make of it what you will.

EVENING. They lie on their cypress boards, dead-still, as only corpses can, their last drastic action performed as always here in our sanctuary. I have been looking at them for some time. When I shut my eyes and try to recall them precisely, I cannot. I open my eyes to study them in their perceptual vividness and again close them to recollect what lies before me. Repeated attempts establish as fact that memory does not record particularity. Yet I think I could, if I wished, draw a detailed image of them "from memory."

To test my hypothesis I've attempted a sketch without looking. Memory, I note, does not furnish a record, in snapshot fashion, of an original. Memory composts time and there's no separating the layers, the whole heap fused by combustions of feeling, perceptions flowing into the gum of the past even as I seize and pull at them. One would like to peel away the present moment clean as a cabbage leaf, but no—the organic leavings of time grow wild, no orderly rows ready for picking, no storehouses of passing moments in all their originality. Yet with my back to them while sketching, I found memory controlling the activity of hand and eye, rigorously limiting it to recreating the original. Mother Florida would be interested in this process whereby the original returns again and again, not in copies but in disclosures. My gift to the dead.

Now the burial. The elegance of Mother Zula's design moves me with its care for my ease, and for efficiency in disposing of their bodies. The simplicity of it. "Simplicity," she would say, "is the last gift—not the first or most important or even the most useful for living, but emphatically the last." The simplicity of her tomb decorations anticipates this moment and its shorn repose—so different from Nongka's consciously primitive work on the sanctuary walls, reveling everywhere in life's joy. I need only push the lever. Rods will glide out smooth as butter, death-boards push apart and guide the bodies down.

There, it is done, the body-disposal staged by this contraption. Mother Florida eased down at a slant while, in the same motion, Mother Zula—as though stimulated by rigor mortis in the withdrawal of support—rolled toward me, rose and leapt into their grave. The fragility and grace of life gone from them, their old bodies fix a powerful finality in the grotesque embrace of death, settled atop Ibo wrapped in the still shimmering blue of Erzilie's robe. Once the lid has been worked back over their tomb nothing remains but to seal it.

MAY 2, 1936. I am today in receipt of the deed to a cottage on the last block of Valencia Street where the ragtag immigrants live, along with assorted poor and colored—this in return for giving up all claim to the property of Frances Florida Boullet, deceased. And, I suspect, for maintaining the fiction of being her West Indian servant Zula's grandchild. For all intents and purposes I, Maria-Louisa Bernard, am no longer to exist. Manumission on my twenty-ninth birthday?

The agreement comes with "the word of the Cane family" not to interfere at any time with me or my work. Randy will hold his father to it. To keep them honest I drew his attention to the numeral "XL" on the spine of this diary; no harm letting him think there are thirty-nine more volumes (a fact if not a truth) any one or all of which might contain evidence damning to the family name. I offered to let him handle it in expectation of seeing the wince of disdain on those aquiline features. It came, with a step back to clear space between us.

Jake Landry has been posted to spy out every inch of the house and grounds. But this little volume works its own power, a buttress for the freedom I have come to think of as "factualizing fictions" (no more powerful than my mothers' way of fictionalizing the facts, but more effective in a world constituted by today's technologies and lifeways). After their death, I fabricated a fantasia orchestrated around the Boullet House and sounded throughout Tarragona. The germ of it was long in the ground, the regional soil of myth. Back in the last century, original sprouts sprang up spontaneously—rumors about grandfather Ibo riding nightly through the Quarter on a white horse, in protection of his people and in vengeance on his killers. I merely watered these roots with tales of him making off with the two old women one winter night—needed their bodies to work as his zombies, that sort of thing— then some hints about being in communication with the African crone called "Nongka" often seen riding with him. Many hereabouts claim to recall her from childhood. Some say she never died, others that she instructs me from beyond the grave in how to carry out her will as indeed, in a manner of speaking, she does.

Within a matter of weeks this humbug was running rampant through the uninhibited pathways of symbolic creation natural to the community. I feed the growing organism as required; it needs little except at boundary points where the limits of sheer confabulation open out like mouths to take in all random facts. I myself do nothing to lend these figments credibility; believers compete with one another to supply their own testimonials. In this way I've learned from the old Quarter how the factualizing of pure fiction empowers it—what modes of validation ground these lies, and the importance of not weeding them out but cultivating them instead. And so the stretch of the Quarter's mythopoeic network to virtually any situation sets the pattern for my own way of life, and its exits.

Randy Cane is among those who neither believe nor half-believe. The life we lead is sure to appear pathological to him, if not pathogenic. I asked whether he would be entering his father's law firm, to which he replied gravely, "No, no, there's that in Tarragona which will not submit to the reasoned processes of the law. New remedies are needed, and there are some exciting ones on the horizon at this time." He's studying medicine, specializing in psychiatry. The "mental hygiene" approach. When I said that my apprenticeship had yielded knowledge at the psychological as well as the chemical and metabolic levels, and that I would willingly take him on for a training period, he turned icy cold as his grandfather the old Judge was reputed to do, refusing to entertain my proposal even in a spirit of play. He's said to be charming. Not so, however, in the presence of what he surely regards as the brash presumption of a blooming lunatic. Isn't he "committed to the scientific approach in all things," aspiring to work with Adolf Meyer at his Johns Hopkins clinic before the great old man retires?

More ignorant, I surmise, than the believers. They at least, mistaking our powers as magical, avoid the error of supposing there are means to curb and contain them. He is prepared to endure our existence only on condition that its disorders be acknowledged and subjected to "treatment." By ridding the world of disease he expects in due course to be rid of us.

Neither the believers nor Cane's kind ever come to grips with the workings of fiction, that casting of a net with death as the nerve center of meaning to which all impulses flow. A simple necessity of time: because I cannot know myself in death, my death must always be a truth ungrounded in fact for me and, so, always remains pure fiction winding aimlessly through my days, set for chance explosions into fact. Mother Florida and Mother Zula understood this better than anyone. The fact of their death has taken on its after-life here in what I and others make of the past. If freedom possesses us fully only in the fictional truth of death, joy comes to us only in the fact of life. And this twenty-ninth year of mine soars with joy under the anarchic power of our freedom.

Some half-dozen children from the Island are due to arrive next month—have already found homes for them and am to take charge of their education. "These children of market women, farmers and fishermen," writes Father, "carry the Haitian energy making an island for all who oppose nature's jubilee of art to violations of justice." I am to transmit to them, he says, balanse in work and rest. His unquestioning trust in my disposition of them reflects his faith that Nongka and Ibo yet draw breath in me. Like an insignia of her deathbed message, I embody some linkage between the few words he heard there and the many he lost. The anonymity I expect to gain in my cottage at the respectable world's edge will be of great practical value, though for short periods I may yet arrange to make use of the sanctuary's protection when necessary. Fortunately, the authorities still fail to notice the appearance of another colored child here or there.

JUNE 15, 1977. I wait and watch closely. The woman from New York who took possession here last month has triggered a new factualizing of things in the closed circuit of the old house. Threadbare yarns reappear in a freshly endowed formation. But the old fiction can no longer accommodate facts unbending to its compass, and this woman's innocent exercise of her power puts her in danger, shuts her off from knowledge of her responsibility for what is happening around her and from any satisfaction she might take in it. She has yet to learn how to read and write what she herself sets in motion.

6

Remains

My right foot's asleep from sitting with it tucked under me all night reading the diary. I stamp it, testing for sensation, and am stopped by a flashback—childhood nightmare (or something I once read maybe?): A rubber leg stored on the top shelf of a wardrobe, like one in our old apartment in Budapest, detaches and reattaches itself to me by some law of its own. I associate it with my dead father. Inert, no sensation

255

or connection to the rest of me. One of those primal figures of disempowerment—not a leg to stand on. Like fiction having no ground. I pitch the diary over on the bed behind me without looking, like a slouchy old hat. What to do with it?

An image of Aimée asleep under her gauzy silk canopy opens on tomorrow. Tomorrow's here already, four a.m., still dark out there, all muffled past my perch of a balcony, Tarragona invisibly asleep on the other side of the Bay—water reaching from shore to shore like the blade of a giant's knife laid down for the night. The conclusion is obvious: If the sanctuary's going on display, a vital piece will be missing without the diary. I could slip it to Aimée at the opening, as we're milling around snacking on canapés and making local history, chatting about the human rights of the Haitians. Then pull out and take off.

But where to and what for? Harding says I'm one of those who move neither in the private nor the public sphere but in some nebulous in-between. No truly private parts for me—nor truly public ones either. "You," she quipped the day she told me about falling into the sanctuary, "live in the 'l' that makes the pubic public, and I came back at her with "the same 'l' that allows passage from the public to the pubic." This only a year or so after she'd come back from Tarragona in the late summer of '77 and I was already making notes on her tales of restoring the Boullet House (minus the part about falling into the sanctuary—nobody ever heard about that, or saw the diary). Idle scratch-pad stuff with no particular focus or direction—jotting down what bubbles up in my mind or what I hear others say is more or less a habit. Not for any future purpose, merely making automatic use of the technology that engages me in the moment. Wild scrawls of the pen. A week later, even a day, I haven't the slightest idea what it says. Forever picking up after myself, affronted by the litter of meaningless missiles.

The public/pubic joke went flat with the eighties' team-up of media, politicians, and guardians of family values to expose everybody's private life. Always in the name of honesty, decency, morality—and the consequent inoculation of politics with pornography and privacy with preaching. How to draw and repair lines between the private and the public, lines damaged, destroyed, knotted beyond undoing? How to become linesman in the media snarl? Time will come—technology will provide—when just about anyone who cares to will be able to access the past in its entirety. We'll have history as a system of high-tech openings to all that has been, from particles and waves to thoughts and feelings and doings of the dead and gone—no more mere interpretations of remains from the past but a three-dimensional show of what happened as it happened. Virtual reality, having overcome perspectival distortion of facts, will reach its heights as the truly omniscient narrator revealing all. No hidden corners for privacy, not with everybody participating in its extinction and tuned in to everything from the Big Bang to the faintest fart from any of us. We'll have the ultimate Public Gaze—not the all-seeing eye of God but the ubiquitous techno-receptor without end. Who or what and where I was will no longer be open to question, only why will not be disclosed.

I rise gingerly, like a geriatric case, take rubbery steps in the direction of the queen-size bed and move the diary to the night table, drop my shoes and strip conscientiously, as if baring my inmost being. (Bodily need forces all of us to become actors in pornographic sequences for our voyeurs of the future.) Pins and needles—my member and I are one again—but the image of the rubber leg in the wardrobe refuses to go away, irrefutable as fate.

This having to decide. . . . *Fatum,* from *fari* (deponent verb): to speak. Metaphor as dead as a doornail. As a rubber leg. The etymology of *fate* and what to do with the diary connect somehow to the question of what's next. What's next for Jael B. Juba, weaver of others' tales and in-between vagrant *extraordinaire*? To speak or not to speak, there's the choice.

Shower on full blast verging on scalding, so steamy I lose all sense of solid objects and give in to the sauna effect. Heavenly endless hot water. I skip the bracing cold rinse, towel my hair dry on the balcony, dozing on my feet. Could that be Tarragona's ghostly contour emerging across the Bay already? At once far and near in this liminal light, as much a phantom of desires past as of the changing middle distance.

Stretched out on the bed I feel oddly carefree, brain activity slowing. Blank intervals, islets of sleep. Dreaming my way through hypnogogic and hypnopompic drifts of remains, and blinks at the dark no-place region of my future. Like Scarlett I'll think about it tomorrow and so help me God will never go hungry again. It's as though I'm there already, idly revisiting scenes of a life put behind me, a book that's written and leafed through one last time—all the voices in it falling together like pages. And the erosion of Harding's restoration stories streaking memory now like float mineral. . . .

ON THE FRINGES of the Old Tarragona historic district, the sitting room of Miss Mary Louise's shotgun cottage. Perfectly square with high ceilings, uncrowded feeling despite books along every wall and pictures hung in every available space between—some unmistakably Zula's, like the one over the mantel, a large watercolor of a room in Cathy's Palm Beach "Minoan Palace": frescoed and stone-flagged, opening into a light-filled courtyard.

At a simple pine table sits Harding in her daily uniform—her summer's labor of love squeezed, now, into little more than a week, inching her way with organized precision out of restoration's workhouse—sipping espresso with Maria-Louisa and Martin Kingston, her nephew from Trinidad. She's gazing at an eighteenth-century chinoiserie cabinet between tall half-shuttered windows, its apple-greens, plums, russets, brighter dabs of green and blue against an alabaster background catching their glow as much from Zula's imaginary light over the mantle as from the late afternoon sun outside. It's one of three beautiful old pieces in the room. Near the front door stands a Louis XV mahogany commode with an elaborate marquetry and, along the opposite wall, a late medieval gothic chest with Moorish carvings and wrought iron mounts—among otherwise functional furnishings.

"Heirlooms from home"—Marty follows her eyes—"left to Grandfather Toussaint by Nongka and to her by her grandfather."

"Carlos," softly from Harding, moved by the intimacy that flows from speaking the names of the dead.

"I brought them here for Maria-Louisa to enjoy," and with the chuckle she's come to listen for, "my entry visa to this house."

Maria-Louisa downs the last of her cup. "Time to pick up the car, Marty, we should leave here no later than 7:15. I'll change meanwhile." She has to get ready for the public KKK teach-in (the Ku Klux Klan's reinvention of itself as an educational organization, hotly debated in the local media all summer long)—history's enactments call for unbroken vigilance, for the scrupulous gathering of facts to plump out the story of what happens. All hell would break loose that night, starting with Jake Landry getting himself killed.

"A friend's car," she explains to Harding as she vanishes into the back of the cottage. Something a bit more sedate and respectable than the pickup Marty uses for hauling historic scraps to the dump. "We'll drop you off; wait for us?" So unexpected, this—sitting among Maria-Louisa's books and pictures, the pleasing blend of plain and fancy furnishings. At rest. Like the ground firming up under her after nearly three months of living with the psychic equivalent of motion sickness. Feeling like . . . like herself again, even Maria-Louisa's diary entry charging her with illiteracy losing its sting.

When she reappears in what seems no time at all, Harding can't conceal her surprise. Dress, bearing, expression—everything's different. Green turban gone, hair pulled back in a casual knot, silvery wisps around the olive-tinted Mediterranean face frame deep violet eyes. Even her walk is subtly changed, less regal and assured. The long-dead criolla of delicate build, Toussaint's Mexican bride, incarnated in her daughter to exhibit the refined charms of aging?

"I take it you think I can still bring this off"—said with a mischievous grin—"in younger days my color depended on how we wanted to live."

"And Zula?"

"Too dark to pass for white. But Mother Florida made an entirely acceptable Creole lady of color in our company, despite not a drop of African blood in her."

Harding turns her empty cup—an old painted Japanese porcelain—this way and that in the soft light. "Unlike you, well . . . my credibility in respect to my own color is questionable. I've long felt myself to be harboring something more than whiteness and had to *learn* for all practical purposes to move in the confines of a white middle-class woman."

A hoot of laughter from Maria-Louisa. "Malleable sculpture-form, the American class mask."

"Fits all sizes—lets you survive any number of permutations and combinations of the social and economic without knowing what you're living through.

"'Got to fix that mask,' Mother Florida used to say. Look at me—anybody, anywhere—see what an easy time I have of it. Money, leisure, property—well, maybe not much, but enough—we always have everything we *want,* don't we?" She lifts the antique cup an inch off its saucer. "Bought this one for a nickel, long years ago. Garage sales and junk stores are my boutiques."

"Mine too—just slumming of course, snapping up bargains for the fun of it."

"Oh how my mothers could style that middle-class mask."

"And oh the energy that goes into the production of it. Humiliation? Never! Turn it into a confession of triumph—moral triumph at a minimum. Starve in silence, freeze in silence, live with rats and bugs in silence . . . never breathe a word about abuse, and die in silence."

"Get caught at it, though, and you'll go down like a cow in the stunning pen! If you escape the compassion of psychiatric care, that is." Maria-Louisa peeked discreetly through the shutter of a front window. "Mother Florida liked to cultivate the political advantages of poverty, seeing that it conferred a bit of the anonymity of color. 'All poor women look alike,' she'd say, 'watch me fade.'"

"And you—you've mastered the art of moving from one color to another without forfeiting one or the other."

"In Tarragona I always was and have chosen to stay black—tonight's an exception. Around here I'm usually Miss Mary Louise."

"Everybody's favorite old art teacher, I hear."

"And medicine woman, don't forget. Believe me, self-love alone gives a pretty secure foundation for the harmony of interests between Maria-Louisa and Miss Mary Louise—that and the invisible presence of my mothers, never to be underestimated. Imagine how they appreciated the irony of their position, virtual outcasts from the middle class community, white *and* black . . . they of all people, authentic bearers of middle-class virtues."

"And 'the Creole Woman'? Neither rich nor poor, black nor white?"

Another little hoot of laughter. "That's what they call me when they're not sure whether I'm too close for comfort or too alien for company. She's handy for projecting a public persona when and as needed. You'll be hearing—and seeing—a lot of the Creole Woman shortly. 'Go public with it,' Mother Zula used to say."

"I bet Zula could shed the anonymity of color like snakeskin—"

"And come out queening or poormouthing as she pleased. But Mother Florida never did quite get poverty and race to hang together right. She could pass herself off with great finesse as just another poor white or even another old washed-out colored woman, but let her try to go public, put colored and poor together, and middle-class whiteness would pour out of her mouth like toad-spit."

"Like me trying to poormouth—doesn't seem to come naturally, to paraphrase a Landry idiom—not unless self-deception lets me forget it's a political act."

"In which case I bet your sincerity admits of no equal!"

"Only when it's on behalf of others—that's the only time I'm convincing—this despite the fact that there were times right after my divorce when my children, Helen and Vanessa, and I were silent candidates for food stamps, and for a good many years after that we hovered somewhere around the official poverty line."

"Not a bad piece of poormouthing. But you're right, you're not a convincing victim. Poverty in your case is at worst a pose and at best an irrelevance."

"Yeah, just the finishing brush of experience to round out my humanity."

"A good job has been done on you. Your white mask is so highly factualized to verify the fiction of middle-class membership—the blinding facts of your education, tastes, speech . . . family, too, I suppose—nobody cares to see any material lack at the core."

"The magic of a decent sham. Makes others comfortable enough with me and assures them I'm no tax burden. Not a humanitarian concern."

"The other side of my mothers' discomfiting magic. Their mere presence in that antebellum house was a public disturbance, a jolt to the comforts of consciousness. You'd have thought they were the source of the old town's evil spring—faith here draws its energy from belief in evil and believers check for it like an electronic monitor."

Maria-Louisa swings the door open as a well-maintained, early sixties Ford Fairlane parks in front of the cottage. "The car," she announces primly, taking up her white knitted bag and a shawl draped over the Gothic chest. Harding follows her out and pulls the door to as instructed.

Will Marty stay with her at the meeting? Heavens no, that would be improper. Marty will wait outside for her like any well-trained chauffeur.

They go down the steps of the cottage together and to the car, two oddly matched white women at ease in each other's company. The middle-aged one, swarthy in her fierce summer tan, not bad-looking if you looked past the paint-spattered work shirt and shorts, the grungy sneakers. The older one, slim to the point of fragility, dressed with a sort of bohemian elegance in a shift of softly woven unbleached cotton, carrying her beauty like a gift of time. Martin Kingston (handsome in a pale blue broadcloth shirt, dark trousers, chauffeur's jacket and cap) directs them into the back seat with a flourish—his aunt on one side, Harding on the other for her one-and-a-half block ride to the Boullet House. Hours of finish-work lying in wait for her.

DEEP DARKNESS in the sanctuary, the night after Jake Landry's murder and discovery of his body thrown over the Boullet fence. The town under horror's voyeuristic spell centered on the Boullet House and all associated with it, living and dead, and Harding asleep on her mat beside the altar, on Maria-Louisa's advice: "Get thee apart." Safe in the secret unseen core of the crime scene after another twenty-hour workday.

The alarm goes off and Harding's on her knees as if on command—*regarde les mains!* Ibo's last cry to Nongka, while his two hooded executioners, the brothers Bob and Jonas Evans, worked the rope between them. In her mind's eye they are sitting side by side in Frances Boullet's parlor, still as manikins—the old, clean scar of Matador's knife down Bob's cheek from eyebrow to chin—only the brotherly hands perpetually in motion. Sinuous, shapely hands. There! Her searchlight freezes on the front panel of the altar: slick with blood, supple hands are twirling a star-shaped badge, its metallic luster leaping eerily back and forth—and, lately mirrored in memory undimmed by time: the hands of her contracting team, Evans & Son, tallying up numbers on a scratch pad ("a fine plumbing fixture don't come cheap, shuga"), joining plastic pipe amid a stream of chatter and cigarette fumes. Like father like son through the generations—blood again, working some phantasmal fit of past and present as eerie as original sin.

What to make of it now, this sanctuary-knowledge received without validation, its birth a mystery buried here? How to tell her story without revealing its source?

She knows she's not dreaming when Monday's paper arrives with a thud on her front porch as it does punctually each morning at six. The *Sentinel*, serving up bloody murder with all the trimmings, buffet style, all you can eat. (All that week, as it turns out, until the day of her departure and beyond.)

MISS MARY LOUISE'S COTTAGE, early Tuesday morning. Maria-Louisa in a rush-bottom chair with the day's *Sentinel* over her lap (headline screaming "New Facts in KKK Killing"), hair falling over an old mauve dressing gown. Harding, doorknob still in hand, unable to take her eyes off the woman who, in dishabille, so resembles Zula's painting of Frances Boullet—the death face. "Still trying to figure out whether I'm a stove-lid or a soda-cracker, are you?"

A stifled moan from Harding in no mood for jokes. "The diary—it's gone . . . disappeared. And all that work left to do . . . can't finish . . . just don't feel up to it."

"Sit, Elizabeth." Maria-Louisa slips on a smutty pair of cotton gloves lying atop some logs beside the hearth. One arm up the flue and out comes an oversized brick. "Like the ones you used to build the front walk, probably the same batch." And up the flue again for something wrapped in a plastic Winn Dixie bag, "you went out one afternoon before the weekend."

"For the chandeliers I had rewired—Friday—all the way across town in rush-hour traffic."

Maria-Louisa flips cinders into the hearth with a glove, draws the diary from the bag and offers it to Harding on the palms of both hands. "Thought you'd realize I'd taken it."

"I've never seen this in the light of day." The smoky old leather has the fragile look of nudity. "Time for another reading?"

"So many facts gathering so fast since you came, especially these last weeks—put them together with the diary and it throws off a scent of what's likely to turn up. What will you do with the house?"

The house! Harding jumps out of her chair—past eight o'clock already—and gives the diary back to Maria-Louisa. "I'll miss this but it's yours, of course."

Maria-Louisa, in disbelief, "No more than yours now, but I'd advise you to install locks on the windows across the back veranda. Meanwhile, I'll hold on to it—until you've decided something, it makes a difference to what we do next." She stands before a mirror propped on a bookshelf to twine her hair into a knot with an easy twist and pulls a long dark green scarf from the pocket of her dressing gown.

"We?"

"Marty and I, and—the refugees from Haiti. Our plans."

Harding lingers by the door, as though she's lost the ability to judge what to do with herself. "I want to sell . . . thought I might list it with Margaret Avery on my way out of town. But can I, and at what price? How much will my little fling down here cost me?"

"In dollars and cents probably nothing"—she winds the scarf deftly around her head, turning herself into the colored woman in the green turban—"you'll end up just about where you started. If you're serious about selling, Chris Stavros is your man."

"Dead serious, just haven't had time or the will—"

"He's right on the Plaza. Stavros, Stavros & Ribaut. One of those two-story cottages near the water, upstairs. Chris is ambitious, Yale-educated—contracts and torts, I believe—looking to buy a restored building big enough to expand in. Stavros senior's retired, he's the one you see walking his dog every evening."

"An ambitious lawyer about to hang his shingle on the local house of horrors, blood-stained again as of this past weekend?"

"Listen to yourself, Elizabeth! Think what it means to own a restored historic property on the scale of the Boullet House! As for the murder, you can be sure all-around forgetting will set in as soon as decently possible." Through the unshuttered top half of the window, strong August sun lights the turbaned head like a close-up, violet eyes steely with determination. She takes Harding's hand as if to stress the gravity of her words: "Remember, you need the secrecy of privacy in fiction-making, but for the facts we have to go public; leave that to me. Don't try to see me anymore this week—*you* keep to your privacy."

Unmistakably now, the Creole Woman talking, in all her readiness to take on the worldly dialectic of power—and shielded by her, Maria-Louisa with the natural fragility of a creature existing in power's dynamic, nothing at stake, looking out from that aging vibrant face amidst the chaotic energy of Nature's young.

HOUSE LOCKED UP AND SHUTTERED, phone off the hook, Harding toiling and sweating like one coerced to earn her body's freedom. Chains rattling off the ever-lengthening workdays. The Creole Woman, meanwhile, going public with the savvy of one at home in the limelight, wherever news is breaking or speculation packaged as such—the paper, the TV, the university lecture

circuit—scripting a highly visible role for herself in the communal murder drama and its simulations of justice served: local history expert, with
knowledge rooted in personal experience of the region's life and people;
spokeswoman for an emerging cultural force.

And virtually stealing the show. Like Nongka at the reins of Ibo's
horse, Miss Mary Louise spurs on the public narrative, insinuating, docu-
menting, highlighting as necessary to spin it her way—managing in the
process to settle some old scores and unsettle quite a few old families. In
short, manipulating local media events with a mastery more occult than
the author's art in a realistic novel.

STILLS FROM THE *SENTINEL*

Two gentlemen of African descent in early nineteenth century
morning dress, identified as "Parson William and Parson James"
(full-page center spread on El Inglés, "Life on a Southern Plantation in the 1830s: Typical or Atypical?" featuring original artwork
of recent murder victim's grandfather, courtesy of Leon County
Museum).
Anthony Krasner ("Missing Link in Landry Murder Case") on
his well-equipped yacht Night Owl, beer in hand, devil-may-care
pose.
Elizabeth Harding Dumot, obviously nettled, dragging a long
piece of molding down the hall of the Boullet House, captioned:
"Restorationist fails to imagine future for her work" (report of attempted interview by Roland B. Markit).
Creole Woman and Aimée Hulin seated amid tropical plants hanging around them in jungly masses in the latter's sunroom on Bayou Caroline, large Haitian primitive in background ("Gallery of
West Indian Art to Open Locally," second floor of Boullet House
above new law offices of Stavros, Stavros & Ribaut).
Leona Evans, wife of Tom Evans, clutching a bulky purse as
granddaughter Adele looks trustingly up at her and the Evans
guard-dogs, Donner and Blitzen, rage on hind legs inside a chain-
link fence ("Police Raid Home of Alleged Porno-King").

MUG SHOTS in a row, front page: *Thomas Evans*, smiling benevolently
as ever, ("Evans Confesses," lead story). *Flanagan J. Prideaux*, "self-
styled black entrepreneur and spokesman for Segovia Villas community" ("Landry Probe Widens," with sidebar depicting vacant unit of public housing project in need of repair). *Dr. Timothy Shibbles* pointing at
limb of live oak curved over dormer window of Boullet House, and

Maria Zamora covering eyes with both hands ("Neighbors Claim Tree Used by Demonic Cult").

I blink awake through a haze of light and a swirl of images. One of them pushes through: Leona Evans's bulky purse with the .38 she always carries there—everything zooms into focus. I'm in Tarragona Beach, sun glittering through glass doors of my hotel balcony, six-thirty a.m. The opening is this afternoon at two.

I swill down a tall glass of water with ice cubes from the mini-bar. Balcony doors shut, curtain drawn, air-conditioning on low, snug under the covers, I'm propped on an elbow to mull over Maria-Louisa's final contribution to the diary: carbon copy on onionskin of a typed letter to the president of DeLuna Community College. She's honored to accept the position of Director of Research in the college's newly funded Studies in Black Cultures . . . important academic initiative in community outreach . . . forging links between Tarragona's black and white (and other) communities . . . enlisting prominent figures, e.g. Dr. Randall Cane III and Mr. Flanagan J. Prideaux, in effort to broaden base for authentication of the new program. The Creole Woman making a start, in the post-Bicentennial 1970s, at an emerging history of Old Tarragona's cultural mixes.

The letter's pasted, Boullet-style, to the stub of a left-hand page, with a short entry from Maria-Louisa opposite. This entry sticks in my mind verbatim, like a code I've been trying to think in lately while working through my thing about the diary—struggling to imagine some cartography of private space for our publicity-besotted age. I flap the page gently back and forth like a dragon fly wing, just this side of weightless.

AUGUST 21, 1977. Comes a time when fiction's public use must exercise prerogative in our writing. Such a time is now mine, viz., my new "composition": the Creole-woman stories from the Sentinel, to be stored in the safe deposit box with Jeremy Wentworth's old papers showing his family's accusations against the Cane men to be more than moot. Records of possible utility in the future, and small reminders that the pull of power (the thrill and security it proffers) and the happiness of existing are not to be confused. Lose sight of the difference and each loses its niche. The coil of silliness in public life animates its horrors with tragic pretension, ousting the comedy of privacy and supplanting it with an apocalypse of ruin. Let the paradox that the enjoyment of power closes us into the sovereignty of me and mine, while the private joys of existing open sharable dimensions among us, work here to insure preservation of this, our sanctuary of drastic action.

May the few who have entered increase in time and become many. My crepuscular eighth-floor hideaway is as hushed as a raft becalmed at sea. Well, then, where does my night with the diary leave me? Their decision to open the sanctuary feels like an authorization, if not a duty, to publish it. Minus errors, slips of the pen, non sequiturs. That's what editors are for. We're minor historians snipping wild shoots from what remains.

No problem—they'll get the text they're after. Post it on the World Wide Web if desired: www.sanctuary-diary.org. My facsimile—state of the art, might pass for the original to an untrained eye—can go on CD-ROM for the research crowd, video showings to the visiting public at an additional fee as is done in other museums. Text or book, what's the difference? For them, none; for me, it's essential, it's all about the *book,* this body of leather and papery filaments—that's what matters. Mark after mark, pen bearing down all those years; and the hand that held it, scissors cutting and pasting—so many pages from volume upon volume destroyed—and leaving this remnant of the burnt offering. The very idea of separating myself from it verges on personal somatic trauma. Child ripped from mother. Mothers, to be precise; they all joined in by the end—Zula, Maria-Louisa, Harding—taking over where Frances Boullet left off her composition, selvedge to her weave. That's what I'm hung up on, the thing itself.

And yet, if *they* don't mind the . . . I want to say "violation" but call it "exposure" . . . if they don't mind, why should I who've never even set foot in the sanctuary? Where possibility is finite and desire interminable consider the options, from strictly curatorial (viz., put the diary on display, under glass, only experts permitted to handle it and then only after making them jump through hoops) to new-age entrepreneurial (like: shred the pages into slips of admission to the sanctuary . . . nice mythic turn here, body of Osiris, Dionysus, etc. . . . relics for modern-day pilgrims to file away in memory lane . . . better yet: make a game of collecting and piecing together the scraps—contests! prizes!).

After all, it's not my body. Or is it? . . . And as for those runaway technological advances to come—equal access to playbacks of, say, my personal history beginning in my mother's womb and ending (I hope) at cremation—I see no alternative. That kind of power promises a range and depth of—vision, is it?—such that we collectively and individually cannot say we will have none of it. Never have. We'll pine, of course, for the old freedom to create the past, but too late . . . all done, all over, and all revealed.

Proposition: You can hide the past only by destroying all trace of it (an ultimate demolition that stymies even the forces of physics). Corollary: Emptying the future of hidden contents from the past is possible only by stopping them from happening in the first place. Take the purge now? (Caveat: Once done—too late—history opens all remains to public access, not to be undone but only to be rewritten. Yeah, tell it again, Sam.)

Any serious fictionalizing will have to turn to the future, we'll start making up this or that *mañana* . . . till then my hypnopompic drifts. I riffle sleepily through Harding's entry, the last one in the diary, and, her voice in my head, snap off the light. . . .

DAY OF DEPARTURE, morning. Harding bounds up the porch steps of Miss Mary Louise's cottage two at a time, crying out "Finished, all of it! It's over—I'm free. Free to go my way." Her voice cracks in the total and sudden weakness of narrow escape.

"So the trading has ended, has it?" Maria-Louisa pulls her forward, to sit beside her on the swing.

"The story of my divestment—"

"A story! Let's hold a proper hearing of it in the sanctuary before you go."

"I have some writing to do first."

"Here's your missing prop—the diary—do whatever you like with it, it's all yours now. I've had my say."

"I never thought I'd make it, I really didn't, you know, just kept plugging away, 'o-o-ne da-a-ay at a time.'" Harding does a reasonably close rendition of the later Joan Baez.

"Never doubted it myself, not from the minute I saw the job you did on the sanctuary hatch."

"This afternoon, then, about three?" Lightly down the steps, feeling Maria-Louisa's eyes on her, she waves the diary triumphantly above her head.

MINUTES LATER, at the corner of the Alley, a honeysuckle vine close enough to the iron palings to grow on them. Kneeling, Harding twines the vine along the fence. Regrets not having had time for the garden, not even enough to make a start on it.

Jimmy Hurd, arms pedaling the air, lopes toward her, the Dollman, basket over one arm, sidling behind with his grin of secret knowledge. "Aw e tai, I say oo maka killn," mumbled in passing. He may look like the town freak, James Stuart Hurd, but he's nobody's fool. Some killing— the check from Chris Stavros in her pocket, all expenses reimbursed and not a penny extra, not a penny for her pains. Three months, one casualty, and out alive.

Jimmy stoops beside her with his usual fixed stare, brushing her hand impatiently away and setting the reluctant vine with a sure touch.

"Yoo aw pa?" Chin jutting in the direction of her car.

"All packed, and leaving today."

Silence. Then, "Wa yoo ga?"

"This?" She holds out the diary for him to examine, "an old book, you write in it, see?"

He's delighted with the way it falls open, sniffs the pages. "Aw fa yoo?"

"No, not all for me only but for all the people like me."

Big smile. "I ray in ee."

Harding sitting back on her heels digs an "EVANS & SON, Plumbing Contractors" ballpoint from the bottom of her purse. He thumbs through the diary to the blank section at the back and carefully lays it on the sidewalk in front of them. Harding points to the space after Maria-Louisa's entry of the day before.

"You always write the date first."

Hunkered down in perfect balance, he holds the pen poised over the page, waits for her to speak, then prompts, "Mondy . . ."

"Monday, yes, the twenty-second. Put down A-U-G-U-S-T 22, 1977. There, now you do your writing."

In deep concentration he sounds out the block capitals one at a time: J-I-M-M-Y-H-U-R-D.

Then lopes back down the alley toward the Hernando—and, suddenly, without turning, rolls his head backwards and sideways for a last look. "Gaw iss oo, Haw-yee." Softly, sorrowfully, almost a whisper.

"I'll miss you too, Jimmy." Him alone, perhaps—Maria-Louisa now more like a presence somewhere close by and she herself already moving to just that interest and concern for the old Quarter and its people which it's said one retains for former intimacies.

Problem: How to position oneself in a future that makes us more intimate with the dead than the living?

THE SANCTUARY, late afternoon of the same day. Harding, darkly tanned, in a casual pale yellow cotton dress and Italian summer sandals. Maria-Louisa, unturbaned, faces her across the casket-altar, seeming with age merely herself, without race or history.

Maria-Louisa (giving Harding a nod): Now for your story, the spirits listen with me. My mothers, Ibo, Nongka, we all hear you and I give voice to the distance you set.

Harding: My story? Tell how stripped I am, brought to this (pointing to herself with the forefingers of both hands)—my shorn body.

Maria-Louisa: Gone that far, has it? Ready for rape by the King of Terrors. Down to final simplicities, I hear you.

Harding: Argue my case?

Maria-Louisa: Yours to bring the case to rest in our sanctum, mine to close it with the speech of deliverance.

Harding: Well then, hear the Act of Sale in the office of Chris Stavros, attorney-at-law and buyer (stopping, in review of details)—

Maria-Louisa: And hear where it takes us.

Harding: To begin with—a handsomely furnished second-story room, good light, antique Tabriz on the parqueted floor, lawbooks lining kingwood bookcases. Between two windows, a walnut desk partly hidden by a Ch'ing coramandel screen, but allowing full scrutiny of a gold-inlaid T'ang ewer at one end. He motioned me to a graceful Louis Seize, paint worn just enough to understate its formality and echo ever so dimly the faded colors of a tapestry cartoon—an eighteenth-century hunting scene—above a small cane-bottomed faux-bamboo settee. I settled snugly into my down cushion.

His receptionist-wife, reeking of femininity, elegant variety, sorry she can't stay and visit (between her two leagues, Junior and League of Women Voters, she hardly has a minute to call her own anymore) served us freshly brewed Sumatran coffee in China trade cups. Members of a collection in a primitive early pie safe facing her work area. When I expressed appreciation for the whole of it, her smile took on the lightness of Southern irony—so much clutter in their house she's taken to hauling off this and that to Chris's office when he's too busy to notice. With what ease all of it will be transplanted to the home I've made for it! Breathing, spreading out, multiplying here in the Boullet House.

He brought a file to the long sake table and took his seat in a winged Chippendale in the Chinese style. I leaned forward for my cup. No heroine ever heaved a sigh of more heartfelt pleasure in that instant than I.

Maria-Louisa: Stripping away the old natural satisfactions destroys neither them nor their power. They remain, once removed, as a breeze may lift smog, a mother die in childbirth, aging lovers recover from orgasm—
Harding: A child grow to maturity, satiety be relieved, or a world metabolize from a touch and metastasize in spirit.
Maria-Louisa: Now for the words, the motile million unseen sentence-seeds.
Harding: Everything's in order, he said. Thanks for sending over the papers from your May purchase, a real timesaver. He spread closing statement and warranty deed before me on the table. Sign below my name . . . here, and where you see the check mark . . . there. Couldn't be simpler, that's the beauty of cash transactions. He laid a pen for my use beside the papers and unscrewed the top—a lovely old Waterman.
Maria-Louisa: A fit instrument for right stitching, this art of future sutures. And so you took the lovely old Waterman in hand for the finishing touch?
Harding: Not just yet. His eyes relaxed, taking me in, their clear medium blue warmly genial, not quite a smile. After a summer in dirty work clothes this more familiar style of dress (and oh, how clearly it met with his approval!) was like an old well-loved costume donned for a special function—but my costume, consigned mine. One I'm thoroughly at home in, and thoroughly at home I was, too, in that chair, that room, the frame of that world: an authentic, well-loved object in a niche of that world. To be protected, preserved, humanely used and enjoyed. Yes, I relished every moment of our transaction.

I eased his bank check out from under the paper clip and took my time reading through the closing statement, then the warranty—all the way through, not because I expected anything to be out of order but because I wished to pause there, without pressure, in that very order.

No questions? he asked, as I signed the deed in acknowledgment of his title to the Boullet House.

I secured the check in the zippered compartment of my purse before responding. Just one, I said. You're sure pride of ownership hasn't blinded you to a rum deal? What appears to be a rare bargain, purchase price on the low side and all, might turn out to be a lemon of the worst kind, what with the notoriety, past and present, attached to the place.

Not a chance, he replied without a moment's hesitation. His confident ruggedness, the same that can range from insipid to obnoxious in self-conscious projections of it in the media, was pleasing in its very innocence, worn rather as a man wears his trusty wristwatch. Such surroundings bring male innocence close, so close I can still be touched by it, though nothing in the past has aroused my nihilistic tendencies more. Not knowing he has no right to it is no small part of its range of privilege, but I was relieved to observe no urge in myself to prick or shatter it. Matter of fact, he was saying, the Sentinel's doing a special on the house next Wednesday, with before-and-after pictures. Put attorneys inside to manage the law and it's a sure winner, you better believe it. Great publicity for our firm.

Maria-Louisa: There you are, the sense of a true master, a chip off the old block, young Stavros.

Harding: He studied me silently over his coffee, as if making up his mind, and came out with: Tell you the God's truth, you're the one getting the short end of the stick.

Hmm, I said, have any reparation in mind?

Better, I've got a Gulf-coast sporting proposition for you: Return my check. You keep the house, move into it and we'll shred these papers before they're officially recorded. You're a sure-fire live ad, woman, don't stop now! Right here's where the future is, you just keep buying all the way through the four-hundred block of Valencia down to the Bay.

What with? I asked. If I give back your check, that's about the sum of my assets apart from my home up North.

Mmh-mmh, it just might be the least of them, he said, letting the tip of his tongue linger between his teeth. With somebody like you in the driver's seat, quite a few of us, me included, could be talked into investing in the restoration business. You've got potential in these parts for backing you never dreamed of. How about it?

Maria-Louisa: Well, well, a proposal that can make you here—preen and posture / feed and feather / Tarragona, forever Tarragona. So how do you accommodate the old natural satisfaction?

Harding: With the facts. For my one restoration, I reminded him, the price has been at least one homicide in the old Quarter. I don't relish the idea of living off that kind of thing. Besides, I probably increase the dangers of an already risky venture—remember what they used to say about having women on board.

Sure thing, he acknowledged, eyes a-twinkle, but what would life be without women and danger? Guess I can't blame you, though, for not wanting to get involved. He looked a question at me and said: not feeling guilty about Jake Landry, are you? That murder stirred up the town's can of homegrown worms but good. Nothing to do with you, though, not your responsibility. Of course hanging him over your fence—my fence now—was out of line, not to mention in bad taste. Next time, we'll find a cleaner solution, I promise. All you need to do is tighten up your game. Satisfied?

Maria-Louisa: Ooh la la, always the wrong question. Poor Chris, forever stuck with the basics: the leg a lever for ascension, the foot a fulcrum of desire, the arm a crank to concession, and so it is that natural satisfaction homes in a tool put to full use. Can a tool be denied full use?
Harding: I took his question seriously. Feeling guilty, no, I said, I don't go in for that. Responsible? Of course, who isn't? As for satisfied, you bet I've been satisfied. To the hilt. After all, get a stranger dabbling in the town's business and something's bound to come of it—every restoration uncovers a historical mystery and every mystery has to have its death.

He seemed to understand perfectly. I will admit, he ventured, there's been a certain feeling that . . . well, time was ripe for this murder, like he had it comin to 'im, relief you always feel when the bad guys finally get theirs, so maybe the good guys have better odds that way.

Yeah, I said, and you start waiting for it like the coming of the cavalry. Or the barbarians.
Maria-Louisa: No more bugles, howls, birds of ill omen beyond the walls, no flight to inner voices, feeling or memory-trace, only the body-tool bracing itself, breathe in, breathe out, ghastly hand flexed, yes, for the butchering. And how accommodate the ancient ecstasy of organic dismemberment, part by part?
Harding: You're a woman who doesn't shrink from the brutal facts, he said—so you don't take a hit today, you get another go. Another crisis, another chance.

That's *your* gamble, I said—wanting to force the issue—didn't the very newspaper preparing a feature on the successful restoration of the Boullet House give most of its space last week to blood and gore and scandal at the self-same address? All part and parcel of the old festival, right? Same story broken down to the daily spread of bits and bites by the news media, minute serializations making the little daily difference and never a hint as to whether it's the full story, the true story, or even the right story—just more bits and bites.

Maybe that's the only way we get something like an overall view, he shrugged. Boil it down to facts, straight scoop of information proving nothing one way or another. Don't tell me that's what you find so unpalatable?

I knew what he meant. Feasting, these days, is more like endless snacking. And when you're consuming illusory matter, the hard reality of bits and bites, those little taste-particles it breaks down to may seem better than nothing, even when you always need more and more to get your fill, approximate the old festive finish. To him I said: Doesn't it all smack of leftovers to you?

Judging from your restoration, he replied with a gentleman's easy charm, I'd say you have a real feeling for what to do with leftovers. Look, this time it would all be different . . . we'd work out some mutually advantageous deal with Margaret Avery . . . the other Board members too. He was making himself unmistakably clear: things would roll along smoothly for me, no snags. I'd made a place for myself in Old Tarragona.

Maria-Louisa: The place of a body-tool bloated with add-ons, yes. More and more, to extend the body's reach, multiply its uses. Empower. Empower.

Harding: I could see he was really caught up in his scenario of investing in my future as a restorationist. And I, realizing that the act of sale could be annulled even now, felt a surge of panic and was barely able to follow his brief of my great expectations in Tarragona, although I did grasp the force of it.

Maria-Louisa: Bits, bites, but and be, the hunger for technology. Choose one and you own its range of violence.

Harding: Point taken, I said, you're offering me an interest in Restoration's Future, Unlimited—I had involuntarily clutched my purse with his bank check in it and, seeing him interpret my gesture as a temptation to accept his offer and return the money, I relaxed, smiled, and leaned back into the seductive comforts of my chair—but no thanks, it's an opportunity I'll have to pass up.

Maria-Louisa: Refuse one and out goes the tease from the stripping game. Shorn bodies don't tool.

Harding: Sure now? he asked. Last chance . . . I'd give you a few days to think it over, but with my lease here expiring I need another place of the right kind to move into. Matter of timing, you understand. Perfectly, I said, and yes, I'm sure.

Maria-Louisa: Stripped to birth's duarchy, the two of you face to face again. But never the same two, never only you two.

Harding: He uncrossed and recrossed his legs with an amiable air of having nothing to lose and everything to gain either way—a win-win situation—then picked up the papers, sorted out my copies, and slipped them into an envelope imprinted with his firm's name and address. I held out my hand for it.

Maria-Louisa: Certificate of departure. Affidavit of your naked singular.

Harding: We sat in silence, comfortably for a few moments, finishing our coffee, comrades parting from a worthy cause, me thinking that the real question about his ownership was whether, with changing times, inflation, and scarcity of skilled labor, a busy lawyer and family man would give his property the care needed to keep it from running gradually down again. Does he know he's bought a time bomb? A lot to handle there . . . in any case no longer my problem.

Maria-Louisa: The course of our self-divestment now: freedom from the power of story. The child's legacy lost, O Death, O Life, at what cost?

Harding: Still leaving today? he inquired when I put my cup down and rose to go. I dangled the keys to the Boullet House in front of him and said, I'll be out and away in not too long, before sundown, for sure. Shall I throw them down the well or leave them in the mailbox when I go?

Just like me to overlook the key factor, he quipped. Last time I'll be keying you in, I said over my shoulder. He grinned and reached in front of me to open the door.

Maria-Louisa: The blind child's beauty never fades, the fine vein of nostalgia winds away from her to the once-trusted, perfect keeper and user.

Harding: We stood there for a second and then another, he with his hand on the doorknob. Nothing intrusive or demanding in his look, merely a signal of his availability for appropriation, as if he were making an unashamed offering of himself.

Maria-Louisa: Still and always there roots in a technology-empowered species desire for the omnipotent tool.

Harding: I hitched my purse over my shoulder, he opened the door and watched me go. Before starting down the slightly turned staircase, I looked back, wanting to hold him clearly in memory: a gentleman in the best tradition of what I had loved lasting. And yes—O let it be said here—on the pillar of my body, the feelings of a natural woman inscribed for my reading. He could not have understood what I got out of the deal and could only have seen it as a loss for me, something like a failure of nerve in the face of risk and rutting.

Maria-Louisa: The species is his, and yours to disown its compass. He has his birthright, you a space free and clear of his past. A good trade has been made.

Harding: Free and clear, shattered as I knew myself to be by the whole affair, I took a turn around Hernando Plaza, the drama running its course in the old Quarter already distanced. And now that I'd certified my choice to own no piece of it and to play no part in it, here I was thoroughly at home in it. The old dump truck parked in front of that little fallen-down Victorian cottage at the end of Delgado and the gloomy figure beside it were well-known to me. I hailed Mr. Ware and inquired concerning his health.

I be out here in the sun doing my job, he replied as he mopped his brow and studied me, approval overcoming surprise, and, Mislizbit, you looking mighty fine today.

Thank you, Mr. Ware, I'm leaving this afternoon. Back to New York, to my daughters.

You acting right too, Mislizbit, this ain't no place to live down here, specially for cheeren. Schools ain't much count, don't teach nothin but a little readin 'n writin.

I walked on to Miss Mary Louise's cottage for the diary and back to the sanctuary for my say in it while waiting to sound the story one on one and hear its reverberations amid these remains of time.

Maria-Louisa: Where we privilege no right but that of the body-tool to the shorn condition of privacy—no part of it for others' uses be they ever so small or grand.

Harding: The bare body gladdened and safeguarded by right, by its own proper solitude, yes.

Maria-Louisa squirts tiny coils of primary colors from tubes of oil on to a cardboard palette and passes it along with two brushes. Picks up a bit of charcoal, eyes flicking over the painted expanse of the sanctuary's north wall and motioning Harding to follow her; draws a face—in the branches of a tree—that Harding recognizes as her own; takes a brush and energetically streaks bright green paint across the forehead, turns and looks at Harding, who, palette in hand, assumes the position of an artist engaged in self-portraiture and fills the other brush with paint for a blue nose. Without stopping they do all but the eyes. Maria-Louisa quickly dips her brush and dabs at them—a pair of red smudges flecked with green and yellow—then steps back to view their work, side by side. The face sinks into its ground, leaving only the expressionist blaze of fiery eye-patches.

"Remarkable likeness of your leave-taking," murmurs Maria-Louisa.

FAREWELLS MADE—house restored and sold, car packed. Harding looks her last on the ranks of white ibis above the roofline of the Boullet House, away to roost, the twisting white string announcing sunset and she impatient to follow their example. Time enough for a four or five hour start on her ride north. She coasts once more past Miss Mary Louise's cottage but, instead of turning left at the end of Valencia toward the Interstate, swerves on impulse in the direction of the ibis gliding downward—to a little road marked "Private" that leads out to the Bay.

At a creeping pace she follows the shell drive through bougainvillea-lined thickets of trees: wide-branching moss-strung oaks, regal magnolias with huge waxy leaves, cool cedars, camellias, jasmine, fruit trees scattered throughout—citrus, peach, crabapple, fig. A clearing opens on to a sandy beach, palmetto scrub fanning the ground, water fowl stalking their dinner. Ahead, a mature well-maintained garden, English style, fronts an eighteenth-century coquina house on a slight rise overlooking DeLuna Bay crinkled, on this late August afternoon, by a light breeze from the west. Sheltered as a lake. Her involuntary, barely audible gasp express-es the peculiar mix of pleasure and pain that comes with the penetration of beauty—there again, that suffusion of what she can only call "love." Leave it to the Canes to have possession of all this.

What brings her here to Segovia Crescent? Not any need, certain-ly, to bid Dr. Randall Cane III and his family good-bye; her '68 Chevy with its Empire State plates, washed down for the trip and showing its age, so clownishly out of place. She gets out and leans against its warm flank to watch the dark-haired woman of delicate creamy complexion on the raised veranda: lemon-yellow dress loosely gathered at the waist and draped around her hips in lyrical good taste as she snips at a potted plant on her way to a hand-fashioned swing on old iron chains and sits down. Looking out over the water—the green of those eyes, it seems to Harding, distinctly visible even at that distance, flitting over her and her car. Dis-missing them both.

Harding stands her ground, this ground that is anything but hers. Recalls Bill Simmons saying once that "Miz Cane" wouldn't give an inflated American dollar for folks that don't keep the home they live in fixed up. And what if you fix one up but don't live in it? Bill thought the Canes incapable of making that kind of distinction; for them, living in a place was the same as fixing it up and vice versa (though not, of course, simultaneously).

As if called to her post, Sophie Cane rises from the swing and takes a few steps directly toward Harding before half turning again to the Bay. The breeze lifts her full sleeves in a diaphanous flutter of Nikean wings as, raising one arm over her head and letting her hand rest on a porch column, she surveys the brilliant horizon of water spread out in the distance. And still Harding waits, looks on, knowing herself privileged to behold the pal-ladium of the place.

The woman glances her way, Harding shading her brow with one hand to see as clearly as possible until, their eyes meeting at last, she receives the other's gaze, its wash of humiliation over her and her car. Like a purge. From the insignificant, Mrs. Cane turns once more to the boundless view, the spit of island on the other side barely discernible in all that shimmer.

Harding circles the shell drive through the garden with a billowing of release, waves and chuckles to herself at the pursed mouth (so hard—she can empathize with the distaste in those green eyes—so hard to live without the invasion of trash these days). And, having looked on the face of her Tarragona anima in the glow of a Gulf-coast sunset, chugs contentedly up 29 North, past the towering bright orange billboard with the black handgun and the legend: THREE YEARS TO LIFE A real law-and-order state she's leaving.

At twilight she forages two little Florida peaches, late Indian Reds, from her food bag and, savoring their sweet juicy whiteness, swings onto Interstate 65 to Birmingham and points north.

Past eight a.m. and sure to be business as usual out there, beyond the artificial night seal of my waterfront hotel room. The diary snuggles between my fingers with all the unthinking assurance of a beloved object. I close it and hold it between both hands, like a face I'll never consensually allow another to touch. A personal belonging of no estate value. The text, of course, will have its place in history for all to read, no going back on that.

My turn now to take care of what matters. I stake my bet that no one who experiences the Public Gaze without sanctuary, in that future sure to arrive, will choose to live under it. Bifurcation of the past is going to be the only available choice—into the certainties of playback and the indeterminacies of fiction, with bumper to bumper traffic between the past that happened and the ones that didn't.

A future that I, as an in-between kind of person moving about in the nebulous split of private and public, can begin to feel at home in. My terrain will very likely acquire a populace—and then it hits me: her voice! Captivating and close, resonant with feeling and the self-awareness of an inner feedback system, Harding's voice is gone! So companionably at my disposal these many years, so naturally it's like a part of myself thinking, luring me all the way down this path of seduction, lost now like a radio signal when you drive out of range. I'm on my own. Exit—out she goes like passion's candle. In a rush of abandonment I flip the pages to her piece entered that last day in Tarragona, Monday August 22, 1977, after Jimmy Hurd's name.

> The tradition has worked its way through me. I can't say how it is
> that I know this is the end of it. I can't even say for sure that I love
> the end any more than the beginning or middle but I can say for
> sure that I hate the beginning and I don't hate the end. . . .

And on for quite a few pages, no paragraph breaks, so that it's like a single drawn breath.

Ordinarily, the tale of Harding, who renounces her own future, twines time and space for me in a sensuous architecture of conscience crafted moment by moment. Lately, though, this pattering down here on her trail—it's almost as if I'm trying to write a different ending for her, somehow revise her sense of the end. Smooth over her break with the past, lead her into a closer relation to it . . . and to the sanctuary. Return her to the Boullet House with conviction of her place there, as though she could have made some adjustment to Tarragona after all the miasma of blood and politics and plain old dirt, eyes wide open, entrepreneurial future in the offing—just worked the house into her life somehow. Like a seductive old flame that fades into a friend of sorts, affectionately held where the old passion is either contained or dies out naturally in time. She could have, after all. She had the chance. Call it a third way.

Alchemy, Jael, alchemy—to paraphrase Nongka. Some things, even if possible and appealing—here it is again—aren't palatable. Not really wanted. Not right. How would Harding put it? Something like: "Being an insider of any historic community requires you to become a surveillant of its life, and I preferred not to. The Neighborhood Watch syndrome held and holds no allure for me." It's her voice more or less—temperamentally, she's no insider—but I had to work at it, it no longer comes naturally, of its own accord like schizophrenic visitations. And I'm no restorationist. Familiar as I am with the ways and works marking that life, it's not for me.

I slide my pillow under the light to see better. Harding's handwriting—each letter flowing smoothly into the next, the words distinct and whole—comes across to me as an intimate reminder that I've let myself be carried away. But her last sentence stops me cold, its import striking home for the first time:

And so, goodbye, dear Diary, as I close my daily genealogical
tracings and leave a blank page for our next entry.

A single page for some as yet nameless communicant with precious little to say once present. Mine, I realize, though I won't presume it was intended for me all those many years ago. Someone like me, with a tendency to be at a loss for words—les mots justes at the critical moment . . .

Must have dozed off—is she really gone for good? Been passing in and out of range for some time now, me filling in for her.

No, there she is again, at a great distance, on the road—the home stretch, only a few miles out of Athena—taking care to avoid the zigzags of a banged up red Duster demanding recognition of equality, blaring its horn irately at the sporty Porsche pulling ahead of the pack—verse after

verse tumbling out of her in a funky Big Mama Thornton / Janis Joplin
style highway song commemorating the couple in the red Duster—
> they're all ridin free
> over their coun-tree
> and the tank ain't empty yet!

—one hand simulating percussion on the dashboard, a hard rock 'n' roll
beat with a bluesy feel to it and the raucous cry of Jimmy Hurd careening
along Hernando Alley—Helen and Vanessa would get it right off—
> they don't plan real far
> ain't they got their own car?
> they go together like a stripe-an-a-star!

And now let's hear it for the Porsche duo—
> they stay outta rain
> in his yacht and his plane
> they're hitched together like a ball-an-a-chain!

> they don't say thank you
> and their kids won't neither
> cause we all deserve what we get!

All together, everybody—
> yeah we're all ridin free
> over our coun-tree
> and energy ain't run out yet—sing it, sister!

> all ridin free
> over our coun-tree
> just awaitin for a hydrogen bat-te-ry.

I set my alarm and float off and under all the way, laughing and lullabied
by Harding's farewell to me.

Oh but I do feel buoyant today! As always when, racing through turmoil,
slathered with slush, I set out on a track of action like a thoroughbred mud-
der. Dress, check out, grab an Egg McMuffin—on to the mainland over the
causeway. Well before noon.

Last minute preparations are in progress all over the Boullet House.
Aimée has everything under control. Maria-Louisa thrusts a copy of the
guest list at me, so I can take a good look at it for the full picture. Feeling instructed to make myself scarce, I lose no time getting to the sanctuary. Library steps—sturdy new ones with handrail, custom-built for a safe,

easy ascent to the dormer. I miss, just for an instant, the gymnastics of Harding's broken-backed chair. (And what happened to the originals, the handsome wooden steps to be donated by Randall Cane?) The wide open hatches are a shock even though I expected as much. I take my time going down, marveling to see it all intact—or as intact as it can be now, exposed to the whole world.

A good half-hour has gone by before I realize how artfully concealed lights, moving and fading indiscernibly like sun rays, direct attention to Nongka's panorama of the spirit-world. In its presence I turn to the frescoed altar where images form an energy band that works on me with the light touch of a healing hand. Minutes pass. I'm oblivious of what I'm here for until the hem of Frances Boullet's dress draped over the edge of the altar breaks my trance. Almost guiltily, I slip the diary under it, a smoky edge showing beneath the creamy white silk. That does it. I cast frantic eyes up at her dress hanging innocently from the rafters, consult her vibrant old face in Zula's altar fresco. Can't think what for, certainly not because I'm still expecting some kind of a sign.

If it were up to me alone the diary would stay here and the sanctuary would remain closed forever. Period. But it's too late for that now and that's that—if there's anything I have in common with these women, it's the rudimentary sense that what it means for a thing to exist, large or small, is to embody a time of its own. To destroy a thing is to take away its time rather than letting it self-destruct in its own way, use up its own time. With time as our mantra we come to the love that maintains a preserve for the mystery of one another.

I remove the diary and leave a scribbled message to the public in its place: "Here lay Volume XL of Frances Boullet's diary. Reproduction available for viewing upon request, limited first edition forthcoming."

Maria-Louisa and Aimée appear satisfied with my message when I run it by them on my way out to the garden. They're much in demand—with caterers, florists, and early guests milling about. Neither asks for any kind of explanation, it's understood I'm doing what's necessary for our conversion of the sanctuary into an exhibition space.

I amble into a secluded niche near the back, sit down on a stone bench behind shrubbery in the shade of the old wall and, without further ado, open to the last page and make my entry.

May 27, 1993. There's to be no sanctuary for my writing, so the age decrees. At best a reasonable facsimile—opportunities like now in a garden where the moment, between the coming and going of others, is mine and my pen joins me with those who used the sanctuary, knowingly, to render what possessed them. Hardly the worst of all possible worlds for jobbing a tomb. That this remainder of their passion may be preserved I myself become a sanctuary for it—where this my passional goes so go I.

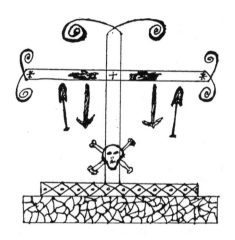

7

The Opening

Maria-Louisa and Aimée join me in the kitchen where I'm looking over the guest list. Everybody, and I do mean everybody, has been invited. All the Wentworths, Hurds, Wares, Canes, Stavroses, Simmonses, even the Evanses (minus Tom, who succumbed to a heart attack after the murder charge against him was dropped), top brass of the police department including Chief Thomas F. Buckminster and family, Deputy Chief Leon Zamora, Lieutenant Mickey Peaden, Sergeant John Gorrie, plus the *Sentinel*'s upper echelon—Editor-in-chief Roland B. Markit with a crew of senior photographers and staff writers—sundry professors, administrators, and support staff from DeLuna College (formerly Community College), also Margaret Avery, Flanagan J. Prideaux, Mr. and Mrs. Greeley Connor, Jimbo Townsend, and Maria Zamora, to name just a few of the locals familiar to me among many others.

And that's only the first part of the list, the Tarragona contingent swelled by names from all over Florida: the Steins of Palm Beach, Jon Howard of Miami Beach, the Tates of Tallahassee (John Henry, I hear, probably won't make it due to unspecified business claiming his attention somewhere between the Indian Ocean and the North Pacific), Anthony Krasner of West Palm Beach, the Picketts of El Inglés Plantation—many, I realize, Howard and Cane connections but a goodly number, too, of unrelated professionals and academics, two small film companies, and a smattering of agencies and foundations headquartered on the Gold Coast. Three plainclothes police officers are posted in and around the house.

This is not what I expected, definitely not just a newsworthy local event. Well over a thousand invitations sent out all told, individualized for recipients by a cadre of artist apprentices under Aimée's supervision. Maria-Louisa threw in a few of her own but won't say which.

I have mine with me—indelibly Maria-Louisa's style, Harding remarked the instant she laid eyes on it. Pen and ink drawing of a woman in an attitude of rapt attention, as though waiting for someone to speak—listening with trancelike stillness—inside an oval of throbbing color pushing its way out of a splash of inky darkness. Around this image runs the hand-lettered invitation: "The Haitian Gallery of Art requests the honor of Jael B. Juba's company at the Boullet House in Tarragona, Florida, for the opening of the women's sanctuary, May 27, 1993, 2–6 p.m." A printed insert reads:

> The sanctuary, built into the historic Boullet House at its inception, served for over a century as a secret women's *ounfò*, or inner sanctum for Vodun *seremoni*. Brilliantly decorated throughout, it is the only such structure known. Its opening to the public, revealing extraordinary aesthetic dimensions shared among women inheriting the Haitian soul, is a major event in the art world.

The second part of the guest list, three times as long as the Florida list, is an eye-opener: representatives of museums and galleries, the media, corporations nonprofit and otherwise, organizations for refugees—ambassadors of various persuasions, drawn (strategically, it's obvious) from around the world. I browse through the addresses: Kathmandu, Tehran,

Munich, Cairo, Istanbul, Zurich, Oxford, Johannesburg, San Francisco, Prague, Bombay, Montreal, St. Petersburg, Dakar, Copenhagen, Seoul, Lisbon, Jakarta, Shanghai, New Orleans, Lagos, Rhodos, Melbourne, Osaka, Tunis, Madrid, Kuala Lampur, and points between. Sublists for Haiti, the other Caribbeans, Central and South America. Not a bad census of a global village with access to the information highway under construction.

"Quite a crowd," I venture, "for what I thought would be a semiprivate by-invitation-only event lasting maybe a couple hours." My voice betrays some question I haven't processed.

"Don't worry," replies Maria-Louisa, "most won't show today—but sooner or later they will."

"When it works, that's how it works?"

Emphatic nod from Aimée. "That's the beauty of it, invitations to the opening will take on more meaning—and value—in time."

They point to a soup tureen in an out-of-the-way kitchen cabinet where they've stashed name-slips, each clipped to a dollar bill—bets with each other about who will and won't attend. RSVPs don't count for much with this crowd. Aimée holds out a handful of blanks: Would I like to place a few bets? "Make mine win-all/lose-all," I say, taking one strip. "Dr. and Mrs. Cane will attend," I write and hold it up for them to see. Eyes roll with the glee of those who know this one has been fixed—mine's a sure loser—as I drop it in the betting bowl.

I'm starting to feel underdressed. On second thought, what I am is undercostumed for this media affair. Aimée and Maria-Louisa are the height of elegance in the appropriate, if rather dramatic, fashion of hostesses. Aimée in a lamé gown of such fine gold and silver threads it swirls like falling stars around her calves with the smallest movement, her subtly streaked ash-blond hair tossed up as if by chance and held in place by tortoiseshell combs as palely amber as her skin. Maria-Louisa, like a Fauvist portrait: *Aged Caribbean Beauty.* Handwoven fabric in an abstract of earth tones, topped by a matching scarf tied Haitian-style at the back, huge ear loops evoking Victorian images of West Indian mambos. Still, there's something to be said for my navy silk, bold enough with a pale green tooled Moroccan belt not to look drab, recessive enough to let me mingle without attracting attention.

They're pouring in now, cameras snapping the arrivals. Individually designed invitations germinating.

We're all wearing name tags and most are circulating. Lots of approach-avoidance activity as always in these situations, and taking stock—others' IDs, and, less overtly, outfits, hairdos, postures and posturings. Everybody so busy socializing—making the move, the right contact—they've forgotten the main attraction, reminded of it only by the line forming on the staircase. "Excuse me . . . sorry . . . ," I squeeze past and into the library. The better to watch the spectacle as they enter and exit the sanctuary.

To one side of me: Tibetan monk smiling and looking serene, with business woman, Amy Ton, Global Networks, Inc., Singapore, reading his tag aloud in a marked pitch accent, "Jam-Yang Paljor, Dre-pung Monastery, Vancouver, Canada."

He smiles even more pacifically, taps his tag, intones something beginning with Jam-Yang that sounds like an extension of his name.

Amy Ton pays close attention and translates triumphantly with rising pitch, "He says he rest so we must not feed him to birds yet—Ja-tor, you know." She's addressing a trio of Indian women behind me wearing finely threaded silk saris. Zeta Pradesh, Visiting Professor, Center for Population and Development Studies, Harvard, regards the monk speculatively and turns with a low, pleasant Hindi inflection to Neeta Shiva, Women's Health Organization of India, New Delhi, and to Gina Jibanānanda, Forestry Institute, Calcutta. Neeta remarks in a nimble Oxbridge patter, "Yes, well, he's not yet an old and naked man and so can't prove he would count death as happiness."

Thoughtfully from Gina Jibanānanda: *"Ter nana ke nano ho!* I was born down below." And to me, "I say, have you by chance met up with the representative from the World Resources Institute?"

Before I can reply, someone has taken my hand and is shaking it warmly. "Been trying to track you down," he says, "they said you were in the garden." The look of him—sixteen years older, he's more gorgeous than Harding let on—and the West Indian melody identify him at once: Martin Kingston, Haiti Reborn, Quixote Center, according to his tag.

Martin introduces me to some people he has in tow, all Haitian Americans and all some years older. Wearing little iron crosses around their necks. "The first of the refugees to be sheltered in the sanctuary," he explains, "they're here for a reunion—to commemorate its opening for them back in the fifties."

I'm thrown off balance, I'd forgotten. There's a sense in which the sanctuary has been open for over forty years—to Haitian refugees nobody was supposed to know about. A secret opening. An invisible crack in the wall of privacy for destitute strangers to pass through, without sound or trace.

And now that I think of it, it seems provident, a kind of transition to today's big show. Smiling dreamily, Jacques Hugo, Society of Small Crosses, Miami, lifts his emblem between thumb and forefinger and whispers, *"Garde Corps,"* nodding toward the sanctuary, "from the hounfor." At this, Félicie Breux, Society of Small Crosses, Key West, tosses her head tied chicly in a chartreuse scarf to one side and, with eyes closed, flings out her arms, moaning and swaying in suggestion of halcyon ecstasy.

Soft drum beats follow her movements as if summoned by them. A six-foot-plus, sensuous streak of a man the hue of antique elm and dressed in immaculate white, Nation of Islam style—with dozens of small crosses on tiny black-linked chains draped over the crook of his left elbow—slinks down the stairs from the dormer entry, then steps aside like an emcee introducing a talent show, a group of African and Asian American teenagers, four girls, four boys, behind him on the stairs. They're decked out colorfully, each in his or her own idea of what a vaudunist looks like, little drums that say ALL PROCEEDS GO TO SEGOVIA PROJECTS DESIGNS strapped around their necks. He lines them up against the dormer wall—the crowd steps back, he's got their attention—claps hands and snaps fingers in rhythm, which the kids pick up in a muffled beat on their toy drums.

"Yo!" he calls out and the tops of all eight drums flip open like one. Hands delve inside and back out waving object after object before the eyes of rapt onlookers. "Thunderstones," he whispers in a velvety rich expulsion of breath, *"assons!"* He reaches for and shakes a beaded rattle. "Special lotions and potions made to order for you ladies, suit your needs, *ouangas! Simps!"*

He fingers a sheaf of rubberbanded crow feathers and confides with a wicked tremor in his voice: "This here *some* bad medicine, man, don't need that gun no more, the times, they're changing!" He snatches a little tintinnabulum from one of the hands and, tinkling it delicately, takes his bow: "Flanagan Jones Prideaux, Segovia Project Designs, at your service."

The boys and girls file out holding thunderstones aloft, humming in unison. "You ladies and gents been looking at the future businessmen and women of the world, they'll be along the fence as you go out—and, hey, show a little respect when you pass, know what I mean? Ain't no drugthugs out there." Flanagan J. Prideaux with his elbow of small crosses dangling in front of his face—like a hip version of a veil—swaggers back to the dormer stairs, takes a step up and pivots toward the crowd, raising a palm outward as if to ward off the rush of consumers, "Sorry folks, no commercializing *inside*." Swinging the crosses over his shoulder in a virtuoso gesture, he invites the first ten guests to follow him into the sanctuary. Those in line behind them are instructed to wait and proceed one by one as others come out—"and don't nobody linger too long below, this ain't the Museum of Natural History here." He extends a hand to a Chinese beauty on the stairs and, disappearing with her into the sanctuary, waves those behind to follow. They do so, audibly counting their numbers.

Martin Kingston and the original refugees look at one another with a mix of appreciation and irony. Félicie Breux, Society of Small Crosses, crosses herself and says, "Is becoming a refugee camp everywhere, *non*?"

"De whole damn world," Jean Mulet, a fellow member of the Society, agrees.

"Then all the more reason," I say, giving in to one of my many surges of wishful thinking, "why the whole damned world must be turned into a sanctuary."

Martin Kingston, leading the original refugees toward the steps, nods. "How about we start with Haiti and branch out from there?"

Jane Fonda and Ted Turner, surrounded by two or three other notables and more wannabes, push between us. But Jean Mulet has taken my arm and calls up to the other originals, "Hear what she say, she one of us, dis lady," and, removing his iron cross, he slips it over my head and adjusts it squarely on my chest. Then in a low serious tone as if completing a rite, "Welcome to the Society, Mamzelle Juba," before stepping regally through the notables' retinue to catch up with the others.

Back out in the hall, laughter and chatter, uberous and exultant, issue from the erstwhile bedrooms of Francis Boullet, Zula, and Nongka, now all hung with Haitian art. Spanish-speakers are finding each other: Cubans from Havana and Miami, Puerto Ricans from New York and San Juan. Colombians, Costa Ricans, Nicaraguans, Guatemalans, contingents from Santo Domingo, Caracas, Santiago, Buenos Aires, and a lively cluster from Mexico City, Guadalajara, Merida, Texas and California. I wander among them noting that here, as a group, they vie in numbers with the Anglos.

Someone else has noticed: "The same with any phenomenon, material or cultural, economic, political—start a trend and there's no stopping it. Forget the ups and downs, bumps and cracks, it's only done when it's finished, to paraphrase the Bard." Dr. William Albright, Professor Emeritus, West Florida University, chatting up Roland B. Markit of the *Sentinel*.

"Is that the latest demographic thinking? The conquistadors started it, their spirit's gone but the course they set just keeps on rolling, taking little unexpected curves and turns that reset and redefine the direction from time to time?" Same old Markit. Can't wait to tell Harding that, despite professional advancement, his rap hasn't changed. Barely kept up with the times—half showing off his special talent for tuning into others, half turning it into his idea of a highbrow joke.

Dr. Albright is pursuing his own course. "Only a couple of hundred years have passed," he reflects, "since not just the Floridas but everything west of the Mississippi, except the Pacific Northwest, was Spanish territory." (Taught American history at the Community College in Harding's

time, I recall.) "I've always had a special interest in Spanish Americans"—
he's trailing off—"Hispanics . . . umm, Latinos, as we say now." Markit
has another go at his fractal theory of the historical event in formation:
"The Spanish discovering each other throughout the hemisphere, passing through a point of instability, wobbling steadily through its shattered
shape to a new communal configuration"—he breaks off to peer at my
name tag since I'm so obviously hanging on to his every word—Jael B.
Juba, Homeless, Classless, No Profession, No History, No Future. The
one I had Aimée print out for me this morning when I realized I'd left my
"Writer" tag on the dresser in my hotel room.

I shake his hand and, even as Dr. Albright extends his, am literally
swept out of the room and along the hall to the staircase by a vigorous
tide. A snatch of a poem I recognize drifts past in a beautifully modulated
voice, ". . . *A largo amor nos alce / esa pujanza agras / del Instante . . .*"
Surrendering to the flow, I follow them down.

Aimée and Maria-Louisa are both at the door welcoming new arrivals
and seeing others off. One of the plainclothes types, no name tag, milling
around them. Videos trained in every direction and a few generation-Xers
following excitedly from room to room.

Maria-Louisa breaks through the traffic and steers a woman of decidedly French stamp, about my age, with one arm and a decidedly German-
looking man with the other to where I'm standing by the newel post.

"You three can surely find common ground for disagreement or what
have you, *n'est-ce pas?* But don't forget to sample the wild mushroom
pâté—on the little table just inside the garden room." And she's back in
her place by the door.

We're left eyeing one another's tags.

"*Ah, une Dadaiste.*" Jacqueline Vallois, Poet, Algiers, smiles at me
and then, surveying Gerhardt Strauss, Art Critic, Munich, adds, *"Et voici
l'autre genre de nihiliste."* He's ash-blond with glints of silver and good-
looking, like a poster boy for the great National Socialist Hope declining
into cosmopolitan rumpled middle age.

"*Et vous, Mademoiselle Vallois—quelqu'une de votre sorte, que pour-
rait-elle avoir en commun avec une bête noire comme moi?*"

Not to be left out in the cold, I take it on myself to answer for her:
"Cherchez le négatif, Herr Strauss."

"Aber nein, Fräulein Juba, nein—"

"La coquette est une piquette," the French poet quips.

Herr Strauss beams down on us both and, with a winning Bavarian lilt,
wraps up the matter, *"Was wir also miteinander gemein haben, geehrte
Damen, ist ein ganz klein wenig Gemeinheit, n'est-ce pas?"*

"Kommen sie," poet to art critic, *"il faut que vous montrez du doigt les chefs d'oeuvre Haitiennes."*

He maneuvers us to one of the galleries and proceeds to expound on a trio of acrylics covering an entire wall in densely packed fantasias of color suggesting a strife of enchantments. "Reminiscent of Hippolyte," he comments, "but more exotic—how shall I say?—*sauvages, visionnaires.*" To be featured in an exhibit of Caribbean art he's consulting on in Munich next month and, after that, Paris. Texaco has contracted to buy the lot for an undisclosed sum.

Trim business type from Tokyo, with distinguished shock of hair and Italian designer suit (looking aggressively Western on him), steps forward, presents a packet of miniature photos, each with his address on the back. Japanese artworks—doing double duty as business cards. "You will please keep," he directs the art critic, "arrangements for exchange very easy. I post anywhere in Europe, you send to me anywhere in Japan."

"Awee fren! Awee fren!" Jimmy Hurd in the doorway, urgently pointing me out to Annie Hurd, dressed up in a two-piece knit suit. I excuse myself from the transnational scene and walk with them down the hall to the garden room where guests cluster around two enormous punch bowls, one at each end of the stone table. "So you remember me," I say to Jimmy, "Harding's friend."

Jimmy herds me possessively through the punch-bowl throng, past tables of plates, napkins, canapés, to a contingent of home folks in lively conversation, overflowing from the French doors that lead down the steps into the garden. "Awee fren! Awee fren!" he's practically jabbing me along with his index finger and repeats his introduction several times until all eyes briefly turn my way.

Stephanie Wentworth leans on her brother's arm like a Gainsborough young matron in K-mart's finest, with a mouthful of perfect teeth—too perfect, I recall, to be her own. "Billy and me," she's saying, "we was on to it when we was kids. It was so-o-o spooky! the noises up there and the footsteps on the stairs, and Billy always telling me to hush my mouth. 'It's voodoo, and we gotta keep out of it, Steph,' he'd say—me 'n Billy, we grew up right here in these very rooms!"

"Yeah," says Billy, "I went upstairs into that big front room once, poked all around, not a cat's lick of anything. Granddaddy Jeremy found out and said we'd never ever have the eyes to see what was going on. Have to be born to it—he had the eyes, he said, but the blood in the rest of us done thinned down so much we was liable to be struck blind if we kept on meddling upstairs. Them spirits up there, he said, sent him messages and he just got the message they was watching every move I made. I never went back, couldn't see nothing anyhow, not having that kinda blood." He flexes the muscles of his free arm and tosses his ponytail to the other side. Body builder, pushing forty.

A chorus of claims breaks out—suspicions and funny feelings so old as to acquire the certainty of pure unadulterated fact. One tall gaunt man, weather-beaten as a sun-dried apricot, states he was pretty sure for as long as he lived in the Hernando—and he lived in it on and off for over fifty years—pretty damn sure, well actually he *knew* all along, having been a witness to it with his own eyes time and again when he cut through the backyard at night—the things going on up in those big windows! "Never said a word to a soul, people get the wrong idea."

Only Annie Hurd denies the knowledge: "I never seen a thing. Too busy looking after everbody, I guess."

Jimmy, who has been deep in thought, looks into my eyes and states with absolute certainty, "Awee—Awee nooo."

"Yes," I say, "Harding knew."

"Tole you," a voice behind me insists, "I said it then, that woman got something back a that wall she want to hide." He's imposing, very dark with a fine head of dreadlocks. Mo Benson, Architectural Treasures, Tarragona, and he's telling it to Mrs. Mo Benson, Architectural Treasures, Tarragona, and Johnson K. Benson, Architectural Treasures, Tarragona, a lanky teenager about his father's height, hair cropped halfway up the head Spike Lee style.

"If it was me, man," declares the latter, "I'da knocked a big hole in that wall and stepped right on in, I'da known everything."

"Sho you would, and Johnson Ware woulda knocked a hole in *you*, boy—your grampa never did believe in wasting his time on white folkses trash. It was always 'If'n you not paid to do it, leave it be.'"

"Ain't that just what you selling out your warehouse," the son sneers, "all that old junk you so particular about?"

"Don't matter what you call it, son, I gets paid for it and that's what buys your jeep and your high-tops." Mo Benson firmly closes the discussion and directs wife and son down the steps into the garden. I follow and overhear him, now out of sight in a spot nearby: "You take that hunk a stone column there, son—could've come straight outta one them ancient temples, right? Well, it come straight outta my warehouse, one of eight off the old Simmons place we tore down, early Greek Revival. Onliest one that broke, but I sold every scrap of it for good money."

"Pardon," says a thirty-something redhead associated with the Florida Council of the Arts. I'm blocking the turn she wishes to take. She seems to know her way around and is showing an elderly gentleman of the Tongin Foundation the garden.

"It always strikes me as sad," she speculates, pausing to let him take in the path ahead, "that gardens, the most ephemeral of all arts, are almost never taken seriously—as if they're not really art until they've lasted like Versailles. Time does it, the longer the better."

"And opening them to the paying public, my dear. As long as Sissinghurst was Vita's garden, it was her property, not an art object. Once anybody could buy a ticket of admission—and she'd been dead a proper time of course—Vita's garden became Vita's art, the moral being that time, people, and money in judicious combination decide what art is."

"Well," she seizes the moment, "whatever it is, art does *belong* to the public, don't you agree? That's why we felt you would be interested. . . . "

I'm about to leap in with an opinion here although I haven't clearly formulated one yet. An impulse, in the presence of such discussions, to push them to complications too extravagant, or too loaded, for conversational purposes—about to come out of my mouth is something about art as work: a crafting action that reproduces itself in the finished thing, this being vaguely aimed at putting the materiality of art out front. But a pair of couples, student types, grabs my attention. Adele Evans, Duke University, Class of '93, accompanied by Alex Stavros, Harvard Law School, and—I recognize the young Vietnamese American from the Tarragona Visitors Bureau (William Wentworth, DeLuna College) who's with Cynthia Buckminster, U. of California, Santa Cruz, '96.

I introduce myself using Jimmy's moniker for me: "Harding's friend." It's obvious though, they've no idea who Harding is. With that slightly dashed sense of boring the young when you enthusiastically refer to acquaintances of their parents, I explain her relation in time to the Boullet House, and—surprise—they perk up and center on me with unmistakable interest.

"You mean the one that restored the house and then sold it to Dad without breathing a word about the sanctuary?" asks Alex Stavros, presumably son of Chris, attorney-at-law. Dark, clean-cut.

"That's Harding."

And from Cynthia Buckminster—daughter of Chief Buckminster, Tarragona's deputy chief in Harding's time—"The woman who told the story to the paper, about 'The Murdering Hand'!? You know, how the dead guy made a sketch of this hand and wrote that label on it, like right in front of her eyes the very day he got killed. Cree-py." She's a honey blonde, very pretty, thinking of majoring in psych, I'd bet.

"Yes, Harding reported the incident to your father after the murder."

"That sketch—Mr. Landry showed it to us too, Grandmomma and me, not long before he was killed, and . . ." in a soft, troubled tone, ". . . it certainly did look a lot like Dad's hand and Grampa's too, and. . . ." Adele Evans covers her eyes with long slender fingers and shudders.

"And," I say, "just like the bloody ones in the sanctuary, twirling the marshal's badge. Family resemblances can be profoundly misleading— not much help, really, as Harding always said, in determining who shot Jake Landry."

All four nod emphatically and begin to talk at once, Will Wentworth taking the lead. He's extra-mural, just finished his first year in personnel management. They're here at the opening, he says, in a last-ditch effort to turn up evidence that would clear Adele's dad and granddad. They've been a team since childhood, these four, drawn together despite age differences by the murder and all the other stuff going on in the old town—one thing for sure, the Boullet House must be at the center of it, everybody always talking about the place being haunted and his mom and uncle Billy just about positive that it was. He himself was too little when the family moved out to remember anything.

"When Dad had his office in here," Alex recalls, "I snuck in a couple of times after dark and went over it from top to bottom. Later, Will and I even played Hamlet and Horatio once—stayed up all night in it watching for ghosts. No show."

"And after *my* Dad got to be chief of police," from Cynthia, "Adele and I like hung out at the precinct and browsed the files—you know, kinda like Nancy Drew stuff in your day—got a copy of the murder investigation report, no problem, and fixated on it for days—well, mostly Adele did, I was still too young to keep my mind on it. Not a single solitary clue."

"Well," says young Wentworth, "opening the sanctuary's cleared up part of the mystery at least—just knowing those were real noises made by real people hiding out up there. Proves my family's not as wacko as everybody thought." The Chief's daughter slips her hand in his and agrees, declaring it's time to put the whole thing behind them, get a life.

Adele Evans, under Alex's protective arm, has kept the fingers of one hand pressed to her forehead in pained thought, engagement diamond glinting. "Your friend," she now asks, "the professor—*she* doesn't believe Grampa was guilty? He kept saying he did it, even after it came out that he and Dad had an alibi—never changed his story up to the day he died."

"No," I say, "Harding was never convinced either Tom or Aubrey Evans did the shooting."

"There," says Alex, "I always said the old man was protecting somebody—probably one of his buddies. One of those KKK characters."

"The only people Gramps would have gone to such extremes to protect would be me and . . . ," she stops and glances uncertainly at the others.

Again I take up where she's left off, "That old news photo of you and your grandmother carrying a big purse—made a few days after the murder—is she still alive?"

"In a nursing home; she had a stroke when Grampa died and never really came back. Grandmomma and her purse, she holds on to it day and night like it might get away from her or something. . . ." She's staring into my eyes already putting it together, and I nod ever so slightly.

This is between me and her, for her to do with as she chooses, I don't think the team will be in on it. Alex maybe, but not the others. Her big blue eyes are round with the shock not, I think, of remembering but of understanding a memory we share—hers from experience, mine from an old *Sentinel* story about little eight-year-old Adele Evans falling asleep in the car, that night of the murder, after overhearing her grandmother talk to Landry in the parking lot. And Harding's remark: "Tom Evans once told me Leona was never without a little .38 in her purse and he'd taught her to use it."

Adele breaks from Alex's arm and drops her head on my shoulder, murmuring, "Grandmomma, Grandmomma"—so much grief, as though I'd been the bearer of a death message. I don't give easy reception to sentiment, however deeply felt, but this kind of bodily expression of trust moves me like no other.

"I know, I know," I whisper, my arms around her in a fragile effort to contain the moment. The others, not in on it, look vaguely uncomfortable. I push her gently away, "Today's opening ends the old story—Cynthia's right, you can move on now."

She smooths back her hair, eyes narrowed with certain knowledge, and smiling at me with that same trust, says, "Thank you" before turning to Alex. He echoes her thanks, then Cynthia and Will, and all shake my hand with the formality of young people paying their respects to a rarely seen aunt at a family reunion.

I wind my way through the garden maze to the privacy of the niche where I wrote my diary entry. Just this morning, was it? My need to assimilate, think—where to go from here?—has reached gut proportions. But my thinking seat is occupied by—serves me right, I feel—a slim, coppery-hued man about my age. So much at home here, so engaged in his work he can't be a mere visitor. More like one of the propertied squeezed by economic necessity to open his historic home for a season each year—English lord, say, disguising nobility. Dispossessed Indian chief seems a surer bet in his case. Whatever, his presence is a stimulant to my weakness for TV movie plots.

No name tag. The large piece of driftwood he's so energetically burnishing has the shape of a shield or coat of arms. He scoops up a string of gold spangles from the bench beside him and starts to wind them speculatively around the wood.

"The necklace! You've got the Shakespearean necklace!" I point at it with what can only be coming across as accusation.

He doesn't look up, goes on with what he's doing and says, "That's what's fascinating you so?" Startled that he's been aware of my scrutiny for some time, I don't reply. He smiles, easy and confident, "You betcha, I've got it, but the vintage is not Shakespearean—this necklace is bona fide Alligator Injun, of which I'm the last" and, seeing my eyes widen, "guaranteed legit, passed down from my great-grandmother."

"The Bride of Freedom?"

"Bride of . . . haven't heard that in an age. You must be Howard kin, they're the only ones ever talked like that. Mom and Pop called her the Alligator Mother. I'm Jon Redman Howard, named after my grandfather." He stands up, awkwardly holding the wood with the necklace draped around it in front of him, and leans over to read my name tag.

"Definitely not, you see, a Howard—like you," I remark acidly.

"Definitely not, but 'homeless, classless . . . ,' seems you're having a few problems of your own."

We laugh and he sits back down, the driftwood on his lap. "Maybe," he says, "you can suggest a use for this fantastic found object, looks like the seasons have been sculpting it for something."

"Think it needs a more anthropocentric function in the world, do you?

"Well why not, no point letting it go to waste." He smoothes it tenderly.

I sit down with him, stroke the burnished edge jutting toward me. "Kind of like me," I say, "not quite junk, not quite marketable, not quite anything. Drifting around. I do a little teaching, write a little fiction, an article or two here and there, hand to mouth—what I need is a profession, something to steady me."

"Something centering—ok, what'll it be? Take me—I'm out to save the Everglades. Wildlife ecologist. Money's not that great but I'm good at it. For a profession, it's got to be something you'll be good at—how's that for starters?"

"Something right for me? The kind of rightness that reveals itself in childhood, I take it, something so easily, so unthinkingly, spontaneously and methodically done it passes through your days like warp and woof."

"You said it—showed up in how you spent your time, what you concentrated on with the fascination and response that marks genius. Like Mozart or Leonardo—gotta find your own . . . gift, they say."

"I secretly concentrated that way only on certain things going on around me—interactions, I mean—between people, sure, but animals too, bugs, plants, objects, anything within sight. Interactions so distinctive of their participants that . . . it was like an invisible frame set them off from all else until their ways of being were uncovered—not explained but stilled in a passing light. It took an alertness that made for a curious mix of paranoia, distanced observation, and investigative rigor."

"An early eye for detail?"

"An insatiable desire, I'd say, to see what comes of details and how. The desire of a lover—not love in the romantic or familial or sexual or any sense you've heard of, not love as usually talked about but somehow the opposite. And not a desire for love's enemy—don't get me wrong—hatred, far from being love's opposite, snuggles in its bed."

Jon perks up. "A new kind of love you got on to as a child?"

"The oldest, most ordinary love of all in my experience—the love that profoundly engages with its other. Nothing mystical, I mean the way our bodies work with each other like wheels of fortune. I seemed to have this natural aptitude for following a transaction to its clarified moment—a public flash—a burst of hidden and unintentional particulars displaying an end in time. Not the insight of intuition or the unconscious laying out its devious sense of things, merely a moment's disport without message or purpose. A conglomeration of accidents."

"Got it, you could fill a professional supply gap there—become a spiritual guide, not exactly a shaman or a guru, just somebody that brings others to realize the pointlessness of—"

"Doesn't suit my temperament," I say, "besides, how can you enter a profession when you abhor the act of professing?"

"Maybe one so standardized it doesn't take much professing, you just follow the game plan—let's look into all the possibilities starting with the world's oldest."

"Which I've hardly dabbled in . . . on the other hand, how about one so nonstandardized there's nothing to profess! An anti-profession from start to finish."

"Create your own practice, that's a start."

"A private one. Set my own hours, big comfy work space, books galore, art, stereo, clients accepted on per-case basis, one on one. Highly labor-intensive, you can see that, especially since this will be a practice that . . . umm . . . makes up what the case is—completed only when client gets a language for it and puts it in writing."

"Made-up cases? Like fiction, you mean?"

"Yeah—a fiction so individualized its rhythms can only be heard in our improvised dance to its beat. A coupling universal in sweep, unspeakable in range, deep in reach and subtle in variations—like sexism, say."

"Sexism?"

"You know, a fiction so body-cogged, so familiar it can't be detected except in its grossest manifestations—there's my cue, Jon! I'll be a detective, feet on desk in the office, hooked on tracking this infinitely intricate chameleon of a fiction to its telltale flashes. Hearing tail-ends in the dyadic play of my client and me."

"Sounds like a cross between Sherlock Holmes and New Age consciousness-raising. A novel brand of psychotherapy maybe?"

"Except I don't intend to treat, tail, or contribute to the welfare of others. I propose to be paid for a kind of collaboration with my clients— where I "hear" the client by sort of becoming the client, off and on that is. A new kind of hearing with no purpose beyond its momentary happening. Client will be able to witness the shaping up of a double, namely me. And this doubling of fiction-making will show how the client and I-as-client arrive at our personal pronouns—above all, our 'we.' A dual being with one 'I' doubling the other 'I'—a couple—'you' and 'I,' bound by nothing beyond the doubling of fiction-making. Get it?"

"Yeah, you been gigging around, boned up on psychosomatic jives, and now you wanna get paid for psychedelic jam sessions—so it's you solo and I'll solo and we'll live together in our blowing room. I'm with you, but I'm wondering if there're any no-nos built in here like, say, sex with clients?"

"Definitely a no-no. An anti-profession can remain anti only as long as there's no expectation of service of any kind, including the world's oldest . . . not exactly taboo but emphatically not included. Still, love does figure into this somehow, in fact it's basic—I'll be a philo-something or other, strictly without quid pro quo."

"Oh . . . well, whatever . . . I got just whatcha want to get your thing going"—he flashes a postcard in front of my face like a magician—"South Beach five-story, queen of art deco, unusual set-back, rare ocean view"—and points to a canopied window in passing. "The perfect office, built-in bookshelves, luxurious apartment to go with it, you'll love it. Small old hotel in SoBe I'm converting to rental condos. But location's your ace, location's everything for starting a dead-end profession so new nobody ever heard of it. You'll be needing access to clients so loaded or loony or risk-oriented, deluded, desperate, or just out for fun and sharing kinky experiences—"

"Or plain tired of the old rat maze and the old rigamarole for making sense of it. Think I'd fare better by answering the personals?"

"Naah, wait'll you walk into this and see who's passing by, all cruising for something to bite on. Hang out a catchy sign and you'll have a client before you can reel in your line, guaranteed. Trust me."

"Perfect office in perfect location. For that I probably won't be able to shell out the first month's rent. Sorry."

"Aha, gotcha, here's where my bait wriggles. On this one, there's a first month's rent cancellation, give you time to move, settle in or change your mind—enticement for right renter in prime property—and if you're not happy with it we nix your yearly lease, no questions asked. Unhappy renters make unhappy owners—forgot to mention you'll have an option to buy."

Light as his tone is, there's no doubt he's serious. Not me. I've merely been babbling out loud, giving little or no thought to what I was saying. Playing around, partly I think in response to him—his manner invites it. Still, hearing my own babble, there's something in what I've been saying.

He picks up the driftwood and declares, "Now this here is pure-dee genius: For the ideal office in the ideal place you need the ideal sign." He unwinds the Alligator necklace to demonstrate how the lettering will go along the top: WORLD'S YOUNGEST ANTI-PROFESSION—and, tracing a space at the bottom—"Logo fits here if you want, and your name centered here, JAEL B. JUBA, followed by type of service—'scuse me, nonservice—all hand-painted in bold colors. Rain-proof storage below for your brochures—I'll leave those to you while I personally design and get your shingle ready to hang in front of your office, can't miss it from the street."

Well, why not, I have to start somewhere. "Get out your paints, Jon," I say, "I'll drive down to view the setup in a day or so."

"Great decision, congratulations." We make our way through the garden maze, he thoughtfully winding the necklace around the wood again, then stashing it behind a greening bronze as we pass by. "Safe as a bank vault— I'll be back for this quicker'n you can say 'see ya later, alligator,' then down to SoBe at top legal speed, get things in order for my new tenant."

We walk up the back steps into the house—silent, both of us a bit dashed, I suspect, by my snap decision. The garden room is packed with Caribbeans. Martinique, Guadeloupe, St. Martin, Trinidad, St. Lucia, Haiti . . . they're all represented in force, dressed as casually as if receiving visitors at home, with the motley, vaguely bohemian air of creative people. Lots of "Painter" tags, along with "Poet," "Sculptor," but mostly just "Artist." It feels like a cross between an Olympic event, all poised for victory, and Carnival—all churning with expectation and shot through with explosive tension. Perhaps the effect of premium quality rum. A party having graciously brought several cases to the opening, the punch bowls are brimming, voices raised, speaking over and interrupting each other. I understand next to nothing of what's being said. But I can't miss the Barbadian intonation of the sculptor beside me who inquires: "What kind of shit is this? You talk like snow queens, I never had any French influence on me, and I'm not settling for chocolate flavor with vanilla ass cream."

Jon knows some of them and understands the Creole dialects. An argument is under way. Once the CIA gets the USA in to force the junta and their death squads out—one of the Haitians is predicting—Aristide will be back and so will tourism; he's heard this little Tarragona gallery is just the U.S. branch of the Port-au-Prince headquarters to be lodged in a specially designed building big as the Louvre. Francophones are adamant the new collection should in no way accommodate outside influence— French is okay—since Haiti has little or no commerce with the English-speaking islands and the only thing they ever have in the offing is one or another sort of exploitation; Anglophones indignant, one Trinidadian boasts he's got the contacts to sink any proposed cultural exchange between Trinidad-Tobago and the French Caribbean, and he damn sure will unless his people get equal time and space. Other Anglophones insist it's only right for them to have preferred treatment given Haiti's long self-inflicted isolation—this pipe dream about Aristide will remain just that unless and until he can get the States behind him. Not bloody likely that *les Français* are about to cross the ocean to help Père Aristide; the French are all talk and no guns. The very mention of the States sets the Francophones bristling—they're more inclined towards Europe and will never under any conditions submit to postcolonial Americanization. Vital matter of artistic integrity—keeping their art West Indian and not standing around letting it degrade into some branch of U.S. consumer culture like dolls with pins in them. Debate is growing more heated with each round of punch.

I may not grasp the nuances but I'm preternaturally alert to the short ends of fuses. I grab Jon's hand and squeeze through the crowded hall in search of Maria-Louisa or Aimée. The garden room will be a bloody mess unless somebody—the police?—takes fast action. At the front door, still welcoming late arrivals and bidding farewells, Maria-Louisa accepts Jon's arm before she's even heard me out and heads back for the melee.

And we're just in time, the room more or less split down the middle with two painters in a shouting match and some Haitians holding back the crowd as if protecting the arena of conflict. A Guadeloupeyan has faced off against the Trinidadian, each professing not to understand the other. The Haitians are translating. "De Guadeloupe on say he feeling fine and want we join togedder in Panama," according to one.

"What the Guadeloupeyan said," Jon whispers, "was 'All the fools I see cracking their jaws belong here in Florida or with the CIA in Panama.'"

Whatever, the Trinidadian understands perfectly well, it seems, and replies, "De fools in my face just up and show it dere place in bed wit Noriega. What dey call art, dass drug-lord territory for steerers and dealers."

"Come, Jon, you're going to put me on top of the table," Maria-Louisa tells him.

"Say what?"

She yanks him, me pressing behind, through the thick of bodies and stops at Aimée's stone table. For a second, I think she's going to try punch-bowl pacification. "Here," she tells Jon, "pick me up and stand me in the center." On her feet between the punch bowls, Maria-Louisa hunches dramatically forward, drops her shoulders, sticks her thumbs in her ears with fingers fanned out and heehawing and guffawing with such zest she looks donkey-possessed. One forgets that, among her many talents, she's a brilliant mime. With all eyes on her and all voices quieted, she snaps to her usual erect stance, hands on hips, and slowly surveys all with withering contempt.

Now first in Creole, repeated in Spanish, then in English: "Fellow fools—for all artists must be fools—your throats make words aplenty but mean about as much as a cock's crow, a lamb's bleat, a lion's roar, an alligator's bellow! Would you become as cocks and lambs, as lions and alligators? Then do it like proper fools and crow about our mission to work beyond the divide of words, bleat and bellow to all and for all, vociferate about whatever happens our way, in whatever places we come to. Island must roar to island in a Caribbean art beyond language, and mark a Caribbean place in time. Sing Caribbean, fellow artists, sing Caribbean, Samba."

"Ayibobo," from the Haitians. A calypsonian starts a rendition of "Doh Stop De Carnival," and all, smiling broadly now, mingle and dance as freely and easily as if in a domain where the past has indeed passed. Maria-Louisa holds out her arms to Jon like a trusting child and is lifted down.

We come upon Aimée in Maria-Louisa's place by the door, where Jon and I take our leave, he with a winking allusion to "Jael's unique and world-shaking private practice," in aid of which I'm renting an office and an apartment from him in South Beach.

"So," says Aimée to me, "we'll be seeing you—often I hope."

Maria-Louisa is making jottings on the back of one of the printed cards. "Of course we'll be seeing her," she says, handing me detailed directions for getting to my new place in SoBe. "Jael's been infected with Harding's spirit—and now she carries this around her neck too." The token of my honorary induction into the Society of Small Crosses, already forgotten by me.

"And this in my bag," I take out the diary and place it in Aimée's hands. "Still a sliver of blank space at the end, waiting for you—you'll be the last to have a say in it."

"My space," Aimée says in deep thought over the band of white below my own brief entry, "and I want to keep it this way—mine will be the space of silence in it. But oh what a book!" She's fingering and examining it with the intentness of one at home in the book-making arts. So concentrated are we both, she on the diary and I on her, neither of us notices the two elegant guests on the veranda, a Hispanic beauty years younger than I supporting a well-coiffed, snowy-haired woman about Maria-Louisa's age who demands with the ease of position not to be denied, "Aimée, what treasure have you got there?" as she takes it into her own hands.

"So . . . the infamous diary, is it? Can't wait to read it." She leafs through it absently and declares, "See here, Aimée, Mary Lucy and I've come to inform you in no uncertain terms that this silliness between you and Randy must stop, the sooner the better. I absolutely refuse to be shut up in that house another day—you're going to come around tonight after your opening and that's that, make it up with him."

"Aunt Aimée," Mary Lucy interjects, "we women have to stick together; Aunt Sophie needs our support, don't let us down."

"I'll hold on to this," Mrs. Cane announces, "you and Mary Lucy can read it to us—my eyes, you know, and we can't expect Randy to do it, can we? But now you must show us the sanctuary."

"That would be my pleasure, Mrs. Cane—Sophie—I'm Maria-Louisa, Frances Boullet's granddaughter. But this you don't need," and, taking the diary from her, she relays it casually to me, "because you'll soon be receiving, compliments of the house, a copy of the forthcoming limited first edition in print. Much easier reading." They link arms and slowly walk upstairs together, Sophie more delighted than she can say to meet the Creole woman in person, Mary Lucy trailing behind and nodding over her shoulder in self-satisfied confirmation.

With book in hand I'm first to recover speech. "So," I bid Aimée farewell for the time being, "I win half my bet and lose half, how about we call it a tie?" She gives me a warm hug and I leave her shaking her head in disbelief.

The kids from the project are still lined up on the sidewalk, along the fence, with their toy drums. Impulsively, I drop a tenner into one of them, whereupon the kids all follow me with a rhythmic tapping that—so the girl pointing at the intersection of the Alley with Valencia informs me—will be heard by the crossroads spirit. When we reach my car, she hangs a miniature black top hat with skull and crossbones on it over the rearview mirror—"Papa Gede go with you, we get 'im for you, special." They see me off singing "Legba mia mia."

Got several hours' head start last night (like Harding, but in the opposite direction) and slept sound and deep in one of those anonymous Comfort Inns sprouting everywhere at welcoming discounts. Completely refreshing, like after you've made a long deferred decision or resolved to close up and move on. Been driving since just after dawn, straight down the backbone of Florida fast as they'd let me, then off on one of the lesser routes due south, as instructed, and with Lake Okeechobee somewhere off to my left, made a couple of half-intuitive turns through the northern rag end of what was once Everglades to where I am now, wherever that is—a long flat snake of a little country road without a number as far as I can tell.

As for traffic, I seem to be pretty much it—who'd dream these remnants of a long-gone Florida could be thriving without state protection in this rural patch midway between two booming coasts? Swampy undergrowth, hardwoods with vines tumbling over them, manes of Spanish moss, even a few cypresses (though I'm miles from the Big Cypress itself). Two or three alligators asleep on embankments and half on the road shoulder, long-legged wading birds in those postures they take as if posing. Except for the blacktop—and my intrusion—the whole of it feels like an allusion to some prehuman (posthuman?) semi-tropical wilderness. I coast through it no more than ten miles per hour in my rented Shadow, hand lightly on the diary beside me.

Call it an overactive imagination revved to an unrealistic pitch by the setting, but there's a distinct pulsing under my hand and I pull over as soon as I've got enough shoulder room. Walk along a narrow alligator-free bank into the marsh and what I'm here for comes clear as truth. I prop the diary against a scrubby oak and build a book-sized pyre out of dry twigs and clear a circle of safety all around. I open my gift from the sanctuary just about in the middle, face-down, light a match to the twigs and listen to the flames spark and dance and crackle. In no time it falls like a flaming star and buries itself in the cone of fire. Ash swirls to my feet—and a finger-sized slip of leather. I pick it up and drop it gently into the embers, then douse them with my liter water bottle for good measure. The burning of what matters done, the last rite of passion mingles it with all manner of wild things. Ashes cooled, smoke thinned down to nothing, snakebirds dry their wings in the sun.

Back in the car, I lay pen and notepad beside me on the seat, this in case a name for my new anti-profession surfaces. "Philo-something," I said to Jon—I'm a died-in-the-wool lover, but of what? Love: the thrill of pure motion, always going some place, always on the road to satisfaction of this or that desire and setting off again (always coming and going, sexually speaking), grateful for rides and rest stops, making do with the carnival of road-pleasures, but to what end? To have what? A longing to possess what?

By sheer luck I'm back on 29 South, moving right along. And then it's due east on Alligator Alley, and south again toward Miami as the afternoon wanes in a wilderness of surging traffic on all sides as far as the eye can see. Reasoning à la Plato, what I as lover never reach is any illumination of love's being—the end of love—the flash of love at rest. My final resting place where what is does not move and, so, remains what it has become forever. (I must say that as the Unmoved I would prefer not to be a Mover but, given no choice, being an unmoved mover is ok since I won't be doing anything and can't be held responsible for how anything ends.)

What I am, it seems, is a lover of Being—a philousiac. Not as patently dangerous as a maniac but unlikely to attract clients. Something elitist about the word "philousiac" (meaning nothing to any but word-hoarders with a handle on their Greek roots) even though you could argue that a vocation with no pedigree, no history of inclusion and exclusion, is anything but elitist. Philousiac work would place client-and-me on the death-trip life is from day one. A place for hearing the lies we create to tell time. ("I'll do this or feel this or be this way until I die," so goes the work ethic of the dying, their credo of "this-is-me-staying-alive.") Time—the fourth dimension, travel mode of us lovers ever nearing the anarchy of freedom—takes your mind off the trip's end. Your body's all the while a dying workhorse in a barnyard of fiction. Make that: perfumery of fiction, life's workplace for distilling the stink of death.

The more I get into this the harder it is to see how consorting with a philousiac could be made to sound inviting. But, then, an anti-profession is bound to have a problem with market appeal.

Wouldn't you know—Maria-Louisa's directions to my new address, having led me through Florida's heart and gut, are now taking me into the thick of Miami's Little Haiti, signs in Kréyol beckoning. *Travay maji*—magic work, says one. Work—sure, that's what I've come here for, *travay.* But *sans* the *maji.* True, my undeveloped childhood gift for turning an eye to whatever was going on—hearing the fiction in motion—had the personal cast of a child's eagerness to discern what good, if any, would come of it. I wanted to *be good*—feel good, do good, but most of all, just come to a good end. Like some magical transport. Truth is, I want another to hear with me the stir of goodness in righting truth and fiction. I jot down "travay" at the next stoplight and scribble "philousiac" beside it as the bus driver behind me honks loudly.

Cross Bicayne Bay on 79th, a right on Collins. Keep going, she says, but I need to stretch my legs and get my bearings before facing the reality of new premises in SoBe; it's been a long day. I cut out of the traffic to a side street and park.

Between 22nd and 21st, a delightful old keystone building with park-like grounds invites relaxation—Bass Museum of Art, already closed. I amble around for a bit under the banyans, stroll on past the museum through a couple of blocks in semi-decline and halfway around the massive convention center that seems to dominate this area. I'm about to turn back when, just ahead, the museum's little outpost School of Art catches my eye, a pleasant, low stucco behind which clusters of oldish men intently play chess in the pre-twilight cooling of day. I walk softly past them to a footpath along a narrow grassy canal that separates this mini-enclave of peace and quiet from the traffic drone of a busy boulevard on the other side. To my left, fenced off with an effect of emphatic seclusion, a jungly arboretum distantly recalls Nongka's sanctuary paintings—and there a slender dryadic form in weathered stone, half-hidden in the growth under a gnarled tree.

Trying to get a better look, I lose her entirely as the path ends and I step out into the sun's last, low, blinding gleam over a pond of water lilies and wading birds so breathtaking I'm sure I've blundered into the privileged domain of someone's private, very private, space. Beside me is a sculpture of a woman with two children in her arms, all lying fast asleep—dead?—on a raised stone slab. More . . . more . . . I resolve to trespass if necessary, and continue along the curve of the lily pond beneath a white bougainvillea arbor, to the startle of a colossal number-tattooed forearm in greening bronze reaching skyward with its tensed hand. Sure now I'm on sacred ground, here by some accidental route of admission beyond my ken, I draw near cautiously, a harrowed music of young voices in my ears, down a narrowing, lowering stone passage toward a child in bronze crouching at the tunnel's mouth—and then, stepping into the softening light of sunset, I am among all of them, alone, in pairs, groups, women, children, men, a multitude of naked ones crowding towards the arm raised skyward in the sculpted bronze-green grotesqueries of their death throes, clutching and climbing over one another in the scramble for breathing space.

I back into the tunnel, I know now where I am—Dachau, Babi Yar, Sobibor, Majdanek, Belzec, Treblinka, Auschwitz are etched into the warm pinkish stone—and scrooch down against the wall under a shaft of waning light. Here in the confines of the memorial I've entered by chance, I sketch out this much:

Welcome to a hospice for the eternally dying. Join me in the practice of hearing: even as death's impress of meaning empowers stories, so does a life of hearing disempower them. Mine is a gift for birthing truth, laying bare the corpse—of fiction, that is—in the moment you yourself cannot (or will not) hear the end on your own. And this not by any method but merely by being who I am, a philousiac hearing with you the resounding silence of truth's clarity: Juba booking your passage to the kill. Two and only two players, you and me coupled in the sport of not-knowing, a union created by the doubling of imagination and consummated in the kill, life quarries playing love without power by ear. Cost for philousiac benefactors will be the sum total of my expenses, bi-weekly in advance, plus fringes like health insurance, time-out and retirement benefits. Duration determined by the natal frolic itself—days, months, possibly years. We'll see. The first to receive this coupling grace shuts the door on all others until our play is done. Until you're ready to write our story, the text-kill of our outing. Then another opening for another benefactor. No predetermined rules or expectation of results.

This surely won't pass for a flyer to be stashed in the rainproof pocket of my professional shingle—or will it? Must avoid as much misunderstanding as possible about what people are getting themselves into.

Lights are appearing out on Meridian Avenue as I wend my way back to the Bass Museum by a longer, more public route and cross over to Wolfie's to study their menu for future reference, then drive south along Ocean Boulevard to Jon's converted art deco, all just as he described, post in place for my sign-to-be:

JAEL B. JUBA, *Travay Philousiac*
first and last practitioner

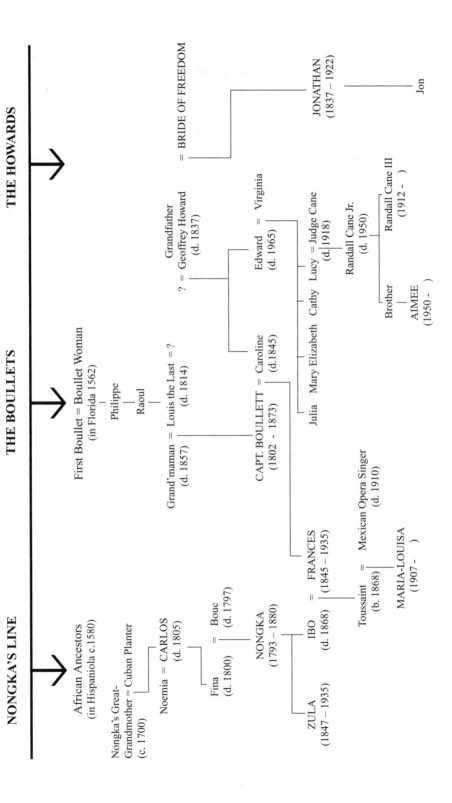

NONGKA'S LINE   # THE BOULLETS   # THE HOWARDS

African Ancestors
(in Hispaniola c.1580)

First Boullet = Boullet Woman
(in Florida 1562)

Nongka's Great-
Grandmother = Cuban Planter
(c. 1700)

Philippe
|
Raoul

Noemia = CARLOS
(d. 1805)

Grand'maman = Louis the Last = ?
(d. 1857)   (d. 1814)

Grandfather
Geoffrey Howard
(d. 1837)

? =

= BRIDE OF FREEDOM

JONATHAN
(1837 – 1922)

Jon

Fina   =   Bouc
(d. 1800)   (d. 1797)

NONGKA
(1793 – 1880)

CAPT. BOULLETT = Caroline
(1802 - 1873)   (d.1845)

Edward = Virginia
(d. 1965)

ZULA
(1847 – 1935)

IBO
(d. 1868)

= FRANCES
(1845 – 1935)

Julia   Mary Elizabeth   Cathy   Lucy = Judge Cane
                                            (d.|1918)

Randall Cane Jr.
(d. 1950)

Toussaint =   Mexican Opera Singer
(b. 1868)   (d. 1910)

Brother

Randall Cane III
(1912 -   )

MARIA-LOUISA
(1907 -   )

AIMEE
(1950 -   )

Library of American Fiction
The University of Wisconsin Press Fiction Series

Marleen S. Barr
Oy Pioneer! A Novel

Dodie Bellamy
The Letters of Mina Harker

Melvin Jules Bukiet
Stories of an Imaginary Childhood

Paola Corso
Giovanna's 86 Circles: And Other Stories

Joyce Elbrecht and Lydia Fakundiny
Hearing

Andrew Furman
Alligators May Be Present

Merrill Joan Gerber
Glimmering Girls

Rebecca Goldstein
The Dark Sister

Rebecca Goldstein
Mazel

Jesse Lee Kercheval
The Museum of Happiness: A Novel

Alan Lelchuk
American Mischief

Alan Lelchuk
Brooklyn Boy

Curt Leviant
Ladies and Gentlemen, The Original Music of the Hebrew Alphabet
and Weekend in Mustara: *Two Novellas*

David Milofsky
A Friend of Kissinger: A Novel

Lesléa Newman
A Letter to Harvey Milk: Short Stories

Ladette Randolph
This Is Not the Tropics: Stories

Sara Rath
The Star Lake Saloon and Housekeeping Cottages: A Novel

Mordecai Roshwald
Level 7

Lewis Weinstein
The Heretic: A Novel